Tami Hoag's novels have appeared on international bestseller lists regularly since the publication of her first book in 1988. Her work has been translated into more than 30 languages worldwide and over 35 million copies of her books are in print. Tami is a dedicated equestrian in the discipline of dressage and shares her home with two English cocker spaniels. She lives in Florida.

You can discover more about the author at www.tamihoag.com

THE BITTER SEASON

After moving to the Cold Case unit, Detective Nikki Liska misses the rush of pulling an all-nighter and the sense of urgency when hunting a murderer on the loose — her current homicide case dates back twenty-five years, and there is little hope of finding the killer. Most of all, she misses her old partner, Detective Sam Kovac . . . Sam is having an even harder time adjusting to Nikki's absence, saddled with a green new partner younger than pieces of his own wardrobe. But he is distracted from his troubles by an especially brutal double homicide: a middle-aged husband and wife hacked to death in their home with a samurai sword. One woman might link these mysteries — but she is being watched. Can Liska and Kovac find her before it is too late?

Books by Tami Hoag
Published by Ulverscroft:

DUST TO DUST
DARK HORSE
KILL THE MESSENGER
DEAD SKY
THE ALIBI MAN
COLD COLD HEART

TAMI HOAG

◆

THE BITTER SEASON

Complete and Unabridged

CHARNWOOD
Leicester

First published in Great Britain in 2016 by
Orion Books
an imprint of The Orion Publishing Group Ltd
London

First Charnwood Edition
published 2017
by arrangement with
The Orion Publishing Group Ltd
London

A catalogue record for this book is available
from the British Library.

ISBN 978–1–4448–3171–9

Published by
F. A. Thorpe (Publishing)
Anstey, Leicestershire

Set by Words & Graphics Ltd.
Anstey, Leicestershire
Printed and bound in Great Britain by
T. J. International Ltd., Padstow, Cornwall

This book is printed on acid-free paper

1

November
Minneapolis, MN
Twenty-five years ago

Ted Duffy loved to swing the axe. He loved the motion — pulling back, stretching his body taut like a crossbow, then releasing the power in his muscles. He probably put more into it than was necessary to get the job done. He didn't care. This was his workout, his therapy, his outlet for the toxic emotions that built up inside him all week.

Swing, crack! Swing, crack!

There was a rhythm to it he found soothing, and a violence he found satisfying.

Day in and day out he dealt with people he would sooner have sent to hell: the dregs of society, sickos and perverts. The things he'd seen would have made the average citizen vomit and given them nightmares. He lived in a horror story, fighting a losing battle with no end in sight.

He'd been working Sex Crimes for seven years now. His initial efforts to remain detached from the grime of it had gradually worn him out. His plan to do a brief turn in the unit and then use it as a springboard to a more prestigious position in another department had eventually crumbled and collapsed in on itself.

Turned out he was damned good at the job that sucked him into the filthy gutter of human depravity. And the longer he did it, the better he became. And the better he became, the harder it was to escape. The harder it was to escape, the bigger the stain on the very fabric of his soul. The deeper the stain soaked in, the greater his understanding of the minds of the predators he hunted. The greater his understanding, the more his idealistic self was chipped away, the more the filth soaked into him until the only thing he recognized of his original self was the face in the mirror every morning — and even that was eroding.

He had always been a good-looking guy, with chiseled features and smooth skin and a thick head of jet-black hair. The face that stared back at him these days as he shaved had aged twice as fast in half as much time as his twin brother's. Every day, the lines seemed deeper, the eyes emptier, the hair thinner and grayer. He was becoming something he didn't want to recognize, inside and out.

So he chopped wood on the stump of an elm tree out behind his house.

Swing, crack! Swing, crack!

He lived in an older neighborhood of square two-story clapboard houses with front porches that had mostly been closed in against the brutal Minnesota winters, and yards separated by tall, weathered privacy fences. His property backed onto a large, rambling park that surrounded one of the city's many lakes. The park let him have the illusion of living in the woods.

2

Mr. Lumberjack, living in the woods, swinging his axe.

Swing, crack! Swing, crack!

Despite the cold, wet weather, he was sweating inside the layers of clothing he wore: thermal underwear, a flannel shirt, a down-filled vest. He hated this time of year. Every day was shorter than the last. Night began to fall in late afternoon. Winter could arrive on any given day and stay until April. They had had an ice storm on Halloween and a blizzard on Veterans Day, followed by three days of rain that had caused flash flooding in low-lying areas. The odd day of stunning, electric blue skies and a paltry few lingering fall colors couldn't make up for the stretches of bleak gray or the damp cold that knifed to the bone. It buried its blade between his shoulders as he wiped the moisture from his face on the sleeve of his shirt and hoisted the axe again.

Swing, crack!

The temperature was dropping quickly. The intermittent spitting rain that had been falling off and on all afternoon was giving way to a pelting snow that cut like tiny shards of glass, stinging his ruddy cheeks.

Every winter he bitched about the Minnesota weather and vowed to move to Florida the day he retired from the police department. But if he moved to Florida, he wouldn't have any reason to split wood. What would he do for his sanity then?

Like he stood any chance of getting away from here anyway, he thought, looking up at the house, where lights had come on in the kitchen and in one bedroom upstairs. His family all lived in Bloomington. Barbie the Ball Buster's family was entrenched in the southern suburbs. The kids had all their cousins and friends here.

Maybe he should go alone. Maybe everyone would be happier if he did.

He sighed and picked up another chunk of wood, set it on its end on the stump, stepped back, and swung the axe.

Mr. Lumberjack. Mr. Sex Crimes Detective of the Year. Featured speaker at conferences all over the Midwest. Expert on the subject of human degradation.

Swing, crack! Swing, crack!

He tried to concentrate on the silence between the small explosions of the axe striking the wood. He sucked cold air into his smoke-blackened lungs. His heart pounded too hard from the effort. The muscles in his shoulders cramped. He felt like he might have a heart attack at any moment.

Barbie would revive him and kill him again with her bare hands, furious to be left with the kids and the mortgage and the Catholic school tuitions.

Theirs was a marriage in the way of many couples: a partnership of paychecks that didn't stretch far enough, intimacy a thing of memory, the future a projected image at the far end of a treadmill that ran too fast.

More and more all he wanted was off.

They resented each other more days than not. His wife had ceased to think of him as a man. He

4

was a paycheck, a roommate, a pain in the ass. He had sought validation and comfort elsewhere. It wasn't hard to get. Consequently, it didn't mean anything. And the spiral of his life went down and down. He didn't like what his marriage had become. He didn't like what *he* had become.

His grandmother had always warned him about purgatory. Hell's waiting room, she used to call it. Purgatory had become his life.

Sometimes he wondered if death could be so much worse.

Swing, crack! Swing, crack!

Crack! Crack!

The final two sounds seemed to come from far away, like an echo.

Ted Duffy was dead before he could wonder why.

The first bullet hit him between the shoulder blades as he held the axe high over his head. It shattered bone and deflated a lung, and tore through a major artery. The second bullet struck him in the head, entering above the right ear, exiting below the left eye.

He dropped face-first to the ground at the base of the tree stump, his eyes open but seeing nothing, blood pooling beneath his cheek and seeping into the new-fallen snow.

2

November
Minneapolis, MN
Present Day

'Duffy was a great guy.'

'That's not one of the criteria for picking a cold case,' Nikki Liska argued.

Gene Grider narrowed his eyes. He had a face like a bulldog, and breath to match. 'What the hell is wrong with you? Do you need a Midol or something?'

She wrinkled her nose at him. 'What decade did you crawl up out of, Grider? Smells like 1955.'

Grider had worked Homicide before her time, but not *that* long before her time. He had put in thirty years, doing stints in Homicide, Robbery, and Sex Crimes. His last few years on the job had been spent working special community initiatives — jobs Nikki would have thought required a lot more charm than Grider could scrape together on his best day.

'It's twenty-five years since Duff was gunned down,' he said, slamming his hand down on the table. 'Twenty-five years this month! It's a disgrace that this case has never been solved. This is what I'm coming out of retirement for. We're finally getting a dedicated cold case unit. This case should be front and center!'

6

'It's not like nobody's worked the case,' Liska said. 'People have worked the case all along.'

'On the side, with no money,' Grider complained.

Which was exactly how the majority of cold cases were worked all over the country — piecemeal, if at all. Cold case units were far more common on television than in reality. In the real world, police departments operated on taxpayer dollars, funding that was continually being cut to the bone. Homicide detectives all had their old unsolved cases that they continued to chip away at when they could, and passed them on to other detectives when they transferred or retired. It was a wonder any of the cases got solved, considering.

'The same as all these cases,' Nikki pointed out.

She had spent the last two months going half blind reviewing cold cases dating back to the mid-seventies. Of the two hundred cases she had evaluated, she had pulled sixty-seven for the final round of reviews. Grider had looked through another two hundred and pulled fifty-nine. They had whittled the list down to a hundred, and now had to prioritize. They would be lucky if the federal grant money being used to set up the unit got them through half the cases on their short list.

'This isn't the same thing,' Grider snapped. 'Duff was one of us. Where the hell is your loyalty?'

'This isn't about loyalty,' Nikki said. 'It can't matter that Duffy was a cop — '

'Nice to know what you think of your peers,' Grider said, sneering.

'Oh, get off your high horse,' she snapped. 'It's about solvability. We've got a limited budget. We have to go after the cases we have a hope in hell of closing. You couldn't close Duffy's case in twenty-five years for a reason: There's jack shit to go on. He was shot from a distance. There were no witnesses, no fingerprints, no DNA, no trace evidence of any value,' she said, ticking the points off on her fingers.

'We're supposed to spend money and man hours going back over a case not likely to ever be solved?' she asked. 'What case doesn't make the cut because we're giving priority to an unsolvable crime? The serial rapes from 1997? The child murder from 1985? The hit-and-run death of a father of six? Which one do we leave out? All those cases have forensic evidence that can be retested with better technology than before. All of them are potentially solvable.'

The new Homicide lieutenant, Joan Mascherino, looked from Liska to Grider and back like an impassive tennis umpire.

She was a neat and proper woman with auburn hair cut in a neat and proper style. Perfectly polished in her conservative gray suit and pearl earrings, she was Liska's height — short. Kindred spirits in the world of the vertically challenged — or so Nikki hoped.

Nikki had learned long ago to take any advantage she could get in this profession still dominated by men. She certainly wasn't above playing the girls-gotta-stick-together card when she could do it subtly. But Joan Mascherino hadn't gotten where she was by being a pushover. Now in her mid-fifties, she had come on the job when discrimination against women was a way of life, and had still worked her way up the ranks to lieutenant. Running Homicide was just another feather in her cap on her way to bigger things. Rumor had it she would be going upstairs to rub elbows with the deputy chiefs in the not-too-distant future.

Homicide's last boss, Kasselmann, had used the closing of the Doc Holiday murders as a springboard to being named deputy chief of the Investigations Bureau — as if he'd had anything to do with solving the serial killer's crimes. He had just happened to be sitting in the office at the time.

Mascherino had come over from Internal Affairs just in time to be handed the plum task of putting together the Cold Case unit, which would, initially at least, be high profile and put her in the media spotlight.

Gene Grider, retired for eighteen months, had come back to work this unit, offering himself at part-time pay, which made him very attractive to the number crunchers trying to squeeze every penny out of the grant money. But it also augmented Grider's pension, and allowed him to bring his own agenda along with him.

His agenda was Ted Duffy.

So went the law enforcement food chain.

Nikki had her own agenda, too. She had leveraged her role in closing the Doc Holiday cases to get Kasselmann to recommend her to

9

this unit. When she caught a case in Homicide, it wasn't unusual to be on for twenty-four hours or more, straight. In Cold Case, there was no urgency. There were regular hours, giving her more time with her boys.

She had spent the better part of a decade in Homicide. The unit was her home away from home, her family away from family. She loved the job, was very good at the job. But R.J. and Kyle, at fourteen and sixteen, were growing into young men, struggling around the pitfalls of adolescence as they made the transition from boyhood to independence and maturity. They needed an adult available, and she was it. God knew their father didn't qualify for the job.

It had been during the height of the Doc Holiday hunt that Nikki realized she didn't know enough about what was going on in the life of her oldest son, Kyle. The lives of teenagers were so much more complicated now than when she was a kid. Her sons could be lost so easily while she was looking away — lost literally and figuratively. No matter how much she loved her job, she loved her boys a million times more.

News of the grant money coming in for a cold case unit had started circulating at the perfect time. She would still be investigating homicides, but the urgency and long hours of a fresh case would be removed. The challenges would be different, but she would still be fighting for a victim.

Except that, at the moment, she was fighting *against* a victim. Another detective, no less.

'If Ted Duffy's murder isn't on this agenda,

I'm out of here,' Grider threatened.

Like he was some kind of supercop. Like he was Derek Jeter coming out of retirement to save the Yankees or something.

'And every cop in Minneapolis is going to be up in arms about it,' Grider continued, cutting a hard look at Liska. 'Except this one,' he muttered, and then put his attention back on the people he wanted to sway. 'Duffy's is the only unsolved homicide on the books involving a police officer. It's a black eye on the department. And I would think now — especially now — that would mean something.'

Liska sat up straighter, incredulous. 'Is that a threat? Is that what you're trying to so cleverly slip into that rant? You'll set a fire amongst the rank and file if you don't get your way?'

Grider shrugged. 'I'm just saying people are already on edge.'

'You're a fucking bully.'

Lieutenant Mascherino cut Nikki a disapproving look. 'We can do without the language, Sergeant.'

Nikki bit her tongue. Great. She had a mouth like a sailor on holiday, and a schoolmarm for a lieutenant.

They sat at a round white melamine table in a war room commandeered from Homicide. Round tables were supposed to foster feelings of equality and cooperation, according to the industrial and organizational psychology expert the department had wasted taxpayer dollars on during the last remodeling of the offices. The same expert had recommended painting the office walls mauve, and had told them they needed to remove the U bolts from the walls and floors in the interview rooms, so they had nowhere to cuff violent offenders if the need arose, because the threat of physical restraint might be deemed 'intimidating.'

Nikki could still see the look on her partner Kovac's face as they listened to the presentation. Nobody had a better 'Are you fucking kidding me?' face than Kovac.

Weeks later a suspect had yanked a useless decorative shelf off the wall of an interview room and cracked Kovac in the head with it. He still had a little scar. Nikki had kneecapped the suspect with her tactical baton before he could do worse. Thank God Kovac had a head like granite.

Mascherino exchanged a look with Chris Logan, the chief assistant county attorney. Logan was a big, handsome man in an expensive suit, tall and athletic with a thick shock of Black Irish hair streaked with gray. Fiftyish. Brash. Aggressive. Intimidating in the courtroom or in a conversation.

Logan's role in this meeting was to give his blessing to cases he thought might have the potential to be prosecuted successfully. The Duffy case offered nothing for him to sink his teeth into as a prosecutor. He would want witnesses, evidence, forensics — at the very least, a viable suspect at this stage of the game. Yet, he didn't jump in to dismiss Grider's sales pitch.

Logan was certainly aware of the contract tensions between the city and the police union, recently made worse by the mayor's threats of deep budget cuts and layoffs. But if any of that concerned him, he wasn't going to show it. He had to be a hell of a poker player.

He rubbed a hand along his jaw as he weighed the pros and cons.

'We owe Duff one more try,' Grider pressed. 'All we need is for one person to talk. That's all it takes to crack a case like this.'

'After twenty-five years, why would anyone talk?' Nikki asked.

'Maybe they got a conscience,' Grider said, 'or found Jesus, or now hate the person they were protecting back then.'

But none of that seemed likely, and even if someone talked, there was still no physical evidence to speak of. They couldn't go to trial with nothing but hearsay or uncorroborated accomplice testimony. Nikki sighed.

The cold case she had pulled as her number one candidate was the 2001 rape and murder of a young mother. There were two solid suspects. They needed only a couple of puzzle pieces and a little luck to make the case. The victim's mother had already been in touch with her to lobby on her daughter's behalf.

'Have you read the entire Duffy murder book?' Logan asked her.

'Enough to know there isn't — '

'That's a no,' he said. 'Maybe you need to take a closer look.'

'I've personally read through sixty-seven other cases that are more promising.'

Logan didn't blink.

'Re-interviewing friends, family, co-workers. Going through the file with a fresh eye,' he said. 'That's not a huge investment of time. A few days. A week at the most. If nothing turns up, at least we gave it a shot.'

'It's a good case for the media,' Grider said, sweetening the deal. 'The twenty-fifth anniversary of the murder of one of the city's finest. The news coverage might shake something loose.'

And there was nothing a politically ambitious prosecutor liked more than a free media spotlight. It was no secret the current county attorney was considering running for the U.S. Senate. Everyone assumed Logan was next in line to take over as top dog for Hennepin County. If he decided to champion the Duffy case, he could get that initial news exposure that would come at the launch of the new unit, and curry favor with the police union at the same time. Two birds, one stone. To the cops, he would look like a hero for reopening the case, and if, after the media had moved on to other news, the case didn't get solved, that would be the fault of the investigators. No downside for Logan.

Nikki sat back in her chair and crossed her arms over her chest. She wouldn't admit defeat, but she would have to accept it. Fine. Let Grider have his one case. It would keep him out of her hair while she devoted herself to her dead young mother.

Unlike Homicide, where the detectives worked together, and had multiple cases going at the same time, in Cold Case each of them would be working one case at a time, until it was either solved or all hope had been exhausted, and then they would move on to the next one.

Logan drummed his fingers on the tabletop and gave a decisive nod. 'Let's do it. That's our headliner.'

Mascherino stood up and went to the long whiteboard on the wall behind her. 'All right, then. We start with the murder of Ted Duffy.'

She chose a marker and wrote Duffy's name at the top of the board in neat cursive. Grider looked at Nikki and smiled like a shark. She rolled her eyes away from him and toward the third member of their team, Candra Seley, who shrugged and spread her hands, mouthing her opinion: *He's such an asshole!*

Seley, on loan from the Business and Technology unit, would primarily be reviewing evidence, processing and reprocessing test results, performing witness and suspect background checks, compiling witness lists, and constructing time lines. Liska and Grider would be the feet on the ground.

Grider got up from his chair, smoothing his tie over his protruding belly. 'I'll get right on it.'

'No,' Mascherino said calmly. 'The Duffy case goes to Liska.'

'What?!' Liska and Grider blurted out simultaneously.

'That's my case!' Grider argued, his face turning red.

'It's time for a fresh pair of eyes,' the lieutenant said firmly. 'That's the whole point of a cold case unit — getting a fresh take on an old

15

crime. I'm sure Sergeant Liska will appreciate your input when she asks for it, but this is her case now.'

'But I know this case inside and out! I *know* these people!'

'That's just my point. I want someone who doesn't know any of the people involved. Someone who has no preconceived ideas going in. That's the only way a case this stale has any chance of being solved.'

Grider paced behind the table. Nikki could hear him breathing in and out like he'd run a hundred yards.

'She doesn't even think the case deserves to be investigated!' he shouted, pointing at Nikki as if he were fingering her for a witch.

'I don't think it deserves to be a priority,' Nikki corrected him, pushing her chair back and standing. He was still half a foot taller than she was.

'You said it was unsolvable.'

'Well, in twenty-five years you certainly haven't proven me wrong.'

'So it'll be just fine with you if you don't solve it, either,' Grider said sarcastically. 'You've already got your excuse ready.'

Nikki felt like the top of her head might blow off. Furious, she walked up on him, her hands jammed at her waist. 'Are you implying that I won't do the job? You think I'm a bad cop? Fuck you, Grider! I didn't ride in here on a powder puff. I've worked my ass off to get where I am. I'll put my record in Homicide up against yours any day of the week. I don't have any moldy age-old unsolved murders with my name on them.'

Grider looked at the lieutenant. 'How am I supposed to work with her?'

'You're not,' Mascherino said. 'You've got your own case to work. Take your number two and run with it. Nikki, you've got priority for Candra's time, however you need her.'

Logan unfolded himself from his chair, looking at Nikki. 'Press conference at five in the government center.'

'Today?' She glanced at her watch. It was nearly four.

'Plenty of time to go powder your nose and put on some lipstick,' Logan quipped.

'Speak for yourself,' Nikki snapped, gathering her notes from the table. 'I've got a case to review.'

3

'The guy's a freaking twitch,' Sam Kovac said. 'The first thing he did when we got him in the box was puke on the floor.'

He sat at his desk watching the feed from the interview room on his computer screen. His new trainee — he refused to use the word *partner* — was just down the hall, taking his turn trying to get information out of Ronnie Stack. Stack — thirty-four, meth head, bone thin, pasty white — was a nervous rodent type: furtive, thin lips quivering, narrow eyes darting all around the room, rubbing his hands together like he was washing, over and over.

'Is he high?' Tippen asked, watching over Kovac's shoulder like a vulture. He was built that way, too: long and bony, with a permanent slouch, a beak of a nose, and keen dark eyes. He'd been a detective nearly as long as Kovac, which made the two of them old as dirt.

'No, but I'm sure he wants to be.'

This fact would, Kovac hoped, tip the scales in their favor. Stack wanted out of that room — maybe badly enough to give them what they wanted: information on the murder of a drug dealer known as BB. Stack was a known associate of BB's, and had reportedly been with the dealer shortly before somebody stuck a knife in his throat and caused him to drown in his own blood.

Stack was not under arrest. This was a noncustodial interview. He was free to get up and leave anytime he wanted. It amazed Kovac how few people exercised that right. They seemed to think that option was some kind of trick.

'How's the kid doing?' Tippen asked, helping himself to the other desk chair in the cubicle.

The kid, Michael Taylor, fledgling homicide detective, was Kovac's third trainee in as many months. Of the other two, one had gone back to his old job in Sex Crimes, and the other had transferred to a sudden opportunity in the Business and Technology unit. Neither had been cut out for Homicide as far as Kovac was concerned — an opinion he had made abundantly clear.

Bottom line: He didn't want a new partner. He was too old and cranky to break one in. He and Liska had been partners for so long that they were comfortable together, their styles meshed; they had learned to tolerate each other's annoying habits. They were like an old married couple that never had sex. He wanted that back. Instead, he had to take this kid and try to make him into something he could live with.

Taylor showed some promise, Kovac admitted grudgingly. He had been an MP in the army. After two tours in Iraq he had opted out of the service and come home to Minneapolis. He joined the force and set his sights on making detective, rising quickly through the ranks. He had come to Homicide from Special Crimes, to bulk up his résumé before he was fast-tracked to

19

further stardom. At least, that was what Kovac believed. The kid was too handsome and too sharp to loiter in the trenches with the rest of the grunts. He had Big Things written all over him. His sheer perfection rubbed Kovac the wrong way.

He shrugged at Tippen's question. 'We'll see.'

He turned up the volume on the computer speakers. Taylor was sitting looking relaxed, looking like he could sit there for the next two or three days. He had his shirtsleeves rolled perfectly halfway up his forearms. Even this late in the day his shirt still looked freshly starched, perfectly tailored to showcase his broad shoulders and trim waist.

'Good thing Liska transferred out,' Tippen said. 'She'd be all over Taylor like stink on a billy goat.'

Tippen resembled a billy goat, Kovac thought, with his long homely face, sporting a goatee and mustache these past few months. His vintage beatnik look. He claimed it played well with the coffee-house chicks.

'The guy is hot,' Tippen went on. 'If I was a woman, I'd fuck him.'

Kovac made a pained face. 'Oh Jesus, don't put that in my head!'

'Taylor's too young for Tinks,' Elwood Knutson announced, joining them in the cramped gray cubicle, and taking up all remaining available space. He was built like a Disney cartoon bear, and had a similar pelt of hair.

'Don't tell Tinks that,' Kovac advised. 'She'll

pluck your eyeballs out and feed them to you.'

'Merely an observation,' Elwood murmured, hunkering down closer to the screen. 'She's not the cougar type.'

'He's not that young anyway,' Kovac muttered. The kid made him feel like a dinosaur. 'He's thirty-four.'

'And how old are you now, Sam?'

'Old enough to remember rotary telephones. I've got shoes older than this kid,' he confessed. 'And a couple of neckties, too.'

He turned his focus back to the computer screen.

'You know,' Taylor was saying to Stack, 'we're just not making the progress here I thought we would, Ronnie. You seemed so eager to cooperate, but you're not telling me anything I don't already know.'

'Maybe I don't know anything more than you know,' Stack said, pushing his limp blond hair back from his face.

Taylor shook his head. 'I don't think I've overestimated you. I think you want to help us out here,' Taylor said. 'BB was your friend, after all.'

Stack's eyes darted from side to side. 'He wasn't really my *friend*. I mean, I *knew* him, but . . .'

Taylor leaned forward a bit. Stack leaned back.

'Now, there you go, trying to distance yourself when we have witnesses who put you with BB shortly before his death,' Taylor said. 'Now you're suddenly telling me maybe you and BB weren't such good friends after all when I know you'd been staying at his house. You have to know what this makes me think, Ronnie.'

Stack nibbled at a hangnail as he curled in on himself, turning into a human comma on the other side of the table, trying to make himself smaller and smaller, as if he thought he might eventually become so small Taylor would find him physically insignificant and let him disappear.

'It makes me think maybe we should be looking at you as a suspect instead of a possible witness.' Taylor's voice was quiet and even, matter-of-fact. 'Should we be looking at you that way, Ronnie?'

'N-no.' The twitch wiped his arm across his forehead. 'It seems really hot in here. Aren't you hot?'

'Me? No. I spent two years in Iraq fighting for your freedom in the ninth circle of hell. I know what hot is. It's not hot in here. I mean, we've got the fan going and everything.'

Without another interview room available, they had had a janitor come in and clean Stack's vomit off the floor, and then had brought in a little desk fan to blow on the wet carpet and dissipate the smell of puke and cleaning agents.

'Did you have some kind of beef with BB, Ronnie?'

'No!'

'Did he have some kind of beef with you? Maybe you pissed him off. Maybe he caught you stealing.'

'No!' Stack protested — too fervently. Like a guilty man. 'I'm not like that. I'm a nice person.

I'd do anything for anybody. I'd give you the shirt off my back,' he said, tugging at the collar of his dirty, puke-stained, olive-colored sweater. The color made him look like maybe he had a liver disease — or maybe he *did* have a liver disease. Fucking junkie.

'I'm always getting blamed for shit I didn't do!' he whined.

'But isn't it true you were mooching off BB for a long time?' Taylor asked in that calm, even voice that was somehow more unnerving than a shout. 'You were sleeping on his couch, eating his food, taking advantage of his kindness.'

'It's not like I didn't help him,' Stack said indignantly. 'I watched his dogs when he was out of town.'

'You watched his dogs while you were sleeping on his couch and smoking his dope and eating his food and helping yourself to the meth.'

'He owed me something for all I did.'

'You felt entitled,' Taylor said, nodding.

'I did all kinds of stuff for him,' Stack claimed.

'Like selling his dope and sticking the money in your pocket? How did he feel about that?'

'I never did that! He would have killed me!'

'So you did it only while he was out of town and you were looking after his dogs?' Taylor said. 'Because you were entitled to that much.'

Stack shifted in his seat, agitated. 'No! I told you. BB would've killed me.'

'So maybe you beat him to it.'

'I'm really hot,' Stack said, tugging again at the collar of his sweater.

'It's probably just nerves,' Taylor said. 'I mean,

here you sit with a homicide detective telling you you might be a suspect in the death of your friend. Maybe I'm trying to visualize you sticking that knife into BB's neck, shoving that blade down his throat, listening to him gurgle as he drowned in his own blood. Hell of a way to go, sucking that blood down in big gulps.'

Stack twisted and turned in his seat. He looked like he might puke again. Taylor rose from his chair, smoothing his tie down with one hand.

'I'd be nervous if I was in your place, too, Ronnie,' he said. 'You've got a couple of drug busts on your sheet already. BB was a drug dealer. Most people won't have to try too hard to stretch that story to fit. You know what I'm saying? I'll guarantee a jury isn't going to be interested in all your 'poor, poor Ronnie' sob stories.'

'Fuck you!' Stack spat the words at him.

Taylor ignored the insult. He hadn't changed the tone or volume of his voice since the beginning of the interview. Pretty damned impressive, Kovac thought, though wild horses couldn't have kicked that confession out of him.

'Tell you what, Ronnie,' Taylor said. 'I'm going to step out for a moment to confer with Detective Kovac. I'll tell you right now, he wants to hold you on this. He's not as patient as I am. While I'm out, you try to refresh your memory for me. Otherwise, Kovac's going to come down on you like Thor's hammer. Trust me, you don't want that to happen.'

'Who's Thor?' Stack asked stupidly. 'Oh. Like in the movie?'

Taylor just looked at him, and then left the room.

'Well played, young man,' Tippen said, impressed.

'I like his style,' Elwood agreed.

Kovac growled a little in his throat, as if to say he wasn't convinced just yet.

As soon as Taylor was out the door of the interview room, Stack got up and started to pace, holding his stomach, bending over a little.

'Oh man. Oh man,' he muttered.

'I don't know,' Taylor said, joining the small crowd in the cubicle. 'We've been at this for two hours already and he hasn't given us anything useful.'

'Except that he now sounds more like a suspect than a witness,' Elwood said. 'Well done.'

Taylor shrugged it off. He had shoulders like the fucking Rock. No possible way he bought his shirts off the rack.

'Ronnie Stack didn't stick a knife in a drug dealer — not face-to-face,' he said. 'He doesn't have the balls for murder.'

'No, but I'd say there's a good chance he knows who did,' Kovac said. 'We'll go back in together. If he knows anything, he'll tell us now.'

'Can we take a couple of minutes?' Taylor asked as Sam got up from his chair. 'The smell in that room is making me nauseous. I think the dude ate a head of cabbage for lunch. Anyhow, I don't know how much more we can squeeze out of him before he uses the *L* word.'

'That all depends on what you mean by that,' Elwood said, pointing at the computer screen. 'I think he's about to squeeze out something right now.'

Kovac turned his attention back to the screen. 'What the fuck is he doing?'

Ronnie Stack was hopping from foot to foot as he undid his pants, chanting, 'Oh shit, oh shit, oh shit!'

'Oh no!'

'No fucking way!'

'Aw, MAN!'

Even as they shouted their protests, their interviewee yanked his pants down and squatted over the room's tiny wastebasket, his ferret face squeezed tight.

'Oooooooh!'

'Not seriously!'

'I'll call Maintenance,' Taylor said, turning away, looking a little green beneath his tan.

'Good luck with that,' Kovac said. 'They're not coming back after the puke, not the guys on this shift.'

'Welcome to the big leagues, kid,' Tippen said, slapping Taylor on the shoulder. 'You scared the shit out of him, you get to clean it up.'

'Noooo, no, no,' Taylor said, shaking his head. 'I'm calling in a hazmat crew. I'm ready to puke right now. I'm not going back in there!'

'Somebody better go back in there,' Elwood said, pointing at the screen again.

Stack was crying now, crawling on his hands and knees across the floor, his pants still undone.

'What now?' Kovac asked, watching their

person of interest make his way toward the fan. At first he thought Stack was just trying to get away from the smell. Then he picked up the cord of the fan, raised it to his mouth, and tried to bite into it.

'Fuck!' Taylor shouted, bolting for the interview room.

The rest of them watched the action on the screen — Taylor bursting into the room, shouting, yanking the cord of the fan out of the wall before Stack could light himself up like a Christmas tree.

'Oh my God!' Taylor said, reeling at the stench. 'What the hell is wrong with you?'

He pursued Stack as the junkie jumped up and stumbled backward, hiking up his pants. 'Were you born in a barn? Shitting in the trash can? Seriously? Who does that? We have plumbing here!'

Stack stepped back, stumbled, kicking over the wastebasket and spilling the contents onto the floor. Overwhelmed by the stench, Taylor unloaded his lunch all over their suspect, to the groans and shouts of his fellow detectives.

'The kid gives his all,' Tippen said.

'We're going to have to burn sage in that room,' Elwood murmured seriously.

Kovac shook his head at the ridiculousness of it all. 'I'm getting too old for this shit.'

★ ★ ★

Kovac thought about that as he stared into his drink. He wished he was as young as he was the

27

first time he said he was too old. The big five-oh was looming large on the horizon. He was on the steep downhill side of making his thirty years on the job. He had always said he would make his thirty and move to a climate where he could wear bad Hawaiian shirts year round. Now that thirty was looming on the horizon, he had to admit he hated Hawaiian shirts and that the idea of retirement scared the crap out of him.

'Hey, move over, Methuselah. I need a seat and a stiff one,' Liska said.

'But would you like a drink?' Tippen asked.

Liska gave him the finger. Ever the lady.

They had a corner booth at Patrick's, an Irish bar owned by Swedes, conveniently located halfway between the sheriff's office and the police department. Any fool trying to rob the bar would have thirty or forty guns drawn on him all at once. The place was always packed with cops — off-duty cops, retired cops, cops just finished with their shifts, cops grabbing a meal before they went to work.

'To what do we owe the pleasure of your company, Ms. Liska?' Elwood asked. 'Isn't it a school night?'

'Speed is taking the boys to a wrestling meet at the U of M,' she said, sliding into the place they had made for her.

'Hot sweaty guys groping each other, and you're not going?' Tippen asked, arching a brow. 'Are you unwell?'

'Momma needs a vodka. What a rotten day.'

'Please. How can you even break a sweat in

Cold Case? Your vics have all been dead for years.'

'Like my love life,' Liska lamented on a sigh.

'Maybe that'll pick up now that you don't have to worry about going on a date smelling like a fresh corpse.'

'Always looking on the bright side, Elwood. I miss that,' she confessed, looking around. 'Where's the noob? I spent all day staring at Gene Grider's ugly mug. I need some eye candy.'

'He had to go home on account of the stench,' Kovac said.

They filled her in on the fiasco.

'That's so gross!' She laughed. 'You guys have all the fun!'

'See what you're missing out on, Tinks?'

Kovac had given her the nickname Tinker Bell on Steroids when she first came into Homicide. Tiny but fierce — and woe to the person who crossed her — she wielded a mean tactical baton. The name had quickly been shortened to Tinks for practical purposes. She was five feet five inches of dynamite with silver-blonde hair cropped short and sticking up all over in one of those trendy finger-in-the-light-socket cuts. Her blue eyes had a gaze that could cut steel.

The waitress brought her a vodka and tonic without Liska having to ask. She took a long drink.

'Don't rub it in,' she grumbled. 'So what happened to the twitch?'

'We had to call him trying to bite through the electrical cord a suicide attempt,' Kovac said. 'So, he's in the loony bin at HCMC on a psych hold. Now, of course, he's going to get a lawyer, and that'll be that. Taylor had him that close to spilling his guts,' he said pinching thumb and forefinger nearly together.

'He actually did do that, just not the way you wanted,' Liska said. 'I suppose none of you saw me on TV, seeing how you were in the midst of a literal shit storm. The Cold Case unit is officially launched. I'm the poster girl, thank you very much.'

'Did you wear a bikini?' Tippen asked.

'You're such a perv.'

'Don't undersell me,' Tippen said, pretending offense. 'I am *the* perv.'

'Whatever,' Kovac snapped, not in the mood for their usual banter. 'What case gets the big spotlight?'

'Ted Duffy.'

'That's stupid,' he said. 'No one's ever going to solve that case. There's jack shit to go on.'

'My words exactly,' Liska said. 'But Grider bullied it through. Then Mascherino gave it to me. I thought Grider's head would explode.'

'They were pals back in the day,' Kovac said. 'Grider and Duffy.'

'Did you know Duffy?'

'Yeah. He was a prick.'

'Salt of the earth, best cop to ever walk the earth — according to Grider.'

'Yeah, well, he's a prick, too,' Kovac said as he raised his burger to his mouth.

'I've already seen that for myself. Was he a good cop? Duffy?'

He chewed, nodded, swallowed. 'Yeah, he was.

30

I had just made detective the year Duffy bought it. I was low man on the totem pole in Sex Crimes. Duffy took all the plum cases, the high-profile stuff. But he solved them, so who was going to complain? He was Sex Crimes detective of the year three years in a row. Plenty of rapists and pedophiles hated him. When he got whacked, everybody figured it was someone he'd put away, but nothing ever panned out.'

'And now it's all on me,' Liska said with a facetious cheer. 'Yay!'

'Maybe the new media attention will shake something loose, get somebody to talk,' Elwood said.

'I hope so. After I spent an hour trying to convince everybody the case is unsolvable, I all but guaranteed Grider I can close it.'

'Don't let your mouth write a check your ass can't cash, Tinker Bell,' Kovac warned.

She reached over to his plate and stole some French fries, like she always did. 'You've got to quit eating this junk, Kojak. Between the fried food and the cigarettes — '

'I quit smoking.'

'Yeah, like twenty-nine times. Are you smoking these days? And remember, I asked a question I probably already know the answer to.'

Kovac scowled. 'Then you probably also know I'm going to tell you to fuck off.'

'I expected nothing less.'

This was how it was with them. She nagged him like a wife, always had. But there had never been anything sexual between them. She was more like an annoying kid sister he would have

31

walked through fire for.

He couldn't fault her reasoning for transferring. She wanted to be a good mother to her boys — and she was. She had managed to raise two good boys with no real help from her jerk-off ex-husband. Kovac just missed her. That was the plain fact of it. They worked well together. He felt a little like he was missing a limb without her.

'Everything changes, Kojak,' she had said to him months ago when she made her decision.

'That doesn't mean I have to like it,' he had answered.

4

Everything changes, Kovac thought to himself as he drove home through a cold, bleak rain, but he absolutely *didn't* like it. His mood matched the weather. He hated this time of year, this bitter season of raw cold and gray skies, knifing winds, and days that grew shorter and shorter. The year was old and dying like the few remaining leaves on the trees. It made him feel empty and alone. And he felt it most coming home to his nondescript box of a house in his tired, nondescript neighborhood.

This night, he didn't even have the energy to hate his next-door neighbor's lunatic mishmash Christmas decorations, which already cluttered his yard: plywood cutout snowmen and tin soldiers crowding around a nativity scene; an army of Santas mounting an attack on the house. At least the cranky old bastard wouldn't light it all up until the day after Thanksgiving.

It occurred to Kovac that he was probably also considered a cranky old bastard by most of the neighbors. He didn't fraternize. It was tough for him to relate to civilians, and vice versa. What did he have to talk about? Death, depravity, autopsy results, potential suspects who shit in trash cans for fear of having to speak to him.

He wasn't exactly party material, unless the party was full of cops swapping war stories and

33

engaging in gallows humor. Like a more-than-average number of his peers, he had two failed marriages to his credit, but the neighborhood ladies of reasonable age shied away from him because of his general attitude. He had been assured he wasn't scaring them off with his looks, even though his hair was more gray than brown and his face was a slightly asymmetrical road map of his life. He had character, like a beat-up old alley cat. Liska advertised him as a 'poor man's Harrison Ford,' whatever the hell that meant.

Anyway, he had pretty much abandoned the relationship idea as a self-fulfilling prophecy of wary anticipation, disappointment, and ongoing bitterness.

Feeling sorry for himself, he fell into his recliner and turned on the television. The Travel Channel was showing something left over from Halloween — *A Killer's Tour of London*, a guided tour of gruesome historical murder sites with costumed reenactments of the crimes. Further proof that people were just plain nuts, he thought glumly.

'Chin up, Kojak,' Liska had said to him tonight as they left the bar, giving him an elbow in the side and a cheeky, if forced, grin. 'Maybe you'll get a good juicy double homicide tomorrow. That'll cheer you up.'

If that was the best thing he had to look forward to, what the hell did that say about his life?

★   ★   ★

34

The house was quiet and dark at last after the chaos of the boys coming home. And when she thought 'boys,' Nikki included her ex-husband. In many ways, Speed Hatcher had never matured past seventeen. When he spent time with Kyle and R.J., he didn't play the role of father as much as big brother. He wanted to be friends with them. He wanted to be the good guy, never the authoritarian, never the disciplinarian, never the one to soothe hurts or sort out problems. He wanted to clown and show off and be one of the guys. That was Speed: an overgrown boy living out the badass fantasy.

Kyle was long since over it. Her quiet, serious, sensitive boy tolerated his father, but he hadn't fallen for Speed's best-buddy bullshit for years. He had long been more mature than his dad in most ways. R.J., two years younger, had always been more little boy to Kyle's little man. Now, as a teenager, he was beginning to see who his father really was, but he made a conscious decision to pretend otherwise.

When they came home from these outings it was always the same: Speed, too exuberant, too loud, trying too hard to sell himself. Kyle, too quiet, with an underlying current of anger. R.J., mirroring his father's behavior, but lacking the same bravado, confused and agitated by his feelings. And Nikki, simmering and ready to snap at her ex, wanting to protect her sons from the emotional damage he did with all good intentions.

At least she had invested in therapy, so she understood her shortcomings, even if she did continue to make the same mistakes again and again. At least she knew why.

'What do you want from me, Nikki?' Speed said with the usual exasperation as they had their usual argument after the boys had gone upstairs to bed. 'It's always the same bullshit with you! You rag on me for not spending enough time with them, then you rag on me when I do!'

What she wanted was for him to become an entirely different person inside the Speed suit. That wish was no more realistic now than it had been during their marriage. The reckless bad boy with the sexy grin had caught her eye when they were both in patrol uniforms, but what made him a hot, exciting lover lost its charm in the long term. Much as she hated to admit it, she had been one of those stupid girls who believed that men would change for them.

'It's nearly midnight and the boys are just getting to bed,' she said. She sat back against her desk in her tiny home office and crossed her arms. 'It's a school night, Speed. I asked you to have them back by ten.'

He shrugged this off. He stood in front of her with his hands jammed at his waist. His square jaw was set, his blue eyes narrowed and glinting like steel. He was shaving his head these days. The sharply carved mustache and goatee had been dyed dark. The shoved-up sleeves of his University of Minnesota T-shirt revealed the lower half of an inked mural on his left arm: the archangel Michael vanquishing Satan.

It suited him. He worked undercover narcotics in the St. Paul PD. Half the time even he didn't know if he was the good guy or the bad guy. He slipped in and out of character as easily as changing his shirt.

'So we're a little late — '

'The wrestling meet was over at nine thirty.'

'We stopped for burgers — '

'You stopped for pizza on the way there.'

'They're growing boys.'

'Who need their sleep.'

'Oh, for God's sake, Nikki. So they go to school tired one day. Big fucking deal.'

'Kyle has an algebra test tomorrow,' she said, trying to hang on to her temper. 'If you ever bothered to show up at a parent-teacher conference, you would know he struggles with math.'

He made a face. 'He wants to be an artist. He'll never use algebra in his whole life.'

'Except to get into a good college.'

'Whatever.'

Nikki shook her head, as if in amazement, though there was no surprise here. 'And there it is.'

'What?'

'The attitude.'

Speed threw up his hands and turned around in a little circle. 'Here we go again! Don't you ever get sick of singing the same fucking song, Nikki? 'Cause I sure as shit get tired of hearing it.'

'That's funny,' she said on a bitter laugh, 'because I'm pretty sure you never listen to anything I say. Or is it that I just sound like the teacher in a Peanuts cartoon to you: *Wah, wah,*

wah, wah, wah, wah.'

'That's about it,' he agreed. 'If Kyle wanted to stay home and study, why didn't he? He could have said no.'

Nikki slapped a palm to her forehead. 'Oh my God, you are so fucking obtuse! First, why should Kyle be the adult in the equation? That's supposed to be your job. Second, of course he wants to spend time with you more than he wants to study algebra. You're his father. He loves you at least as much as he resents you.'

'Ouch! Fucking low blow, Nikki!' he said, cringing. 'You're such a bitch since you changed jobs. Don't take it out on me that you left Homicide — '

'I did that for the boys,' she shot back. 'It's called making sacrifices for your children — a concept completely unfamiliar to you, I know.'

'Yeah, yeah. I'm an asshole and you're Supermom.'

'I do what needs to be done. You do whatever you want.'

'Then you won't be surprised when I leave.'

'Why would that surprise me? You do it all the time.'

R.J.'s voice came down the stairway. 'Mo-om! I don't feel good!'

Nikki gave her ex a nasty look. 'That's your cue to leave anyway — parental duty calling.'

'Suck it, Nikki.'

'Go home,' she said, tired of dealing with him. She pushed past him on her way to the stairs. 'I don't need another child to deal with. Two is my limit.'

★ ★ ★

Nikki sat on the bed beside R.J., his head on her shoulder as they waited for the antacid to soothe his upset stomach. He was already bigger than she — taller and heavier, and stocky like his dad — but that didn't stop him being her little boy when he didn't feel well.

In the shadowed amber light of the lamp on the nightstand, she took in his room. Posters of sports stars, a pennant from a Twins game, a shelf with trophies and awards he had won in football and hockey. His new passions were wrestling and Brazilian jiu-jitsu — also one of Kyle's sports. Several family room lamps had paid the price for witnessing their matches.

Kyle was her neat freak. Everything in his room was just so, bed made, clothes put away. R.J.'s armchair was overflowing with laundry — dirty, clean, and borderline. Athletic shoes littered the floor.

R.J. had inherited his father's blond cowlicks. His dimpled smile was all Speed. He was going to melt a lot of hearts. Unlike his father, R.J. was utterly lacking a talent for lying. Everything was right on the surface with him. If he did something to get in trouble, he was the first one to say so, telling Nikki the story in great detail, admitting any and all culpability. He didn't have a devious bone in his body.

Nikki hugged him tight.

'Feeling any better?' she asked quietly.

'A little,' he said. She could sense the weight of gravity in his pause. 'I wish you and Dad didn't hate each other so bad.'

Nikki winced internally. 'I don't hate your dad, R.J. We just push each other's buttons, that's all.'

'I hate it when you guys fight,' he said with a hint of little-boy whine in his voice. 'And you fight all the time.'

Speed wasn't around enough to qualify for 'all the time,' Nikki thought, but she didn't say this. She didn't want to call attention to the obvious. At any rate, that would only open the 'But you made us move away from him' argument.

She *had* moved them away from their dad, leaving St. Paul for Minneapolis on the excuse of a shorter commute to work and Kyle's scholarship to a top arts high school. In truth, she had not moved to keep Speed away from the boys, but to keep the boys from noticing that their father didn't give a shit most of the time. The list of times Speed had disappointed them by not showing up was long. Nikki had decided it was better if they blamed her for moving than thought about how many times their father had let them down.

'You fight because of us,' R.J. said, a little tremor in his voice. 'Because of me and Kyle.'

Nikki wanted to crawl in a hole. She and Speed at least tried to keep their voices down when they were fighting, as if that would keep the boys from feeling the pall of bitterness between them. Kids were so much more astute than adults ever gave them credit for.

'Your dad and I love you both so very much. Don't ever think we don't,' she said, holding him close, wondering how much of his upset stomach was junk food versus the stress of hearing his parents argue. 'We just don't agree on how to show it.'

'Well, I wish you'd figure it out,' he said with just enough petulance that it was almost funny. Almost.

'I promise we'll work on it,' Nikki said. 'You know I lie awake nights worrying about screwing you guys up for the rest of your lives. I'm trying not to. You get that, right?'

'You do okay, Mom.'

'Thanks.'

'And Dad does the best he can,' he said. 'His best just isn't the same as your best, that's all.'

Out of the mouths of babes.

'I'll try harder to remember that,' Nikki said, closing her eyes against the sudden rise of tears.

'Good. Thanks.'

'You're welcome. You're pretty darn smart, you know.'

'I try hard,' he said. 'That's the most you can ask from a guy.'

She thought her heart would burst with love for him.

He drifted off to sleep not long after. Nikki stayed, sitting on the bed beside him, watching him sleep, listening to him breathe. She had always loved this part of motherhood when they were small, just being with her boys as they slept, when the house was quiet and dark and she could pretend that their lives could be perfect and free of hurt or trouble.

Unwilling to make herself get up and leave, she dozed off, propped up against the pillows beside R.J., to the *tic tac, tic tac* of sleet tapping against the window.

5

The whispers came in the night, seductive and sinister, like snakes sliding into bed beside her.

Trust me. Let me help you . . .

Trust me. Let me comfort you . . .

Trust me. Let me touch you . . .

In the dream, she was eight, she was twelve, she was seventeen, nineteen — all at the same time. Her reaction was instant: fear, dread, her heart rate doubling, a terrible chill running through her like the blade of a sword. She woke with a gasp, a cold sweat drenching her. But she made no overt movement. Out of old habit, she lay as still as possible as she took in her surroundings, just in case she had awakened into a nightmare.

She made a visual inventory of the room in the glow of the nightlight: the bedside table draped in soft blue fabric, the chair with her robe tossed across the seat and arm, her slippers, the blue drapes that flanked the window . . .

As the roar of her pulse subsided, she became aware of the *tic tac, tic tac* of sleet against the windowpane.

She was home, in the present, safe. Her husband, Eric, sighed and stirred on the other side of the bed. Evi held her breath, hoping she hadn't disturbed his sleep. He turned over and settled, and she relaxed a little.

As many times as he had told her he didn't

mind waking up with her in the night, she still hated doing that to him. It upset him to know she was upset and that there was nothing he could do about it. He couldn't erase her bad memories. He could only help her try to make better, happier ones. Every day they were together accomplished that.

She slipped from the bed like a wraith, barely disturbing the covers, and moved soundlessly out of the room. The house was cold. She wrapped her robe and her arms around herself and went down the hall to her daughter's room.

The same amber nightlight as in her own bedroom glowed in Mia's room — and everywhere else in the house, for that matter. She couldn't tolerate absolute darkness. The light just kissed Mia's cheek as she slept, letting Evi see her daughter's long eyelashes and rosebud mouth, her small hand curled beside her pillow. At five years old, Mia declared herself no longer a baby, but her thumb was always at the ready as she slept, just in case.

Evi crept into the room and carefully rearranged the blankets around her daughter's shoulders, making sure the nose of her teddy bear poked out above the covers. Her heart swelled with love as she watched her child sleep. And just at the edge of that love lay the familiar fear that this couldn't all be real. She couldn't have such a perfect life with such a perfect family. How could she have met a man as good and kind as Eric? How could she be lucky enough to have him love her? How was it the universe had given her this beautiful child to call her own, to raise and love?

'Too good to be true' was the theme of her daily existence.

She and Eric had been married six years now. Maybe when they had a decade together she would start to let her guard down, stop waiting for the other shoe to drop.

Doubt was the last and biggest hurdle she circled around and around, never quite brave enough to attempt to clear it. At least the pace at which she ran around it had slowed from frenetic to familiar over the years. Her therapist was satisfied with that much. She didn't share Evi's disappointment in herself at her inability to be completely happy.

She had the perfect husband, the perfect child, the perfect home, the perfect job. Why could she not be perfectly happy? Was she ungrateful? No. Nothing could be further from the truth. Was she weak? Did she know deep down that she didn't deserve any of it? That was her greatest fear — what if that one remaining voice of criticism was right after all?

'You have to convince yourself that voice is wrong,' Dr. Price had told her so many times over the years. So many times that Evi had long ago become too embarrassed even to bring up the subject anymore.

Leaving Mia's room, she went downstairs to the living room and curled up in a corner of the sofa with her knitting, and turned the television on to keep her company and distract her from her anxiety.

The nightmares left an emotional aftertaste

that lingered. She didn't have them every night, or even every month. When she had gone without one for a long time, she could almost convince herself they would never come back. And once they returned, she despaired of their ever letting her sleep in peace.

A local channel was rerunning the ten o'clock news, showing the weather advisories and preemptive school closings. Temperatures were hovering just at freezing, with precipitation coming in a mix of rain and sleet. The only vehicles advised to be on the road overnight were the trucks from the Department of Transportation that were out laying down sand and salt in anticipation of intrepid morning commuters.

Mia would be disappointed not to have school. Unlike Evi, her daughter was a social butterfly, friendly and confident. Those were traits Evi had to work at. She loved her job and the kids she worked with. She was proud of the work she did and the accomplishments of the Chrysalis Center, but none of it came easily to her. Her daughter, on the other hand, had the confidence of a child who had never known what it was not to be loved completely. Mia would always have that. No matter what else happened in her life, she would always know that she was loved absolutely.

That had to be one of a mother's greatest accomplishments, Evi thought. She wondered how differently her life would have turned out if she'd had that kind of unconditional love as a child.

No matter, she told herself, because her life

had turned out like this: perfect. And as she thought it, and as she smiled wider, she felt the residual anxiety from the dream fade away.

She focused on her knitting: a winter scarf in shades of pink. She had a stack of scarves in a variety of colors and textures already stashed away in the gift closet, Christmas presents for the girls she worked with — her extended family of troubled teenagers.

'Isn't the news depressing enough the first time around?' Eric asked as he came into the living room in red plaid flannel pajama bottoms and a faded black T-shirt that had been through the wash too many times. He slouched down onto the sofa beside her, blond hair tousled, a sleepy smile on his handsome face.

'I missed it the first time around,' Evi said. 'I was doing your disgusting hockey laundry.'

'You are so beautiful,' he said. 'Have I told you in the last two minutes how beautiful you are?'

He smiled at her like he was trying to pick her up, like he was sharing an inside joke, shining brown eyes always ready with a wink.

'You are the perfect husband. But your hockey laundry still stinks.' Evi chuckled. 'FYI: Mia doesn't have school tomorrow.'

As a firefighter, Eric was twenty-four hours on and forty-eight hours off. He took full advantage of his days off to be the house-husband and be involved in his daughter's life. He was, in the opinion of all Evi's friends, the perfect modern man.

'If this sleet keeps up, we'll all have the day off,' he said.

'I've got a big meeting — ' Evi started.

Eric narrowed his eyes. 'I don't want you driving if the roads are bad. Never mind that you're a safe driver. These first bad weather days leading into winter people lose their minds. You'd think they lived in Miami and had never seen snow.

'Stay home and play *Frozen* with us,' he suggested. 'Mia might let you be Elsa. Once. Only once. I get to be Kristoff *and* Olaf.'

'I've been informed I don't sing well enough to be Elsa.'

'I love you anyway.'

'Thanks.'

'Trouble sleeping tonight?' he asked, trying to slip that in casually.

'I'm fine,' Evi said. 'I woke up and couldn't get back to sleep. A little TV, a little knitting . . . I'm fine.'

'It's the pressure of being a local celebrity,' Eric said teasingly.

The Minneapolis *Star Tribune* had recently run a weekend feature story on Chrysalis and its work with victims of sexual abuse, domestic violence, and sex trafficking. In her capacity as the center's senior social services case worker, Evi had been pictured and quoted, speaking out about the difficulties faced by victims who had aged out of the foster care system but didn't meet the requirements for most women's shelters.

'I'm last Sunday's news,' she said.

She had been a little uncomfortable with the spotlight, brief as it had been, but publicity for the center was always welcome. The article had generated interest from several local TV and radio stations in the week that followed, but media attention had since moved on to new stories.

Evi dropped a stitch in her knitting as one of those new stories filled her television screen with photos and graphics. Her heartbeat quickened. A strange cold flush ran over her from head to toe.

NEW COLD CASE UNIT TARGETS UNSOLVED HOMICIDES.

The photograph took her back in time. Ted Duffy in a suit, looking authoritative, his face set in stern lines as he accepted an award, his wife, Barbie, and his twin brother standing in the background clapping.

'Using half a million dollars in federal grant money, the Minneapolis Police Department, in conjunction with the Hennepin County Attorney's Office, will launch a dedicated cold case unit this week . . . '

The unit's first case would be the unsolved murder of decorated sex crimes detective Ted Duffy.

Eric looked from Evi to the TV and back. 'What? Do you know that guy?'

'No,' she lied, setting her knitting aside. She turned back to her husband with a smile. 'A dedicated cold case unit will be a godsend for a lot of victims' families from back when. Kate Quinn will be knocking on the door of that unit first thing tomorrow.'

'While we sleep in,' Eric said, getting up from the couch. He held his hand out to her and pulled her up and into his arms. 'Let's go back to bed, Mrs. Burke. We've got some serious snuggling to do.'

Evi pressed her cheek into his shoulder and hugged him tight. 'That's the only place I want to be.'

In the here and now with the man of her dreams. But when she closed her eyes, she saw only the faces of her past.

6

Sleet began to pelt the windows at around one thirty in the morning. The sound woke Professor Lucien Chamberlain from a shallow sleep. He fumbled for his glasses on the nightstand and checked the time on his phone.

Beside him, his wife slept on, undisturbed by the rapid *tic tac tic tac* of the ice pellets striking the glass. Of course, she had taken to wearing earplugs to bed because she claimed he snored. Ridiculous. He didn't snore. *She* snored. She snored especially when she had been drinking, and she had been drinking more than usual lately.

She thought he didn't notice. She thought she had become so adept at hiding it over the years that she could fool him. The truth was he didn't care anymore. As long as she didn't embarrass him in public or in front of his peers or their neighbors, he ignored her.

That was, and had been, the state of their marriage: tolerance and cohabitation. He had no interest in her as a woman any longer. He never really had. His life was about his career. She had her committees and charities. They were companions for social events.

She had never been a beautiful woman, he thought as he looked at her in the dim light from the bathroom. She had started leaving a nightlight on after stumbling into the shower stall by mistake one night, injuring herself badly enough that she had needed to go to the emergency room.

The hospital staff had jumped to the conclusion that Lucien had beaten her, and had called the police. It still made him furious to remember how shabbily the police treated him, and how the neighbors reacted when Sondra's eye blackened and her bruises ripened — the surreptitious stares and quickly averted eyes. As if they could believe he, a highly respected member of the faculty at the University of Minnesota, would ever have been so stupid and brutish as to punch a woman in the face.

He had resented Sondra for putting him in the position to be judged and gossiped about. Her overly eager attempts to explain away the bruises had only made him seem all the more guilty. And the more irritated he became, the more obsequious she became, until he questioned the logic of ever having married her in the first place.

No, she was not a beautiful woman, and at fifty-eight her plainness was giving way to a heavy, matronly look he didn't like at all. He told her to diet and exercise. It didn't help. He believed she secretly ate sweets and hid the evidence. He once went through her dresser drawers when she was away visiting her mother, but had found nothing incriminating, only a vast collection of foundation garments she never appeared to wear.

He had married her for her family connections and, to a lesser degree, her money — better, more logical reasons than looks or lust. They had been together nearly thirty years.

He watched her sleep now, envious. He had always been a light sleeper. His brain was always working. Now he would lie here, driven mad by the incessant *tic tac tic tac* while his mind worried at the day-to-day annoyances of academia, and the power struggle going on in the History Department.

He fretted because he hadn't published anything recently. And that thought automatically brought the rush of bitterness that he had never been able to sell his book on the comparative similarities and differences in the warrior cultures of medieval China and Japan, his masterwork.

He should already have been named head of East Asia studies, not be fighting for the title. If he had a published book that was well received by his peers, the university would not have been able to deny him. He would have been the clear front-runner. Instead, he was in competition with Ken Sato and some Vietnamese woman from UCLA.

Sato, who never failed to irritate with his unconventional lifestyle and his unconventional teaching methods. Lucien suspected Sato was being considered for the job largely because he was Japanese, and the chosen star of that pompous ass and committee member, Hiroshi Ito. Lucien had considered suing on the basis of racial discrimination if Sato — or the Vietnamese woman, for that matter — were to get the position. He was far more deserving. Then again, he worried what a lawsuit would do to his reputation. Reputation was everything in academia.

If Sondra's father had still been alive, his influence at the university would have negated all other issues. What terrible luck that he had died of a heart attack nearly a year past. Lucien was beginning to feel that the powers of the universe were against him. And now, to further complicate his life, was this ridiculous business with Diana and the Office for Conflict Resolution. The mere thought of it infuriated him. The conniving little bitch — jeopardizing his promotion, forcing him to take the actions he was about to put in motion . . .

No wonder he couldn't sleep.

Tic tac tic tac. The sound was relentless.

Then came a sound out of time, out of place. A sound that seemed to come from another part of the house. Downstairs.

He sat up in the bed and strained to listen. They lived in a lovely old established neighborhood. But there were plenty of criminals in the run-down parts of the city. Crime was no longer a rarity in Minneapolis. Lucien blamed Minnesota's overly generous public assistance programs for ruining the work ethic of the poor minorities.

He'd had a home security system installed years ago. Sondra had the jewelry she had inherited from her mother. He had a valuable collection of Asian antiques he had accumulated over the years, most notably artifacts of generations of samurai and ninja warriors. Had Sondra forgotten to set the alarm after dinner? It was her responsibility. He often worked late in his study, too engrossed to be bothered with household details.

Tic tac tic tac tic tac . . . thump.

Or was it just the wind? There was a shutter loose on one of the study windows. Someone from the handyman service was supposed to have come four days ago to fix it, but it had been banging against the house earlier in the evening. He had snapped at Sondra for hiring the incompetent fools in the first place.

She had originally called them to clean the rain gutters and put on the storm windows. The service was unreliable, its workers rude. Lucien wrote a scathing review of their work on Yelp after the storm window fiasco. The owner promised to rectify the situation in a timely fashion, but they had yet to show up. They were in no hurry to do a job for which they would not get paid. Now the shutter, which they had probably purposely loosened in the first place, would drive him mad the rest of the night with the syncopated combination of *bang, thump,* together with the *tic tac tic tac tic tac* of the freezing rain on the windows.

He wasn't going to get a minute's sleep, and first thing in the morning he had yet another meeting, with Foster, the department chair; the director of undergraduate studies; and Hiroshi Ito, professor emeritus. He needed to be sharp, to present himself at his best. The decision on the head of East Asia studies would be made before the Thanksgiving break. He would go into the meeting with confidence, sure in the knowledge that he had an ace to play that Ken Sato could never trump, but still, he wanted his sleep. He wanted to look as confident as he felt.

Maybe if he closed all the doors between the stairs and the study, the sound would be muffled enough not to bother him. It was on the other side of the house from the master bedroom.

Giving his sleeping wife another resentful glare, he threw the covers back and slipped out of bed. A creature of habit, he put on his dressing gown, adjusting the sleeves of his pajamas so the cuffs showed and tying the belt in a tidy knot. He paused at the head of the stairs, just in front of his pair of eighteenth-century Qing dynasty carved rosewood chairs and the spotlighted Qing period portrait on silk. He paused and listened.

Thump bump, thump bump, thump . . .

Yes, the shutter. After his meeting tomorrow he would take a moment to go on Yelp and write another scathing review of the handyman service.

He made his way down the stairs with the bearing of a king, the amber glow from the tiny art spotlight floating ahead of him, ever dimmer and more diffuse. He didn't bother turning on a light at the bottom of the stairs. The white of the streetlight at the end of the block came in through the transom above the front door. Turning, he made his way toward the back of the house. His study was just beyond the dining room. He would shut the study door, and shut the heavy pocket doors to the dining room on his way back.

Bang thump . . . bang thump . . . bang thump . . .

The sleet tapping on the windows seemed louder to him down here for some reason. His level of irritation rose as he realized he must have neglected to turn off the lamp in the study. The glow came into the dining room from across the far hallway. The dining room seemed cold and drafty. The diaphanous white curtain at the French doors to the patio drifted into the room, fluttering like a ghost in a movie.

The chill he felt then came from within.

One of the doors stood open a foot or so — just enough for a person to slip inside.

Lucien stood frozen, unable to think, unable to move.

The dark figure came from the direction of his study. A ninja! he thought in astonishment. A silent intruder dressed entirely in black, even the hands covered; even the head was covered in black, only the eyes showing. Eyes looking straight at him, shining black, like an animal's.

Lucien drew a breath to call out, but no sound came out of his suddenly bone-dry mouth. It felt as if the walls of his throat were stuck together, cutting off his air, as if an unseen hand had him by the neck.

In the next instant, the violence began like a sudden, terrible storm. The ninja came at him, and was on him before he could do more than stagger back and slam into the dining room table. The strength and power of the assailant was overwhelming. He felt like a frail old man, like his bones would snap and crumble to dust beneath the other's strength.

And they did. His collarbone shattered beneath the first strike. He could raise only one arm up to protect his head, and it went numb as he was struck on the wrist.

The attacker's fists were like iron, raining down blow after blow. Lucien scrambled to get away, falling toward the open patio door, landing on one knee on the hardwood floor. His kneecap exploded with pain. Even as he tried to crawl for the door, he looked back over his shoulder.

The faint light caught for a second — not on the fist of his assailant, but on the weapon he clutched in one hand. The *nunchaku*: two handles fashioned of iron-hard oak connected at one end by a short horsehair rope. The ninja wielded the weapon as a club, bringing it down with vicious intent, striking Lucien's head once, then twice.

His vision blurred as his eye socket collapsed. He heard the crunch of his skull fracturing beneath the second blow. He lost consciousness before he could register the next strike. He was unaware as the assailant kicked him viciously in the ribs and then stepped behind him and brought the *himo*, the horsehair rope that linked the two handles, beneath his chin and used the ancient weapon as a garrote to choke him until his tongue came out of his mouth, swollen and purple.

The assailant dropped him to the floor in a heap, and dropped the bloody *nunchaku* beside him. Shards of bone penetrated the left frontal lobe of Lucien's brain, severing neural pathways, disconnecting the structures vital for forming thought and emotion. The damage set off an electrical storm, sending random signals to his limbs. His arms and legs jerked and twitched like those of a marionette in the hands of a mad puppet master.

★　★　★

The assailant stood back and watched by the silvered light that fell through the patio door, mesmerized as the victim's arms and legs jumped and flopped. The movement subsided slowly until the man lay still on the floor.

The face was caved in like a smashed jack-o'-lantern's. His right cheek was lying in a pool of blood. The left eye hung from its shattered socket by a tangle of nerves and blood vessels. The nose was a lump of mush. He was still breathing in irregular fits and starts, gurgles and wheezes, causing tiny bubbles to form in the bloody mess of his mouth. Several teeth lay scattered on the Oriental rug.

The weapon lay near the man's mangled left hand, as if he had been the one wielding it. Blood and hair stuck to the heavy oak handles.

Pulling a cell phone from a pocket, the killer leaned down close and took a photograph of the victim's face, and then took another from slightly above, making sure to get the weapon in the picture, feeling almost giddy with the rush of excitement.

Killing felt good, satisfying, exciting. *Very* exciting. Empowering.

In no hurry, not concerned about being found, not concerned that the police might be coming, the assailant rose and went back into the study. A small lamp gave enough light to view the collection of ancient weapons mounted on the walls and in display cases. Knives and daggers, helmets and fearsome painted face masks of long-dead warriors from the other side of the world. And swords. Long, curving swords, some with elaborate scabbards and handles of carved wood, some with etched steel blades, some simple and plain. All of them deadly.

One of the swords was chosen and carefully lifted down to admire, and an idea formed and slithered through the killer's mind like a viper. The blade hissed as it was slipped from its scabbard. The light shone down the length of it. The edge was tested against the pad of a thumb. A tiny bead of blood welled up and ran down the blade. The sight of it brought an almost sexual stirring within.

'Lucien?'

The woman's voice was far away and tentative.

'Lucien? Are you down here? You should be in bed! You have that meeting in the morning.'

The voice was growing louder, coming closer.

The assailant went very still. Dead calm.

'Lucien? I hope you're not eating something at this hour. You'll get your acid reflux back,' she said as she came into the dining room. 'Why do you have the door open in this weather? Everything is getting wet! What are you thinking?'

She came around the side of the table,

stopping at the sight of her husband lying dead in a pool of blood.

'Lucien!'

She looked up and shrieked as Death came straight at her.

The scream died in her throat as the sword struck her in the side of the neck.

7

'So, I'm leaning toward Stench,' Kovac said as he walked into the cubicle with his third cup of office coffee.

He'd had the better part of a pot of the stuff at home, trying to rouse himself from a listless night's sleep. Liska had given him a modern cup-at-a-time machine with all the lights and bells and whistles, but he turned his nose up at the fussy little flavored pods that went in it as 'not real coffee.' He still used a Mr. Coffee machine from the last century. He and Mr. Coffee produced a brew that was capable of stripping varnish — not unlike the stuff that came out of the office coffeemaker.

Taylor looked up from his computer screen, green eyes bright and clear, no bags under them. 'I'm sorry? What?'

'For your nickname. You need a nickname. I've been lax with that, I admit. It doesn't usually take me this long. I'm off my game,' Kovac confessed.

'That's okay,' Taylor said, going back to his work. 'I don't need a nickname.'

'Sure you do. We can't just keep calling you Noob. It's too generic.'

'That's okay.'

'Did you have a nickname in the service?'

'Taylor.'

'That lacks imagination.'

Although, that might have suited him, Kovac thought as he looked at Taylor's workspace. It was devoid of the ridiculous tacky and vulgar stuff Tinks had collected to clutter the place up — her coffee mug full of crazy pens, the cop cartoons printed off the Internet and pinned up on the walls, the voodoo doll of her ex, the framed photos of her kids. Taylor didn't have so much as a Post-it. Boring. Finally, a flaw.

Kovac's work area was a mess: binders and file folders in precarious stacks, notes and reminders hastily scribbled on scraps of paper and stuck haphazardly to the cabinet doors and the bottom of his computer screen. On the shelf above the computer a human skull sat with a fake severed finger in its nose hole and a cigarette clenched between its teeth.

He set his coffee mug on the desk — black with a ceramic gun for a handle. The taste went bitter in his mouth, and his mood soured. Michael Taylor was the modern detective in a nicely tailored charcoal suit and shined shoes, a business executive with a badge. His side of the cubicle could have belonged to a bank vice president. Kovac, on the other hand, felt like he'd slept in his clothes. He had nicked himself shaving. He looked like he was on the backside of a three-day bender, with his bloodshot eyes and the dark smudges beneath them, while his partner could have been a model for *GQ* magazine.

'I like Reek, myself,' Tippen said, wandering over from the giant whiteboard where all active cases were listed on a grid. 'It has a medieval feel to it.'

'Maybe we could put this off until I do something more impressive than puke on a suspect who shit all over the interview room,' Taylor suggested.

Tippen shrugged. 'We could, but seriously, how are you going to top that?'

'How about a double homicide with a samurai sword?' Elwood asked as he joined them.

'What are the odds of that happening?' Kovac grumbled.

'Better than even. The call just came in. You guys are up.'

★ ★ ★

The city looked like it was made of glass, all the trees and bushes, parked cars and fire hydrants encased in a thick layer of ice that had turned the entire metro area beautiful and treacherous overnight. The sleet and freezing rain that had begun after midnight had eventually turned into a light snow as the temperature dropped, covering the ice, doubling the danger. The ERs would be full of car accident victims and slip-and-fall broken hips and wrists.

Taylor had snagged the car keys before Kovac could reach for them, and drove them across town like a grandma, carefully avoiding the fender benders that littered the streets.

'I'd like to get there before they mummify,' Kovac complained, drumming his fingers impatiently on the armrest.

'I'd like to get there in one piece,' Taylor countered. 'They aren't going to get any deader.'

Kovac scowled. 'You know, I've probably been driving longer than you've been alive.'

'Yeah. It's a pure damn miracle you've made it to this ripe old age. I'm just making sure I get as far along as you.'

'Yeah, well,' Kovac grumbled. 'By the time we get to this scene . . . '

Two radio cars were parked at the curb in front of the address. A news van had already staked out a spot on the opposite side of the street. Barricades had been put across the sidewalk and the end of the driveway to keep the vultures at bay. If the words *samurai sword* had gone out over the radio waves, every reporter and kook with a scanner would be rolling up at any minute.

'Bad news travels fast,' Taylor said as they pulled in behind the crime scene van.

'Faster than you,' Kovac returned, getting out of the car.

The house was a formal two-story brick Colonial that would have looked at home in Boston-white trim, with black shutters and a black lacquered front door with a big brass knocker and a wreath of wheat and fall leaves that said 'rich but homey.' The kind of place upper-middle-class families had Thanksgiving dinners as depicted on television: everyone slender and well dressed, smiling and laughing. Not the kind of place where people were found hacked to death.

That was the thing with murder, Kovac thought as he flashed his ID at the uniform on the front steps: The emotions that fueled violence didn't discriminate. People of all socioeconomic classes were equally capable of hate and rage, and equally capable of dying in a puddle of their own terror.

'Taylor! Mr. Bigshot homicide detective,' the uniform said with a grin.

Taylor ducked his head, sheepish. 'Dave. How's it going?'

'It's a fucking bloodbath inside, man. Hope you didn't eat a big breakfast. I hear you've developed a delicate stomach.'

'Ha ha,' Taylor said without humor. 'Were you first on the scene?'

'Yeah. The university called for a welfare check. The male DB was a professor of something or other. He didn't show up for a big meeting, didn't answer on any of his contact numbers. We came, did a walk around the house, spotted the bodies through the patio door to the dining room. Looks like that's where the killer went in — knocked a pane out of the French doors, reached inside, and let himself in.'

'Any footprints?'

He shook his head. 'Had to have happened before the snow.

'We went in and checked the house for other possible victims,' he went on. 'It's all clear. Looks like a burglary gone bad. The home office and the bedrooms were gone through.'

'Have there been any recent burglaries in the area?' Taylor asked.

'A couple B-and-Es, no violence, no home-invasion shit. This is a nice quiet neighborhood.'

'Suspects on the burglaries?' Kovac asked.

'Not that I've heard.'

'What's this bullshit about a samurai sword?'

'No bullshit, Sarge. You'll see. Down the hall and to the left. These people were killed by freaking ninjas.'

'Ninjas didn't use samurai swords,' Taylor said. 'Samurai used samurai swords.'

'There's a difference?'

'That's why you're still in a uniform, Dave.'

'Fuck you, dude,' he said with a laugh. 'I'm not stupid. I just lack ambition.'

'I don't remember any questions about ninjas on the detective's exam,' Kovac said as they went into the front hall of the house and put sanitary booties on over their shoes.

'I was a ninja in a past life,' Taylor said, deadpan as he pulled on purple disposable gloves.

Kovac looked around the hallway they had come into. As the exterior of the house suggested, everything was prim and proper: cream-colored wainscoting and drab gray wallpaper, an expensive-looking Oriental carpet runner leading the way down the hall. To the left was a formal living room. The furniture looked stiff and uncomfortable, the chairs upholstered in silky fabrics that didn't invite anyone to sit on them. It was a 'kids, don't touch anything' kind of a house, a museum of antiques and formality. At the top of the staircase a spotlight shone on a huge painting of an ancient Chinese man scowling down on them with disapproval.

Taylor looked from the staircase to the front door, frowning. 'That's bad feng shui.'

'What?'

'The Chinese never want a staircase to end directly opposite the door like that. All of your good chi will go out the door. It's very unlucky.'

Kovac's brows pulled together. 'Who are you?'

Taylor shrugged. 'I grew up on *Karate Kid* and *Teenage Mutant Ninja Turtles*, then Bruce Lee and Jackie Chan. I've always had an interest in the martial arts and the societies that practice them.

'These people have all this Chinese and Japanese art and antiques. They were allegedly killed with a samurai sword. Too bad they didn't extend their interests to philosophy. They should have at least hung a mirror over the door to bounce the good chi back in before it could escape.'

'Their good mojo went out the front door, and this is why a ninja killed them?'

'If you buy into the philosophy,' Taylor said, snapping photos of the offending staircase and front door with his iPhone. 'There's a whole faction of people who believe Bruce Lee died because the design of the house he was living in flew in the face of feng shui.'

'Are you one of them?' Kovac leveled a flat stare at him. 'Don't even think about trying to feng shui the cubicle.'

Taylor held his hands up to ward off the idea. 'Hey, man, I've got my shit together. Your life force is not my business.'

'That's right.'

As they proceeded down the hall, the stench of a violent death scene wafted out of the dining room to greet them: blood, urine, and shit, the stink of absolute terror.

Kovac cut his partner a look. 'Don't puke on my scene, ninja boy.'

'Don't worry,' Taylor said, brows pulling low over his narrowed eyes as he put his game face on.

'Mr. Culbertson!' Kovac called out as they stopped in the wide doorway to the scene of the crime.

The room was busy with a swarm of people in jumpsuits collecting evidence, photographing the scene, dusting for fingerprints. Culbertson, the ME's investigator, had his back to them, hands on his hips as he stood over a body.

He was the first person to physically examine the decedent at a death scene. No one touched the body before he did, for any reason. It was his unpleasant task to take the temperature of the corpse to aid in figuring out the time of death. It was his job to assess and make note of the visible wounds and a hundred other minute details.

Culbertson turned around to face them, blocking their view of the scene. Lean and vaguely scruffy, fast-talking and shifty-eyed, he was the kind of guy who looked like he would step out of a dark alley in a sketchy part of town and try to hustle you out of something or into something. Kovac had known him for years. They had polished off more than a few bottles of whiskey together, burning the taste of death out of their mouths at the end of a long night.

'It's about time you got here, Kojak. I thought sure the words *samurai sword* would get even your jaded ass excited about a couple of stiffs. You're slowing down in your old age.'

'Fuck you very much,' Kovak said without much rancor. 'Steve, Michael Taylor, who drives like an old lady despite his dashing good looks. Taylor, Steve Culbertson, ME investigator and all-around reprobate.'

'Another noob?' Culbertson asked, arching a dark, bushy brow. 'What happened to the last one?'

'He reconsidered his career path.'

'I can't imagine why. Was it your sunny disposition or the fact that you drive like a drunken Formula One reject? You look like hell, by the way.'

'Thanks. I'm trying to dispel that whole 'fifty is the new thirty' myth.'

'Job well done.'

'Can you introduce us to our host and hostess here?' Kovac asked. 'I'm sure we'll find their personalities more agreeable than yours.'

'Be really careful where you step,' Culbertson warned, going into professional mode. 'There is literally blood everywhere in here. You can't see it so much on the red walls, but it's on the ceiling, the chandelier, the drapes. This was your basic massacre.'

Culbertson stepped to the side, clearing the sight line to the carnage on the dining room floor. The scene stopped Kovac in his tracks.

The contrast of the fussy, formal room and the raw animal violence that had ended these people's lives was jarring. The victims' bodies had been so abused that Kovac's brain

70

automatically wanted to reject the idea they had ever been living, breathing human beings. His last tiny sliver of raw, unjaded humanity, he thought. The thought lasted less than the blink of an eye.

He had seen people decapitated, disemboweled, burned, drowned, strangled, beaten, run over. Not that long ago he and Liska had a case where the assailants had poured acid on the victim's face while she was still alive. There was no end to the ways people could destroy one another.

'One assailant or two?' Kovac asked.

'I'd say one. Looks like one set of shoe prints in the blood.'

The female victim lay on her back, spread-eagle, with her head at Kovac's feet. She was, quite literally, bathed in blood. It was impossible to determine her hair color, difficult at a glance even to distinguish her race. He could see she was a woman because her nightgown had been torn, exposing one large, bloody breast that had been sliced diagonally.

A horrific gash cleaved the left side of the woman's face, from her partially severed ear, across her cheek, completely opening her mouth. The edges of the lips curled back in a macabre grimace, exposing muscle, tissue, bone, and teeth. Another gash cut deep into her neck where it met her shoulder.

That had probably been the first blow, Kovac thought. The one that knocked her down, but not the one that killed her. She had been slashed and stabbed in the torso multiple times. The weapon that had been used to kill her stood upright. Her killer had run the sword through her stomach so hard the blade had penetrated the floor and stuck there like a steel exclamation point.

'Sondra Chamberlain,' Culbertson said. 'Fifty-eight years of age, and her husband, Professor Lucien Chamberlain, forever fifty-three. They were just starting to go into rigor when I got here. So I'd say they were probably killed between one A.M. and two thirty. Obviously, they died right where they are. You can see what happened to the wife. The husband was bludgeoned, strangled, and stabbed in the back — probably postmortem. Toss up on cause of death. He took a hellacious beating with the handle end of the nunchucks.'

'Nunchucks?' Kovac repeated.

'Surprised a thief?' Taylor speculated.

Kovac gave him the eye. 'How many burglars carry nunchucks around with them?'

'We'll get to that,' Culbertson said. 'Looks like this patio door was the point of entry.'

'No security system?' Taylor asked.

Culbertson shrugged. 'Maybe it wasn't on. My mother is eighty-two and she refuses to turn her alarm on.'

The professor lay facedown, head pointing in the opposite direction of his wife's, beaten down in his pajamas and bathrobe. Something about that struck Kovac as extra sad. He guessed the professor had probably been a fussy little man who had creases pressed into his pajama bottoms. He had gotten up in the night and put

72

on his bathrobe and slippers to meet the Grim Reaper.

Kovac picked his way around the bodies to find a place he could hunker down and get a better look at the damage done to the man's head. The left side of the skull had been caved in with terrible force, like a hardboiled egg that had been smashed with a hammer. Shards of bone spiked the exposed brain. The left eyeball hung out of the shattered socket, lolling against the man's bloody, broken cheek.

Lying on the bloodstained Oriental rug a foot or so from the dead man's hand was the apparent murder weapon: wood-handled nunchucks covered in blood, strands of the victim's salt-and-pepper hair sticking to the ends.

'Ever see anything like this before?' Kovac asked Taylor as he straightened.

'Yeah,' Taylor said quietly. 'I have. But not in this country.'

'Looks to me like whoever did this enjoyed himself,' Culbertson said.

'So, we've got a sword-wielding maniac running around the city,' Kovac declared. 'Great. A fucking wack job.'

'He left his weapons here,' Taylor pointed out.

'I don't think he brought them to the party,' Culbertson said. 'These were weapons of opportunity. Come see.'

They followed a trail of bloody footprints out of the dining room and to a study full of dark furniture and a darker collection. Weapons lined the walls — swords, daggers, knives, Chinese throwing stars, stuff Kovac had seen only in movies. Glass cases displayed iron helmets and painted face masks from ages past. Several of the cases had been shattered, the contents taken.

'Safe to assume our assailant helped himself to the weaponry,' Culbertson said. 'It's a homicidal maniac's wet dream.'

Kovac put his reading glasses on and took a closer look at the deadly beauty of the weapons: swords impressed with intricate carvings in the handles, etchings on the blades. Small plaques beneath each piece gave a description, a date, and a place of origin.

'So,' Taylor said, 'the question is did he know the weapons would be here, or were they a bonus once he got in the house?'

'That's for you guys to figure out,' Culbertson said. 'I'm going to go do my job. I've got a bus coming to transport the bodies as soon as you give the go-ahead, Sam.'

'Okay. Thanks, Steve.'

'This one has to be worth a couple of rounds at Patrick's tonight, don't you think?'

'At least. You buying?'

'Shit, no. The noob's buying, right?'

Taylor looked confused. 'Why am I buying?'

'Because you're celebrating your first scene working with me,' Culbertson said on his way out. 'Kids these days. No appreciation for tradition.'

Kovac rested his hands on his hips and looked around the study. A couple of desk drawers that had probably been locked had been forced open and rummaged through. Books had been cleared from shelves and lay scattered on the floor.

Someone had been looking for a safe, most likely. There were a number of empty spaces in the wall display where only the small plaque beneath described the pieces that had been there.

'So, maybe this mutt came looking to steal specific items,' Kovac speculated. 'A collector with a bad attitude? Who would know this stuff is here?'

'Family, friends, colleagues, maybe other collectors. His students, maybe.'

Kovac scratched a hand back through his hair and sighed as he thought about the other recent burglaries in the neighborhood. No violence, the officer had said. No violence, no witnesses. There probably hadn't been nunchucks or samurai swords at the other houses, either. Sometimes the only difference between a thief and a murderer was opportunity.

Many a killer began his career by accident — in the heat of passion, in a moment of self-defense, in a split-second's rage when a weapon was within reach. He struck out and killed — and then came the rush of adrenaline, the surge of power as he realized what he'd done. Few things were more intoxicating to a person with no conscience than the omnipotent control over life and death.

Absorbed in that thought, Kovac retraced the killer's footsteps to the dining room, where the crime scene people were marking evidence and measuring distances. He stood in the doorway imagining the possible scenario: rushing at the professor with the nunchucks, swinging his arm, crushing the man's skull. If that was how it had happened, the killer had gone back to the study to get the sword and then had waited for the wife to come looking for her husband.

One death hadn't been enough. The overkill spoke to frenzy — either a wave of rage or a sick euphoria. The sword that pinned Mrs. Chamberlain to the floor like a bug in a collector's display case was a statement, an artist's signature.

'What are you thinking?' Taylor asked.

He was thinking they had better hope someone had hated these people enough to do this terrible thing, because the alternative was a monster on the loose whose thirst for blood was not likely to fade.

'I'm thinking you were right,' he said soberly. 'About that feng shui business. They should have hung that mirror over the door before their luck ran out.'

8

' . . . here in this beautiful, normally quiet neighborhood, now the apparent scene of a brutal double homicide. While there has been no official statement from the police as to the names of the victims, the home belongs to Professor and Mrs. Lucien Chamberlain.'

'Way to notify the next of kin, asshole,' Nikki muttered at the television on the kitchen counter.

'Who's an asshole?' R.J. asked.

'You are,' Kyle muttered, helping himself to more bacon.

'Don't say 'asshole,'' Nikki corrected half-heartedly.

'You do.'

'I'm the Mother of Dragons. I can use bad language if I want.'

'Can I get a dragon tattoo?'

'When you're thirty-five. Now shush. I'm trying to listen to this.'

With school canceled because of the treacherous road conditions, the boys had slept in. With Nikki working Cold Case, there was no urgent need for her to go in to the office. She had brought a stack of files from the Duffy case home with her to review, anyway. This was just the kind of scenario she had imagined when she first thought of leaving Homicide: being able to take a snow day with the boys and fix them a big breakfast instead of the usual hastily grabbed bowl of cereal or toaster waffles.

But now, with the local news reporting live for half the morning from the scene of a double murder, she was feeling jittery, wanting to know more — from inside the yellow tape. She wanted to be in on it.

'Chamberlain is listed on the university's roster as a professor of East Asian history,' the reporter went on, looking suitably grim. He was standing in the street with the background of an old established, well-off neighborhood crawling with police and crime scene investigators. 'Reports of an attack by a sword-wielding assailant are unconfirmed at this point . . . '

'Maybe they were attacked by one of the Knights Templar!' R.J. said excitedly. He jumped from his stool at the kitchen island and began to pretend he was fighting with a sword of his own.

'You're such a dork,' Kyle commented.

'You're a nerd.'

'Mom, Master Gracie says he's getting a new instructor who teaches escrima. Can I sign up?'

'Me, too!' R.J. exclaimed.

'What's escrima?'

'Filipino fighting sticks.'

Nikki gave him a look. 'Right. That's all I need: the two of you beating each other with sticks. No.'

'But, Mom — '

She held up a finger to stave off his argument, her eyes fixed on the TV. Kovac and his new partner, Taylor, were in the shot, behind the reporter. They stood in front of a lovely brick

78

house, deep in conversation with Lieutenant Mascherino and Deputy Chief Kasselmann.

The double homicide of a U of M professor and his wife in their own home would bring out the brass and local political muckety-mucks — at least for the first few days of the investigation. Sam would hate that. To his way of thinking, they would be nothing but in the way and underfoot. They served no useful purpose at best and fucked things up at worst. Kovac liked to keep a tight rein on his investigations, and that meant keeping a tight rein on the flow of information to the media. A well-placed leak to the newsies could be a valuable tool. Information vomited out by a politician with an agenda never failed to make the detectives' jobs more difficult.

Nikki thought of her own case, and how the media attention could only have helped her. But now the attention of the press and the public would all be on the sensational slaying of a respectable couple in their lovely home, and the long-cold case of Ted Duffy, a Sex Crimes detective shot to death in his backyard twenty-five years ago would literally be yesterday's news.

She had gotten up early to read more of the Duffy file, and thought about it now as she cleaned up the kitchen. She would start at ground zero, go to the scene and get the feel of the place. While Duffy's wife had eventually remarried and moved out of the house where the tragedy took place, Nikki hoped some of the neighbors had remained. Still, twenty-five years was a long time. People moved away, got old, lost

79

their memories, died. There had been nothing significant in any of the neighbors' statements given at the time. It was doubtful any of them would have much to say about it now, even if they could be found for an interview. Still, Candra Seley was already working on trying to locate Duffy's family, friends, and neighbors.

According to the weather and traffic reports, the roads would be clear by noon. The bad weather of the night before had given way to a day with a bright sky and warming temperatures, a brief respite until the next system of bleak gray and damp cold rolled in.

By one o'clock the boys were antsy and off to hang out with their friends. Nikki picked Seley up at City Hall, and they headed to Ted Duffy's old neighborhood.

'I'm so excited to get out of the office, I can't stand it!' Seley said, looking around like a woman just let out of prison, dark brown eyes bright and wide and a big smile lighting up her oval face. 'I'm no good at sitting still.'

'Seems an odd choice then that you work at a computer all day,' Nikki observed.

'Yeah, it's not my nature,' she confessed on a sigh. 'I loved working patrol. That was where I started. That was my thing. Every day is new and different on the streets. But it made my husband a nervous wreck, then Hunter and Brandy came along, and I had to realize my life wasn't just about me. I worked Special Crimes for a while — Crimes Against Children. I couldn't take that. I wanted to kill someone every day. Then I went to Community Initiatives.'

'Did you work with Grider there?'

'Well, I didn't so much work *with* Gene Grider as work *around* him. He probably doesn't even remember I was there. He's one of those guys that seems not to see or hear women if he can help it — which was fine by me.'

'I've dealt with my share of those over the years,' Nikki said. 'I can't help myself, though. I have to get in their faces. I used to keep a giant dildo in my desk, and I would take it out and smack guys with it when they were trying to shut me out. I'd get it right under their noses and shake it and say 'Look at that, asshole! I've got the biggest dick here, so back off!' '

They both laughed at the mental image.

'Nikki, you're something else. If you were as tall as me, you would take over the world.'

'Forget that. If I were as tall as you, I wouldn't have to climb on my kitchen counters to reach the high shelves.'

'That is a definite benefit to being five-eleven.'

'So, how did you end up in Business and Technology?'

'I took a nasty fall off a horse and hurt my back. I had to go on desk duty. They had an opening in B and T, and I'm good with computers.' She made a little shrug and looked out the window. 'It's okay. Rex, my husband, is happy.'

'And what about you?'

'I'm hoping Cold Case gets funded permanently,' she confessed. 'It's the perfect compromise. How about you? You miss Homicide?'

Nikki groaned. 'Yes. Even as we speak, my old

partner is working the scene of a double murder — respectable couple in a respectable neighborhood, possibly killed by a sword-wielding maniac. I admit it gets my adrenaline running. But, on the other hand, I had a great breakfast with my boys this morning, and I won't be pulling thirty-six hours straight while they fall into juvenile delinquency from lack of parental interest.'

'This is the place,' Seley said, pointing to a square white two-story house on a block of similar houses.

Nikki parked at the curb, and they got out of the car.

'The property has changed hands four times since the Duffys lived here,' Seley went on. 'I called the current owner and warned him we'd be stopping by to have a look. He's at work. He said to feel free.'

From the front, the place didn't look much different from the photos taken twenty-five years ago. Someone had added blue shutters. The landscaping had been updated. A newer, taller privacy fence cordoned off the backyard.

They let themselves in through an unlocked gate. The tall fence blocked ground-level views into the yard on two sides. But at the back of the property, a simple post-and-nail fence allowed the homeowners a beautiful view of a wooded park beyond.

The shots that killed Ted Duffy had come from that park, from up the hill or in a tree, judging by the trajectory of the bullets. He was shot at a downward angle with a small-caliber hunting rifle, probably from no more than fifty yards away. The visibility that day had been poor, with intermittent spitting rain mixed with snow. The crime took place late in the day, when darkness would have been gathering. Duffy had been chopping wood at the time. One bullet struck him in the upper back. The second shot hit him in the back of the head as he fell. Despite an extensive search of the area it was believed the shots had come from, no shell casings had been found.

'He was standing about here when he was shot,' Nikki said, spreading her arms.

The stump Duffy had been using as he split firewood was gone. Nikki had used the garage windows to estimate the spot based on her memory from the crime scene photos.

'Come stand here,' she said to Seley. 'He was about your height, a couple of inches taller.'

Seley took her place on the spot, her back to the woods. Nikki stepped back a few feet, imagining where the first bullet would have struck Duffy, and then looked toward the park, up the wooded slope. There would have been few people in the park at that time of day, certainly not back here, where there were no trails and nothing to see but the backside of an ordinary neighborhood.

This was deer hunting season, but there was no hunting allowed within city limits; nor were rifles allowed for hunting deer in this part of the state anyway. That wasn't to say no one in the city owned rifles. Plenty of Minnesotans took them across the St. Croix River to hunt in

Wisconsin. But Ted Duffy, a man chopping wood in his backyard, had not been mistaken for a deer. He had been deliberately killed. Someone had come hunting him.

Duffy's three children, ages five to nine, had been in the house at the time, along with a thirteen-year-old foster child. Two days before Thanksgiving, his wife, Barbara, had been grocery shopping. A second foster child had been at a school event.

'Sad way to go,' Seley said. 'Back here in the dark, in the rain, all alone.'

'As far as I've seen, they're all sad ways to go,' Nikki said.

'My grandmother passed away in her own home surrounded by people who loved her. That's how I want to go.'

'I want to go in my sleep,' Nikki said, 'dreaming that I'm having wild hot sex with Dwayne 'The Rock' Johnson.'

'Hey there!' a man's voice called out sharply. 'What are you doing back there?'

Nikki looked around, then up and next door. A man, heavyset, red-faced, salt-and-pepper crew cut, leaned out a second-story window. She put him in his late sixties.

'Mr. Nilsen!' Seley called, stepping out of her role as substitute Duffy. 'I'm Sergeant Seley! We spoke on the phone earlier today. This is Sergeant Liska.'

He looked less than impressed.

'Can we come over and have a word with you, Mr. Nilsen?' Nikki asked.

He didn't look thrilled about that, either. He

pulled his head inside and shut the window.

'Pleasant sort,' Nikki remarked, starting for the gate.

'He's the only neighbor I found who was living here at the time of the murder,' Seley said as they left the backyard and headed next door. 'He was home, but says he didn't see anything, and he doesn't see why he should have to talk to us.'

Nikki rang Nilsen's doorbell.

'I didn't see anything,' the old man said irritably as he opened the door. 'I've told you people that from the get-go.'

'Can we come in for a few minutes?' Nikki asked, pressing forward. He stepped back automatically. 'I'd like to ask you a few questions about what was going on around here at the time. Get your general impressions. I'm sure living here — how many years? — makes you the expert on this neighborhood.'

'I've lived in this house thirty-seven years,' he said.

'That's impressive.'

'Why?' he demanded. 'Because I'm too damn stubborn to move? I'll stay in this house 'til the day I die. I don't care what anyone thinks.'

He let them into the entryway and then stood with his arms crossed over his medicine ball belly, barring them from going any farther into his living room, where the television was still playing coverage from the scene of Kovac's double homicide.

The house smelled of mothballs, old man, and boiled kielbasa sausage. A deer's head stared at them from the wall above the electric fireplace

85

on the far side of the living room.

'I'll see some ID,' Nilsen snapped.

Each produced her identification. Nilsen looked through smudged reading glasses and sniffed in disapproval. 'I remember when women were meter maids.'

'Yeah? Now they let us have guns. Crazy, huh?' Nikki said. 'How well did you know the Duffy family?'

He scowled harder. 'I've answered all these damned questions a hundred times.'

'Well, it's all new to me. I have to investigate this case as if it happened yesterday. So, please bear with me because I haven't heard your answers before, Mr. Nilsen.'

'The police don't keep records of these things?'

'How well did you know the Duffy family?' she asked again.

'As well as I cared to.'

'You didn't like them?'

'Too many kids, too little discipline, too much noise. You would have thought they were Italian.'

'Did you know Ted Duffy personally?'

'I knew him to say hello. I didn't care for him. He let his wife run the show. But he was a decorated police officer. He worked hard. I had to respect him for that. Now, if the wife had stayed home and taken charge of those kids — but no, she had to have her little job on the side . . .'

'Mrs. Duffy was an emergency room nurse,' Seley pointed out.

Nilsen just looked at her, underwhelmed by

the excuse. 'She had three small children. She should have been home with them, but he didn't make enough money, she said. Then she brought those foster kids in for babysitters. That was clever, I suppose, if they hadn't been a couple of little tarts.'

'What did you do for a living, Mr. Nilsen?' Nikki asked.

'I sold life insurance.'

'Did you ever sell any to the Duffys?'

'He was covered by the city. This has all got to be in a file somewhere,' he complained, looking frustrated.

Nikki glanced around the room as he went on, her gaze settling on old family photos on the wall above a small cabinet cluttered with mail and keys and a bulging old wallet. Nilsen had the same unpleasant expression in his family portrait from twenty-some years past: that of a man in constant pain. Despite his expression, he had been handsome in a rugged way. He hadn't aged well.

'Is your wife around, Mr. Nilsen?' Seley asked.

'No!' he barked. 'She left. I haven't seen her in years.'

The wife had been an attractive woman with a shy, pretty smile, Nikki noted, never failing to marvel that women routinely married less than they deserved — herself included.

'Does she still live in the area?'

'I have no idea.'

'And your son?' she asked. 'Was he living here at the time?'

'What's the matter with you?' Nilsen snapped.

87

'You don't like my answers? You want to talk to people until you find someone who will tell you what you want to hear?'

'Not at all. But when it comes to potential witnesses in a cold case investigation, the more the merrier. We need all the help we can get to put the picture together.'

'Where's the last detective who investigated this?' he demanded. 'He at least knew what he was doing.'

'He had gender reassignment surgery and left the force,' Nikki said.

Seley doubled over, coughing to cover her laughter.

'What the hell?' Nilsen looked horrified at what Nikki had said. Seley could have fallen and died at his feet for all he cared.

'Excuse me!' Seley said hoarsely, a hand at her throat, eyes wet. 'I just need to step outside.'

No one paid attention to her as she went out the front door.

'How old was your son at the time of Ted Duffy's murder?' Nikki pressed on.

'He wasn't here when it happened.'

'I know that, but did he know the Duffy kids or the foster kids? Looks like he might have been in high school at the time. If he knew them, they might have spoken to him about the family.'

In his high school senior picture, Young Nilsen was a lean, more refined version of his father, but with the same unhappy expression. Nikki didn't remember seeing any mention of the boy among the interviews in the Duffy files. Kids sometimes got overlooked or discounted in investigations, as if they were invisible.

'He had some sports event that day. I've said it a hundred times. I was home, my wife was home, and I didn't see anything.'

'Still, I'd like to talk to him.'

'Good luck with that. He's dead,' he said coldly. 'Now get out of my house. You're an idiot! I don't have anything more to say to you. If you people haven't solved this crime in all these years, stop wasting our tax dollars and do something about the crime rate now. People are being murdered in their own homes by sword-wielding maniacs, for Christ's sake!'

★ ★ ★

'Misogynistic prick,' Nikki muttered as she descended Nilsen's front steps.

'That's redundant,' Seley pointed out.

'For emphasis,' Nikki said as they walked back to the car.

'Could we have some kind of signal for when you're about to say something outrageous?' Seley asked. 'I almost peed my pants!'

'A signal would require premeditation on my part. I just open my mouth and stuff comes out.'

'The mental image was too much for me. I instantly saw Grider in drag. I'll never be able to look at him the same way again.'

'And you just know he's hairy everywhere,' Nikki said as they got in the car. 'A plunging neckline is not going to be a pretty look.'

She shuddered at the thought, and looked at Nilsen's house. The old man was standing in the doorway, staring at them, a cell phone pressed to his ear. He was probably calling the department to complain that detectives packing vaginas had come to his house.

His original statement given at the time of Ted Duffy's murder had been less than a page long. He didn't know anything. He hadn't seen anything. Nikki was puzzled: He was the kind of neighbor with his nose in everyone's business — by his own admission, he had been bothered by the noise from the Duffy household in general — but he had not stuck his head out a window at the relentless sound of Duffy splitting wood or at the sound of two gunshots. He had spied her and Seley in the Duffy yard quickly enough, but he hadn't seen Ted Duffy lying dead on the ground. Duffy's body had been discovered by his wife at around six o'clock in the evening.

'See if you can find his ex-wife,' Nikki said. 'I want to know more about the Nilsens.'

'Will do. What next?'

'We meet the Widow Duffy.'

9

'I don't know what to say.'

Forrest Foster, chair of the History Department, had turned the color of chalk. He sank down into the chair behind his desk looking like he might pass out. He was a rail-thin man in his fifties, dressed like a history professor from Central Casting: shirt and bow tie, burgundy sweater vest, tweed jacket, horn-rimmed glasses. His hands were trembling as he placed them on the desktop.

Located in Heller Hall on the U of M's West Bank campus, Foster's office was small, with a tall, narrow window that allowed him a view of the next brick building.

'I knew when Lucien didn't show up for the meeting this morning something had to be wrong,' he said quietly. 'I thought an illness, maybe, or a car accident. With the way the roads were . . . But then when Sondra didn't answer her phone, either, or the house phone . . . '

The Chamberlains' landline had been cut. The fact that the wife had not called 911 on her cell phone suggested the murder of her husband had been as quick and efficient as it was brutal. Chargers had been found on the nightstands in the master bedroom, but no phones. No laptop computers. No iPads or tablets of any kind. The wallets of both Professor and Mrs. Chamberlain had been cleaned out of cash and credit cards.

Jewelry boxes had been raided. A lockbox in the master bedroom closet had been forced open and left on the floor. Anything in it that might have been valuable was gone.

A nice slick burglary with an unexpected side of murder.

'What was the nature of the meeting?' Taylor asked.

Foster blinked like a man waking from a nightmare, relieved for the distraction of a mundane question. 'A very generous alumnus has donated a substantial amount of money to the university to be used to expand our programs in East Asian history and art history. It's very exciting,' he said with no excitement at all. 'We'll be adding two faculty positions, and will be naming a head of East Asia studies. Lucien was one of our final four candidates.'

'Does this new job carry a lot of prestige?' Kovac asked.

'Our Asian studies program has always been small but well regarded,' said Foster. 'With this new influx of money, and expansion, yes, the title will carry cachet in the academic world.'

'And money?'

Foster's answer stuck in his throat as the implication struck him. 'You don't think — surely you can't believe — no. No, no. That's insane.'

'Yeah,' Kovac said, nodding. 'So is what happened to the Chamberlains. We'll need to speak to the three other candidates.'

Foster pulled off his glasses and pinched the bridge of his nose, mumbling, 'Oh my God. This is unbelievable.'

'It's routine procedure, Professor,' Taylor assured him. 'We have to examine every possibility, even the far-fetched variety.'

'Ken Sato,' Foster said, looking through a file on his desk. Too nervous and flustered, he sat back again. 'Ken is already on staff here. A very dedicated, innovative teacher. Dynamic. Popular with the students. Then we have a candidate currently teaching at the University of California — Los Angeles. Hanh Luu. Our interviews with her have been via Skype up to this point. She's flying in this Friday.'

'And the fourth one?' Taylor asked, glancing up from his note taking. 'You said there were four finalists. Chamberlain, Sato, Luu, and . . . '

'There were four. This is just all the more tragic . . . ' He shook his head in disbelief. 'Stuart Kaufman. Professor of East Asian art history. He passed away suddenly about two weeks ago. We're all still reeling from his loss.'

'Passed away of what?' Kovac asked, on point.

'Pancreatitis and kidney failure. It was terrible. He went home with the stomach flu one day, and the next day he was dead. We were all so shocked.'

'Had he been ill prior to that?' Taylor asked.

'He had been hospitalized for pancreatitis once before several years ago. I understand once you've had it, you're susceptible to it.'

'Was there an autopsy?'

'I don't know. I don't think so. He died of natural causes.'

Kovac just stared at him.

Foster blinked and looked away. 'I can't

believe any of this is happening.'

'These three professors — Chamberlain, Sato, and Kaufman — how did they get along with each other?'

'They were professional acquaintances. Lucien and Ken Sato, being in the same department, had their differences, but they went to all the same functions and never tried to kill one another. That's just absurd even to consider. Stuart ran with the Art History crowd. He didn't have that much to do with either Lucien or Ken.'

'How long have the three of them worked here?'

'Stuart had been on the faculty for twenty-five years. Lucien came here from Macalester College in 2001. Ken has been with us only the last five years — '

'And he was being considered for head of this new department?' Taylor asked.

'He came to us highly recommended by one of our retired professors, Hiroshi Ito, whose brother had Ken as a student in the graduate program at the University of Washington. At thirty-eight, he's already published two well-received books on Japanese history. Like I said, Ken is a very dynamic individual. He's the face of the future for the department.'

'What did Lucien Chamberlain think of that idea?'

Foster's mouth turned like he'd tasted something sour. 'Lucien was predictably not happy about that. He felt Ken was jumping the food chain. But it wasn't his decision to make.

Hiroshi Ito is on the committee, so of course Ken would be considered for the position.'

'What was Professor Chamberlain like?' Kovac asked. 'Was he a nice guy? Did he get along with his co-workers?'

'Lucien . . . was a very intelligent man,' Foster said, obviously choosing his words with the care of a man walking across a minefield. 'Very professional.'

'You don't have to be diplomatic with us,' Kovac said. 'I'm sure you don't want to speak ill of the dead, but we're not the media. We're investigating a double homicide here. Let's call a spade a spade. If he was a pompous ass, then we need to know that.'

'He could be difficult,' Foster admitted. 'He held his students and his peers to a high standard, and tended to put himself on a pedestal.'

'Did he have any enemies in particular?'

'I wouldn't go so far as to call anyone an enemy.'

'But people didn't like him.'

'He isn't the kind of man who has friends. He has — *had* colleagues, rivals. He was a bit of a narcissist.'

'That's like being a little pregnant,' Kovac said. 'What you're saying is people didn't like the guy, and not without reason.'

Foster sighed. 'This is so uncomfortable. Egos are a common commodity in the academic world, Detective. Lucien's was bigger than some and smaller than others. We're educators, not thugs.'

'And yet we have a dead professor.'

'I thought it was a burglary,' Foster said. 'That's what they were saying on the news: that Lucien and Sondra probably interrupted a burglar.'

'That very well might be,' Kovac said. 'There appeared to be things missing from the house, including pieces from the professor's collection. Do you know of anyone who can help us understand the significance of what we're looking for?'

'Lucien's collection is impressive.'

'You've seen it?'

'The tour was always the highlight of their annual dinner party. Ken Sato will be able to help you understand what you're looking at there. He was practically drooling when we walked through the house last winter. Chinese New Year,' he added, thinking back on a happier event. 'They always have their party on Chinese New Year.'

'We'll need contact numbers for the Chamberlains' next of kin,' Kovac said. 'By the family photos, it looks like they have a couple of kids.'

'Yes, a son and a daughter. My secretary can give you their information. Charles and Diana.' He made a bit of a face. 'Sondra was caught up with all things royal and British. Her family name was 'Spencer.' They were somehow distantly related to the family of Princess Di.'

'Thank you for your time, Professor,' Taylor said as they all rose. 'Sorry for your loss.'

Kovac placed his business card on the desk. 'If

you think of anything we should know, just call. We'll be in touch.'

'Was Professor Chamberlain going to get the job?' Taylor asked as they moved toward the door.

Foster's brow furrowed as he frowned. 'We haven't made the decision yet.'

'But . . . ?' Kovac prompted.

'He was high on the list, and then his student assistant filed a complaint against him with the Office for Conflict Resolution.'

'A complaint about what?'

'She alleges his behavior is — was demeaning, condescending, and sexist, and created a hostile work environment. You can imagine we don't want to start off this new chapter in East Asian studies with something like that making the news.'

'Who should we speak with about that situation?' Kovac asked.

'Inez Ngoukani. The office is in this building, on the sixth floor. I'll call down and let her know you'll be coming.'

'How did the professor feel about his assistant ratting him out like that?' Taylor asked.

'Lucien was extremely upset about it, as you might imagine, but the girl wouldn't back down. He finally agreed to go through mediation in the hope of ending it. We wanted the matter settled and put to rest before we had to make our decision.'

'We'll need the name and contact information for the student, too,' Kovac said.

'Yes, of course,' Foster said with a rueful look.

'It's Diana Chamberlain. Lucien's daughter.'

★ ★ ★

'So this guy was some kind of a dick,' Kovac said as they got on the elevator. 'His own kid reports him for being an ass right when he's up for a big promotion. Families. Gotta love 'em.'

'You don't think the daughter could have killed them, do you?' Taylor said. 'Beating the old man to death with a pair of nunchucks? Running her mother through with a sword? Hard to picture a woman doing that.'

Kovac shrugged. 'She could be a freaking Amazon for all we know. I'm not going to think anything until we meet her, except that dear old narcissist Dad must have been royally pissed with her for messing up his chances for the big dream job.'

'It had to take something pretty obnoxious for the daughter to make a formal complaint. I mean, she's his grad student. Why would she take that on in the first place — and why would he have her in his department — if they didn't have a good relationship to start with?'

'I had a feeling about that guy,' Kovac muttered. They walked out of the building, and he stepped off to the side, digging a cigarette out of his coat pocket.

'Which guy? Foster?'

'Our stiff. Murdered in a silk dressing robe.' He lit up, thought of Liska, felt guilty, and then took a long, satisfying drag and blew it out slowly. 'What kind of guy puts on a silk dressing robe to go downstairs in the middle of the night? He's gotta be gay or he's gotta be a prick.'

'I know what not to get you for Christmas.'

'I don't want pajamas, either,' Kovac said. 'I don't see the point of wearing clothes to bed.'

'That's more information than I needed.'

Kovac took another pull on his smoke, imagining the bruise he would have ended up with if Liska had been there. She would have hauled off and socked him in the arm as hard as she could.

'What's your story, anyway, Stench?'

Taylor's eyebrows sketched upward. 'You want to know what I wear to bed? This is getting weird.'

'No. What's your story? Your family background.'

'I grew up in Plymouth. Mom, dad, kid sister.'

'Nice family? Good family?'

'Nice family, yeah, middle class, living in the 'burbs. My dad worked for Pillsbury. My mom made us go to church on Sunday.'

'Your parents loved you, raised you right.'

'Yeah.'

'You joined the army, but you came back here to settle down, to be near the family.'

'My dad passed away. Head-on crash with a drunk driver. I came back to help my mom out.'

'You're a good kid,' Kovac said. 'You probably never did anything to give your parents ulcers.'

'I don't know about that.'

Kovac laughed. 'Oh come on. I know. I can tell by your haircut. You were captain of the football team, lettered in three sports, took the homecoming queen to prom, and always used a condom.'

Taylor scowled a little. 'Is there a point to this conversation?'

'Sure,' Kovac said. He blew out one last hard jet stream of toxic fumes. If he smoked only half the cigarette, that wasn't so bad. He stubbed it out on the sidewalk and palmed the dead butt. At least he wasn't a litterbug.

'Here's your lesson for the day, Junior. If there's one thing I can assure you about working Homicide, it's that you are going to see some of the most mentally fucked-up people and family situations you can imagine. After all the years I've been doing this job, just when I say I've seen everything, somebody comes up with some new and different way to be a sick, perverted wack job.

'Never judge a family by their address or bank account,' he went on. 'And never underestimate the power of the American public to utterly shock and disappoint you.'

★   ★   ★

The director of the Office for Conflict Resolution was waiting for them. Inez Ngoukani was tall and elegant, an ebony sculpture with long slender limbs and full features beneath a tight cap of steel gray hair. She invited them into a conference room as graciously as if they were at her home for a pleasant chat.

'May I offer you something to drink, gentlemen?' she asked in a beautiful, cultured accent. Kovac felt like he should have gone and washed up and brushed his teeth before coming in the room.

'We have cucumber water,' she said, gesturing gracefully to a glass pitcher on the table. 'It's very refreshing.'

'Thank you, ma'am,' Taylor said, and poured glasses for all three of them.

Kovac took a long drink, hoping to wash the smoke out of his mouth.

'Professor Foster broke the news to me about Lucien and his wife, Sondra,' Ngoukani said. 'Terrible. So terrible to imagine what they must have gone through. The more educated we are, the less we believe violence can touch our lives. But it can and it does. I saw Lucien on Monday, and now he's gone.'

'What was his mood when you saw him?' Kovac asked.

'Ooooh,' she said, raising her pencil-thin eyebrows nearly to her hairline. 'He was in a foul humor. So angry.'

'Did he say why?'

'No, and I didn't ask. I've been trying to help him come to a calmer, more reasonable place in his mind. He would have none of that Monday.'

'Did you find that unusual?'

'No, to be honest. Lucien is a difficult man. If something doesn't go his way, he throws a tantrum like a spoiled boy. This ongoing clash with his daughter has not gone well for him. His temper has been terrible.'

'His daughter was his student assistant,' Taylor said. 'That seems like an unusual situation.'

'Highly. And a recipe for disaster from the start,' Ngoukani said. 'Professor Foster told me he tried to discourage them, but the two of them seemed bent on it. Who can decipher the tangled motives of a parent-and-child relationship as complicated as that one? One might think Diana wanted her father's acceptance and approval, and that Lucien wanted to support her effort to follow in his footsteps, yet they butted heads constantly.'

'So, how does this work?' Taylor asked. 'The daughter filed a complaint. Could he have gotten fired?'

'No. Not at this point. The Office for Conflict Resolution is a neutral and independent office where the faculty and staff, including the student workers, can raise concerns,' she explained. 'We advocate for neither management or nonmanagement. We facilitate discussions between the parties involved, consult with them individually, and offer coaching. We offer mediation in the hope of resolving the issue before it can escalate to the point of having to be reported to Human Resources or to the General Council for more serious consideration with the potential for career-impacting consequences.'

'But according to Forrest Foster this complaint was still going to create a problem for Professor Chamberlain with regard to his possible promotion,' Taylor said. 'How does that work if this office is confidential?'

She gave him a look like he should have known better. 'The university can be a very small and incestuous world, Detective. It was hardly a secret within the department that Lucien and Diana weren't getting along. Diana came to this office with her complaints. Her father went to Forrest Foster with his outrage, trying to head his daughter off at the pass, so to speak, thinking if he could discredit her with his friend, the head of the department, that would be the end of it. But Forrest wasn't willing to look the other way. He couldn't. There's too much at stake, and he is an honorable man. He encouraged Lucien to try to solve the issue through this office.'

'Did the daughter's complaints hold water?' Kovac asked.

'Oh yes. Her father can be a tyrant. She's not the first of his assistants we've heard from. Diana, of course, believed he was being particularly hard on her. If not for the fact that I am to remain neutral in these things, I would have to agree with her.

'Diana recorded several of their arguments on her cell phone. She played them for me.' She shook her head in disapproval. 'Not to say Diana can't dish it out, but Lucien doesn't hesitate to make an argument personal, to go for the raw nerve.'

'And what did he have to say for himself?'

'That Diana was being vindictive and ridiculous. He felt a great deal of pressure because of the circumstances and the timing. A cornered narcissist is a cornered cobra. He will strike out at anyone, regardless of their intent.'

'He struck out at you?' Taylor asked.

She waved the suggestion off like a bothersome fly. 'I manage conflict for a living,

Detective. We were all working very hard to try to bring the situation to a calm conclusion. Professor Chamberlain wanted Diana to drop her complaint. She would not. However, Forrest had finally talked Lucien around to sitting down for mediation.'

'It doesn't sound like he was in the mood for mediation on Monday.'

'No, but I don't know why. Perhaps they'd had another fight.'

'Did you speak to the daughter?'

She shook her head. 'I haven't heard from her this week. We were supposed to meet later this afternoon — the three of us. Of course, that won't be happening now,' she said sadly. 'Have you spoken with Diana?'

'She's our next stop,' Kovac said, rising.

'Please give her my condolences,' Ngoukani said, showing them to the door. 'And please let her know I'm available for her. All she need do is call.'

10

Two years after the death of her husband, Ted, Barbie Duffy married his fraternal twin brother, Thomas 'Big Duff' Duffy.

'Clever girl,' Seley said. 'Think of all the money she saved not having to change all her monogrammed towels.'

'It's kind of creepy, if you ask me,' Nikki said.

They drove south on 77, across the Minnesota River, to the suburb of Apple Valley, and to a development where the houses were large and the lots were larger.

'There's something sort of Stepford about it,' she continued. 'Lose your spouse? Pick up a clone! Or were the Stepford wives robots? I forget.'

'It's biblical, really. Isn't there something in there about a man having to marry his dead brother's wife?'

Nikki shuddered. 'If I had to marry my ex's brother, I'd become a lesbian.'

The last Duffy house they had been to could have fit into the current Duffy house twice with room left over. Instead of tired white clapboard, this one was faced in stacked stone and brown stucco. The pillars that held up the front portico looked to be fashioned from massive tree trunks. Prairie style on steroids. The heavy wooden front door was adorned with big black studs and fake strap hinges that looked like they had been hand-forged by some sweating, muscular shirt-less artisan with a big hammer.

'It's safe to assume this brother isn't living on a cop's salary,' Seley remarked.

'No. He owns Big D Sports.'

'He's Big Duff? From the commercials?'

'The one and only.'

The Big D Sports commercials were local favorites featuring Big Duff dressed in Elmer Fudd hunting garb, and a guy in a silly, cheap moose costume: Melvin D. Moose. It was the kind of goofy humor that made guys guffaw. Speed and R.J. loved them and mimicked them, making each other fall down laughing.

'He had just started his first store around the time of Ted Duffy's death,' Nikki said. 'Twenty-five years later, he's got stores all over the upper Midwest.'

Stores that specialized in hunting equipment, including guns, she reminded herself. But at the time of his brother's death, Big Duff had allegedly been two hours away, at his cabin near Rice Lake, Wisconsin, getting the place ready for a Thanksgiving weekend party. Ted and some buddies had been set to join him for a few days of deer hunting and hanging out. Pre-cell phone, a family friend had driven to the cabin to break the news in person. Big Duff had reportedly been inconsolable over the death of his twin.

Two years later, he had married his dead brother's wife.

One big happy.

The heavy door swung open as they approached.

'Mrs. Duffy, I'm — '

'I know who you are,' Barbie Duffy said impatiently.

Nikki's first thought was that Barbie Duffy did not look sixty. Her hair, which hung just past her shoulders, had been artistically streaked ash blonde and carefully coiffed to look like it hadn't been done at all — which undoubtedly cost extra at the salon. She'd had work done, but done well — a little lift here, a little filler there, a spot of Botox, a boob job. Dressed in leggings and a yoga top, she had a figure that would have been coveted by most women in their forties.

She had worked as an ER nurse when she was married to Ted Duffy. She had traded up a few economic levels with Ted's brother. No doubt she had plenty of time to devote herself to all the latest exercise crazes. She probably spun, Zumba'd, and Pilates'd herself that flat stomach and those skinny legs, and CrossFitted herself a pair of toned arms.

Nikki's second thought was that Barbie Duffy was not happy to see them.

'I don't see why we couldn't have done this over the phone,' she said as she led them through the foyer. 'I have a barre class at five. I have to be out of here by quarter to.'

It was four o'clock. She was allowing forty-five minutes for the discussion of her first husband's unsolved murder.

'We'll try not to take up too much of your time . . . '

. . . *trying to figure out who murdered the father of your children.*

'What a beautiful home you have,' Seley said, looking around at some designer's idea of Northwoods chic: exposed timbers, chandeliers fashioned from the antlers of a herd of elk, bronze sculptures of wild animals. 'This should be in a magazine.'

'It has been,' Barbie said with the fake smile of a popular girl. 'Several times.'

She showed them to a living room with furniture made for giants — huge sofas and armchairs covered in leather and textiles that might have been handwoven by native people in some far-flung corner of the world. Nikki felt like a little kid taking a seat in one of the armchairs. She had to perch on the edge of the cushion or her feet couldn't touch the floor.

'As you know,' she began, 'your husband's case has been chosen for review by the new Cold Case unit.'

'Yes, I know that. Gene Grider called me days before you did. I don't understand why he isn't in charge.' Barbie Duffy sat on the edge of a leather chair, her back ramrod straight, lower legs twisted together elegantly. A stack of bangles rattled on her wrist as she made a gesture. Her manicure was immaculate, her nails painted a perfect fall crimson. 'He's worked on Ted's case all these years — '

'And the case has never been solved. Why would you want a man who hasn't solved the case in twenty-five years to be in charge of trying to solve it now?' Nikki asked with a little edge to her voice. 'Do you not *want* the case closed, Mrs. Duffy?'

She expected a burst of outrage, real or manufactured. What she got was more complex.

'Honestly?' Barbie Duffy asked, chin up. 'Honestly, I want it to be over. Do you know how many times we've been dragged through this over the years — opening and reopening the wounds? And for nothing. It's like being victimized again and again.'

'You don't want your husband's murderer brought to justice?'

'Is that even possible?' she asked. 'I don't think so. Would it be worth what we have to go through? I don't think so. Will it bring Ted back? No, it won't,' she said, blinking back tears. 'Nothing will ever bring Ted back. That's my bottom line. So why go through all this — '

She paused for a moment to compose herself, then started again.

'Our phones have been ringing off the hook since the announcement yesterday. We've been deluged by our friends, and family, and all of their emotions. And reporters — literally dozens of reporters. Can they come to the house? They want to do a feature on us. Would we be willing to go back to the old house and shoot it in the backyard where Ted died?'

She blinked her eyes hard as if in amazement. 'Do I want to go back to the scene of my husband's murder so they can capture my grief and pain for the ten o'clock news? Would you want to do that?'

'I don't know,' Nikki admitted. 'I do know the families of most murder victims would beg for that kind of publicity. My phone's been ringing off the hook, too, with the families of dozens of murder victims who want to know why their loved one's case isn't a priority. I think they might jump at that chance.'

'Would they? Then feel free to open their lives up so they can relive their worst nightmare,' Barbie said. 'I'm tired of it. You will be, too, soon enough. You've already said you don't think it can be solved. Gene told me. So why don't we just skip the dance? You won't have to go through the motions, and I won't have to go through the rest of it.'

Nikki wanted to go find Gene Grider and kick him in the shin. What an asshole, telling Barbie Duffy she had fought against choosing this case in the first place. No matter that it was true. The victim's family didn't need to hear about her misgivings. By telling Barbie Duffy, Grider had sabotaged Nikki's chances at a clean start on the case.

'Mrs. Duffy, let me be perfectly clear with you on this,' she said. 'I think your husband's case is a difficult one. I believe we have a lot of other cases pending that are more solvable. But this is the case I've been assigned. It was assigned to me specifically because I have no history with it. I have no preconceived ideas about anyone involved. That will allow me to pick up on things a detective who has been over this ground many times may have overlooked. And now that the case is mine, I will dig at it like a terrier. If there's anything to be found, I'm going to find it. If it's even remotely possible to get my hands on the person who killed your husband, I will.'

Barbie Duffy clapped her hands slowly, a sardonic smile twitching up one corner of her perfectly painted mouth.

'Points for a passionate speech,' she said. 'You should have saved that for a camera.'

Nikki wanted to call her a bitch for the remark, but she wouldn't. She had dealt with hundreds of family members of homicide victims over the years. No two reacted exactly the same way. No two had exactly the same experience. And she had been at the center of a number of high-profile cases where the pressure of the media was so intense and abrasive, and the public scrutiny so harsh, that it was crushing.

Still, she couldn't imagine losing a loved one and just letting go of the fact that someone had ended that person's life with malice afore-thought. As many times as she had wanted to kill Speed with her bare hands over the years, she would have gone to the ends of the earth to track down someone who had killed him. He was the father of her boys. She owed them that much.

'Does your husband feel the same way?' Seley asked Barbie Duffy, breaking the silence. 'We were told this morning he's willing to up the reward for information leading to an arrest.'

Barbie Duffy closed her eyes and sighed, shaking her head. 'Of course he is. Duff wants it solved. It nearly destroyed him when Ted died. Ted was his little brother by twelve minutes. Duff went through depression, alcohol abuse . . . He was so angry. It took a long time for him to come to some kind of resolution. But every time you people come around trying to peddle hope, he buys a load of it and then is crushed all over again when nothing happens.'

'I'm sorry you feel that way,' Nikki said, 'because the first thing I learned when I started working Homicide is that I work first for the victim, and my obligation to the victim is to get them justice. It can't matter to me if you want to do this or not. I have to ask the questions and dig through this. I'm sorry.'

'I doubt that you are,' Barbie returned. 'Being the one to solve Ted's case would be a nice feather in your cap, wouldn't it, Detective?'

'Why are you trying to make me your enemy?' Nikki asked.

'It's not personal. I don't know you. I don't care to know you. I just don't want to do this again.'

'So you think you might as well make a bad situation worse by being difficult? You should consider going back to school. You'd make a hell of a lawyer.'

Barbie laughed at that. 'Don't forget I know exactly how much of an insult that was. I was married to a cop.'

'And how was your marriage in the months leading up to your husband's murder?'

She arched a brow. 'Oh, you're going straight for the jugular. You forget, I've been asked these questions a thousand times. You aren't going to shock me or surprise me.'

'Good. Then we can skip over the niceties. How was your marriage in the weeks leading up to your husband's death?'

'It was very ordinary for people married ten

years with three kids and not quite enough money. It was a partnership. Ted had his job, I had mine. When we had time together, we were too exhausted for sex, so we argued about money instead. Occasionally we both got enough sleep to wake up and remember how much we used to like each other.'

'Were either of you dissatisfied with that arrangement?'

'I think both of us were dissatisfied with that arrangement, but that's life. At that stage of the game, I didn't know any couples that were entirely happy. Are you married, Detective?'

'Divorced.'

'Kids?'

'Yes.'

'Do you have enough time for everything? Is there ever enough money? You dumped your husband for a reason — or he dumped you.'

'I dumped him for a reason, all right,' Nikki said. 'What about Ted? Was he the kind of guy who fooled around? And remember: I am a cop, and I know cops. My ex was a cop. I know that animal.'

'I don't know if Ted was fooling around,' she said, glancing down at the arm of her chair, pretending to pick at a piece of lint. 'I was too tired to care at the time.'

'So you wouldn't know if there was a jealous husband or boyfriend who might have wanted to eliminate the competition?'

'No.'

'How was Ted acting around that time? Up? Down? Distracted?'

'Well . . . he was either the most generous, caring guy you'd ever met, or the biggest prick on the face of the earth. It depended on what kind of case he was working. The sicker and more depraved the case, the darker and angrier he was.'

'Did he talk about his cases with you?'

'No. He said the things he had to deal with were too horrible to bring home. He didn't want it touching the kids,' she said. 'He'd been glum. He always hated this time of year — the shorter days, the rotten weather. He always complained that everything died in November. I always thought he had that seasonal disorder. But the Duffy men are just prone to their moods. That Black Irish thing, you know.'

'Had there been any strange calls to the house?' Seley asked. 'Was he acting secretive?'

Barbie Duffy rolled her eyes. 'Do you know how many people have asked me these questions in the last two and a half decades?' she asked impatiently, checking her watch. 'You have to have all these answers in a file somewhere.'

'Yes, but see, we're here right now,' Nikki said. 'So we can ask you in person, and that's always better. You might arch an eyebrow, or tip your chin, or look down to the left, and all of that means something.'

'That sounds like you think I'm a suspect.'

'Why would we think that? You were at the supermarket when it happened.'

'There were people who found it suspicious that Big Duff and I ended up together,' she said. 'You probably do, too. Some people thought we must have conspired to kill Ted so we could be together.'

'Did you?' Nikki asked, just to see her response.

She didn't bite.

'Of course not. We didn't even like each other before Ted died.'

'You've been married a long time,' Seley said.

'Yes. That all seems like a lifetime ago. I guess it was,' she said quietly as she glanced at her watch again. Then she took a deep breath to conjure up more energy. 'Anyway, I was at the supermarket buying cranberry sauce, and Big Duff was in Wisconsin, so no, we didn't kill Ted.'

'We'll need to speak with your kids,' Nikki said, knowing they were running out of time.

'They won't have anything to say that they haven't already said. They were little then — five, seven, and nine.'

'Still, we'll need contact info.'

Barbie Duffy huffed a sigh. 'They've lived their whole lives with this investigation. The children of a murdered cop. Jennifer had to see a therapist off and on for years, she was so traumatized by the aftermath of Ted's death. Thank God for insurance.'

'And you had a couple of foster kids living with you at the time?'

'Yes,' she said coolly. 'I'm sure you have their names somewhere. They're probably in jail or dead.'

'They were difficult?'

'They were teenage girls from broken homes with drug-addicted mothers and their mothers'

115

abusive boyfriends. They had a lot of issues. I sent them back after Ted was killed. I had enough to deal with. I couldn't cope with their problems, too.'

'Your neighbor made a comment to us about the girls being' — she looked to Seley — 'what's the word he used?'

'Tarts.'

'Tarts.'

'What neighbor said that?'

'Donald Nilsen.'

Barbie Duffy rolled her eyes. 'Dirty old man. Maybe he should have spent less time looking in our windows and more time minding his own damn business.'

'Do you mean that literally?' Seley asked. 'He was looking in your windows?'

'He would complain to Ted about the way the girls dressed. Their shorts were too short. Their skirts were too short. Their tops were too short. He was worried they would tempt his perfect son. It was like living next door to the Taliban. Ted told him to stop staring at the crotches of teenage girls or someone might get the wrong idea and call the cops on him.'

'How did Nilsen react to that?'

'He blew a gasket, but he didn't complain again after that.'

'What was the son like?'

'He was quiet. He minded his own business — unlike his father. He mowed our lawn in the summer and shoveled the sidewalk in the winter. He never said anything more than 'yes, ma'am,' 'no, ma'am,' and 'thank you, ma'am.' I found him a little odd, but why wouldn't he be, with those parents?'

'Was he 'distracted' by the girls?'

'Not that I ever noticed. He mostly looked at the ground.'

'Do you know how he died?'

'He died? I had no idea. It must have been after we moved away. I remember him giving his condolences at the funeral.'

'There must have been a thousand people at that funeral,' Nikki remarked.

'Yes, there were. But I remember because his father wasn't there. The son and the mother came.'

'What about Nilsen's wife?' Nikki asked. 'Did you know her?'

'Not really. I had a job and five kids. I didn't have time for coffee with the housewife next door. I hardly ever saw her. What difference does it make, anyway?' she asked, glancing at her watch again. 'Do you think Susie Homemaker killed Ted?'

'Just getting a feel for the neighborhood,' Nikki said. 'So you didn't keep in touch with her after she left the husband?'

'I didn't even know that she left the husband,' she said, standing up. 'Good for her. And speaking of leaving, I have to go. I'm going to be late.'

'I'll have more questions,' Nikki said, following her to the front door.

'I'm sure you will,' she said, opening the door to show them out. 'But don't be surprised if I'm difficult to contact. I've moved on with my life.

It's time the police department does, too. What's done is done.'

★   ★   ★

'That's an interesting attitude she has,' Nikki said as they got back in the car. 'There's no statute of limitations on murder. Apparently the same can't be said for Barbie Duffy's feelings for the former love of her life.'

'It's been a quarter of a century,' Seley pointed out. 'That's probably longer than she and her husband even knew each other. I agree, it doesn't make her seem like the most compassionate person, but she's had to live through all of it. We haven't.'

And that was the whole point of their being there, Nikki thought as she drove them back into the city. They had yet to see the whole picture of Ted Duffy's life and death. She only hoped they could bring it into focus. His death had to mean something to someone — even if that someone wasn't the person who should have cared the most.

★   ★   ★

Homicide was crowded when they got back. The shift had changed, but no one seemed to have left. Kovac's double murder, Nikki thought, straining to pick up bits of conversation as she passed through on her way to the Cold Case unit's borrowed office space.

A professor from the U and his wife, murdered

118

in their own home. The brass would be clamoring for the case to be closed ASAP, all the while getting as much air time and management mileage out of it as possible. She could see Mascherino in her office with Deputy Chief Kasselmann, deep in conversation. The sense of energy and urgency that came with a high-profile case was palpable in the room.

Tippen was on the phone at his desk, scribbling notes. He glanced up as she passed, held the phone to his shoulder, and said, 'You're missing a big one, Tinks!'

'I have my own big one, thanks.'

'I know that. But I'm talking about a case.'

She flipped him the finger and kept going, her mood darkening even as he laughed in her wake. She hated feeling left out of a job she had left by choice. But she had her own job to do.

She had stewed on Barbie Duffy's attitude all the way back from Apple Valley. The fact that Grider had fouled the waters for her before she had a chance to establish a rapport with Ted Duffy's widow was burning like an ulcer in her gut. Bad enough to start from zero with a case as cold as this one. He had made sure she was starting in a hole.

And there he was, ten feet in front of her, stuffing a sandwich in his fat mouth as he stood shooting the shit with one of the Homicide guys, no doubt drawn into the room by the same energy they all felt when a big case was getting off the ground.

Nikki saw red.

'Grider!' she snapped, walking up on him.

'What the fuck do you think you're doing?'

'Having a sandwich,' he said, with his mouth still half full. 'What's your problem?'

'You're my problem,' she said, toe to toe with him, wishing she didn't have to crank her neck to look up at him. 'I just came from interviewing Barbie Duffy. Imagine my unpleasant surprise when she told me you called her yesterday. What the hell is the matter with you?'

Nikki realized her voice was raised. She could feel the attention of the room turning toward them. She was too angry to care.

'Just letting her know it's your case now,' Grider said.

'And telling her I'm gonna do a shit job? Fuck you!' She jabbed him in the sternum with a forefinger. 'Keep your big ugly mug out of my case!'

Seley touched her on the shoulder. 'Nikki — '

Nikki shrugged her off.

'Or what?' Grider challenged.

'I'll have your ass on a platter, that's what!'

'Nikki — ' Seley started.

The next voice that came made Nikki cringe. Mascherino.

'Sergeant Liska. My office. Now.'

Fuck. Well, there was nothing for it now but to go all in. She grabbed a handful of Grider's shirt and turned toward the lieutenant.

'He's coming with me.'

Mascherino frowned. 'I want to speak to *you.*'

'He's the reason you want to speak to me,' Nikki said. 'If you're killing birds, you might as well get two for one.'

'All right,' the lieutenant said, turning her frown on Grider. 'Both of you.'

'She attacked me!' Grider whined.

'Right now,' Mascherino snapped.

She turned on her heel and marched. Nikki fell in step behind her, glancing over her shoulder to make sure Grider was coming. Everyone watched silently as they passed on their way to the lieutenant's office, and started talking again the second they'd gone by, the noise of their voices swelling like a wave behind them.

'Close the door and sit down,' the lieutenant ordered as she went behind her desk and turned to face them.

Nikki was too angry to sit. She crossed her arms over her chest and stood behind a chair, glaring at Grider, who took the other seat in front of the desk. Mascherino let it go.

'I'm running a Homicide unit, not some dive bar where people start brawls on a nightly basis,' she said. 'I will not have my detectives shouting expletives and threats in this office. Is that understood, Sergeant Liska?'

'Yes, ma'am,' Nikki said, choking on the explanation and accusations that wanted to come spewing out of her mouth.

'She attacked me!' Grider said again.

The lieutenant gave him an icy look. 'We'll get to you,' she said, and turned back to Nikki. 'You will calmly explain to me what this is all about.'

She took her seat behind her desk and waited. Nikki blew out a breath and sat down.

'He called the widow of my victim and led her

to believe I'm not all that dedicated to this case, putting me in an adversarial position with her before I could even introduce myself.'

'What do you have to say for yourself?' Mascherino asked, turning her steely gaze on Grider.

'I've known Barbie Duffy for thirty years,' he said. 'I called her to let her know the case had been reassigned. We had a conversation, and I gave her my opinion.'

'I gave her my opinion, too,' Nikki said. 'If you haven't solved her husband's murder in twenty-five years, why does she want you on it? She should have decided you were incompetent a couple of decades ago.'

'Nikki . . . ' Mascherino warned.

'Seriously, Lieutenant,' Nikki said. 'Seley was with me. She'll tell you the same thing. Barbie Duffy couldn't get rid of us fast enough. She doesn't want us reopening the case at all. She was perfectly happy with the lack of results this one gave her,' she said, hooking a thumb in Grider's direction.

'What the hell are you implying?' Grider asked, his face darkening as his blood pressure rose.

'I don't know,' Nikki said, shrugging. 'I'm just stating the facts. Maybe you can enlighten us. Why would she rather run off to her exercise class than talk to people who want to solve her first husband's murder? Maybe there's a reason this case was never solved on your watch.'

'Are you accusing me of something?' Grider demanded. 'Ted Duffy was my friend. You think

I didn't want to close his case? I'm the one who brought it up for review!'

'So you could keep not solving it?'

Grider shoved himself out of his chair. 'I don't have to listen to this shit from you.'

'Sit down!' Mascherino ordered.

He backed down reluctantly, and planted his ass back in the chair.

'You will not interfere in this investigation,' the lieutenant said to him. 'This is no longer your case. I don't want to hear again that you've contacted someone involved and offered your opinion or anything else. Do you understand me?'

Grider rubbed a hand across his mouth like he was trying to push his opinion of the situation back down his throat.

Mascherino waited, staring him down. She might have a sweet picture of her three grandchildren sitting next to her pen holder on her desk, but there was no sweetness in her as a boss. She was going to make everyone toe her line, Gene Grider included.

He tossed his hands up as if in defeat, but he was shaking his head no even as he said, 'It's all yours.'

Nikki bit her tongue. He was no more going to stay out of it than he was going to stop breathing. He'd said it himself: He'd known the people involved for thirty years. He had gone back to them time and again over the decades.

The lieutenant turned her gaze on Nikki and pointed in the direction of the squad room. 'I will not have another outburst like that in this office. Is that understood?'

'Yes, ma'am. I'm sorry.'

'You're not,' Mascherino said. 'But I'll take it anyway. Now go, the both of you. I've got a press conference to prepare for.'

Ever the gentleman, Grider walked out ahead of Nikki.

'Are you happy now?' he grumbled over his shoulder, as they went down the hall toward their own office. 'Tattling to the principal. Nice cunt move, Liska. You and the Mother Superior there can have a good laugh over it while you're rolling your own tampons later on.'

Nikki cut in front of him and stopped, facing him, hands on her hips. The hall was empty but for the two of them. Technically, they were out of the Homicide office proper. Grider stopped and mirrored her stance.

'Now what?' he asked. 'You're going to report me for gender insensitivity?'

'You listen to me, you fucking dinosaur,' Nikki said, keeping her voice low. 'I've had worse from better than you. So don't think for a minute that you can intimidate me. You can take your last-century misogynist bullshit attitude and stick it up your ass. And if you want to make this a fight, metaphorically or otherwise, you'd better know, I will break you in two and beat the shit out of both ends. Stay out of my case.'

She let that hang in the air. Grider said nothing. He just stood there staring at her with cold eyes, his resentment oozing out of his pores like rancid sweat. He had come on the force during another era. Having to stomach the fact that women were equal to or ranked above him stuck in his craw like a chicken bone.

Slowly, Nikki started to back away like a thug leaving a gang confrontation, mean-mugging all the way into their office. Grider followed, but went directly to his desk, grabbed his coat, and left without a word.

Seley sat at her desk, eyes wide. 'Can I be you in my next life?' she asked. 'You're a total badass.'

Nikki ignored her, staring at the open door Grider had gone out, and thinking the very first thing he would do when he got out of the building would be to call Barbie Duffy.

'Generally speaking,' she said, 'who doesn't want a crime solved?'

'The perpetrators of the crime,' Seley answered.

'I'll see you tomorrow,' Nikki said. 'I'm going to go home and read every scrap of paper on this case again.'

11

Diana Chamberlain didn't answer her phone. She lived in a shabby neighborhood near the commercial district known as Dinkytown, not far from the U of M campus. An area where the big old box-style houses had been cut up into cheap apartments for students, and where the sidewalks were buckled from the massive roots of the old trees that lined the boulevards. An assortment of older cars took up all the parking spaces on the street.

The sun that had melted the morning's ice was gone, and its meager warmth along with it. The temperature had dropped just enough to freeze the slush into ruts and turn the puddles back into little skating rinks.

Taylor cruised past the address, pulling into the parking lot of a dirty little strip mall a block down the street. He parked in a space reserved for customers of a small dry cleaners with a flickering red-neon Open sign in the front window. A pissed-off-looking tiny woman in a hot-pink sari stood in the doorway with her hands on her hips.

'Parking for dry cleaning only!' she shouted as they got out of the car.

'We're here on police business, ma'am,' Taylor said politely, holding up his shield.

'Police dry cleaning business?' she asked pointedly.

'Uh, no, ma'am.'

'I thought not. Then take your handsome self away from here and park elsewhere. I have a business to run.'

'We're from Homicide — ' Taylor started.

'No one has been murdered here. I have no need of you.'

'We have to go deliver some bad news — '

'I'm so terribly sorry to hear it. Don't let me delay you,' she said. 'Get in your car and go deliver your bad news of a murder that did not happen here at Star Dry Cleaning.'

Taylor looked at Kovac, clearly not used to being denied anything by a female.

'What time do you close, ma'am?' Kovac asked.

'Six o'clock.'

'It's almost six now.'

'In seven minutes it will be six o'clock. You are taking the parking space of customers who must rush in to get their dry cleaning at the last possible moment, and this will cost my business money.'

'It's only four minutes by my watch,' Kovac said. 'We can drag this out for four minutes and park for free or you can accept our gratitude and let us get on with our business.'

She arched a brow. 'How much gratitude?'

He looked at Taylor. 'Give the lady ten bucks.'

'Ten bucks?' Taylor said with a tone of protest as he dug out his wallet. 'It's three minutes.'

'You are a cheap man,' the woman scolded, snatching the bill out of his hand. 'Cheapness makes you less handsome.'

'It's ten bucks more than you would have had without us,' Kovac pointed out.

A brilliant smile split her face. 'This is very true. I thank you, gentlemen. Excuse me now while I close my shop. Good day to you.'

'We could have just parked there,' Taylor grumbled.

'Don't be a piker. It's important to foster good community relations,' Kovac said, flipping up the collar of his coat. The damp cold dug into his shoulders like talons. 'Besides, it did my heart good to spend your money.'

'I'm so happy for you.'

Diana Chamberlain's apartment was located on the ground floor of a huge, ugly brown house with a sagging wraparound porch. The front door was open. Three different kinds of loud music leeched through the thin walls into the first-floor hall, the volume rising and falling as apartment doors opened and closed. Taylor rapped on the door marked 'B,' and they waited. He knocked again.

The door of the house opened and a college kid with dreadlocks came in with a bicycle and muscled it up the stairs to the second floor.

Taylor knocked again. 'Miss Chamberlain?'

The door cracked open and a fit, good-looking Japanese man in his late thirties stared out at them. 'Can I help you?'

Taylor held up his ID. 'Police. We're looking for Diana Chamberlain.'

'Finally. She had to see the news on TV first. Nice job, guys,' the man said sarcastically.

'And you would be . . . ?' Kovac asked.

'Ken Sato.'

'*Professor Ken Sato?*'

'Yes.'

Kovac cut Taylor a subtle 'What did I tell you?' look.

'Do you live here?' Taylor asked. 'We have a different address for you.'

'No, I came over for Diana,' Sato said. 'She called me, hysterical. She'd seen the news coverage at the gym while she was working out.' He shook his head in disbelief. 'I knew something had to be wrong when Lucien didn't show for the meeting this morning. I never imagined anything like what happened. Was there really a sword involved? That's a hideous thought.'

Doors opened and closed above them, and feet thundered down the stairs, accompanied by talk and laughter.

'We'd like to come in and speak to Miss Chamberlain,' Kovac said.

'She's resting. She's had a rough day.'

Taylor had the better angle to see into the apartment. He was looking past Sato, his suspicions rising just as Kovac's were. For all they knew, Sato had massacred the Chamberlains and had come here to cross the daughter off the list.

'Yeah, well, I'm afraid we have to insist,' Kovac said. 'We have a few questions we need answered.'

'She just lost her parents. This can't wait until tomorrow?'

'No. It can't,' Kovac said firmly.

Sato frowned, not moving from the doorway. A woman's voice came from somewhere behind him.

'Ken? Who is it?'

'The police. They want to speak to you.'

'Oh, we'll want to speak to you, too, Professor,' Kovac said. 'You being so close to the family and all.'

Unhappy, Sato stepped back and motioned them inside. He was dressed in jeans and a long-sleeve Henley T-shirt that skimmed broad shoulders and a tapered waist. No bow tie, no tweed jacket. His Clark Kent glasses only made him look hipper. His thick black hair was shaved close on the sides of his head, and left long on top, to spill across his forehead. The sleeves of his shirt were pushed halfway up to his elbows, revealing intricate sleeves of tattoos on both forearms.

Diana Chamberlain was taller than Sato by several inches. She had to be close to six feet, an angular, athletic-looking girl in her mid-twenties with tumbling waves of streaky blonde hair. Her face was an interesting oval of slightly asymmetrical features. A bump on the bridge of her nose suggested it had been broken once. Her eyes and nose were red and puffy, presumably from crying.

Kovac introduced himself and Taylor. She looked Taylor up and down like he might be on the menu for dinner.

'We're sorry for your loss, Miss Chamberlain,' Taylor said.

'We're sorry about the way you found out,

too,' Kovac added. 'The media ran with the story before we could stop them.'

'Was it true?' she asked. She backed up to a sagging couch and curled her long legs beneath her like a foal, settling back into a corner and pulling a blanket around her shoulders. She never took her eyes off Taylor. 'What they said about my parents being attacked with a sword — is that true?'

There was no emotion in her voice as she asked, no fear, no horror at the idea. Nothing but morbid curiosity.

'There was evidence to suggest that, yes,' Taylor said.

'That's so terrible,' she said, wide-eyed. 'With one of Daddy's swords?'

'We can't really get into those details yet,' Kovac said.

The apartment smelled of weed and incense. Everything in it looked thirdhand and worn out. The sink and counter of the kitchenette were piled with dirty dishes. It was a far cry from the home the girl's parents had died in.

'Do you know which sword it was?' she asked. 'Did they use more than one?'

She wasn't crying now. She wasn't tearing up at the thought of her parents being hacked to death. She wanted to know which sword their killer had chosen to use.

'I can't comment on that,' Kovac said again. 'I wouldn't know one from the other at any rate. We were hoping you might be able to help us in the weaponry department, Mr. Sato.'

Sato sat down on the couch a foot away from

the girl, touching her reassuringly on the shoulder. 'Absolutely. Whatever you need.'

'Did they suffer?' the girl asked. 'I wouldn't want to think my mother suffered.'

She sounded like she was talking about a stray animal that had been run over.

Kovac took a seat on a hard, straight wooden chair to be at her eye level. He thought of Sondra Chamberlain lying spread-eagle on the floor of her dining room, a quarter of her face sliced away, a samurai sword planted through her abdomen. 'It looked like it happened pretty fast.'

The girl blinked her wide gray eyes. Vacant eyes. He wondered if she was on something.

'When was the last time you spoke to either of your parents?' Taylor asked. He took the other hard wood chair and balanced his notebook on his thigh as he scribbled his notes.

'I was there for dinner Sunday. It was my father's birthday,' she said. 'And my mother called me every day. I didn't answer her call yesterday, though.'

'What time did she call?'

'Around eight thirty. I don't take her calls after dinner. I can't stand to listen to her when she's been drinking.'

'How would you know she'd been drinking if you didn't speak to her?' Taylor asked.

She looked at him like he was an idiot. 'My mother drinks in the evening. Every evening. I would drink, too, if I lived in that house, but I wouldn't live in that house, so I don't want to hear about it.'

'Your father was a difficult man?' Kovac asked.

'An egotistical, misogynistic megalomaniac.'

'But you went to his birthday dinner?' Taylor said.

'It was a command performance. I didn't say I enjoyed myself.'

'You were his grad student,' Kovac said. 'Did he twist your arm to do that?'

'It was a prestigious position with one of the leading scholars of East Asian history in the country.'

'We were told you filed a complaint against your dad with the Office for Conflict Resolution. What was that about?'

'That was about him treating me like dirt in my capacity as his assistant.'

'I'm getting the impression you didn't get along with your dad,' Kovac said dryly. 'Did you really think it would be any different working with him? In my personal experience, if people are assholes, they're assholes all day long. Or did you think having the subject in common might soften him? Was that where your interest came from? You wanted something in common to share with him?'

Now her eyes filled with tears and her face went red from trying to hold them back. She sprang up from the couch and ran into the adjacent bedroom, slamming the door behind her.

Kovac looked at Sato.

'Obviously Diana has a difficult relationship with her father. It's a long story.'

Kovac sat back and spread his hands. 'We've got nothing but time.'

The professor sighed, not happy to be put on the spot.

'Diana has issues.'

'Such as?'

He glanced at the bedroom door as if he thought she might be listening on the other side. The muffled sound of her sobs filled the silence.

'Diana was adopted when she was four or five. She has abandonment issues. She's insecure. An insecure girl shouldn't have Lucien Chamberlain for a father. Life revolves around him, his needs, his career. Children have to have their needs met, too.'

'She's not a child anymore.'

'We're all children with our parents, aren't we?' Sato asked. 'She went through a rebellious stage: drugs, drinking, dropped out of school, in and out of rehab. When she came out of that, she decided to start fresh, finish school, and try to mend her relationship with her father.

'She's a very bright girl,' he continued. 'Lucien could appreciate that when she applied herself within his rigid construct of how students should learn. But not every student responds to the traditional methods.'

'He rejected her?' Taylor asked.

'Nothing as simple as that. Rejection implies defeat. Lucien would rather make a student quit than admit he needed to change his methods.' Sato shrugged. 'He was who he was, and she is who she is. The two of them working together was a train wreck waiting to happen.'

'He must have been angry when she filed the

complaint against him,' Taylor said.

'He was livid. He believed she timed it to sabotage his bid for the promotion to head of East Asian studies.'

'Didn't she?'

Sato looked again at the closed bedroom door. 'Probably.'

'And what's your role in this family drama?' Kovac asked. 'Is she sleeping with you to piss off her old man? Or are you sleeping with her to piss off your colleague?'

'I'm just a friend, Detective,' he said, his expression carefully neutral. 'I'm just a shoulder to cry on.'

'You're not sleeping with her?'

'No,' he said, but he couldn't quite hold eye contact as he said it.

Liar, liar.

'She seems very . . . comfortable with you,' Taylor said.

'I've known Diana for five years. I could see from the start the struggle she was having with her father, and I could understand it, too. My own father is controlling and manipulative. We have that in common. And I've had my own struggles with Lucien.'

'What kind of struggles?' Kovac asked.

'I'm from a more modern school of teaching. I believe in challenging old ways and old thoughts. Lucien found me threatening because I pull students out of his dull rut and let them open their eyes.'

'Were you a threat to him?'

'Not in the way you mean. Not physically.'

'But professionally and as a parental figure,' Taylor said.

'I wasn't trying to steal Diana away from him — as a teacher or a father. I was trying to help her. We commiserate over how difficult her father is — was, and let her blow off some of the anger and frustration she feels,' Sato explained. 'I appreciate Diana's spirit. She needs someone to encourage her to reach her full potential, not criticize and belittle her, or try to make her live in a cage inside her own mind.'

'So you've become *special friends* with the troubled daughter of your biggest professional rival,' Kovac said. 'How'd that go over with her father?'

'Lucien didn't know. He would have misconstrued the relationship.'

'And gotten your ass fired?' Kovac asked. 'I have to think the university frowns on professors and students being special friends.'

'I wouldn't get fired,' Sato said with confidence, like he had someone on the inside greasing the wheels for him.

'But you wouldn't get that promotion, either, would you?' Kovac asked. 'If Lucien Chamberlain made some claim of impropriety against you, whether or not you were guilty, it wouldn't look good, would it?'

Sato looked at him as the implication sank in, his dark eyes steady. 'I wouldn't kill for it, if that's what you're thinking.'

'When did you last see Professor Chamberlain?' Taylor asked.

'Yesterday at work.'

'And where were you last night?'

'At home.'

'Can anyone vouch for that?'

He cut another quick glance at the bedroom door. What would be worse: to have an uncorroborated alibi, or to say he was in bed with the dead man's daughter? He was a suspect either way. So was she.

'I was alone.'

Kovac raised his eyebrows just to mess with the guy. *That's the answer you picked? Huh.*

'Okay,' he said, getting to his feet. 'We'll be in touch about the weaponry.'

Sato walked with them to the door. 'Anything I can do to help.'

'We'll need you both to come in and get fingerprinted for elimination purposes.'

'Me?' Sato said, surprised. 'I haven't been in that house in a year or more.'

Kovac smiled at him. 'Better safe than sorry. I can't just assume they have the world's greatest cleaning lady. It's no big deal, really. It takes two minutes.'

'Yeah, sure,' Sato said with no conviction.

'We understand Professor Chamberlain's collection is valuable,' Taylor said.

'It's incredible.'

'How could he afford that on a professor's salary?'

'They've always had money. Sondra's family was connected to some chemical-pharmaceutical fortune. Lucien made sure people knew. He liked people to think he taught for higher reasons — like his ego.'

'You didn't like him,' Kovac said.

'Nobody liked Lucien. He wasn't a likeable man. People respected him, or they envied him for what he had: his position, his possessions — '

'His collection?' Taylor said. 'Something someone would kill to have?'

Sato frowned. 'I hope not.'

'I hope so,' Kovac said. 'Because if someone killed those two people the way they killed them just for the hell of it . . . '

He let that hang as he handed Sato a business card. 'We'll be in touch,' he said.

Ken Sato saw them the ten feet to the door and locked the dead-bolt as soon as they were on the other side.

'That's some messed-up shit right there,' Taylor said softly, glancing back over his shoulder as they went down the hall to the apartment house's front door. 'The daughter sleeping with Dad's rival for the big promotion. I can't wait to meet the son.'

'What'd I tell you?' Kovac said. 'The all-American family. It's Norman Fucking Rockwell on acid.'

★   ★   ★

Sato tapped on the bedroom door. 'Diana?'

No answer. No sound. She might have fallen asleep. She might have slit her wrists. Either was possible in her current state of mind. He opened the door and slipped inside.

The bedside lamps were on. She was naked, kneeling on the bed, touching herself, her eyes already glazed, her mouth wet and open. Her body was beautiful, lithe and subtly muscular. Her nipples were pierced with small silver rings. A ruby studded her navel.

She grabbed him by the waist of his jeans and pulled him closer.

'Diana.' He breathed her name as she undid his pants and took him in her mouth.

The sex with her was crazy and hot, as addictive as crystal meth. She went to a dark, desperate place in her mind he didn't want to know about, but he willingly went along for the ride.

She rode him hard, sweating, gasping, crying, and when the end came for her, she pounded her fist against his tattooed chest over and over and over, like she had a knife in her hand.

Then, exhausted, she collapsed on top of him and drifted into unconsciousness on an anguished whispered word: '*Daddy . . .* '

12

'You're here about my parents,' Charles Chamberlain said as he opened the door to his apartment, his expression grave, his voice quiet and a little unsteady. Nerves. Emotions. Both. He was pale, though whether that was natural or caused by the circumstances, Kovac couldn't guess.

He appeared to be a modest, unremarkable young man — early twenties, medium height, medium build, medium brown hair cut in a medium-length, conservative Everyman style. He wore nerdy glasses, and was neatly dressed in khaki pants and a button-down shirt, tucked in.

'Professor Foster called and broke the news. He said you'd be contacting me. I didn't know if I should call the police department or go downtown or go to the house, or what,' he said. 'How does anyone know what to do when something like this happens?'

'They don't,' Kovac said. 'Everybody gets the crash course.'

'We're sorry for your loss, Mr. Chamberlain,' Taylor said.

'Thank you.'

'I know this is a tough time,' Kovac said, 'but we need to ask you some questions. It's important that we get as much information as we can as fast as we can.'

'I understand.' He stepped back from the door, inviting them in. 'Professor Foster said it was probably a burglary, that someone might have targeted them — maybe for my father's collection. Is that true?'

'There appear to be elements of a burglary,' Taylor said. 'There have been a couple of burglaries in the area recently. But we don't know anything for sure at this point.'

'How could someone break in? What happened to their alarm system?'

'We don't know yet. Were they good about arming it?'

'Yes, every night after dinner. It was part of my mother's routine. She took the dishes to the kitchen, set the alarm on the back door keypad, then started cleaning up.'

'What time did she start drinking?' Kovac asked bluntly.

The kid gave him a look, like he wanted to express outrage and denial, but in the end he said, 'She liked a glass of wine with dinner . . . and maybe another after dinner. So what? She wasn't a falling-down drunk, if that's what someone told you.'

'Did you speak to her last night?' Taylor asked.

'No. I was working. I turned my phone off. I have a deadline,' he said. His brows knit and his eyes filled. 'I had a message from her when I turned it back on this morning. Just wanting to talk. She gets lonely. I guess by the time I picked up the message . . . '

By the time he picked up the message, his mother was already dead on the dining room floor. He was seeing some version of that in his head now.

'Try not to beat yourself up, kid,' Kovac said. 'We can't foresee bad stuff coming; otherwise we'd stop it from happening.'

He was regretting not taking the chance to have had one last conversation with his mother. People always did. They wanted to believe they would have had some incredible moment of clarity about how much they loved that person they were unknowingly about to lose; how whatever petty arguments and angry words they held against one another would have magically dissolved, and they would have had the most beautiful, meaningful conversation of their lives.

The truth was if Charles Chamberlain had answered that call from his mother, he would have been irritated because she was interrupting his work when he had a deadline. He would have heard the lonely, wine-soaked self-pity in his mother's voice and thought, Here we go again. They probably would have had unpleasant words about his father or his sister. And he would now be feeling guilty for that conversation because he hadn't been patient, and he hadn't consoled her, and now she was dead and he hadn't told her he loved her.

The kid showed them to his living area, just to the left of the front door, and they all sat down. Like his sister's place, most of the apartment could be seen at a glance: a tiny kitchen, a counter to eat at, a living room, a hall that led to a bedroom and a bath. Unlike his sister's place, Charles Chamberlain's small home was modest, not cheap, and neat as a pin. There were no dirty dishes visible. It didn't smell of weed. The furniture might have been from the fifties or sixties — or at least made to look that way — low and clean, with straight lines and no frills. Jazz music played softly in the background from fist-size speakers beside a twenty-three-inch flat-screen TV on a console made from some kind of industrial serving cart. A laptop computer sat open on a small desk in one corner, two filing cabinets with a slab of glass for a top.

'I don't know what to say,' the kid murmured, almost to himself. His hands were trembling as he rested them on his knees. 'It's surreal. I keep thinking there must be some mistake. Who would want to kill my parents? And then I turned on the television when I got home, and there was the house on the news. It's crazy! They were killed with a sword?'

He looked straight at Kovac, clearly wanting a denial that was not forthcoming.

'Oh my God.'

He had that haunted look in his blue eyes, like someone who had seen something unspeakable. He shook his head as if he might be able to shake the images out of his brain.

'Who could do something like that?' he whispered, a shudder passing through him.

'Can you think of anyone who might have had a grudge against one or both of them?' Taylor asked.

Chamberlain laughed abruptly, in the way people do when they're shocked. 'Sure. But they're professors who think my father is an ass. They're not people who go around committing murder! My mother has her charities. She goes to her book club. Who could she possibly offend?'

He pulled his glasses off and rubbed a hand across his face. His fingernails were bitten to the quick. He picked at a cuticle as he breathed in and out with purpose, trying to pull himself together.

'It had to be some kind of thug or a homicidal maniac or something, right?' he asked, glancing up with that light of desperate hope in his expression that Kovac had seen so many times. When it came to violent crime, everyone wanted to believe in the bogeyman. No one wanted to think they might know a killer.

'We have to consider all possibilities,' Kovac said. 'Right now we're just trying to get a picture of your parents' life and the people in it. Had they mentioned having a problem with anyone? A neighbor, someone doing work on the house, anything like that?'

'The one neighbor, the Abrams, have already gone to Arizona for the winter. They've lived next door forever. My mother and Mrs. Abrams are friends. The house on the other side of them is vacant. It was sold over the summer. The new owners are renovating,' he said. 'My father complained about the noise on the weekend.'

Kovac would set Taylor to the task of checking out the construction crew. Maybe someone had a record. Maybe someone had a temper, or a screw loose, or both.

'Had your parents had any work done on their own house recently?'

'Oh, well, there was the Yelp incident,' he said, as if they should know what that meant.

'What's that?'

'My mother hired a handyman service to do some work around the house. My father didn't like the job they did, and he went on Yelp and wrote a nasty review. I guess he and the guy running the business got into it over the phone a couple of times. But people don't kill people over bad Yelp reviews.'

'You'd be surprised,' Kovac said. 'You run into the wrong person, they'll kill you for having blue eyes. That's why we need to know anything at all that might fit into the picture. Even if it seems insignificant to you.'

Taylor stared intently at his phone, flipping through the photographs he had taken earlier. He stopped on one, enlarged it with his thumb and forefinger, and shot a look at Kovac.

'Handy Dandy Home Services. There was a notation on the calendar in the kitchen for last Friday.'

'The guy had offered to come back and do some work for free if my father took the bad review down,' Chamberlain said.

'Do you know if that happened?'

'I don't know. My father said he wouldn't take it down until he was satisfied with the follow-up work.'

'I'll look it up,' Taylor said, tapping the screen of his phone.

'When did you last see your folks?' Kovac asked.

'Sunday. My father's birthday dinner.'

'And how was that?'

He bobbed his eyebrows, looked away, and sighed. 'It was the usual family gathering.'

'What does that mean?'

He didn't want to say. He stared down at his hands and picked at the loose piece of cuticle.

'We've already spoken to your sister,' Kovac prompted. 'You might as well give us your version.'

Another sigh as he considered what to say.

'My mother tried too hard to be festive. My father played the role of tyrant, my sister got belligerent, and we all ended up screaming at each other.'

'That's the usual?'

'It is for us. In case no one's told you, my father is a raging narcissist, and my sister is bipolar. It's not a good mix. Our mother drinks to take the edge off.'

'And what do you do?'

'I try to keep my head down.'

'Have you spoken to your sister today?'

He shook his head and gave in to the nervous urge to bite off the offending loose cuticle. 'She won't pick up. She isn't answering text messages, either. She's punishing me for not taking her side Sunday. I didn't take his side, either. But she didn't care. You're either for Di or you're against her. She doesn't believe in neutrality.'

'Who's the oldest?' Kovac asked.

'She is.'

'But she's still a student?'

'She had some . . . *interruptions* along the way.'

'Are you a student, too?'

'No. I'm a paralegal at Obern and Phipps. Family law.'

'Decided not to follow in the old man's footsteps?'

'There's more call for paralegals in the workplace than for scholars of ancient Asian history,' the kid said. 'I didn't have any desire to go into his field and be his rival.'

'But your sister felt differently?'

'We're different people. She still has some idea that if she pleases him, he'll be proud of her. The thing is it's virtually impossible to please him.'

'So, you became a paralegal, and you don't have to live up to your old man's reputation or expectations?'

'I wouldn't say that,' he mumbled. 'He doesn't limit his criticism to his own field of expertise. But I don't care,' he declared in a way that made it clear he *did* care. 'I figured him out a long time ago. Narcissists love themselves. The rest of us live on a sliding scale of pleasing them or displeasing them.'

'Where did you rank on that scale lately?'

'Somewhere on the lower end of center,' he admitted.

'What was his beef with you?'

He shrugged, as if to say, *Take your pick.* 'I should have become an attorney instead of a paralegal. I should have become a doctor instead of a lawyer. I should have been him instead of me. That's how it works. To try to live up to his expectations is a trap. He just keeps raising the bar — a lesson my sister refuses to learn.'

He went quiet for a moment. 'I guess she doesn't have to now.'

Kovac sat back and scratched the side of his face, thinking he needed a shave, watching the kid's body language. He was uncomfortable talking about his family issues. He was having a hard time sitting still. He kept glancing at Taylor, who was reading something on his phone.

'What was the fight about Sunday?' Kovac asked.

Chamberlain rolled his eyes. 'Diana is — was our father's student assistant. Pretty much the worst idea ever. She filed a complaint about him at school, and he's up for a big promotion. He accused her of sabotaging him.'

'Was she?'

He shrugged. 'I don't know. Probably. Partly. I mean, it's not like he isn't a jerk. He was hard on her. But her timing . . . Everything is complicated with Diana. Her brain is hardwired differently. She doesn't feel obligated to make sense to anyone but herself.'

'What about Ken Sato?'

'What about him?' he asked, his expression carefully neutral.

'He and your sister seem . . . close.'

The kid shook his head again, like a pitcher shaking off a catcher's signs. He didn't want to play this game.

'I mind my own business. I don't get involved in Diana's life.'

'She's truly bipolar? Is she on medication?'

He shrugged. 'She should be. Whether or not she takes it, I don't know. Why are you asking all these questions about her?' His eyes got big. 'You can't think she would — no. No.'

'We're just trying to get a clear family picture,' Kovac reassured. 'We're not accusing anybody of anything.'

Chamberlain looked around, uncomfortable, anxious, probably feeling trapped in his own home. He'd just about had enough. He got up and walked behind his chair, needing to burn off some of the anxiety. He chewed on a thumbnail as he paced.

'Di is a mess, but she would never do anything like that,' he said. 'I mean, she and our father went around and around. That was just their relationship. It was like a sick game.'

'What was your relationship with your father like?' Taylor asked.

'It was . . . fine,' he said, struggling for the right word, clearly not satisfied with the one he chose. 'I have my own life. I saw him when I had to see him. We weren't buddies or anything. That's not who he is.'

'We have to ask,' Kovac said. 'Where were you last night, Mr. Chamberlain?'

The kid looked from one of them to the other. 'I was here, working. I have a deadline.'

'Can anyone verify that? A roommate, a friend, a co-worker, a neighbor?'

'Oh my God,' he breathed. 'Do I need an *alibi?*'

'It just makes our job easier if we can

conclusively put people in place while we figure out the time line,' Kovac said.

'I was home. Alone.' He looked like he might get sick.

'Lots of people are. That's not a crime.'

'I was on my computer,' he said. 'It has a log.'

'Don't worry about it,' Kovac said, rising. Taylor took his cue and stood.

'What happens now?' the kid asked. 'Should I be making arrangements or something? Who's supposed to do that?'

'Next of kin,' Taylor said. 'Do you have any uncles, aunts, grandparents in the area?'

'No.'

'You're it, then. You and your sister.'

'The bodies are at the medical examiner's office, pending autopsy,' Kovac said. 'Five thirty Chicago Avenue. Someone will have to come downtown and make the official ID.'

'Are you kidding me?' Chamberlain asked, horrified. 'We have to come *look at them?*'

'It's an unpleasant formality,' Kovac said. 'They'll let you do the viewing on a monitor.'

Chamberlain looked away, shaking his head. He didn't want to be a part of any of this. He didn't seem to want to be a part of his family at all. He had gone to that disastrous birthday dinner out of a sense of duty. Now duty would drag him to the morgue.

'We can take you down there and bring you back,' Kovac said.

'Now?' the kid asked, incredulous.

'Tomorrow is soon enough.' Kovac took a card out of his pocket and handed it to him. 'We'll be

150

in touch. Sorry for your loss.'

★ ★ ★

'The families I've seen . . . ' Kovac started as they left the apartment building. 'Makes being divorced twice seem not so bad.'

Even as he said it, he thought of Tinks and her boys. They did well as a family — as long as that asshole she had been married to stayed in line or out of the picture.

Kovac had started his own family once. Or so he had thought. His second wife gave birth and then promptly divorced him, took the kid, and moved to Seattle, where she remarried with suspicious haste. It all happened so fast and so long ago, it seemed like some weird bad dream now. He doubted the kid was even his. Kovac had been a convenient source of health insurance, that was all.

'The Yelp review is still up,' Taylor said.

'How bad is it?'

'He called the workmen incompetent, ignorant, filthy, and foul-mouthed, and said that was apparently company policy as evidenced by the behavior and attitude of the manager over the phone. Thirteen people have found the review useful. Three thought it was funny.'

'Funny?'

Taylor shrugged. 'Thirteen 'useful' is thirteen customers lost, to say nothing of the people who read the review but didn't comment. That's dollars lost to a small business, plus a bad reputation in a good neighborhood.'

'See what you can find out about the business. Let's pay a visit to the manager. For now, let's go back to the office. I want to get the war room set up. There's so many people that hated this professor, I already need a program to keep track of them.'

★ ★ ★

Charlie Chamberlain sat on his sofa for a long time after the detectives had left. He sat with perfect posture, staring into the middle distance, images and arguments tumbling through his mind. Pandora's box had opened wide, and all the memories came spilling out, one running into the next, and into the next.

Him at five in short pants and a bow tie, with knobby skinned knees, and tears on his cheeks. His mother's drunken, angry face; her mouth twisted open like a gash in her face. His father's cold stare.

He saw himself at nine, at twelve, at fourteen. He heard the voices.

Stupid boy . . .

I told you never . . .

. . . so disappointed . . .

Get out of my sight . . .

Worthless . . .

. . . mistake . . .

He saw the hand striking, the belt swinging.

He saw his sister and heard her crying.

He felt the helplessness of a child.

'Such a perfect family,' everyone used to say. They didn't know, and wouldn't suspect.

Appearances were all that mattered. Appearances, accolades, money, the right car, the perfect dinner party. Two children brought out on cue and promptly put away.

Seen not heard.

Don't cause a problem.

Don't say a word.

He didn't know how much time passed as he sat there. Years passed through his head. He might have sat there an hour or all night, lost in a trance, in emotional limbo. So many feelings tore through him and collided that they canceled each other out until he was numb.

What was he supposed to feel?

The doorbell brought him back into the moment. He had no idea of the time. Maybe the detectives had come back to take him to the morgue to identify the bodies.

He put an eye to the peephole and took in the distorted view of his sister — hair disheveled, eyes red, face swollen.

'Di,' he said as he opened the door.

'They're dead, Charlie,' she said, her face twisting in anguish. 'Oh my God, they're dead!'

She threw herself against him and began to sob. He put his arms around her and held her. They had only ever had each other.

'They're dead,' she mumbled through her tears. 'We're free . . . '

Even as he tried to comfort her, he knew that wasn't true. They weren't free. The future might be clear ahead, but the past was something no one could escape but the dead. There was irony. They would always be damaged by their pasts and by the choices other people had made. The only ones free in this story were lying on slabs at the county morgue.

But he said nothing as he held his sister, and they cried together.

13

Nikki read files until her eyes burned and her vision blurred. So much for the idea of no late hours working cold cases. While there may have been no outward sense of urgency in solving a case that had been gathering dust in the archives for a quarter of a century, that didn't change who she was. She was still going to dig and scratch and poke and prod with the focus of a terrier.

At least she got to do it at home.

She had gotten home in time to make a nice dinner for herself and the boys, and had taken an hour to watch some TV with them. Every commercial break included a promo for the local news: *More on the story of the double homicide of a university professor and his wife! Tune in at ten!*

The big news of the new cold case squad and the unsolved murder of Detective Ted Duffy hadn't even managed a twenty-four-hour cycle in the media. Everyone in the metro area was now captivated by the bigger, fresher, more gruesome crime.

She had caught the coverage of the press conference on the six o'clock edition. The mayor, the chief of police, Deputy Chief Kasselmann, and Lieutenant Mascherino, all looking suitably grave as they gave their statements. No Kovac. No surprise. Sam loathed press conferences. He would have been out doing his job, sure not to pick up the message that his presence was required in front of a news camera.

She wanted to call him, to find out what was going on, if they had any leads, but she wouldn't let herself. He was busy, and it was none of her business. He was probably setting up the war room, scribbling all over the whiteboard with his terrible handwriting. Tippen was in on the case, and Elwood would be as well. They'd be up all night drinking bad coffee and eating pizza out of cardboard boxes.

She would be up all night reading about a case that had already happened and had long gone stale, making notes on her own whiteboard in her own little office at home. At least the coffee was better.

At the time of Ted Duffy's death he had half a dozen cases going at work. No one had been able to connect any of those cases to his murder. Considerable time had been spent tracking down guys Duffy had sent to prison over the years who had subsequently been released in the right timeframe. Of those known to be in the vicinity, some had alibis, some didn't, but no one could put any of them in that park behind the Duffy house with a rifle on the day in question.

The hottest prospect they'd had at the time was a rapist, a repeat offender who'd screamed at Duffy in the courtroom that he would get him. He had been released from prison just a week prior to the shooting. After three days of an intensive search in the Twin Cities and surrounding area, it was discovered that the guy had been arrested in Eau Claire, Wisconsin, three days after his release from the prison in Moose Lake, where many of Minnesota's hard-core sex offenders were sent to be rehabilitated. He had gotten out of prison, taken a bus to Wisconsin, and promptly tried to assault a waitress leaving her workplace late at night.

'I guess that rehab didn't take,' Nikki mumbled, setting those reports aside.

She thought a little about the weapon that had been used to kill Ted Duffy: a small-caliber hunting rifle, a .243. It was described as a gun suitable for smaller hunters because of the lighter recoil. One of the comments she had read online regarding this caliber of weapon for hunters: 'A nice rifle for a woman.'

Barbie Duffy had allegedly been out grocery shopping the day of her husband's death. She came home with groceries, but who could prove when she had bought them? There was no store receipt on file, and no mention of any store surveillance tape showing her buying groceries at the time in question. The detectives — Grider being one of them — cut her slack in small ways they might not have had they not known her and her husband. If Barbie said she had been shopping, then she must have been shopping. The grocery bags were probably still sitting on the kitchen counter when the detectives showed up.

Had the Duffys owned a .243 hunting rifle? Ted had been going to join his brother deer hunting in Wisconsin that weekend. But Ted

Duffy was a big guy. He would have used a big gun, not one written up as being 'A nice rifle for a woman.' Nikki made a note to ask Barbie Duffy if she had ever gone deer hunting. But even if Ted Duffy didn't own a .243, his twin had access to every gun there was.

Big D Sports was best known for hunting and camping gear, including guns. Big Duff had allegedly been in Rice Lake, Wisconsin, opening his cabin for the weekend's hunting when his brother was killed. That was where he had been found by the family friend who drove the two hours to deliver the news of Ted's death in person. But that was several hours after the discovery of Ted Duffy's body. Big Duff would have had more than enough time to kill his brother and drive back to Rice Lake. He had been seen in a convenience store near his cabin earlier in the day, but most of his afternoon was unaccounted for.

Whose idea had it been to send the friend to Rice Lake to deliver the news to Big Duff? The cabin had no telephone, but they could have called the local sheriff's office and sent a unit out to inform Duff of his brother's demise. They would have gotten to him much closer to the time of Ted's death — or they might have gotten to an empty cabin, as Thomas Duffy was still making his way back from killing his brother.

If the crime had taken place a week ago, or a year ago, or even ten years ago, they would have been able to track Thomas Duffy's movements via the cell towers his phone had pinged off. But at the time of his brother's death, cell phones were less common, and used differently. Back then, a cell phone was something to have for emergencies.

In one of the many revisitations to the investigation several years after the fact, a harder look had been taken at Big Duff (by a detective *not* named Gene Grider) after he and his brother's widow got hitched. Still, nothing in the way of evidence had been found to implicate him in his brother's death. But there was plenty of speculation to be made.

Barbie Duffy collected a considerable sum of life insurance on her husband's death. Big Duff did as well. Ted had invested as a partner in his brother's first store. The partners had been insured. It was safe to assume that at least some of that money went into the expansion of Big D Sports, and the second Mr. and Mrs. Duffy ended up rich and living in a house that was photographed for magazines. Happily ever after.

Nikki wondered if anyone had spoken to the neighbor, Donald Nilsen, the self-appointed neighborhood morality police, about whether Ted Duffy's brother ever visited when his twin was not at home. If they asked that question, she couldn't find any record of it.

Nilsen had been interviewed many times over the years. He hadn't seen anything. He hadn't heard anything. He had been working in his home office. His wife had been making dinner. His son had been attending a basketball game at school.

In the one and only interview with Renee Nilsen, she had little to say. The Nilsens' son,

159

Jeremy, had also been interviewed just once. It didn't look like anyone had tried to learn about the Duffy household through him, even though he had mown their yard and shoveled their sidewalk, and had probably gone to school with the teenage girls living with the Duffys at the time.

As the mother of a son the same age, Nikki could state with certainty that if Jeremy Nilsen was straight, he would have been very aware of the 'tarts' next door. And those girls would have been very aware of him. He was a good-looking kid — and the quiet type, according to Barbie. There was no animal on the face of the earth more irresistible to a teenage girl than a handsome boy who had nothing to say. A man of mystery! They would have spun tales in their heads about why he was so quiet. They would have fantasized about being the one person he would open up to and trust with all his secrets.

She wondered if Jeremy Nilsen had secrets about what his father was up to when Ted Duffy was being murdered. Unfortunately, Jeremy Nilsen was dead. Whatever secrets he might have had had gone with him to his grave. Nikki kept seeing the trophy buck hanging over Donald Nilsen's electric fireplace. Unless he had bought that thing at a flea market, he owned guns and was a crack shot. He didn't make it a secret that he hadn't liked the Duffys. He had paid far too much attention to the goings-on at the house next door. Ted Duffy had confronted him and leveled a thinly veiled threat at him for ogling the girls.

She went to her whiteboard on the wall across from her desk and made three columns headed 'Barbie Duffy,' 'Thomas Duffy,' and 'Donald Nilsen.' Beneath each name, she jotted notes in black, and questions in red.

Of the Duffys' children, only Jennifer, who was nine at the time, had been interviewed. She was in her bedroom upstairs at the time of the shooting. Her room overlooked the backyard. She said she had been reading a book and hadn't seen anything. The younger two Duffy children were in the family room at the front of the house playing while the younger foster child, Penny Williams, watched and did homework. The older foster girl, Angie Jeager, had been at a school function, not returning home until around nine thirty. The same basketball game Jeremy Nilsen was attending? Nikki wondered.

To the far right on the whiteboard, she wrote, 'TBI' (for To Be Interviewed), and beneath it, the names Renee Nilsen, Penny Williams, and Angie Jeager.

What were the odds of finding any of them? Nilsen claimed to have no idea where his ex-wife was. Barbie Duffy hadn't maintained a relationship with the two girls she had taken in as slave labor and then sent back to the foster care system like stray dogs to the pound. Twenty-five years after the fact, it was doubtful any of them still had the same last name.

'And that's why they call you a detective, Nikki,' she murmured to herself.

★　★　★

161

Someone had already ordered in pizza by the time Kovac and Taylor returned to the office. It was past eight o'clock, but Mascherino was still there, having a slice with the guys. An incongruous picture, Kovac thought: the petite and proper fifty-something lieutenant in her smart maroon suit standing in the break room with the rest of the hooligans, eating pizza off a paper plate. He gave her credit for the effort.

'Sam, Michael,' she said as they came into the room to grab their dinner. 'Get something to eat and bring it to my office. I want an update.'

The three of them went to her office and Kovac filled her in, chowing down on his dinner between segments of the afternoon's events.

'So, basically,' he said, 'Professor Chamberlain never met a person he didn't annoy. Nobody had anything bad to say about the wife, other than that she named her children Charles and Diana, after the royals, and she liked to drink a bit in the evenings.'

'Do you think the murders were personal?'

Kovac gave a halfhearted shrug.

'The robbery looked legit,' Taylor said. 'Not staged. The key rooms were hit for stuff that could be carried and sold: small electronics, cash, credit cards, jewelry — '

'The weapons taken from the professor's collection raise the question of whether our bad guy went there specifically targeting the collection or just hit the jackpot finding that stuff,' Kovac said. 'Sato, the colleague-slash-rival, is going to go through it with us. We'll find out the significance of the pieces that are missing.

'That in itself should be interesting,' he continued. 'The head of the department told us Sato had a pretty serious hard-on for the collection. He wants the same job Chamberlain wanted. He's banging the daughter. That's a lot of checks in his column.'

'But the burglary aspect looks like several others in the area,' Mascherino said.

'I put Tippen and Elwood on that.'

'I spoke to them already. There are two cases that could very well be connected to this one — similar method of entry, neat and efficient burglary. The difference being no one was home at the time.'

'All the more reason for the Chamberlains to have had their security system armed,' Taylor pointed out.

'I've spoken with the security company,' the lieutenant said. 'According to their computer, the Chamberlains' system was armed last night a little after seven, and disarmed around twelve thirty. Of course, they can't tell us who disarmed it or why. Disarming the system with the pass code doesn't raise any red flags with the company.'

'The code number was on a label on the keypad in the kitchen,' Taylor said. 'I took a picture of it.'

'The electronic-age version of leaving the key under the doormat,' Mascherino said, shaking her head.

'People accidentally set the alarm off, they panic and can't remember the code,' Taylor said. 'It's not hard to imagine that happening with

Mrs. Chamberlain's drinking habit. Next thing, the cops are there. And if that happens a couple of times, they're getting fined.'

'That wouldn't have gone over well with the tyrant,' Kovac said.

'So she made a little label and put it on the keypad,' Taylor said. 'People do it all the time. They write the number down on a notepad on the counter. They write it on the corner of their message board by the kitchen phone.'

'They're afraid of the people they don't know,' Kovac said. 'They think danger comes only from outside their world, not from their own circle of acquaintance.'

'So the perpetrator broke in through the French doors,' the lieutenant said. 'They had no glass-break detectors. Professor Chamberlain felt they were an unnecessary expense, since all the openings were wired. No motion sensors, either. No video cameras. He bought a good basic package and left it at that.

'After the bad guy was inside, he had thirty seconds to get to the keypad and disarm the alarm before it went off,' Mascherino went on. 'So he had the alarm code, but not a key to the house.'

'Anyone who has been in the house could have had that code,' Kovac said. 'The cleaning lady, the handyman with the grudge. We're on to that angle next. The professor had a beef with a handyman service. He trashed them online and got into it with the owner of the company, according to the son. They were scheduled to come back to the house and redo some work a couple of days ago.'

'Handy Dandy Home Services,' Taylor said. 'They've got all their paperwork: registered, licensed, insured, etcetera. They've had a few complaints against them on the various websites that rate these businesses. Nothing violent. No big red flags. From what I've read, they rank somewhere in the middle of the pack for price and quality.'

'In keeping with the professor's penny-pinching,' the lieutenant said.

'We're on our way to talk to the owner,' Kovac said. 'Who knows where he gets his workers. Some of those companies are on the up-and-up, and all their workers are on the books. Others — not so much. Guys that work that kind of job can be transient.

'And I want to take a harder look at the family and the professor's associates, too,' he said. 'The daughter is a trip. We know she and the dad were at odds.'

'But could you see her beating her father's head in?' Mascherino asked. 'That beating was brutal. Does she seem like she could be that strong?'

'She's athletic,' Kovac said. 'And she's tall. Bigger than her father. And the brother says she's bipolar. Maybe she just snapped.'

'Bipolar is not the same as psychotic,' Taylor pointed out.

'But bipolar people can be violent.'

'Violent people can be bipolar,' Taylor corrected him. 'Contrary to what the movies and TV would have us believe, the overwhelming majority of people with mental illness are not violent. Statistically, they're more apt to become victims.'

'We're not talking about statistical probabilities,' Kovac argued. 'We're talking about Diana Chamberlain. Is she or is she not a weird chick?'

'She's a weird chick,' Taylor agreed. 'And she's sleeping with the enemy. But could she hack up her mother with a sword? If she attacked her father with nunchucks in a blind rage, and hacked her mother up with a samurai sword, could she just turn that rage off and coldly stage a burglary as slick and professional as this? Not likely. Either she snapped and went ape shit crazy or she didn't. No one can turn that on and off like a faucet.'

Kovac blew out a breath and sat back in his chair, already regretting the pizza. Now he was getting too fucking old to eat pepperoni.

'The daughter's apartment was a pigsty, but at a crime scene she's meticulous?' Taylor went on. He shook his head. 'The burglary points to a pro.'

'And the other professor?' Mascherino asked. 'The one the daughter is sleeping with?'

'Ken Sato. It's easy to argue motive for him,' Kovac said. 'Eliminating the competition for a big promotion.'

'But with Diana messing up her father's chances, bringing a complaint against him with the Office for Conflict Resolution, you could argue Sato already had pretty clear sailing for that job,' Taylor said.

'He could have done it for love, I suppose,'

Kovac offered. 'She hated her father — not without reason, by the sound of it. But is Sato a professor by day and a ninja cat burglar by night?'

'Find out,' the lieutenant said. 'What about the son?'

'Smart, quiet, nerdy kid. He's a paralegal for a law firm. His alibi kind of sucks,' Kovac said. 'He was home alone, working.'

'But we can check his computer,' Taylor said, 'and confirm what Wi-Fi network he was using. We can check his cell phone records and see what towers it was pinging off.'

'He seemed pretty shaken up by what happened,' Kovac said. 'With the sister being a flake, the responsibility for the aftermath is falling on him. We're bringing him to the ME's office for the official ID tomorrow morning.'

'Any hits on the Chamberlains' credit cards?' Mascherino asked.

Kovac shook his head. 'No action on their cell phones, either.'

It was the lieutenant's turn to sigh. 'I'm sure I don't have to tell you this case is front and center until it's solved. You've got Tippen and Elwood full time, and you can borrow anyone else available if you need to.'

'The overtime is approved?'

'Yes. Whatever you need. I want this case solved before it can be used as a political football.'

'Isn't it too late for that already?' Kovac asked. 'I heard the press conference was belly-to-butt with brass and suits. The local stations are running the story practically nonstop.'

'The union and the politicians aligning with the union are going to use this case as an example of what's wrong with the force,' she said. 'Not enough officers, not enough money.'

'And I'm supposed to be against that?' Kovac asked. 'It's the truth.'

'Do you want the public panicking, believing no one is safe in their own home?' Mascherino asked. 'Do you want them thinking we're not doing our jobs, that we're using a high-profile case — the horrible deaths of these innocent people — to extort money from the city?'

'No.'

'That's the flip side,' she said. 'The mayor starts beating his drum about the no-good, dirty police union. Then what?'

Kovac was silent for a moment. 'You're a smart cookie, Lieutenant,' he said, his mouth kicking up at one corner. 'I think I might like you.'

Mascherino smiled like the *Mona Lisa*. 'Yes, I am, and thank you. Now go do your jobs. We've got a case to solve.'

14

'You can't possibly think I did it.'

Dan Franken was thirty-six, six feet tall, and thick bodied. He had a bony, hawkish blade of a nose, and his dark eyes sat back in deep sockets. They had a tendency to dart from side to side, from Kovac to Taylor and back again. His mouth turned downward by nature, a lipless horseshoe centered on planes of heavy five o'clock shadow.

Kovac and Taylor stood silent, Kovac propping himself up against a tall filing cabinet, Taylor looking all military: legs straight, feet apart, hands clasped behind his back. A human guard dog on alert.

'I mean, I didn't get along with the guy, but the wife seemed nice enough. I felt bad for her, having to be married to an asshole like that,' Franken said. His voice was rough with half a lifetime's worth of cigarettes. He shook one out of a pack now and lit up, blowing the smoke up at the low yellowed acoustic tile ceiling. 'I heard on the radio someone hacked them up with a samurai sword. That's nuts, man! What the fuck?'

Franken ran his business out of a tiny, cluttered wood-paneled office in an old commercial park on the North Side. The low buildings made of corrugated steel were part of a U-Store-It complex, and housed an odd variety of businesses: It's a Party! party planning; Faux

Flora, silk plants; B&D Auto Body; the offices of an outpatient drug rehab called Rising Wings; Iron Neck Gym. Franken looked like he might have spent his free time at the last one, Kovac thought. His hands, clenched in loose fists at his sides, were the size of five-pound hammerheads.

'Professor Chamberlain wasn't very happy with your work,' Taylor said. 'We read his review. His son said the two of you got into it.'

'I never met the son,' Franken said. 'I didn't even know he had a son.'

'Did you argue with Professor Chamberlain?'

'Hell, yeah. I argued with him the day it happened, and I argued with him again when I found out about the Yelp review,' he admitted. 'That was a shitty review. People look at those things, you know, especially young professionals. That's a big part of my market.'

He sat back against his desk and tapped his cigarette ash off into an ashtray heaped with butts that testified to an evening spent slogging through paperwork. 'He should have given us the chance to take care of the problems. But no, he had to be a prick and go online and run his mouth. I had other jobs lined up in that neighborhood. I lost two of them because he called the people up and ragged on about how terrible my guys were and what a shit job they did.'

'So you were pretty pissed.'

'Yeah, I was pissed! Of course I was pissed! Do you know how hard it is to get a new business going in this town? I've got plenty of contracting experience, but I don't have the name or the kind of bucks it takes to get into new construction. This is my way in: Handy Dandy. I trademarked the name. My brother-in-law thinks I might be able to franchise it if things go well. I've spent the last three years trying to build a reputation.'

'Chamberlain cost you business,' Kovac said. 'He cost you time, he cost you money. He set you back — who knows how far?'

'So I went to his house in the middle of the night and killed him and his wife so I can lose everything I've worked for and spend the rest of my life in prison?' Franken said. 'You're out of your mind.'

'What kind of work did you do for them that they were so unhappy about?' Taylor asked.

'Cleaned the gutters, put on storm windows. Cheap fucker. The guy has that kind of money and doesn't replace those old windows. A couple of them got broken. He flipped his shit. Of course we would have fixed them right away, that day. He throws a hissy fit and kicks the guys off the property then bitches all over the neighborhood that he doesn't have storms on half his windows.'

'Did you do any work inside the house?'

'They fixed a couple of wonky cupboard doors in the kitchen.'

Taylor glanced at Kovac. The security code was on the keypad on the wall near the kitchen door.

'Did you go back and finish the job?' Taylor asked.

Franken set his jaw like a petulant teenager. 'I

171

told him if he took the review down, we'd finish the job and not charge him.'

'That would be a no,' Kovac said. 'We'll need the names and contact information of the workers.'

'Yeah, sure,' Franken said, but he looked down at the ashtray as he said it, crushing out his cigarette.

'What kind of guys do you have working for you?' Kovac asked.

'They're decent guys, hard workers.'

'Cream of the crop?'

'If they were the cream of the crop, they'd be working for better pay than I can afford.'

'Are they all on the books?'

'Absolutely,' he said, shaking another cigarette out of the pack.

'And they've all had background checks?'

'Yep.'

Meaning no one would be able to prove otherwise. Franken would give them the names of the guys that were legit, not the ones he paid in cash under the table.

Kovac sighed. 'You know, Dan, we don't have time to monkey-fuck around here. We're looking for a murderer. Now, I can go back downtown and waste an hour writing an affidavit, find a judge, get a search warrant, get pissed off, come back here, and turn this rat's nest inside out just for kicks and giggles, and you'll spend the next six months trying to put all your files back together, or you can tell us the truth.'

Franken's expression didn't change. His eyes went still, lids half lowered. 'I don't know what you're talking about.'

'Let's take him downtown, Sarge,' Taylor suggested, impatient. 'He can sit in the box and think about it while we get the warrants.' He turned back to Franken. 'You've got your equipment here? I saw your name on the big overhead doors on the next unit. We should probably get warrants for that space, too, Sarge. Who knows what he might keep in there.'

'Oh jeez,' Kovac grumbled. 'It could take days to inventory all this shit. Days and days of no business for Mr. Franken. All those Handy Dandy customers waiting will have to look elsewhere for their home maintenance needs. And then, depending on what we find . . . '

'I'll sue,' Franken said.

Kovac shrugged. 'That's not our department. We're just trying to solve a brutal double homicide that's all over the news. If you want your name attached to that story as an uncooperative person of interest, that's your choice.'

Franken looked away, the muscles in his jaw working. He swore under his breath. 'I'm just a taxpayer trying to run a business.'

'I appreciate that,' Kovac said. 'And we're not the business police. I personally don't give a shit if you've dotted all your *i*'s and crossed all your *t*'s on your license application. But I'm gonna care a whole lot if you lie to me and a killer runs loose because of it.

'Now, you've got a drug rehab right around the corner,' he went on. 'I'm willing to bet a few of the fine upstanding citizens who attend group

173

therapy and whatnot there need to pick up a little pocket money now and again. Am I right?'

He could see Franken weighing his options, and not liking any of them.

'And I'm thinking it doesn't take a master carpenter to clean the crap out of rain gutters,' Kovac said. 'Where's the harm in throwing a few bucks to a guy down on his luck?'

Franken ran a hand back over his thinning dark hair. 'What happens to me if it turns out I hired a guy who did . . . something . . . bad?'

'From where we stand? Nothing — unless you sent him there specifically to do harm. On the other hand, hindering a police investigation will get your ass thrown in jail.'

Franken swore again and rubbed a big hand across his face. He pushed away from the desk and shifted his weight from one foot to the other. He wanted to pace, but there was no room to do it.

Kovac knew the feeling. He was losing patience, himself. He stepped a little closer to Franken. 'If your guy is our guy, and he's out there right now killing someone else? I will do everything in my power to get you charged as an accessory. How's that for upping the ante, Dan? You can lose everything and spend the next twenty years in prison, or you can answer us honestly.'

'Fuck this,' Taylor muttered, scowling. He pulled a pair of handcuffs out and moved toward Franken.

Franken held his hands up. 'Okay, okay! Yes, I sometimes pick up extra guys from the rehab.

I'm a recovering alcoholic myself. I believe in second chances. Is that a crime?'

'I don't have a problem with that, Dan,' Kovac said, stepping back, lessening the pressure. 'It's karmic. Somebody helped you out, you pay it forward, and the universe lets you save a few bucks. It's all good — except that you don't check these guys out, do you?'

He couldn't look Kovac in the eye. 'I'm a good judge of character.'

'They're addicts. How do you know how recovered they are?' Taylor asked, irritably. 'Or what they might have done when they were using? And you're sending them into people's homes?'

'Desperate people do desperate things, Dan,' Kovac said. 'Drunks don't generally steal, but drug addicts will do just about anything to get a few bucks for a fix — sell their own body, sell their own kids. I once got a call-out on a guy who tried to cut off his own arm with a chainsaw just to get the pain meds. Stealing is the least of it.'

'Yeah? Well, that's not who I pick,' Franken barked back.

'No?' Kovac said. 'You're a fucking mind reader? Look at my partner here,' he said, hooking a thumb at Taylor. 'Good-looking kid. Nice suit. Polite. Do you think he's a killer? He doesn't look like a killer. He looks like freaking Channing Tatum. Do you think Channing Tatum is a killer?'

Franken just glared at him.

'Why would anybody that good-looking and

175

clean cut be a killer? Right? What's he got to be pissed off about?' Kovac looked at Taylor. 'Kid, how many people have you killed?'

'Seventeen, Sarge,' Taylor answered without the slightest hesitation, his green eyes narrowed and unblinking as he stared at Franken.

Kovac shrugged. 'I rest my case. Now, who did you send to the Chamberlain house?'

Franken sighed. 'One of my regular guys, Greg Verzano — he's an idiot, but he's not a killer — and a guy who works at Rising Wings. He's a good guy,' he insisted. 'He's a vet. He had a drug problem, went through the program, and now he works there. They hired him; why shouldn't I? I've never had any trouble with him.'

'Name?'

'Gordon Krauss. He's not your guy. I'm telling you.'

'What does he do at the rehab?' Taylor asked.

'Odd jobs. Security. Janitor-type stuff.'

'Have you seen him today?'

'No, but he's probably over there now. He stays there nights. They've gotten broken into a couple of times.'

'Surprise, surprise,' Taylor muttered, turning for the door. 'I'll start the car,' he said to Kovac on his way out.

'You stay here,' Kovac said, pointing at Franken. 'And don't even think about tipping Krauss off.'

The steady drizzle had picked up, Kovac noticed as he left Franken's office and got back in the car.

'I called for backup,' Taylor said, putting the

car in gear. 'They're three minutes out.'

Kovac looked over at him in the glow of the dash lights. 'Have you really killed seventeen people?'

Taylor didn't answer.

They drove slowly, with no headlights on, around the end of the building to the double row of parking in front of Rising Wings. The rehab took up an entire fifty-by-one-hundred-foot building, the last building at the back of the complex. Twenty yards beyond it stood a tall security fence, and beyond that, a lot full of RVs, fifth-wheel campers; pleasure boats on trailers, all covered with tarps for the winter. Security lights scattered sparingly across the lot cast glowing white balls of light that didn't travel far in the rain.

Warmer lights glowed through the shades in a couple of Rising Wings's windows, and several cars were parked near the building, but there was no way of knowing how many people might be inside. The building had multiple doors, one on each end and two along the side, probably on both sides. Kovac wanted the exits covered before they approached.

'I don't want to just sit here,' Taylor said impatiently, opening the car door. 'What if he comes out? I don't trust Franken not to tip him off.'

'The unit's two minutes out,' Kovac argued. 'They'll be here before I can get soaked to the skin. And there's a big-ass fence on the other side of the building. Where's he gonna go?'

Taylor hummed his disapproval and got out of

177

the car, leaving the door ajar. Kovac grumbled and got out, hunching his shoulders and flipping the collar of his coat up in a vain effort to keep the cold rain off his neck. Damn kid. 'I'll watch this side,' he said with resignation. 'You take the back.'

Taylor hadn't taken ten steps toward the building when a figure dashed out of the shadows, running hard for the fence.

'Well, shit!' Kovac snapped.

Taylor bolted, covering ground like a race-horse, yelling, 'Stop! Police!'

The runner hit the chain link about a third of the way up. Taylor caught him by one leg and the back of his coat and yanked him down. They hit the asphalt with a thud.

Kovac hustled toward them, drawing his weapon, yelling, 'Give it up! We've got you!'

We. Like he was in the mix.

The two men rolled and scrambled on the ground. In the pale glow of a distant security light, Kovac couldn't make out one from the other. He was still thirty feet away. Someone threw a punch. Someone threw an elbow. One grunted, one cursed. Then they were both on their feet, heads together, arms tangled, pushing and pulling as they staggered one way and then the other. Then one broke free, spun around, and kicked the other in the head like something from a Bruce Lee movie.

One man went down like a felled tree.

The other man ran down the fence line, then skidded around the corner of a building and out of sight. By the time Kovac turned the corner, their bad guy had disappeared. *Shit*. He could continue blind pursuit and get himself cold-cocked or worse, or he could turn it over to the uniforms that were just pulling up alongside his unmarked unit.

Huffing and puffing, sucking the cold, wet air into his burning lungs, Kovac turned around. Taylor was staggering to his feet, grabbing hold of the fence to steady himself. Kovac walked past him and went first to the radio car. He sent them running in the direction their escapee had gone, then got on the radio and called for additional units, one of which was to pick up Daniel Franken and take him downtown. Asshole. He could sit in a windowless room for a few hours contemplating the wisdom of tipping off Gordon Krauss.

'I'm getting too old for this,' Kovac said as he walked up to Taylor. 'If the Grim Reaper comes chasing me, he can just kill me and be done with it. I'm not spending my last waking moments running. Fuck that shit.'

Taylor turned away and puked on the ground.

'You okay, Stench?'

'Great. I hear bells ringing,' he said loudly.

'Maybe you should go sit down, kid.'

'I'm fine.'

'Stubborn stupidity is an excellent quality to have on this job,' Kovac said. 'But if you collapse and die from a brain aneurysm, that's a shitload of paperwork on me.'

'I'm fine,' Taylor said again.

Kovac shook his head. 'Great. I'm going in the rehab and find somebody to talk to about this yahoo. You go redeem yourself, Captain America.'

Lights glowed in one of the windows about halfway down the length of the Rising Wings building. Kovac went to the door nearest, rang the buzzer, and knocked.

'Police! Open up!'

He repeated the process twice before a dark, bearded face appeared in the sidelight next to the door. 'Can I see a badge?' the man called through the glass. His eyes shifted toward the patrol car in the parking lot.

Kovac pulled his ID and held it up.

'Hey, sorry,' the man said, pushing the door open. He was short and pudgy in corduroy pants and an untucked flannel shirt. A pair of reading glasses perched atop his bald head. 'You wouldn't believe the stuff that goes on out here at night.'

'Yeah, actually, I would,' Kovac grumbled. 'Who are you?'

'Owen Rucker. I'm the assistant director. What's going on out there?'

'Do you have a man named Gordon Krauss working for you?'

Rucker's open, friendly face closed a little with concern. 'Why do you want to know?'

'I get to ask the questions, Mr. Rucker. I have a feeling you probably know how that works.'

'What's that supposed to mean?'

'It means I doubt I'm the first cop who ever came here looking for someone. Let's try this again. Do you have a Gordon Krauss working here?'

180

'Yes. But — '

'Is he here tonight?'

'I saw him a while ago. His room is down the hall.'

'Mind if we have a look?'

'I do mind. I'm not letting you rifle through someone's personal stuff. Ask Gordon yourself.'

'I don't think he's in,' Kovac said. 'But let's go see.'

Rucker led the way down the hall, turned the corner, and knocked on a door.

'Hey, Gordon? You in there?' he asked, and knocked again, frowning at the implication that Kovac knew something he didn't. He tried the doorknob and breathed in relief when he found it locked.

'Can we have a seat in your office, Mr. Rucker?' Kovac asked. 'I have a few questions.'

They went back the way they had come, and into the assistant director's small office, where music was playing over the computer speakers and the desk was awash in files and forms.

'I had the evening group session,' Rucker said. 'I decided I'd stay and catch up on some paperwork.'

He took his seat and turned the music down, motioning Kovac to a chair. 'What's this all about?'

'Mr. Krauss recently did some work for Handy Dandy Home Services. We need to ask him a few questions about that job.'

'You don't think he's done something wrong, do you? I've known Gordon for two years. He's a

181

good guy. I trust him enough to have him here overnight.'

'Do you know any reason he would feel the need to run from us?' Kovac asked. 'Because someone just did, and I think it's him, and now I've got half the cops on the North Side coming here to look for him.'

'What? I don't understand any of this. What do you think he did?'

'Has he been in trouble with the police before?'

'Not since I've known him.'

'Do you have an address on file for him?'

'This *is* his address.'

'The sign says this is an outpatient facility.'

'It is. Gordon was staying in a shelter downtown before he came to us. The director is a friend of ours. We try to take a couple clients out of the shelters for every thirty or so paying customers.'

'You get some kind of county money for that?'

Rucker shook his head. 'Not for that. We take a certain amount of clients from the county. The rest are private clients, men and women from all walks of life. Our big boss foots the bill for our shelter guys through his own charitable foundation. Less red tape. Plus, he's a veteran himself. He knows the last thing some of these vets want is to deal with the government. They've been screwed over too many times as it is.'

'That's decent of him. Then you hire some of these guys after they make it through the program?'

'We've got connections all over. We try to hook

the vets up if we can.'

'So Krauss is employed by Rising Wings — '

'No. It's a straight-up trade. He helps us, and we help him.'

'Uncle Sam would be unhappy to know he's not getting anything out of that deal.'

'He already got everything he's getting out of Gordon. I've seen too many of these guys come back from this or that hellhole and get jack shit for their trouble. It's disgraceful. We ought to send Congress to war and treat them like how these kids get treated when they come back.'

'If we sent Congress to war, we'd all be speaking English as a second language,' Kovac said.

Rucker laughed. 'True, that!'

'So, tell me about Mr. Krauss. What was his self-medication of choice?'

'I can't tell you that.'

'Sure you can,' Kovac said. 'You're not a doctor or a priest, and he's not a patient or a penitent. This is not a medical facility or a church. And I'm not looking to bust him for drugs, anyway. I just want to know who I'm dealing with.'

Rucker looked unhappy, but he answered anyway. 'Whatever he could get. Oxycodone, weed, booze. Whatever he could get his hands on to dull the pain.'

'He has physical problems?'

'The worst pain isn't in the bones, Detective. It's in the heart. It's in the mind.'

'Is he clean now?'

'As of his last drug test.'

'When was that?'

'Five weeks ago.'

'Has he stayed clean since he got here?'

'He was clean for almost a year. He fell off the wagon around the holidays last year,' Rucker confessed. 'You know, it's a tough season. Short days, long nights, the weather, all the Happy Holidays bullshit. It's hard for people who don't have family.'

And here they were again a year later, Kovac thought. Short days, long nights, shitty weather, Christmas ads running roughshod over Thanksgiving, all the pressure to be happy and nostalgic and part of a loving family unit. He hated it himself.

'So I was told you had a couple of break-ins and that prompted you to have Mr. Krauss stay here nights? What was stolen?'

'Electronics. Some cash out of people's desks. Stuff that could be sold quick and easy.'

'For drugs.'

'Probably.'

'You reported these break-ins?'

'No,' Rucker said. 'You have to understand, trust is a big part of what we do here. If our clients are on edge, worried about the police coming in, we lose ground on what's most important, which is getting them well.

'We didn't lose more than a couple thousand dollars' worth of stuff anyway,' he said. 'The boss didn't even file the insurance claims. It's tough enough to get a rehab insured. Why file some petty claim for stuff we can afford to replace?'

'Did you suspect any of your clients?'

'We kind of had to suspect all of them, past and present, but we never solved it. We upped the security system, added some cameras outside, and started having someone stay here nights. We haven't had any problems since.'

Possibly because they had corralled their thief on their own premises and put cameras on him around the clock, Kovac thought. He would want to get a look at the security footage for the night the Chamberlains were killed to see if Krauss had been there or had gone out.

'Do you have paperwork on Mr. Krauss?' he asked. 'Driver's license? Social Security number?'

'I don't have anything on file for him. I don't even know if he has a driver's license,' Rucker said. 'He doesn't have a car. When he works for Dan Franken, he just goes along in one of Franken's trucks.'

'You're telling me you don't have *anything* on this guy?' Kovac said. 'That's hard to believe, Mr. Rucker. I have to give two forms of ID and promise my firstborn kid to cash a freaking check. How do you have nothing on a guy you let live on the premises?'

Rucker spread his hands. 'Gordon isn't a county patient, so we don't have county paperwork. He's considered a private client, and since the boss foots the bill, and he's not a paid employee, what do we need from him?'

'Does he collect veteran's benefits? His mail must come here, right?'

'No, it doesn't. If he gets mail, he's got a box somewhere. It's none of our business.'

185

Kovac rubbed his hands over his face and muttered, 'Wow. We live in the age of information, and you have no information. This guy could be a mass murderer for all you know.'

'I don't think so,' Rucker said.

'You don't think so.'

'He's quiet, reliable, keeps to himself. He's never caused any trouble here.'

Here, where he had a free bed to sleep in and nobody asked any questions.

There was no point in pursuing the conversation further. Kovac would try to get a search warrant for Krauss's room, but he didn't like his odds tonight. What did he have for probable cause? He couldn't even say for certain their running man was Krauss at all. The guy had cleaned the rain gutters on the murdered couple's house. So what? Chamberlain's public beef had been with Dan Franken. There had been no mention of Krauss specifically in his complaint. They would run Krauss's name through the system for wants and warrants. Maybe something would turn up — or maybe not.

This night was getting longer by the minute.

'Do you have a photograph of this guy?' he asked. 'Or is he invisible, too?'

'That I can help you with,' Rucker said, turning toward his computer.

He pulled an image up on screen — himself and a lean, athletic guy in his forties with a thousand-yard stare, a head full of wavy brown hair, and a bushy beard. Rucker was smiling, looking happy. Krauss looked like someone you wouldn't want your mother to sit next to on a city bus.

Rucker printed a copy of the photograph for Kovac to take.

'Can you please e-mail that to me as well?' Kovac asked, handing Rucker his business card. 'If you see him, call me immediately.'

★ ★ ★

The search continued for another hour among the rows of U-Store-It buildings, and the adjacent lot with the RVs and covered boats. Half a dozen uniformed officers and a K-9, and they never caught so much as a glimpse of their mystery man. He had vanished.

Kovac finally pulled the plug. He would issue a BOLO for Gordon Krauss, and try to squeeze Dan Franken for some answers. If Franken felt enough loyalty to Krauss to tip him off, maybe their connection went deeper than one former addict helping out another.

Wet and tired, he slid behind the wheel of the car. Taylor fell into the passenger's seat like a sulky teenager, swore, and banged a fist on the dashboard.

'I had hold of him! I had him! I let him get away!'

He banged on the dash a few more times, cursing with each punch, then fell back in his seat, clasped his hands around the back of his head, and groaned.

'Don't sweat it, kid,' Kovac said. 'He wanted to get away a whole hell of a lot worse than you wanted to hang on to him. Never underestimate the power of a desperate individual.'

'What if he's our guy?'

'What if he's not even Krauss?' Kovac countered. 'He could be some poor homeless schmuck who crawled out of a doorway to take a leak, and suddenly people are screaming at him and jumping on him. That was some kick he gave you.'

'That was a kick?' Taylor asked. 'I thought he hit me in the head with an iron pipe.'

'That was like something out of a kung fu movie,' Kovac said. 'I wonder if he knows anything about samurai swords.'

'I should keep looking,' Taylor muttered.

'Every cop in Northeast is looking for him now. Don't be a freaking martyr,' Kovac said, putting the car in gear. 'You need your head examined.'

'I'm crazy for wanting to find this guy?'

'No. I'm taking you to the ER so they can shine a light in your eyes and ask you how many fingers you see.'

Taylor didn't protest, which said enough.

'I hate to go home empty-handed,' the kid complained as they headed south.

'We're not,' Kovac said. 'We've got one thing we didn't have when we came here.'

'A concussion?'

'A suspect.'

188

15

Evi sat down for what seemed like the first time all day. She was tired, but in a wonderful way. They had slept in because of the ice, then Eric had cooked them his famous firehouse breakfast, with eggs and pancakes, bacon and hash browns. At Mia's insistence they decorated their pancakes with faces, using banana slices and blueberries and strawberries and whipped cream out of a can. They had played with their daughter, then gently made love while Mia had her nap.

A perfect day, Evi thought as she curled up on the sofa. Eric had convinced her to stay home all day. The center called to cancel the meeting she had worried about missing, making for a guilt-free afternoon. She soaked in the pleasure and joy of it all the more because she would now be without Eric for a day and a half. He had left late in the day to fill in at an ambulance service for a paramedic buddy whose wife was having a baby. His regular twenty-four-hour shift at the firehouse would begin at eight the next morning.

She missed him already, which seemed kind of silly. They weren't lovesick teenagers. They had been married for six years and had dated for two years before that. They should have been slightly bored with each other by now. But she still loved him so much it hurt when he was apart from her. She had never dreamed she could have a love like that. For most of her life she believed she didn't deserve it, and for part of her life she *didn't* deserve it. But she had learned that life is all about growth and change, rebirth and resurrection. And she deserved a chance at happiness as much as anyone.

Having gone through her own metamorphosis with the help of the caring staff at Chrysalis, she had taken her second chance and had returned to the center to give back. She found her job as a social worker for at-risk girls and young women completely rewarding. She didn't think she could ever give back to Chrysalis as much as the center had given her, but she loved trying.

One of her current cases was a sixteen-year-old runaway named Hope Anders, who had been rescued from a sex trafficking ring. She had escaped life with her family in a strict fundamentalist cult, where she had been abused by her older brother, only to be snatched off the street by a pimp; raped, beaten, and tortured for days; and then added to his string of underage prostitutes. Hope had been through a hell Evi knew too well. The staff at Chrysalis would help her make it to the other side of that trauma, offering health care, psychological therapy, social services, and legal aid.

The meeting that had been canceled that afternoon regarded Hope testifying against her brother for molesting her. The girl was terrified at the prospect of her parents' wrath. Even though they had abused her psychologically as surely as her brother had physically, there were still threads left from the ties that bind a child to the people who brought her into the world. As terrible as they were, the Anderses were the only family she had, and there was a part of her that didn't want to let go. If she went forward with testifying against her brother, she would likely never see any of them again, except across a courtroom.

Evi knew firsthand what a terrible thing it was to be that young and feel utterly alone in the world, knowing the people who were supposed to care about you most cared the least.

Hope Anders was terrified. She was afraid of her parents, afraid of the religious cult, afraid of her brother, and she still had every reason to be afraid of the man who had imprisoned and profited off her on the streets.

The pimp, known as Drago, had escaped capture. Rumors were that he could still be in the Twin Cities area. Hope would be a key witness against him when he was finally caught and brought to trial. Her continued existence was not in his best interest.

Evi looked over her notes for the meeting, which had been rescheduled for the following afternoon, while the television kept her company. Mia, worn out from their big family play day, was tucked in bed, sound asleep. Evi planned to follow suit soon. She was already in her pajamas.

Setting her notes aside, she turned up the volume on the TV to catch the day's news, expecting the morning's weather to be the biggest story of the day. Instead, the news crawl splashed across the screen with the station logo read: BRUTAL SLAYING HOME INVASION ROB-BERY.

A history professor from the University of Minnesota and his wife had been killed in their home. Evi listened to the details with shock and horror at the sheer brutality of the attack, making a mental note to triple-check the locks tonight. The neighborhood where the crime had taken place, considered a very safe and desirable area to live, wasn't that far away.

Evi found herself instantly wishing Eric hadn't volunteered to work for his friend. Their cozy little house in their quiet neighborhood suddenly felt like a fishbowl. She realized anyone could be outside, staring in through the windows.

What was the world coming to when someone would do something like this: beating and slashing a middle-aged couple to death in their own home? For what? For whatever the perpetrator could carry away? A few hundred or a few thousand dollars' worth of stuff?

Evi got up before the story was over and went around the house, checking the locks on every door and window, flinching at every shadow as she went. When she came back to the living room, she changed the channel to a cooking show and sat down to sort through the mail, thinking the mundane task would calm her.

Sale flyer, sale flyer, coupon, coupon. NEED A PLUMBER? CALL PETE! Bill, bill, bill. A small envelope addressed to her in block print: EVANGELINE BURKE.

It looked the size of an invitation or a thank-you note. She tried to think if she had been expecting either. There was no return address. No one she knew called her by her full name. She didn't use it. She never had. She didn't use it professionally. She didn't even use it on her checks. She had only kept the shortest version of it possible to save the expense of legally changing it. Who would send an envelope hand-lettered to someone she had never really been?

She opened the envelope slowly, a strange sense of apprehension filling her chest as she extracted the note. She stared at it, a terrible chill spreading through her.

An otherwise blank piece of ivory paper with two lines in black ink.

I KNOW WHO YOU ARE
I KNOW WHERE YOU LIVE

Evi's hands began to tremble. She felt like she couldn't breathe.

Why would anyone send her such a thing? She was no one special, just a social worker, a wife, a mom living a normal life.

The chill went through her again like a shard of ice. She was a social worker for Hope Anders, who had been threatened by a cult and by her own family. Hope Anders, who was potentially the target of a vicious criminal being hunted by law enforcement.

Evi had never equated her job with danger to herself. While the girls and young women she helped may have come out of dangerous circumstances, her job was simply helping them navigate the social services system. She was no threat to anyone. She didn't even know where

Hope Anders was staying. The addresses of the safe houses used by Chrysalis were known to only a few people. Evi was not one of them.

She worked at the Chrysalis offices downtown, in a nondescript building just a few blocks from the Hennepin County Government Center, where the courts were located. Her name wasn't on the letterhead. It wasn't on the door. Grace Underhill, the founder of Chrysalis, was the public face of the nonprofit, along with Kate Quinn, who served as an advocate and liaison between the young women and the prosecutor's office and law enforcement.

But Evi had been quoted in the article the *Star Tribune* ran on the center. She had been included in one of the photographs.

Still, why would anyone seek her out?

She turned the envelope over again, as if she thought a return address might magically appear to answer her questions. Stupid. Then it occurred to her that she probably shouldn't be handling the envelope or the note at all.

She popped up from the sofa and went to the kitchen, her skin crawling at the feeling that someone might be watching her as she passed through the house, catching glimpses of her through the blinds in the dining room as she hurried to get to the kitchen. She pulled open a drawer and yanked out a Ziploc bag, then hurried back to the living room and maneuvered the note and envelope into it, trying not to touch the paper any more than she absolutely had to.

She left the bagged note on the side table and

stood back with her hands on her hips, staring at it as if it might morph into something. Maybe if she stared at it long enough, it would become an invitation to a holiday party or a thank-you for the baby monitor she had given her friend Kim at her baby shower.

I KNOW WHO YOU ARE
I KNOW WHERE YOU LIVE

What should she do? Should she call Eric at work? And tell him what? *A strange thing came in the mail . . . ?*

She didn't want to make a fuss. She didn't want to inconvenience him. She shouldn't disturb him at work.

Old rules with hard consequences came back to her so easily. It didn't matter how long ago they had been instilled, or how long since they had been enforced. She called herself stupid before that terrible voice in her memory could do it.

Why should she bother Eric with her nerves over nothing? The note wasn't even a threat. Would she call the police over it? No. They would laugh at her, roll their eyes, mock her when they got back into their car and drove away. She knew it happened. She'd seen it happen . . . and she knew what happened after they went . . . Not here, not now, not in this life, but the memory of it was so strong she could taste the copper of blood in her mouth.

I KNOW WHO YOU ARE

195

That was no secret.

I KNOW WHERE YOU LIVE

Obviously so. She didn't like that idea, but anyone could look up Eric's name in the phone directory. If the mysterious 'I' knew who she was, then he or she knew she was married to Eric. They weren't living under witness protection.

Her husband was not the only Eric Burke in the Twin Cities, she remembered with the sudden hope that the note had been delivered by mistake. There was another Eric Burke! Eric's second cousin —

But she was the only Evangeline Burke.

No one called her by that name. She didn't use it. She never had.

She hugged herself and paced the small room, chewing on a thumbnail. She shouldn't have looked at the mail. If she hadn't opened the envelope, she would have been in bed asleep by now, blissfully ignorant, dreaming of her perfect day and her perfect life.

Her heart was racing. She was breathing hard. Angry with herself, she went to the front door and checked the locks again. She went to the kitchen and checked the patio slider. She went to the back door and unlocked and relocked the deadbolt.

Enough, she told herself. God, how disheartening it was to have those old thoughts and old patterns of self-loathing rise to the surface like they'd never left her — *because* they had never left her. No matter how she weighed them down with common sense and cognitive therapy, they could always slip loose and rise.

No. No, she wouldn't allow it. She had worked too hard to be stronger. She had tattooed the word on her chest above her heart. STRONGER.

Nothing had happened, really, she told herself. Nothing *could* happen. She and Mia were safe inside their home. She was going to go upstairs to bed, and she was going to sleep. In the morning, she would take the note to work with her and show it to Grace and to Kate, just so they would know, just in case they got one, too. If this was something tied to Hope Anders, or to the article in the paper, all the directors at Chrysalis had probably gotten one just to shake them up. Kate would know what to do with it or about it. That would be that.

Hanging on tight to her false bravado, Evi turned off the television, left the lamp on, and went upstairs. She checked on her sleeping daughter, not allowing herself to go into the softly lit room. She didn't want Mia to wake and sense her mother's tension. Her daughter deserved better than to have her innocence tainted by her mother's bad memories — no matter how badly Evi ached to go in and kneel down beside her bed and kiss her cheek and feel her daughter's soft breath.

She went to her own room and pretended to be normal, brushing her teeth and washing her face. She climbed into bed with just the nightlight on and burrowed into the pillows. She pulled Eric's pillow close and breathed in his scent, trying to calm herself. She went through the exercises she had been taught: breathe slowly, breathe deeply, in through the nose, out through the mouth.

She thought of the perfect day they'd had, and remembered those feelings of warmth and love with her family. She imagined Eric's arms around her as they lay in this bed, skin touching skin, hearts pressed together.

But instead of drifting off to sleep to dream of how she was loved, she began to cry. She pressed her face into her husband's pillow and sobbed, shaking with the fear that some nameless, faceless thing was about to end her dream come true.

16

Cheap Charlie's was as much an institution for Minneapolis cops as Patrick's bar. They had been going to the diner for breakfast for half a century. It was a mean and nasty place in an ugly brick bulldog of a building that squatted at the edge of the vast cracked blacktop wasteland known as Downtown East. For many years the Hubert H. Humphrey Metrodome had been the centerpiece of the area, a sports stadium that rose up from the desolate fields of parking lots like a giant, ugly concrete ottoman. For years the neighborhood had all the charm of a postapocalyptic war zone. Cheap Charlie's had flourished.

The current fear was that while the diner had thrived in a climate of adversity, it might not survive the new wave of gentrification that the extravagant new Vikings stadium was bringing with it. Pricey lofts and green spaces, juice bars and trendy bistros — all had a way of crowding out blue-collar hole-in-the-wall traditions, starving out places like this one with boutique rental rates.

For now the place remained, defiant, too mean to die. Everything about it was original, including the grease on the ceiling. The décor harkened back to the 1950s: chrome and red vinyl, black and dingy white checkerboard linoleum. The waitresses still wore uniforms and took orders on a green pad, writing with the nub of a pencil.

The front window was fogged with the breaths of a full house. Nikki parked across the street and hustled through a nasty drizzle, her shoulders scrunched up to her earlobes against the chill. As she walked in, she was assaulted by the smell of bacon and strong coffee, and a wall of noise composed by two dozen conversations — one of those being led by Gene Grider, on the far side of the room. She stood where she was, staring at him until he noticed her. She made a sour face and walked away.

Kovac sat next to Elwood in a booth, hunched over his eggs like he thought someone might try to steal his plate away. The new guy sat across from him, a big, strapping hunk with shoulders that strained the bounds of his suit jacket.

'Holy fucking shit!' Nikki said, arriving at the end of the booth, laughing as she took a good long look.

Kovac barely glanced up. 'Tinks, meet Michael Taylor. I'm calling him Stench.'

'That's a terrible nickname.'

'Thank you. I agree,' Taylor said, lifting his coffee cup in a toast. He had narrow green eyes under a straight brow line, a jaw cut from granite, and a mouth made for sex fantasies.

'What would you call him?' Kovac asked.

'I like Hottie McHotterson,' Nikki said without hesitation.

'That's sexual harassment,' Taylor pointed out.

Nikki rolled her eyes. 'Call a cop, Sweet Cheeks.'

'I expected more sympathy from a woman,' Taylor remarked, sliding over to make room for her in the booth.

'That's sexist, too,' she said, sliding in beside him, careful to keep her wet coat between them. He was easily the best-looking man she had ever seen walking around loose in the real world — and probably ten years younger than she. 'I have just as much right to be an insensitive jerk as anyone with a penis.'

'Taylor,' Kovac said, completing the introduction, 'Nikki Liska.'

'What did people call you when you came on the job?' Taylor asked her.

'Pissy Little Bitch, Mouthy Cunt, Bull Dyke — which I'm not, just to be perfectly clear,' she said, motioning a waitress over. 'We're not exactly working with poet laureates here — present company excluded, Elwood.'

'Thank you, Tinks,' Elwood said, striking a noble pose. Their gentle giant with the soul of an artist. Nikki missed his insightful observations and his goofy porkpie hats. The hat du jour was made of black oilcloth, to withstand the filthy weather.

'And all these enlightened years later, I still get called all those things and worse,' she said. 'Gene Grider is probably sitting over there wracking his tiny little atrophied brain right now coming up with something dirty and degrading to call me. Last night he suggested that the lieutenant and I roll our own tampons.'

Taylor scowled in disapproval.

Nikki shrugged, trying not to stare at his mouth.

'That's Grider. Class out the ass, that guy.'

'Fuck him,' Kovac growled. 'My money's on you in that fight.'

'It had better be. Hey, did you just insult me?'

'Not intentionally.'

She ordered a coffee and a Spanish omelet. 'I heard you caught the big double homicide. Have you gotten any sleep?'

Kovac looked like he hadn't slept in a week, though he had shaved and put on one of the fresh shirts he kept in a desk drawer at the office. She resisted the urge to reach across the table and fix the crooked knot in his tie.

'Sleep?' he said, like it was something for pussies. 'Maybe tonight. Maybe tomorrow. This one is extra special, you know,' he said sarcastically. 'Seeing how the vics are rich, white, and connected to the U.'

'Killed with a samurai sword,' Nikki said. 'A very sexy case. I'm jealous.'

'Funny, huh? Someone gets it in the throat with a screwdriver, they bleed out just the same, but it's so much less glamorous,' he said, forking up some eggs.

'Suspects?'

'Sniffing around a few. We almost had our hands on one last night. He mule-kicked the kid in the head like a fucking ninja and ran off into the night.'

Nikki looked at Taylor for damage. Taylor frowned at his pancakes and rubbed his neck.

'He's fine,' Kovac said dismissively. 'How's your thing going? That case is so cold it's got freezer burn.'

'Thanks for the encouragement. It means so much.'

'I'm here for you.'

Nikki pulled a list out of her coat pocket and handed it across the table to him. 'I'm guessing you might know most of those guys. They all worked the Duffy case at one time or another. Which one do you think is worth me trying to talk to?'

He looked at the list and ticked them off. 'This one's dead. This one's drooling. This one moved to Costa Rica, the lucky son of a bitch. That leaves Peterson. Your winner by default.'

He gave her a look. 'You could have picked up the phone and found out all of that in ten minutes.'

'Shut up,' she grumbled, annoyed that he saw right through her. 'I asked you and found out in less than one minute. And I'm getting breakfast while sitting next to Magic Mike here.'

'I feel so cheap,' Taylor said.

'I know. It's tough being the sexy one,' Nikki said, patting his arm. 'We all feel really bad for you. So, do you have any tattoos, Mike? And if yes, where are they located on your person?'

Taylor blushed and grinned sheepishly, ducking his head.

'Oh my God, and he blushes, too!' Nikki exclaimed, delighted. 'You are the cutest thing ever!'

'It's lonely back there in the broom closet, isn't it, Tinks?' Kovac said.

They all had a laugh, and it felt good . . . and it hurt a little, too, Nikki admitted. Maybe more than a little. She was a social animal. She thrived on camaraderie. Kovac's character would have been more suited to working cold cases than hers. He at least did a better job of pretending not to need human interaction.

'All right, kids,' Kovac said, hailing the waitress for a check. 'These murders aren't going to solve themselves.'

Nikki's breakfast arrived as the three others left. She stared down at it, not really wanting it now. She sighed and looked around, her gaze going to Grider, sitting at a table on the far side of the room. He had his big ugly head bent down and was deep in conversation with another big man whose back was to her.

She had gone over as much of the Duffy case as she could the night before, until the words on the pages of reports and statements blurred into a swarm of black dashes on white. She hadn't come up with any overt misstep by Grider during his various stints on the case.

Had he gone easy on Barbie Duffy? Yes, but more so than any other investigator? Not on paper. Then again, he had been the one writing the reports on his investigations. He wasn't going to make himself look bad.

No other investigator had hinted at anything wrong with Grider's handling of the case. But that was a problem coming into a case entirely cold: She had only official reports and statements to look at. The real story of an investigation was in the detective's personal notes, where he didn't have to worry about verbiage, and could express his concerns and opinions. Those were the notes detectives took home with them and hoarded in file cabinets and cardboard boxes. She had boxes of her own in her attic. What she would ever do with them, she couldn't imagine, but she kept them just the same. Nobody left those notes in a file, which was why she wanted to speak to one of the guys who had worked the Duffy case — someone not named Grider.

She didn't know Peterson, the only viable choice from her list. Would he think Grider had looked the other way with regard to the alibis of Barbie and Big Duff? Peterson hadn't solved the case, either.

Maybe she was just being a bitch, wanting to place the blame on Grider just because she hated him. What would his angle have been, to drag down the case, if Ted Duffy was such a great friend, anyway?

He wouldn't have been the first guy to fall for his best buddy's wife. But could she see Barbie Duffy sweating up the sheets with Gene Grider? Gross. Even if she could get her head around that idea, the bigger, better theory of the crime put Barbie and Big Duff in cahoots. And why would Grider run interference for either of them, let alone both of them?

As Kovac had taught her, most murders boiled down to one of two motives: sex or money. Barbie had collected on her husband's life insurance and his pension. Big Duff had also collected insurance on his brother's death.

She could ask to get Gene Grider's financials for the months just prior to and after Ted Duffy's homicide. She could only imagine Mascherino's reaction to that request. Then again, Mascherino had come from IA. She might not blink an eye. But even as she thought about it, Nikki felt a little dirty. It wasn't her nature to go after her own kind.

She had other angles to pursue, angles other investigators had discounted or hadn't considered at all. The obvious routes had been trampled down over the years, to no avail. She would consider every possibility, and eliminate all but one.

Grider pushed his chair back from his table and started to rise. Nikki put her phone up to her ear and glanced down at her eggs. She could feel Grider's eyes on her as he walked past her booth on his way to the front door. He left alone.

She looked back to his table. His breakfast companion was still there, one arm gesturing as he spoke with the smiling waitress. He had a booming laugh. A familiar laugh. Everyone around him laughed with him as he stood up and turned to go.

Thomas 'Big Duff' Duffy.

'Grider,' Nikki muttered under her breath. 'You son of a bitch.'

★ ★ ★

Nikki said nothing to Grider as she walked into their office; just gave him a long flat look as she took her coat off and hung it up. He glanced away first, phone pressed to his head.

Candra Seley watched the silent exchange as

she crossed the room to Nikki's desk.

'It's another beautiful day in the neighborhood, I see,' she said as she pulled up a chair.

Nikki rolled her eyes. 'What have you got for me?'

'Jennifer Duffy's info,' she said, handing her a note card with the address and phone number. 'I also sent these to your e-mail, but I'm old-fashioned. I like things written down.'

'Perfect. What about the missing Nilsens?'

'I can't find Renee Nilsen,' Seley said. 'And I mean, I can't find her anywhere.'

'Seriously?'

'Seriously. She seems to have vanished off the face of the earth. The Nilsens never got divorced. She never legally changed her name in this state. She does not hold a current driver's license. She has not used or applied for a passport; nor has she filed a Minnesota tax return.'

'Was she ever reported missing?'

'No.'

'Shit,' Nikki muttered. 'I want to solve one case; now we've got a bonus mystery? I hope for her sake she ran off with a hot boyfriend.'

'That's not all,' Seley said. 'I did a little digging to find out what happened to the son.'

'And?'

'Get this: He enlisted as soon as he turned eighteen, just a couple of months after Ted Duffy's murder. He didn't even wait to graduate.'

'I guess he couldn't wait to get the hell away from the old man,' Nikki said. 'Who could blame him? Especially if Dad made Mom disappear.

Time to get out of Dodge. Then he dies serving his country. That's sad.'

'It would be if it were true,' Seley said. 'He was given a psych discharge nine years ago.'

'Then what happened to him? How did he die?'

'I'm not convinced he's dead. Or, if he's dead, he didn't die in the state of Minnesota. There's no death certificate. There's no obituary anywhere.'

'Ah,' Nikki said. 'So you're thinking he might not be dead; he might just be dead to dear old Dad.'

'Imagine how a psych discharge would go over with that man. I think it's worth checking into. I mean, Jeremy Nilsen could be dead, or he could be living on the street somewhere. You know, a lot of these guys fall through the cracks in the system and just disappear off the grid. He could be anywhere, doing anything.'

'Keep looking,' Nikki said. She swiveled her chair and sighed. 'I was thinking last night that the people close to this murder who were overlooked were the kids. No one really seriously questioned any of them.'

'They were small.'

'Jennifer Duffy was nine. That's not too young to know what's going on in the family. Barbie Duffy said that her daughter had a lot of issues afterward. Why? And the foster kids were teenagers. My boys are teenagers. They're wrapped up in their own stuff, but they're certainly very aware of what goes on between their dad and me, whether they want to be or not. They hear things, they sense things, it impacts them,' Nikki said, thinking of R.J. and his stomachache of the other night, brought on as much by the tension between her and Speed as by too much junk food after the wrestling meet.

'I haven't found anything on the foster kids yet,' Seley said. 'But I've reached out to a woman I know at DCFS. She'll get back to me.'

Nikki hoped Seley's connection would make the difference. The system at the Department of Children and Family Services was a maze unto itself.

'Great. In the meantime,' she said, raising her voice, 'I've got a meeting with Thomas Duffy. I need to ask him how he liked the pancakes at Cheap Charlie's.'

Grider heard her. She could tell by the way he tipped his head, by the tension in his jaw. He was off the phone now, scribbling notes. He didn't look at her. She half-expected him to ask her if she was running to the lieutenant to tell on him. Then again, if he cared about that, he shouldn't have met with the man in a public place — not just a public place, a cop hangout.

What was it to him if he got fired? He was already retired. He had his pension. He didn't need this job. He had only come back to work the Duffy case, and now that the case was no longer his, his number one priority was being a pain in Nikki's ass. She should have wanted him to get fired, but it seemed like a better idea to keep him where she could see him, no matter how annoying he was.

He sat up straighter as Mascherino came into the office looking all business. But the lieutenant's sharp blue eyes were on Nikki.

'Have you spoken with Thomas Duffy yet?' she asked.

Nikki smiled inwardly as Grider turned toward them. Let him sweat, the fucker. 'I have a call in to him. He hasn't called me back.'

'I just got off the phone with the news director from KTWN. They're going to shoot a news segment with Duffy at the Big D flagship store off 494 around noon today. They would like you to be a part of it.'

'Great,' Nikki said. 'I have lots of questions for Mr. Duffy.'

Mascherino gave her the eye. 'Try not to rub anyone the wrong way.'

'Who? Me?' Nikki said, feigning innocence.

'Unless there's something in it for us,' the lieutenant added dryly as she turned to leave. 'Sergeant Grider?'

Grider gave her the blank face.

'You have egg on your necktie. Please rectify that situation before you leave the office. I won't have people thinking my detectives are slobs.'

She was gone before he could say, 'Yes, ma'am.'

'It's okay, Grider,' Nikki said. 'Not everyone has what it takes to make it in television.'

17

'They'll show you one at a time,' Taylor said quietly. 'Look at the monitor, answer yes or no. That's it. Be prepared. They both have facial damage from the attack. It's not going to be easy to look at.'

'Are you sure you want to do this?' Charles Chamberlain asked his sister. 'I can take care of it.'

'They were *our* parents,' she whispered.

They stood in the viewing room of the county morgue, the Chamberlain children facing one another, holding hands, like little kids making a pact. Kovac studied them from a few feet away, the brother looking like Harry Potter grown up, the sister towering over him like an Amazon.

Kovac hadn't expected the sister when they stopped to pick Charles Chamberlain up, but there she was, wandering around his apartment at eight thirty in the morning in a man's shirt, hot-pink panties, and wool socks, her hair rumpled and half in her face as she pressed a coffee cup to her lips. She had insisted on coming, but they had to wait nearly half an hour for her to make herself presentable.

She had emerged from the bedroom looking like a naughty librarian character from a porno — hair pulled back, a pair of large plastic-rimmed glasses, the white shirt buttoned up to the throat, and a pair of black leggings painted

211

on her long, long legs. Deep red lipstick and lots of black mascara.

Who put on come-fuck-me lipstick to identify dead family members first thing in the morning? Diana Chamberlain.

She had preened and pouted and batted her lashes at her little brother in a way that made Kovac's skin crawl. Taylor watched the show with a serious frown, even when the girl cast him a few come-hither glances. The brother seemed immune to it. Charles Chamberlain treated his sister like a child, even though she was a couple of years older, and physically larger.

He sighed now and nodded to Taylor. 'Let's get it over with.'

Kovac kept his gaze on their faces, barely blinking. He knew the second the monitor came on. The young man flinched and turned away almost immediately, swallowing hard and mumbling 'That's him.' Diana Chamberlain stared at the screen, transfixed, unblinking, her face stark white except for the red mouth.

Taylor spoke into the intercom. 'Next.'

When the image of Mrs. Chamberlain came on the screen, the son turned away, went to the far side of the room, and retched into a wastebasket. Diana continued to stare at the screen, then slowly began to tremble, then shake harder, and harder, like she was having a seizure. Screams tore up from the depths of her soul. Shrieking, she flung herself at the curtained window that separated them from the room where her parents' corpses lay. Pounding her fists on the glass, she screamed and screamed.

'Mommy! No! No! No!' she cried, dissolving into racking sobs.

Taylor leapt toward her, catching her by the arm before she could fall to the floor. Her brother hurried to her, and she draped herself over him, pressing her face into his shoulder as she cried. They sank down on the small sofa, holding each other.

Kovac glanced at Taylor to see him watching the pair like a hawk, studying their behavior and their body language. There were times to look away and let survivors grieve. This was not one of those times.

After a few minutes the Chamberlain siblings separated and began to collect themselves. Charles took his glasses off and cleaned them with his handkerchief, his hands trembling. Diana dried her eyes delicately with tissues from a box on a side table. She had had the foresight to use waterproof mascara, Kovac noticed.

She sniffed and looked up at Taylor from under her lashes. 'My mother had a diamond-and-pearl bracelet she would have given to me,' she said softly, her voice fluttering like the wings of a butterfly. 'Do you know if that was taken? I would really like to have it.'

Taylor's jaw dropped a little, but he recovered well. 'Ah, I'll have to check on that. We won't be able to release any personal effects for some time, though.'

'Would you be able to look at your mother's things and tell us what might be missing?' Kovac asked.

'Yes, of course.'

Charles frowned. 'There's a detailed inventory of everything in the house, for insurance purposes. I helped make the DVD. That's going to be the most accurate way to do it.'

'There's a DVD?' Kovac said. 'Great. Do you know where we can find that?'

'He would have put it in his safe-deposit box at the bank. And the insurance agent has one, of course.'

'Great. That'll be helpful. And we'll be walking through your father's collection with Ken Sato today, too.'

The kid didn't seem to like that idea, either. He looked pointedly away from his sister. 'I'd like to be there.'

'Sorry, but we can't have a lot of people traipsing through the crime scene.'

'That's our home.'

He didn't want Diana with them off leash, Kovac thought, and he didn't like Ken Sato. Did he have suspicions of one or the other? Or was it just habit to be protective of his wack job of a sister?

'We understand,' Taylor said. 'But our first obligation is to protect the integrity of the scene. You wouldn't want your parents' killer getting off because someone had accidentally messed up evidence, would you?'

'No.' He got up to move, nibbling at a hangnail as the wheels in his mind turned. 'What happens now? When can we make arrangements?'

'That's up to the ME. It could be a few days before the autopsies are done — '

'Autopsies?' Diana said. 'Why do there have to be autopsies? You know they were murdered. Isn't that enough? You have to have them cut up like meat? That's sick!'

'All violent deaths get autopsies,' Taylor explained. 'There are a lot of things we can learn about the crime from the autopsy.'

Staring down at the floor, the brother pressed the heels of his hands into his temples like his head might be about to explode. 'This is a nightmare,' he muttered to himself. 'I just want it to be over.'

Kovac didn't bother telling him they were only just getting started, or that the road ahead was probably going to get rougher before it got easier. He would be the one making it tougher for them, and he wasn't going to ease into it, either. His obligation wasn't to Charles and Diana Chamberlain, but to their brutally murdered parents lying on cold steel tables in the next room. Sympathy ranked far below manipulation on his list of job requirements. He could feel bad for them later if they deserved it.

Diana excused herself to go to the ladies' room. Taylor escorted her out to the hall to show her where to go.

'So, Charlie — Can I call you Charlie?' Kovac asked, not to be a buddy, but to pick at the kid's tight outer wrapper.

The boy wanted to say no, but didn't, making a stiff half shrug. 'I don't care.'

But he did care. He didn't like it, but he packed his annoyance down and kept it inside. All those years of dealing with a pompous father had taught him to control his own emotions with an iron fist.

'So, Charlie,' Kovac began again. 'Is there a reason you don't want your sister going to the house without you?'

'No!' he said too quickly, looking a little startled. He thought he'd hidden it better.

'You seem to have a calming influence on her. You two are pretty tight.'

'I know her.'

'You understand her. There's a difference,' Kovac said. 'I get the feeling you've spent a lot of time running interference for Diana, trying to head disaster off at the pass. You're a good brother. That's no small job, I'm thinking.'

'She's my sister.'

'You're protective of her. Why do you think you need to protect her from us? We're not the bad guys here.'

He wouldn't quite make eye contact. 'I don't know what you mean.'

'We're not the bad guys,' Kovac said again. 'I know she's been in trouble with the police before, but that's got nothing to do with what I need to accomplish, right?'

'Her juvenile record was expunged.'

'I imagine you helped her with that. Good idea. People shouldn't have their lives ruined because they did some stupid shit as teenagers, right?'

'Why are you bringing it up, then? And how do you even know about it?'

'Having a juvenile record expunged means regular people can't find it,' Kovac said. 'I can find it. Arrest records stay in our system for donkey's years.'

'Then why do you need me to tell you about it, if you already know?' the kid challenged, scowling.

'I know what happened — shoplifting, shoplifting, possession of weed, more shoplifting. I want to know why.'

'Then you should ask her.'

'I'm asking you for your opinion as her brother.'

'I already told you she's bipolar.'

'I'm not asking for a medical diagnosis,' Kovac said patiently. 'A lot of people are bipolar. They don't all go around taking the five-finger discount at department stores. They don't all get into hair-pulling catfights at sporting events. They're not all in and out of rehab in their teens.'

The kid was stressing, breathing faster, wanting to get away. But it hadn't occurred to him yet to say, 'Fuck off.'

'It's important for me to know who all the people close to the victims are,' Kovac explained.

'Diana wouldn't hurt our parents,' Charles said defensively, but his eyes glazed with a fine sheen of tears as he said it. Maybe he wasn't as certain as he wanted to sound.

'I'm not saying she did,' Kovac said, lifting his hands a little, fingers spread wide. *Nothing up my sleeve, kid.* 'But I don't know who her friends are, or were. I don't know that she didn't — or doesn't — have some bad boyfriend, back when she was going through her delinquent phase, and that guy knows where her parents live, and what they have. See what I'm saying here, Charlie?' he asked quietly.

He could see the wheels turning.

'She's always been difficult,' the kid said, giving in. 'Even when we were little. I don't know why. Maybe something happened to her. I don't know.'

'Something like what?'

'I don't know!' he said, exasperated, glancing toward the door, willing it to open.

'Did your parents talk about something having happened to her?'

The kid drew a big breath like he was going to say something more, but the words stayed in his mouth as the door opened and Taylor ushered Diana Chamberlain back into the room.

'Are we done?' she asked. 'Can we go home now?'

'Yeah, we're done,' Kovac said, resting a hand on Charlie Chamberlain's shoulder as he walked with him toward the door. Kovac as father figure. 'This isn't something anyone should have to deal with. I know it's tough. I'm sorry.'

He sent them home in a cruiser, watching as the car pulled away in the drizzle.

'Did she come on to you?' he asked, cutting a glance at Taylor beside him.

Taylor rubbed his stiff neck as he watched them drive away. 'Ooooh yeah.'

'I'd bet my pension she's been sexually abused by someone somewhere along the line.'

'Daddy?'

'You know what they call that.'

'Incest?'

'Motive.'

'Sato said Diana Chamberlain was adopted when she was four or five,' Taylor said as they walked to the car. 'That's got to be tough for a little kid to be uprooted and given to strangers at that age. I'd like to know if she was broken before the Chamberlains got her or what, you know? Does she come from a long line of crazy? I wonder if we can find out.'

'Depends. Maybe the family lawyer can help us with that. Given that the Chamberlains had some bucks, it might have been a private adoption.'

'Poor kid. Abandoned by her real mother one way or another, then ends up with an alcoholic and a narcissistic jerk for adoptive parents. That's some rotten luck.'

'That's a petri dish full of resentment, is what that is,' Kovac said, digging the car keys out of his coat pocket.

Taylor frowned. 'I can drive.'

'You have a head injury.'

'Yeah, well, I'd really rather not get another.'

'I got us here, didn't I?' Kovac said, perturbed, as he slid behind the wheel.

'Yeah, but that bus — '

'Was in the wrong freaking lane. How could you see it anyway? You can't even turn your head.'

'Well, there are these things on the sides of the car,' Taylor said, settling himself gingerly in the passenger's seat. 'They're called mirrors.'

'Whatever. It's five blocks. Don't be such a pussy,' Kovac said as he turned left onto Fifth for the short ride from the morgue to City Hall.

A BMW swerved around them, horn blaring.

'There's two lanes for a reason, asshole!' Kovac shouted. 'Get the fuck over!'

Taylor cringed, then took a deep breath and let it out slowly.

'You survived a war, for Christ's sake,' Kovac grumbled.

'Only to die in traffic.'

'Let's get our minds back where they belong.'

'The road would be a good start.'

'I can drive this in my sleep,' Kovac said. 'I have. What did you think of the kids' reactions to seeing their parents messed up like that?'

'They seemed real,' Taylor said. 'Even Diana's reaction when she saw her mother seemed genuine — genuinely freaked out.'

'She just stared at her father, like he wasn't even real,' Kovac said. 'Could she be that completely cut off from him in her own mind? Did she not react because she had already accepted that he should be dead? Like maybe she's pictured him that way a thousand times.'

'And Mom was a surprise?' Taylor asked, sounding doubtful.

'Maybe Mom was collateral damage,' Kovac said. 'Daddy was the target. Mom's supposed to be sleeping off her evening bottle of Château Blackout, but she wakes up, hears the commotion downstairs, goes to investigate . . . '

'Girls don't go around physically overpowering people, beating people's heads in,' Taylor argued. 'And whoever killed Mrs. Chamberlain didn't leave that sword in her by mistake. That was an exclamation point. And then we go back to the whole thing about the scene being too tidy and the burglary being too slick. I'm not saying the daughter couldn't have had something to do with it, but — '

'But she likes to twist men around her curvy little finger,' Kovac said. 'And there's Sato — '

'You think she's not going to flip out on him if he did that to her mother?'

'That line of thinking would rule out the brother then, too. How could she be around him if he did that to their mother? But she's hanging all over him like a cheap sweater,' Kovac said. 'I wanted to go take a shower watching that. Do you think they're sleeping together?'

'The brother and sister? He doesn't really react to her that way. He seems to know how to handle her. I guess he's had his whole life to master it.'

'Yeah. He doesn't want her alone with us, though,' Kovac said. 'What's he afraid of? What's she going to let slip? Does he think she did it? Does he think she'll rat him out? Are they in it together?'

'We'll find out today who inherits what,' Taylor said. 'What does either of them have to gain besides getting rid of a tyrant?'

'Isn't that enough?' Kovac asked. 'I didn't even know the guy, and I want to punch him in the throat. Add the bonus of whatever that collection of his is worth, and what money Mom was worth, insurance policies . . . '

'I still say the scene says pro,' Taylor said. 'My money's on the handyman.'

'A drug addict in and out of rehab,' Kovac mused. 'Diana Chamberlain has been in and out of rehab. I wonder what the odds are that their paths might have crossed.'

Kovac's head was throbbing with the effort to keep all the threads from tangling and something important from falling through the cracks. He had been up for almost thirty hours, and he was starting to feel it. The adrenaline had finally started wearing off as he sat across the table from Dan Franken in an interview room at oh-dark-thirty in the morning while Taylor was at the Hennepin County Medical Center ER getting a head CT.

Taylor was probably right, Kovac thought. He probably shouldn't have been driving a car, but he was afraid to stop moving. If he had been sitting on the passenger side, he would have been slack-jawed and drooling, sound asleep with his head against the window. That would have been okay with Liska. They'd been together too long to worry about impressing each other. But he didn't want Taylor thinking he was too old for all-nighters — even though he was in fact starting to feel too old for all-nighters.

His mood soured, he parked the car in a space designated for some city councilman he didn't give a shit about.

'Ummm . . . ' Taylor made a half-assed gesture at the sign as they got out of the car.

'Screw him,' Kovac growled. He wanted a gallon of coffee to be delivered intravenously, and to eat a greasy donut just to perpetuate the cop stereotype.

They went into the CID offices and straight to the war room.

'We got a hit on Professor Chamberlain's credit cards,' Tippen said by way of a greeting.

'If you tell me you have a culprit in custody, I'll kiss you on the mouth,' Kovac said, making a beeline for the coffeemaker.

'Pucker up, pal. Suite three, down the hall.'

'Seriously?'

'Detained by security at the Lake Street Kmart. I'll pass on the kiss, though. People will think we're in love.'

'You have a problem with that?' Kovac asked, his mood brightening again with the prospect of a lead. 'I'm hurt.'

'It's not you, it's me,' Tippen said, leading the way down the hall. 'I'll only break your heart in the end, my friend.'

'You're not my type anyway,' Kovac said as they stopped outside the interview room. 'So tell me we have a sword-wielding ninja on the other side of this door.'

'I never promised you the moon.'

What they had on the other side of the door was an angry three-hundred-pound woman with a rainbow-colored hair weave and drawn-on eyebrows like the golden arches of McDonald's. She sat behind the undersize table, her arms crossed atop the wide ledge of her chest, glaring at the cops as they entered the interview room.

'Sergeant Kovac,' Tippen said, 'meet Professor Lucien Chamberlain.'

'You're Professor Chamberlain?' Kovac said, straight-faced.

'Yes, I am,' she said. 'And I demand to be released on my own personal renaissance.'

'*Recognizance*,' Taylor corrected her. 'You can't get that from us.'

'What *can* I get from you, then, you sweet hot piece of man candy?' she asked, batting her long false eyelashes at him.

'You're Professor Lucien Chamberlain,' Kovac said again, moving to block her sight of Taylor. Kovac put his reading glasses on and held up the driver's license Tippen handed to him, as if to compare the photo to the person sitting before him. 'You're a professor of East Asian history at the University of Minnesota? Five-feet-nine-inch, one-hundred-fifty-five pound Caucasian male Lucien Damien Chamberlain?'

'Well, that's an old picture,' she said stubbornly.

'Also known as Millicent Johnson, Antoinette LaPort, Robert Milland,' Tippen said, producing an array of credit cards and driver's licenses as with a magician's card trick. He plucked one from the rest. 'And last but by no means least: Ms. Sparkle Cummings.'

'Ms. Sparkle, where did you get this ID and credit card?' Kovac asked. 'Lucien Chamber-lain's.'

'I didn't steal it, if that's what you think.'

'You're not a cat burglar-slash-martial arts assassin in addition to your many other talents?'

'Are you out your mind?'

'You seem to have a lot of alternate personalities,' Tippen said. 'Did you not steal any of them?'

'I plead the Fifth Commandment.'

'Your mother and father will be glad to hear it,' Kovac said. 'Look, I don't care about any of the rest of those people. I don't care how you came to have their credit cards in your possession. I don't care if you boiled them and ate them. I only need to know where you got Lucien Chamberlain's cards.'

She gave him a look. 'I'm not going to recriminate myself. I know my rights. This ain't my first rodeo, handsome.'

'Indeed, it is not,' Tippen said. 'Ms. Sparkle and her alter egos have been guests of Hennepin County on several occasions — shoplifting, possession, vagrancy, public intoxication, and multiple counts of soliciting . . . ' He gave the woman a sideways look. 'Ms. Sparkle, you naughty girl!'

She laughed, eyes flashing. 'Honey, I ain't giving all this away for free!' she said with an elaborate gesture to her person.

'Honest to God,' Kovac said, bracing his hands on the table and leaning down. 'I'm not interested in sending you to jail if you help me out here, Sparkle. If you help me out, I'll help you out. I'll get you into a shelter if you want. I'll get you into a drug program if you need it. I will have you relocated like a bear to another part of the city. Whatever you want, sweetheart. I need to know where you got these cards.

'But if you don't play nice with me,' he continued, 'I'll flip the switch and be the biggest jerk you ever met. Lucien Chamberlain and his wife are on slabs down at the morgue, and I will be very happy to arrest you for putting them there just because I'm tired and pissed off.'

'I didn't kill nobody!' she protested.

'I don't care,' Kovac said. 'I haven't slept since God was a child. I will throw you in jail and take a vacation to Bermuda. Where did you get these cards?'

'I found them!'

'Found them where?'

'On the ground next to a garbage can.'

'Where?'

The address she gave them was a street lined with check cashing places, bail bonds places, and dive bars; a part of town populated with drug dealers and their customers, homeless people, street hustlers, and prostitutes.

'When was this?'

'Yesterday morning,' she said. 'I like to get out early and look for treasures. People drop things, lose things, throw all kinds of things away when they're drunk or high. I found this weave in the trash,' she said, pointing to the rainbow on her head.

'So these cards were on the ground like somebody just threw them away?' Taylor asked.

'That's the God's honest truth,' she said.

'You didn't see anybody drop them or throw them there?' Kovac asked.

'No. I wasn't out the night before. The weather was bad. I found them in the morning, on the sidewalk all covered in ice.'

★ ★ ★

'What thief throws away credit cards?' Mascherino asked. 'They use them, they sell them, they don't throw them in the trash.'

She had come into the war room for an update and to bring them a gallon of Starbucks and a bag of deli sandwiches. Gold stars for the lieutenant. She sat with them now, nibbling on an egg salad on whole wheat as they filled her in.

'Unless the idea is to throw us off the scent,' Kovac said. 'A misdirection play. We have to run around chasing down these credit cards and whoever happened to get hold of them, wasting time and taking up our manpower while our bad guy is off unloading a fortune in antique weaponry.'

'We just heard from American Express that Sondra Chamberlain's card is vacationing without her in Spain,' Tippen said.

'So was this a theft with two murders thrown in?' Mascherino asked. 'Or was it a double homicide and the trinkets were a bonus?'

'We'll find out this afternoon what the stolen pieces from the weapon collection are worth,' Taylor said. 'Plus Mrs. Chamberlain's jewelry, and the small electronics.'

'The other burglaries in the area,' Mascherino said, looking again to Tippen and Elwood. 'What was taken?'

'Small electronics, cash, and jewelry,' Elwood said.

'Art? Antiques?'

'No.'

'Did these homeowners have anything in common?'

'Anthony and Lillian Johnson are both art history professors at the U,' Elwood said. 'That neighborhood is thick with college professors, obviously, but it might be interesting to note the Art History Department and the History Department are both housed in Heller Hall.'

'What about the other case? Is this a thief targeting university people only?'

'No. The other house belongs to a CPA and his wife,' Tippen said. 'No connection to the U at all. No connection to any of the other victims.'

'Did any of these people know the Chamberlains?'

'The professors were acquaintances, not friends.'

'Lucien Chamberlain didn't have any friends,' Kovac said.

'The wives were friendly,' Elwood said. 'They served on a museum charity together. Mrs. Johnson is pretty broken up about what happened.'

'Had any of these people had handyman work done recently?' Mascherino asked.

'All of them,' Tippen said. 'Two different companies. The CPA used Handy Dandy, and the Johnsons used Lundquist Contracting.'

'What's the proximity of the two houses from one another?' Taylor asked.

'Same street, about a block apart,' Elwood said. 'So, anyone working either job might have cased other houses in the neighborhood. And these houses are about two blocks away from the Chamberlains'.'

'So what's the update on your missing

handyman?' the lieutenant asked, turning back to Kovac and Taylor.

'We don't have one yet,' Taylor said. 'There's no Gordon Krauss in the system.'

'The name is probably an aka,' Kovac said. 'He came out of a church shelter. They didn't care what name he used. The rehab took him as a charity case. They didn't bother with paperwork. Nobody's checking up on this mutt. He could be anyone.'

'If we can get our warrant for his room at Rising Wings, we can lift his prints,' Tippen said. 'Prints don't lie.'

'You'll have it by the time we finish lunch,' Mascherino said. 'Have there been any sightings of him today?'

'Not that have panned out,' Elwood said.

'And Michael, how's your head?' she asked, looking at Taylor.

'I'm fine, ma'am. A little headache and a stiff neck is all.'

'Good,' she said. 'When is the last time a suspect used martial arts to get away from you — any of you?'

'Never,' Taylor said. 'But if this guy is a veteran, then he's had some combatives training. And he's pretty good if he can land a kick like that.'

'I'll be interested to see if he has a pair of nunchucks in his room,' Kovac said.

The lieutenant sighed and pushed the last of her sandwich aside on its little square of brown paper. She may not have been in the office all night, or out in the rain looking for their phantom suspect, but she had stayed late and come in early, and here she was now with her suit jacket off and the sleeves of her crisp white blouse neatly rolled up. That was more than Kovac could have said for a lot of lieutenants.

'I've spoken with the Chamberlains' family attorney,' she said. 'He's been out of the country. He got back late Tuesday evening. He says Professor Chamberlain called his office Monday morning and made an appointment for late Wednesday afternoon.'

'Did he say what the appointment was for?' Kovac asked.

'He didn't know. He said Chamberlain would never have told his secretary. He was a very private man.'

'He and the daughter were supposed to meet with Ms. Ngoukani at the Office for Conflict Resolution late Wednesday,' Taylor said.

Kovac arched a brow. 'Sounds like maybe he decided he didn't care to resolve that conflict after all.'

'But he had to,' Taylor countered, 'or he wasn't getting the promotion.'

'We're missing a puzzle piece,' Mascherino said as she rose to leave. 'Go find it.'

Kovac breathed a long sigh and glanced at his watch as the lieutenant made her exit. They had an hour before they had to leave for the Chamberlain house.

'I'm gonna lock myself in a room for an hour,' he said to Taylor. 'Come find me when it's time to go. Or if you solve the case in the meantime, that'd be good, too.'

An hour of shut-eye would recharge his batteries enough for him to get through the afternoon.

He stepped out of the war room and ducked right.

'Sam Kovac! You're a sore sight for my eyes.'

'Oooooh man!' Kovac groaned. 'The most beautiful woman in my life, and you have to catch me on the backside of an all-nighter? You're heartless, Red.'

'You're working the latest crime of the century,' Kate Quinn said. 'Murder is not a pretty business.'

He'd been in love with her for years, the girl of his dreams: a tall, gorgeous redhead with a quick mind and a smart mouth. But she had always been out of his league (or so he thought), and she had ended up with an FBI profiler who looked like George Clooney.

'What can I do for you, Gorgeous?'

'Can I have a few minutes?'

'You can have as many minutes as you need,' he said, motioning toward the interview room he had earmarked for his nap. 'What's up? How's it going at Chrysalis? I saw the piece in the paper. Nice write-up.'

He had first known Kate as a victim/witness advocate for the county, a job she left when she and the profiler started their family. She came back to the same field, but in the private sector, working part time for the Chrysalis Center as a liaison with law enforcement and the county attorney's office.

'Seeing how there's no end to human

depravity, poverty, and cruelty, we're doing a booming business,' she said, taking a seat. 'We're up to our ears in victims of the sex trade, homeless teenagers who've aged out of the foster care system, young women trying to transition out of rehab to make a life.

'It's rewarding,' she confessed. 'I wish I could give them more hours than I do.'

'So what brings you here?'

'One of our social workers got this note in her personal mail yesterday,' she said, handing him a plastic bag with a note inside. 'She doesn't have any idea where it came from, but she's working with a client who came out of a sex trafficking situation. The pimp is a very bad guy called Drago. He's at large. Meanwhile, the girl has ratted out her eldest brother for molesting her, and it turns out the family is part of some scary religious cult.'

'Has anybody else at the center been threatened?'

'Grace Underhill gets threatened on a semiregular basis because she's the face of the place, but she hasn't gotten anything similar to this or anything specific to the Hope Anders case.'

Kovac turned the note over. 'There's nothing on here that refers to anyone in particular. What makes you think it's to do with the girl?'

Kate shrugged. 'Nothing. It's just the only answer we could come up with for why anybody would target Evi. She's the sweetest thing on the planet. She lives a quiet life. There's no reason anyone should want to threaten her — except that she's working with this girl who's going to eventually end up testifying against several bad people in court.'

Kovac glanced at the note again.

I KNOW WHO YOU ARE
I KNOW WHERE YOU LIVE

'It's not much, as threats go,' he said.

'I realize that. Which is why I'm coming to you.'

'You didn't just miss me?'

'Of course I miss you,' she said. 'How many Sundays have I invited you over for football? And do you ever come? No.'

'Yeah, well . . . '

'Yeah, well, there's that whole having-to-interact-with-people-who-aren't-cops thing . . . '

'So what do you want me to do about this?' he asked, handing the note back to her. 'There's been no crime.'

'You know everybody worth knowing in the department. Can you reach out to someone and get a few extra patrols past her house? Let them know there's a potential stalker situation. Evi's husband is a firefighter. He's gone for twenty-four hours at a time. She's home alone at night with her five-year-old daughter.'

Kovac looked at the address. A neat, unremarkable neighborhood full of houses built in the 1940s and '50s. A mix of blue-collar workers and young professionals starting families.

'Sure,' he said. 'I'll make a phone call. No

233

problem. Anything for you, Red.'

'Thank you, Sam,' she said, standing. She leaned over and gave him a peck on the cheek. 'You're the best.'

'Yeah, that's what all the ladies say,' he said sardonically as he saw her to the door.

Giving up on the idea of sleep, he headed back to his desk to make that phone call.

18

'I wish you wouldn't go,' Charlie said.

'Why? Are you afraid I'm going to take something?' Diana asked. 'Mommy would have given her jewelry to me, not to you.'

'I don't care about the stupid jewelry,' he said, shoveling scrambled eggs onto two plates on the breakfast bar. He pushed one of the plates toward her. 'Here, eat this. There probably isn't any jewelry left to go through anyway. It was a robbery.'

'Then what's your problem?'

'It's just . . . ' How to put it into words that wouldn't set her off? A conversation with Diana was like traversing a minefield. 'I just . . . I don't want them to misconstrue something you might say.'

'And what do you think I might say, Charlie?' she asked, sitting up straighter, setting her fork aside.

He cringed inwardly. He could see the storm building in her eyes. 'I don't know. They're cops. You know they can twist what you say. It's just better to stand back and let them do their jobs.'

'Do you think I did it?' she asked, her voice clipped, angry.

'Diana . . . '

'Do you?'

'No.'

'Do you?' she asked again, sliding off her stool. 'Look at me!'

'No!'

'Do you think I killed our parents?' She picked up the plate and flung it at him, eggs spraying everywhere. 'Fuck you, Charlie! You hated them, too! Daddy treated you like shit, too!'

This was exactly why he didn't want her going to the house with the detectives, not without him. Kovac was right: He had spent his whole life running interference for her. Her temper was volatile at the best of times, but now she was emotional and tired, and probably off her medication. She might say anything just to say it, just to be difficult.

'They're going to start asking questions about insurance,' he said, 'and who inherits what, and — '

'And I don't know anything about any of that!' she shouted.

'No, but you already told them you want a piece of jewelry,' he said. 'You told them that Mother would have given you her jewelry — '

'She would have!'

'That's not the point! Do you not hear how that sounds? Do you not hear how that must sound to detectives who are looking to put these murders on someone?'

'You think I'm stupid,' she snapped. 'You always think I'm stupid!'

'I do not!'

'I'm the one getting my master's!'

'I'm the one who studied the law!'

'You're a fucking clerk! No wonder Daddy was

236

always disappointed in you,' she said, eyes narrowed like a snake's.

The remark cut as sharp as any of the swords in their father's collection.

'You're such a bitch, Diana! I'm trying to help you, and that's what you say to me?' he said, his voice cracking. 'Jesus! I've always tried to protect you!'

'Well, you never have done a very good job of that, have you?' she said bitterly, coldly, glaring at him.

Tears rose in his eyes and burned like acid. He turned away from her and stood staring out the narrow window that overlooked the parking lot. He couldn't look at her, not now, not after that.

He heard the door slam. He didn't go after her. He leaned his forehead against the cool of the window and started to cry. Through the blur of his tears and the rain on the window, he watched her get into her car and drive away. Then he slid down to the floor with his back to the wall, hugging his knees and burying his face, wishing he had never been born.

19

The scene was surreal: Big Thomas Duffy dressed like a cartoon lumberjack in a red plaid flannel shirt over old-fashioned long johns, with hunting boots and an Elmer Fudd-style cap with earflaps. His sidekick: the Method actor from hell. A man in a moose costume, who insisted on speaking in his character's goofy voice without cease.

They stood in front of a Northwoods set with cardboard pine trees against a painting of a lake and a full array of camping gear on display like a prize package on a game show.

This Big D Sports camping package can be all yours, Nikki Liska! Or would you rather have a BRAND-NEW CAR?!!

I'd take the car, she thought. Camping was one of the few things Speed did well with regard to his boys. Nikki's idea of roughing it was a hotel room with no mint on the pillow at bedtime.

Crowding around Duffy and his moose pal was the crew, there to shoot a Big D commercial wherein Duffy would take ad time to talk about his brother's case. And crowding around that crowd was the KTWN news crew, shooting the footage of the production in order to use pieces of it in their news segment. Crowding around all the cameras were the lunch-hour shoppers at Big D Sports, as goggle-eyed to see their local celebs, Big Duff and Melvin D. Moose, as they would have been to see actual movie stars. Nikki wanted to pull an arrow out of the quiver in the display beside her and stab herself in the eye.

The point of the ad, and the news segment they would be shooting, would be for Big Duff to announce the increased reward money for information leading to the arrest of his brother's killer. A good idea on paper, but the reality of a big reward on a cold case was usually a lot of false leads that tied up investigators' time and yielded nothing. If no one had come up with a viable lead for fifty-thousand dollars in the last twenty-five years, chances were not good of anything real materializing now.

Still, Nikki knew that any publicity for the renewed effort at solving the crime held some slim chance of reaching the ear of the right person with the right piece of information. She had to take the opportunity no matter the odds. She should have been glad Thomas Duffy was willing to spend his company's money and ad time asking for information from the public. This wouldn't be just a sixty-second segment on the news that people might blink and miss while they were passing the potatoes at the supper table. People loved Big Duff and Melvin D. Moose. They would pay attention to the ads. Still, it rubbed her the wrong way. It was still a commercial for Big D Sports with a 'By the way, if you happen to know anything about my brother's murder . . . ' thrown in; a 'Hey, we're offering this big-ass reward . . . and THE LOWEST PRICES IN THE TWIN CITIES!' kind of a thing.

She watched the show, standing at the edge of it, her arms crossed, foot tapping, her expression set in stone — a stark contrast to the delighted faces of the shoppers around her. They were loving it. Take after take after take. The moose kept messing up and then falling into comic antics that had the crowd in stitches. Nikki wanted to step in and beat him like a cheap piñata.

Finally the set was restaged for the interview. They all sat on camp stools around a fake campfire, looking like characters in a piney woods Fellini film: the news reporter and Nikki in business attire, Big Duff still in costume, and the stupid fucking moose. Theater of the absurd, Minnesota style.

' . . . and how do you feel about Big Duff's efforts to promote the case, Detective?' the reporter asked.

'Anything that might bring attention to the search for Ted Duffy's killer — '

'That's right!' Big Duff interrupted, trampling over Nikki's air-time. 'We want people to remember! My brother was a decorated police detective! If anyone can remember any detail about that day, call the hotline! The reward for information leading to a conviction of my brother's killer is up to one hundred thousand dollars! *One hundred thousand dollars!*'

By the time the fiasco was over, Nikki's head was throbbing to the point that she wanted to grab a camping hatchet and put herself out of her misery.

'Mr. Duffy,' she started as the news crew

packed up and the moose went to the customer service area to sign autographs. 'I need to speak with you privately — '

'Yeah, sure.' He didn't look at her. 'Thanks, Melvin!' he called out, waving to his cohort. 'Kids! Be sure to get your picture with Melvin!'

'Mr. Duffy,' Nikki started again.

'Great ad, don't you think?' he said, still more interested in his customers than in her. 'I think we might get something off that.'

She wanted to ask if he meant sales or information. 'It's possible — '

'People love that damn moose! They'll pay attention because of that damn moose!' He laughed, amused at his stroke of genius in creating the character of Melvin.

Nikki wanted to kick him in the balls to get his attention on her. He was her least favorite kind of man: the kind who only talked, and who never listened to a woman. A woman's part in a conversation with this Neanderthal was as a placeholder, a blah-blah-blah while he thought of the next brilliant thing he wanted to say.

He chuckled to himself. 'That goddamn moose!'

Nikki waved a hand in front of his face. 'I don't give a shit about the fucking moose,' she said, loud enough that several shoppers in line for autographs turned with expressions of shock and disapproval.

Duffy looked down at her as if she had just sprung up out of the ground like an unpleasant little forest gnome in his surreal camp scene.

He frowned at her. 'I heard you had an attitude.'

Nikki forced an unpleasant smile. 'I can't imagine where you heard that. Do you have an office we can go to, Mr. Duffy?'

He led the way to the back of the store, pulling his hat off to reveal thinning black hair shot through with gray. They passed the restrooms and the employee break room, which smelled of reheated chili and microwave popcorn. At the end of a hallway, Duffy opened a door and walked into the office ahead of her.

'I've told this story a hundred times to a dozen different cops,' he said, rounding his messy desk to drop into the well-worn leather executive's chair.

The store was the Big D flagship off 494, near the Mall of America, a bright, modern building, but the office chair looked like it had been with him from the early days. The wall behind him was dominated by a stuffed blue marlin and a poster of a pair of scantily clad sex kittens posing with hunting rifles.

Nikki sat down across from him. He was a big man, on the flabby side, his face heavy with the beginnings of jowls. With the goofy cap off, the makeup he was wearing for the television camera stood out: clownish red rouge, eyebrow pencil and mascara, black powder to darken his five o'clock shadow.

'And now we have to start all over again with you,' he said, none too pleased about it.

'I continue to be confused by the low standard everyone involved in this case seems to have,' she said.

He gave her a look that said she should know

better. 'It's been twenty-five years.'

'You think the case can't be solved? Is that why you doubled the reward? Because you don't believe you'll ever have to cough up a hundred thousand dollars?'

'Every detective in the city was on this case when Ted was killed,' he said. 'Are you better on a cold case than every detective in the city on a fresh case put together?'

'You don't know that I'm not,' she said, 'despite what Gene Grider might have told you over your Corn Flakes this morning at Cheap Charlie's.'

He sat up a little at that, frowning at the idea that he might have underestimated her. Clearly Grider hadn't gotten through to him with the news that she had seen the two of them together.

'I keep hearing how close you were to your brother,' she said.

'I loved my brother. He was my best friend every day of my life since before we were born. And every year, at this shitty time of year, I get reminded that someone killed him and he's never going to be in my life again. And that sucks like nothing else I'll ever know.'

'Then you ought to be rooting for me.'

'I don't have any reason to believe you can do what nobody else has done in twenty-five years,' he said. 'All you're going to do is upset my wife and family. You're just going to ask the same damn questions and get the same damn answers every other cop has.

'Isn't that what you came in here to do?' he asked. 'Where was I the day my brother died?

Was I having an affair with Barbie? Did we kill him for the insurance money? Blah, blah, blah. The same fucking five questions over and over. Excuse me for not being excited about that or excited about you.'

Nikki considered what he said as she looked at the calendar of UFC ring girls hanging on the wall above a tall filing cabinet. Thanksgiving weekend was X'd out for his annual hunting trip.

Nothing changed. Every year was another year his brother was dead with no resolution to his murder. Every year on the same weekend in November he went to Wisconsin to hunt. Every year he and his buddies probably sat around the fire at the cabin and toasted his absent twin. And every time his brother's case got dragged back out, the same questions and the same theories were raised, with no result.

If Thomas Duffy had been telling the truth all these years, he had nothing new to offer. If he had been lying all these years, why would he stop now?

'You know, you're right,' she conceded. 'There's no point in me asking you the same questions every other detective has already asked you over and over. You're not going to tell me anything you didn't tell anyone else. And the same answers aren't going to get this case solved. It's Einstein's definition of insanity, right? Doing the same thing over and over and expecting a different result.

'So I'm not going to ask if you killed your twin brother to collect on the insurance so you could sink the money into the business,' she said. 'Or if

244

you killed him because you were fucking his wife. Or both. You wouldn't tell me if you did.'

'I didn't.' The desk chair groaned as he leaned back and spread his hands. 'So, what's the point of you being here?'

'I like to know exactly who I'm dealing with,' she said. 'And I want you to know exactly who you're dealing with.'

'Am I supposed to feel threatened or something?'

'Not unless you've done something wrong.'

'I've got some parking tickets I haven't paid,' he said with a self-amused smirk. 'You probably know some meter maids. Maybe you can take care of that for me.'

'Boy, those meter maid jokes never get old,' Nikki said, putting the thinnest veneer of amusement over a pained smile. 'Feel free to call me if you come up with any more of those gems.'

She stood up, took a business card out of her coat pocket, and placed it on the blotter in front of him.

'In the meantime, I'm going to do everything I can to solve your brother's murder. I'm going to look for things nobody else thought to look for. I'm going to talk to people nobody else bothered talking to. Because those are the people who see things — the ones nobody notices. And maybe they haven't talked before because nobody asked them, or maybe they haven't talked because they didn't realize they had anything relevant to say.

'That's who's going to solve this case,' she said. 'Me, and someone nobody ever thought about — a clerk at a convenience store, a neighbor looking out a window, a child nobody paid any attention to.'

'Yeah?' Duffy said, clearly bored with her. He picked up her card and tossed it on a pile of junk mail. 'Well, you be sure to call me when that happens.'

'You'll be the first to know. Maybe you give the reward to that person here in the store, give them one of those giant checks. They can get their picture taken with the moose. Great publicity.'

He made a face that looked like he had a toothache.

'You have a nice day, Mr. Duffy,' Nikki said. 'Don't forget about those parking tickets. They have a way of coming back to bite you in the ass. The past always does.'

* * *

Ted Duffy's eldest daughter, Jennifer, now thirty-four, worked as a librarian at the Pierre Bottineau Library, five minutes northeast and across the Mississippi from downtown Minneapolis. Single, she lived in an apartment within walking distance of her job.

Seley's research had returned nothing remarkable on Jennifer Duffy. She had graduated in the middle of her class in high school and in the middle of her class in college. She had never done anything to make herself stand out in any way. Her mother had talked about her extensive history of therapy, to deal with the aftermath of her father's death, but if she had ever taken her troubles in the direction of drugs or alcohol, she had done so quietly. She had no police record of any kind.

A pair of the beige brick-and-stone Victorian buildings on the campus of the old Grain Belt brewery complex had been beautifully renovated to house the library. When the brewery was in operation, the neighborhoods around it were populated largely by working-class people of Eastern European descent. In recent years, urban renewal had brought an influx of young professionals and artists. Other brewery buildings, warehouses, and old bank buildings had been converted to apartments, offices, studios, galleries, restaurants, and taprooms.

In good weather the area was an interesting place to explore. In the constant cold drizzle, Broadway and Marshall was just another busy intersection as would-be shoppers and diners passed by on their way elsewhere.

Nikki parked on Marshall and walked through the archway and up the brick path to the library. All warm wood and floor-to-ceiling windows, the place had a cozy feel, full of nooks and crannies and private alcoves for reading or surfing the Internet.

Jennifer Duffy emerged from an office on the other side of the main desk. She was a younger version of her mother: blonde, slender, pretty; smartly dressed in a mid-calf green wool skirt with tall brown boots and a brown sweater set with a pretty silk scarf cleverly tied around her throat.

'Can I help you?' she asked in perfect librarian

tone, a polite smile on her face.

'Jennifer Duffy?'

The smile immediately faded. 'Yes.'

'I'm Sergeant Liska. I'm a detective — '

'I know who you are,' the woman said, frowning at the ID Nikki held up. She glanced around surreptitiously, clearly worried that someone might notice she was talking to a cop. 'My mother told me you'd be calling,' she whispered. 'I don't have anything to say to you. I was nine years old.'

'I understand that,' Nikki said. 'I just want to have a conversation with you. I promise I won't take up much of your time.'

'I don't see the point. I don't have any information for you.'

'You don't know what questions I have.'

'You have the same questions as every other detective.'

'From what I've read in the reports, no one ever bothered to ask you much of anything.'

'Because they knew I don't have anything to say!'

She spoke too emphatically, drawing the attention of several people browsing the stacks. A tall elderly gentleman in a fisherman's sweater took it upon himself to butt in, stepping toward the desk.

'Is everything all right, Jennifer?' he whispered, giving Nikki the eye.

Jennifer Duffy's cheeks turned red. 'Yes, Mr. Weisman, I'm fine. Thank you.'

He drifted back toward the shelves reluctantly.

'I'm not going away, Miss Duffy,' Nikki

whispered. 'Just sit down with me for fifteen minutes. Then I can write my report and cross you off the list, and I will never bother you again. Please. I'm just trying to do my job.'

She still wanted to say no, but she didn't turn away.

'Look, I don't want to make a problem for you,' Nikki pressed. 'But my loyalty in this is to your father. He doesn't get to ask you to help. I have to do it for him. And I will be like a dog with a bone, so you might as well sit down with me and get it over with.'

Looking annoyed and worried, Jennifer Duffy huffed a sigh. She turned and said something quietly to another librarian working behind the desk, then turned back.

'Not in here,' she said. 'I'll get my coat.'

They walked in silence through the drizzle to a mostly empty coffeehouse within sight of the library. They ordered at the counter and then sat down at the farthest table, next to the window, away from curious ears. Nikki took the corner seat out of habit, so she could have the best view of the room and the people in it. Jennifer Duffy sat across from her, huddled in her raincoat, looking sullen.

'I don't need everyone at work knowing my business,' she said.

'I understand.'

'If you understood, you wouldn't be here.'

Nikki sighed. 'Why do I seem to care more about finding your father's killer than everyone else in your family combined?'

'Because you haven't lived with it for

practically your entire life,' she said. 'It's new to you. It's like a shiny new toy,' she said bitterly. 'That's the way it always is, every time someone thinks they're going to be the person to crack the case and nothing ever comes of it, and we're all left to deal with our feelings all over again.'

She had a point. Nikki had yet to become disillusioned with the attempt to solve Ted Duffy's case. Jennifer Duffy had been disillusioned again and again.

'It's like having someone ransack your house over and over,' Jennifer Duffy said. 'They never stay to put it all back together.'

'I'm sorry no one has ever been able to give you closure on this,' Nikki said. 'I sincerely hope this will be the last time.'

'I hope so, too,' she said, though she had clearly run out of hope for that a while ago.

The waiter brought them their coffees. When he had walked away, Nikki said, 'Your mom told me it was especially hard on you when your dad died. You were close to him?'

'No. I don't have that many memories of him, to be honest. He was working all the time. So was my mom. One was gone or the other one was gone.'

'How was it when the family was all together? Did your parents seem happy?'

'I'm not going to trash my parents' marriage,' she said. 'I'm not going to tell you my mother was having an affair with Big Duff or anyone else. Or that my dad was doing something he wasn't supposed to be doing. That's the bush you're beating around, isn't it? I wouldn't know the answer. I was a child.'

Nikki didn't try to argue. She had already stumbled over these same ruts. Her whole point in being here, talking to Ted Duffy's eldest child, was to find new ground. She sat back and took a sip of her coffee.

'Was he a good dad when he had the chance?'

'He was tired,' she said with a weariness of her own. 'He had bad moods. We were always being told not to bother him. Daddy has a hard job, Mom would always say. I could never understand why he didn't just get a different job so he wouldn't be so unhappy all the time.'

Nikki tried to imagine her at nine. She would have been one of those pretty, ladylike little girls. It wasn't hard to picture her in her green plaid Catholic school uniform and black patent leather Mary Janes, her hair in two neat braids with bows. Quiet, Nikki thought, shy, even. She might have had her mother's looks, but she didn't have her mother's edge. She seemed more delicate, internally fragile.

When she spoke, Nikki could hear the echo of loneliness in her voice, the confusion and rejection of a child pushed to the side. Every little girl wanted her daddy's love and attention. Jennifer Duffy hadn't gotten much of either from her father, by the sound of it. Those were the emotions she didn't want to have to relive every time another cop came calling with the promise of solving her father's case.

'I have two boys,' Nikki said. 'Their dad and I are both cops. We're divorced now, but we had our years like that, too. He was gone, working undercover narcotics. I was gone working my shift. When he was home there was always tension. Even though I was a cop, too, he thought I couldn't really understand his world. I know it's the same way with the Sex Crimes detectives. What they're exposed to on a daily basis is so filthy and so foul. Even if it was possible for their spouse or their family to comprehend it, the cops don't want to share it. They don't want it polluting everyone's lives. That isolation takes a toll on the family.'

Jennifer Duffy nodded almost imperceptibly as she looked down at her coffee.

'My dad was a cop, too,' Nikki went on. 'He worked patrol his whole career. Old school. Never talked about the job. Never. And we weren't supposed to ask him. If he had a bad day on the job, how would we know? He wouldn't tell us, and we couldn't ask. How were we supposed to know he wasn't mad at us? Kids think everything is about them.'

'You end up feeling like he's just a man who sometimes stays overnight,' Jennifer murmured, the memory pressing down on her.

'It's hard.'

'But you became a cop yourself.'

'Yes. I suppose in part to feel closer to him,' Nikki admitted. She took another sip of her coffee. 'Or maybe to make up for what he lacked as a parent. I'm very close to my boys. I don't ever want them to feel separate from me the way I felt from my old man.

'Even so, it's not easy being a cop's kid,' she continued. 'It makes you different. It sets you a

252

little apart from the other kids.'

'Yes, it does,' Ted Duffy's daughter murmured, as she stirred her coffee with a stick of rock sugar.

'I read in the file that you were in your room reading when your dad was shot.'

'He was chopping wood,' she said quietly. 'I could hear him chopping wood. He did that when he was upset.'

'Did you hear the shots?'

'I suppose I did, but I didn't realize it.'

Nikki pictured the scene in her mind: Jennifer Duffy propped up by pillows on the bed as she lost her loneliness in the pages of a book. The distant *crack* of the axe striking the wood. The distant *crack* of a rifle shot. A nine-year-old child wouldn't have known the difference. And even if she had been looking out the window the instant it happened, she never could have seen into the gathering gloom of the woods where the shot had come from.

'Then it was quiet,' Jennifer said. 'It was quiet for a long time. I just kept reading. I thought he must have come inside, but he was lying out there, dying.'

The mother in her made Nikki want to put her arms around the young girl in the memory. Jennifer blamed herself in the way children did because they believed their worlds revolved around them. In the active imagination of Jennifer Duffy's nine-year-old mind, she might have been able to save her father if only she had known he was out there wounded. If only she had realized something was wrong. Instead, her father had bled out lying on the ground beneath her bedroom window.

'He was killed instantly, you know,' Nikki said softly. 'There was nothing you could have done.'

She made that slight nod again, but she was still far away in her mind. 'That's what they said,' she whispered.

Now, as she put the pieces of Jennifer Duffy's answers together, Nikki could see why she had been the one to take her father's death the hardest. He had never been the father she wanted, and her hope for that to change had died with him. Her father hadn't seen her off on her first date, hadn't seen her graduate, would never walk her down the aisle — and somewhere deep down inside there was still a tiny remnant of that nine-year-old girl that believed she was somehow responsible.

'So you grew up to be a librarian,' Nikki said, to move her memory away from the dark corner of her father's death. 'Were books a refuge for you as a kid?'

'You can go anywhere in a book,' she answered, smiling slightly. 'Be anyone. And life has to make sense in a book. Real life doesn't have to make sense. In real life, good people can turn out to be bad people, and bad people can get away with murder . . . and worse. I'll take a good book over that any day.'

She used both hands to lift her cup to her lips. It rattled on the saucer as she set it down.

'My oldest boy is an artist,' Nikki said. 'He draws his own comic books. That's his escape. He says the same thing. In comic books, the bad guy always gets it in the end. There's a lot of comfort in that.'

Jennifer Duffy stared out the window, her mind years away, in a place where a nine-year-old girl had to hide away from a bad reality. Her father's death? Her parents' struggling marriage? Their unhappy family? Her own unjustified guilt . . .

'Can you tell me about the girls who were living with you at that time?' Nikki asked. 'Angie and Penny?'

Jennifer Duffy looked at her, confused. 'Why? What could you think they would have to do with anything? They were teenagers.'

'I'm fishing,' Nikki confessed. 'I spoke with your old neighbor Mr. Nilsen. He said the girls were kind of wild. Maybe one of them had a bad boyfriend or got in trouble with people in the drug culture. Or maybe they had someone in their family background who was unhappy with them being in the foster care system,' Nikki suggested. 'Or someone who didn't want them talking to a police detective.'

'That sounds like a movie,' Duffy said. 'They were just teenage girls. I don't think anybody cared about either of them.'

'Did you like having them around? It had to be kind of like having instant big sisters, huh?'

'I never liked Penny. She was mean when she babysat for us. And she was a liar and a thief. I wasn't sad to see her go.'

'And Angie? She was the older one?'

'I liked her. She was quiet, and she was nice to us. She liked to read, too,' she recalled. 'She would read to me sometimes,' she admitted, smiling a little at that one small fond memory. 'I loved to be read to, but I was supposedly too big to be read to, so I never asked my mom to do it. She didn't have time anyway. I was the one who read to my little sister and brother at night.'

'And then Angie would read to you?'

'She would sneak into my room, or I would sneak into hers, and we would curl up in bed and take turns reading out loud.'

Her expression changed slowly as she looked inward. A happy memory was slowly overtaken by one not so pleasant, like a cloud passing over the sun.

'Anyway . . . I should be getting back to work,' she said, pulling herself away from the dark thought.

'Angie wasn't there when your father was shot,' Nikki said, pressing forward. 'Do you remember where she was?'

'No,' she said, gathering her purse and pushing her chair back. 'Something at school. Really, I need to get back to work.'

'I'll walk with you,' Nikki said. 'I'm parked on Marshall.'

Jennifer Duffy didn't look happy about having to spend another three minutes with her. They went back out into the damp. The librarian set a brisk pace.

'It must have been hard for you,' Nikki said. 'Losing your dad and then losing your surrogate big sister. Did you stay in touch with Angie after she left?'

'No. I never knew where she went. No one would tell me.'

'Do you remember the kid that lived next door? Jeremy Nilsen? He mowed your grass.'

'He was in high school.'

'I know. So was Angie. They must have known one another. Were they friends?'

'I wouldn't know,' she said curtly as she pulled open the library's outer door. 'And I really don't see the point of this. How could it matter? I have to go back to work. Thank you for the coffee.'

'Thank you for your time,' Nikki said as the glass door closed in front of her. 'And you *would* know,' she murmured, watching Jennifer Duffy disappear into the library. 'That *is* the point.'

20

'I don't understand why I can't come in,' Charlie Chamberlain said stubbornly.

They stood in the drizzle on the front walk of the house: Charlie, Diana, Ken Sato, Kovac, and Taylor. Kovac had purposely made sure that Charlie knew the time they would be meeting, in the hope he would turn up, despite the fact he had been told not to come. Kovac did so for the express purpose of literally shutting the kid out. If Charlie Chamberlain didn't want his sister left alone with the cops, it was worth messing with him to find out why.

'I told you, kid,' Kovac said curtly. 'I can't have people wandering around the crime scene. We're here for two reasons. One, so I can walk through the collection with Professor Sato, and two, so your sister can look over your mother's jewelry with my partner. I don't need a third wheel here.'

'I have a DVD of the collection,' Chamberlain said, pulling a plastic DVD case out of the patch pocket of his rain jacket. Mr. Helpful. 'I stopped by the attorney's office to talk about making funeral arrangements, and I remembered he had a copy — '

Kovac took the case and handed it to Taylor like he couldn't be bothered with it. 'Thanks, that's great. You can go now.'

'This is my home,' Chamberlain argued. 'I

have as much right to be in it as anyone.'

'No,' Kovac snapped. 'This is *my* crime scene until I say it isn't, and you don't have any rights here until I say you do. That's how this works. Now, I'd like to get out of this filthy weather before pneumonia sets in, so . . . '

'It's fine, Charlie,' Sato said. 'It's all fine.'

Sato went to put a hand on the kid's shoulder. Charlie Chamberlain shrugged him off, shooting Sato a look that could have cut glass. 'Nothing is *fine*. No part of any of this is *fine*, Ken.'

'Oh my God, Charlie,' Diana said impatiently. 'Why don't you just shut the fuck up and go do whatever it is you do when you're not butting into my life.'

'Oh yeah, this is all about *you*, Diana,' Charlie bit back. '*Our* parents are dead.'

She rolled her eyes like a teenager.

Kovac resisted the urge to raise his eyebrows. Something had shifted in the dynamic between the siblings since that morning, when they clung to one another, crying over their mutual grief. He caught Taylor's eye and knew he was making note of it as well.

'And unless you know something the rest of us don't,' Kovac said, 'Detective Taylor and I are in charge of solving their murders. Do you have something to contribute to that conversation, Charlie?'

The kid huffed and looked away and back, shoving his clenched fists into his jacket pockets as he struggled with his temper. 'No. I would just like to see for myself the state of the house.'

'We're not pocketing the silverware, if that's what you think.'

'I'll video,' Diana said and walked up the steps, dismissing him.

Kovac made a show of relenting. 'Look, kid, go sit in your car if you've got time. I'll walk you through when we're done.'

They left him standing on the sidewalk looking like an unhappy wet puppy.

Inside the front door, they shed their dripping coats, hanging them on an iron coat tree. Taylor handed out booties for everyone to cover their shoes.

The house still carried a hint of the smell of spilled blood and the faint stink of cigarettes. While no one was allowed to smoke in a house being processed as a crime scene, plenty of the people on the job ducked outside for a break during the hours it took to do the job, bringing the smell of smoke back inside with them.

'Where were they killed?' Diana Chamberlain asked. True to her word, she held up her phone and took a video of the foyer and the staircase.

'The dining room,' Taylor said. 'We won't be going in there.'

'I think I should.'

Sato gave her a disapproving look. 'Di, no.'

'I should,' she insisted, turning to him with her bravest and most earnest expression. 'It's the last place their souls were,' she said with all the drama of a soap opera actress. 'That's where I should say good-bye to them.'

'We really can't have people in there,' Kovac said. 'We need you to go upstairs with Detective

Taylor and look through your mother's things.'

He turned to Sato. 'Professor, you and I are going to the professor's study.'

He didn't look any more like a professor today than he had the day before. He was in black jeans and a black hoodie with several glossy black Japanese characters running down the left side of his chest.

'Do you have some kind of history with the boy?' Kovac asked. 'He doesn't seem too happy to see you.'

'Charlie thinks I'm an anarchist because I don't fit in any of his neat little boxes.'

'What the hell does that mean?'

'It means he can't control me, and control is everything to Charlie. Control the emotions. Control the situation. Move the chess pieces around on the board to create the best defense.'

'Defense against what?'

'Life,' he said, looking around as they went into a fussy formal sitting room that was lined with dark wood bookcases crowded with leather-bound tomes and framed family photos.

'These aren't the best circumstances, but he seems pretty uptight for a twenty-four-year-old kid.'

'You would be, too, if Lucien were your father,' Sato said. 'Charlie always tried to be the peacemaker. Given the personalities involved, that's a stressful role. He's a sensitive kid.'

'He's very protective of his sister.'

Sato didn't comment. He stood in the center of the room with his hands on his hips and looked around. 'It's strange to be in here knowing Lucien and Sondra are gone.'

'Did you come here often?' Kovac asked.

He laughed. 'No. Lucien invited me once a year to their annual Chinese New Year party, so I could see what a successful life he had.'

'And you don't have a successful life? You're a professor, too. You're in line for the same promotion.'

'I'm not married to money.'

'You could be,' Kovac said, watching him carefully. 'Now you could get the girl, get the job, get the money. It's clear sailing. You'd probably end up with the collection, too. Half of it, anyway.'

Sato's expression hardened. 'You brought me here to accuse me of murder?'

'I'm not accusing you of anything. Just pointing out the obvious.'

'Am I seriously a person of interest?'

'Did you seriously think you wouldn't be?' Kovac asked, giving him a look like *Come on.* 'Everyone connected to the Chamberlains is a person of interest until I'm satisfied they're not.'

'What about this manhunt for some drug addict carpenter I heard about on the news?'

'He's someone we need to have a conversation with,' Kovac answered, peeved that the media was running away with that story. Dan Franken would probably threaten to sue the department before the day was out. The fact that his illegal employee was being hunted in connection with a murder investigation would be bad for business. 'We have to consider all possibilities.'

'The fact that this guy is on the run says

enough to me,' Sato said. 'Innocent people don't flee the police.'

'He could be guilty of something. That doesn't make him guilty of this,' Kovac said. 'Anyway, why don't you enlighten me about some of this stuff?'

Sato gestured to the painting over the fireplace, a fearsome-looking elaborately dressed warrior of some kind, sword drawn. The colors were bold and solid — black, dark blue, bright white. The matting and frame probably cost a week's pay.

'It's a late-nineteenth-century *ukiyo-e* — a Japanese woodblock print.'

'Is it valuable?'

'No, not very. It's in pristine condition, and it's a beautiful example of the art, but they're not rare. After Japan opened up during the Meiji Restoration in 1868, tons of these came west. Japan and all things Japanese were all the rage in Europe and in the States.'

'So this collection of Chamberlain's is just a bunch of tourist trinkets from back when?'

'Oh no. We haven't gotten to the good stuff yet.'

'How about any of the stuff on these shelves?' Kovac asked, more interested himself in the family photos: a wedding picture of the professor and his bride; photographs of Lucien Chamberlain receiving various awards, of him traveling in far-flung corners of the world. Photos of the professor outnumbered the rest of the family three to one.

'I don't know that much about the art objects,'

Sato said. 'That's not my area of expertise.'

'I guess Stuart Kaufman would have been the one to help us with that,' Kovac remarked.

From the corner of his eye he could see Sato bristle.

'Do you think I killed him, too?'

'I don't know that anybody killed him. But it would make me a little nervous if the candidates for the job I wanted were dropping like flies.'

'Stuart got sick and died. People do. I don't see that one death has anything to do with the other. It's an unfortunate coincidence.'

Kovac bobbed his eyebrows and made a noncommittal humming sound as he looked at a photograph of the Chamberlain children dressed up in their white karate outfits, standing ramrod straight, bare feet wide apart, arms crossed, their expressions grave. They must have been around eight and ten, he thought. Even then Diana towered over her brother.

'Did you know Diana when she was in and out of rehab?' he asked.

'She put that behind her several years ago.'

'Has she ever talked about any of the rehabs she went to?'

'No. You don't think she could be connected to this handyman suspect, do you? He came out of a drug rehab, right?'

Kovac didn't answer.

'She doesn't hang with any of those people.'

'That's not to say someone couldn't remember her, and think her family is loaded,' Kovac said. 'You see?'

He led the way down the hall to Lucien

Chamberlain's study. 'Watch your step. The crime scene unit has already processed the scene, but I still don't like to mess up blood stains and footprints if I can help it.'

Sato tiptoed around the dried bloody shoe prints like a cat.

'Charlie tells us Diana is bipolar,' Kovac said. 'Do you know if she's on medication?'

'You'd have to ask her,' the professor said, his voice chilly. He was about done with the subject of Diana. He looked pointedly at his watch. 'Can we get on with this? I have an appointment in an hour.'

'Sure,' Kovac said. 'We'll get the insurance report on the values, but I want you to look at what was taken and tell me if you think the thief knew the significance of what he was stealing.'

'Okay. Let's start here,' Sato said, gesturing to an empty display case. The glass had been shattered. A brass plaque described the missing item as SAMURAI MEMPOß-ÆAPANß-©IR. 1800. '*Mempo* was the mask worn by the samurai in battle,' he said. 'This one covered the entire face and was made from leather with a detachable iron nosepiece. It's lacquered white on the outside with red accenting the lines of the face, and lacquered bright red on the inside. The hallmark of these masks is a terrible grimacing facial expression, meant to intimidate the enemy. The missing one also had a horsehair mustache. They added those so that decapitated heads on the field of battle wouldn't be mistaken for women's heads and discarded.'

'There were women on the battlefield?'

265

'More than you would think. There were actually female warriors — *onna-bugeisha*. They participated in battles a lot more than the history books say. The remains of a hundred and five bodies at the Battle of Senbon Matsubaru in 1580 were recently DNA tested. It turned out thirty-five of them were women.'

He shook his head at a memory. 'Lucien and I actually argued about it. Misogynist that he was, he tried to find every alternate explanation he could to diminish the significance of the *onna-bugeisha*. And yet, he has their weapon of choice in his collection — the *naginata*. Fucking hypocrite,' he muttered.

Kovac looked up at the wall to a thing that appeared to be a spear on one end and a curved sword on the other, and imagined a pack of angry women armed with them.

'He also chose to adamantly ignore the samurai practice of *wakashudo*,' he said with disgust. 'Ridiculous homophobic dinosaur.'

Kovac raised an eyebrow. 'There were gay samurai?'

'They didn't label people that way. Like the Spartans, they accepted and actively encouraged relationships among the warriors. *Wakashudo* literally means 'the way of the young men.' It was a normal part of a mentor-student relationship among warriors. It wasn't until Westerners and Christian missionaries came to Japan that homophobic attitudes were imposed on the society.

'Opening to the West was the demise of samurai culture in every way,' he continued.

266

'And the Victorian attitudes of Westerners kept details like the *onna-bugeisha* and *wakashudo* — truths they didn't approve of — out of the history books.

'That's where Lucien's soul lived — in Victorian times,' he went on. 'He was rigid, judgmental, sexually repressed. The irony, of course, is that the Victorians were secretly some of the most sexually deviant, fucked-up people ever.'

'Do you think Chamberlain was that, too?' Kovac asked. 'Deviant? Some of what I see in Diana's behavior makes me wonder if there's a history of abuse.'

'I wouldn't know,' Sato said, but he looked away as he said it. 'Anyway, back to the mask — I recently saw one for sale that was not quite as old or quite as nice as this one. The guy wanted three grand for it.'

'Is there a black market for this kind of stuff?'

'Sure, for the ultra-rare pieces. Men all over the world are enamored of the samurai and their culture. Wealthy men like expensive toys. But the average bozo thinks samurai and ninja are cool, too. So, a common thief might take that mask or a sword or dagger just because it excites him, not because he understands the historical or monetary value.'

He went to a blank spot on the weapon wall and tapped a finger on the brass plaque. 'This was a *kubikiri tanto*, a head-cutting knife from the middle of the Edo period. Rare. Valuable. The blade is seven to eight inches long, with the cutting edge on the inside of the blade. This

267

would have been carried by a high-ranking samurai, who had the honor of removing the heads of slain enemies in the field as trophies. A hard-core martial arts movie groupie might know what it is. But it's rarely seen in Western collections, so a knowledgeable thief would definitely want it.'

Kovac rubbed a hand across his forehead and sighed. 'Well, why should this be easy?'

'One of the things that makes Lucien's collection stand out,' Sato said, 'is that he got his hands on these things most Westerners couldn't. It's a small collection, but the quality is special. He traveled and studied extensively in Japan and China when he was younger — an opportunity that allowed him to make connections. Money talks louder than tradition to some people,' he muttered.

Sato clearly didn't approve of Chamberlain having these things. Kovac wondered if that disapproval stemmed from jealousy or bigotry, or loyalty to long-dead ancestors. Ken Sato was as American as anyone, but the blood of ancient Japan ran in his family. He talked about Westerners like he wasn't one.

'What's the most valuable thing in the collection?' Kovac asked.

'There are three swords that are worth low five figures apiece,' Sato said, going to the center section of the display wall, where the long swords were mounted one above another all the way to the ceiling, some with matching shorter blades directly beneath them. 'The top three here.'

It would have required a ladder to get them

down from the wall, Kovac noted. Not burglar-friendly. The lowest one in that section was gone. The only long sword that was missing was the sword that had been used to murder Sondra Chamberlain.

'The samurai carried a pair of weapons called *daisho*,' Sato said. 'Individually: The long sword, *katana*, and the shorter weapon, *wakizashi*. The *katana* was the iconic weapon of the samurai. *Bushido* — the warrior's code — says the samurai's soul is in his *katana*. The *wakizashi* was for stabbing in close combat. It was also the weapon used for *seppuku* — ritual suicide.'

'Like hari-kari?'

'Harry Caray was a baseball announcer,' Sato said with the thinnest edge of condescension. '*Hara kiri*. It refers to the act of slicing open one's own abdomen.'

'That's harsh.'

'Death before dishonor.' Sato indicated a blank spot on the wall at about eye level. 'That's the blade that's missing here: a *wakizashi*. A nice one.'

'Did Chamberlain do anything with this stuff besides collect it?' Kovac asked as he looked through the glass doors of a cabinet at the collection of various types of nunchucks and throwing stars. 'Did he know how to use any of it?'

'Lucien was all about possession — possession of knowledge, possession of things, possession of people,' Sato said, not quite able to keep his disgust at bay. 'Possession of the position of power . . . It's such a bad joke that he tried to possess all things samurai but had no true grasp of *Bushido*.'

'But did he know how to use a sword?'

'He liked to say he did.'

'Do you?'

Sato gave him a long, narrow look, trying to decide if this was some kind of trick; trying to decide if he should play the game. The tiniest of unkind smiles turned just the very corner of one side of his mouth.

'It would be helpful to know if our bad guy was familiar with the weapon or was just hacking away,' Kovac said. 'If he knew what he was doing would there be a pattern to the wounds?'

'If we're talking about a trained swordsman, yes.'

'And how would that go?'

Sato said nothing as he weighed his choices. Then he turned and chose a sword from the wall, unsheathed it, and set the black lacquered scabbard aside on the credenza. He took a stance in front of Kovac, taking a moment to carefully position his grip around the handle of the *katana* and test the weight of the weapon in his hands. His expression grew hard and dark as he looked down the length of the blade.

'The *katana* is made for slashing,' he said quietly as he flexed his wrists, raising and lowering the tip of the sword methodically. 'The first strike would be an overhead cut.'

He raised the sword over his head and brought it down slowly, at a slight angle, aiming for the place where Kovac's neck met his shoulder. He stopped just shy of touching him.

Kovac stood stock still, never taking his eyes off Sato's.

'When a *katana* was made, it was tested by cutting through the limbs of prisoners,' Sato said. 'Or they would pile corpses one on top of another to see how many bodies the sword could cut through in one slice. A good blade could cut through three bodies in a stroke, flesh and bone. An exceptional blade — as many as seven.'

He stepped back, drawing the sword all the way to the left, across his body. 'The second strike would be a sideways stroke,' he said, moving in slow motion as he swung the blade almost like a baseball bat. 'High to decapitate. Or low to disembowel.'

The tip of the blade, which looked just as lethal now as it probably was two centuries ago, passed within an inch of Kovac's stomach.

Sato stepped back again, into some kind of ready stance, and then brought his feet together and bowed deeply.

'And that,' he said as he straightened, 'is *shinkendo*: the real way of the sword. Was that helpful, Detective?'

'One way or another,' Kovac said as he watched Lucien Chamberlain's chief rival sheath the sword and reverently place it back on the curved rests that held it in its place of honor on the wall. *One way or another . . .*

★ ★ ★

'This looks good on me, don't you think?'

Diana Chamberlain lifted her streaky blonde

271

waves up in two messy handfuls and admired herself in the mirror over the dresser. She had put on one of her dead mother's necklaces — a thick twist of dark gray beads that brought out her pale gray eyes.

The costume jewelry had been left untouched by the thief — the necklaces left hanging in the closet, the earrings in trays stacked on the dresser, the bracelets in a dresser drawer that had been pulled open but left alone. The large lacquered rosewood tiered jewelry box that sat atop the dresser had been emptied.

Taylor stood near the door to the master bedroom like a guard and watched Diana in the mirror, his face carefully neutral. She had changed her look from that morning, abandoning the studious glasses and letting her hair loose, unbuttoning the man's white shirt one button too far for modesty, giving glimpses of a lacy black bra when she moved. The red lipstick had been refreshed, he noticed as she pursed her lips and batted her eyelashes at her reflection — and at his.

'Don't you think I'm pretty?' she asked, her voice dark and smoky.

His inclination was to ignore the question, but Kovac had given him a job. *Put those looks to work, Junior. See what you can get her to say.*

He had always been acutely aware of the power of his looks, but not necessarily comfortable with that power. He didn't like being given things for no other reason than that he was handsome. Nor did he like using his looks as some kind of bait. It wasn't his nature to be disingenuous.

'You're a very pretty girl,' he said flatly, like it was a dry fact. 'Were you close to your mom?'

She pouted for a second at his apparent lack of interest in her beauty. 'She was my mother. Of course I loved her. She was the sweetest person.'

'Except when she was drinking?' Taylor said. 'How long had she been doing that? Did she drink when you were little?'

'How would I know?' she asked quietly. 'Everything is normal to a kid.'

'I knew it was normal for my Uncle Phil to smell like beer,' Taylor said. 'I knew it was hard to understand him when he talked. I knew to stay away from him if he'd had one too many. And when I was old enough, I figured it out that Uncle Phil was a drunk.'

'What does it matter if she drank?' she asked. 'Who could blame her? My father wasn't a nice man to live with.'

'She could have divorced him,' he said, taking a couple of steps closer to hear her better.

She shook her head as she fingered through a tray of earrings. 'People always think they know how easy someone else's life should be.'

She chose a big red button of an earring and put it on. It matched her lipstick. There was something exotic about her, something a little too eccentric or untamed for the stuffy formality of her parents' bedroom, with its drab gray-green walls and heavy silk draperies.

'What about your life?' Taylor asked. 'It's tough on kids when their parents don't get along. Was that hard on you and Charlie?'

She raised a shoulder and let it drop. 'We had each other.'

'You watched out for each other. Is Charlie adopted, too?'

'He was here first.'

'But he's younger than you.'

'They adopted Charlie as an infant. Two years later they adopted me. They decided to skip the baby phase the second time,' she said. 'Too loud and messy. So they went out and got me — walking, talking, and already potty-trained. They thought that would be easier. Joke's on them!' she said with a bitter smile. Then she sighed, and just looked sad. 'Poor Mommy. All she wanted was a nice little family. She renamed me so Charlie and I went together like a set.'

'And what did your father want?'

'For us to be quiet, to speak when spoken to, to reflect well on him.'

'Was he abusive?'

'Daddy has expectations,' she said, slipping back into the present tense, as if she thought her father might still be watching her.

'And if you didn't meet them?'

'*When*,' she corrected him.

'When . . . ?'

'Then Daddy doesn't love you anymore,' she said, putting on the second earring. 'Mustn't disappoint Daddy.'

She picked her phone up off the dresser and took a selfie in the mirror, and then turned the camera on him.

'I'm tired of answering questions. What about you, Detective Taylor?' she asked seductively, slowly coming toward him. 'What's it like to spend your life investigating gruesome murders? Do you like it? Does it excite you?'

Just like that, she turned on the sexuality, like flipping a switch. He could feel it emanate from her like heat. Diana Chamberlain had a master's degree in disingenuousness. He wondered if the hyper-sexuality was part and parcel of her bipolar disorder, or if it was, as Kovac thought, the result of sexual abuse as a child — either before or after the Chamberlains adopted her.

'Come on,' she said, with a sexy one-sided smile. 'The camera's rolling. Your turn to confess something. What's it like to stand over a dead body? Can you feel their souls? Are they still in the room?'

'They're long gone by the time we get there.'

'Where do you think they go?'

'I don't know. Where do you think they go?'

'I can't decide,' she admitted, still videoing him. 'If someone is bad, I hope they go to hell, but I don't want to go there.'

'Why should you go to hell?' he asked. 'Do you think you're bad?'

'Oh, I'm a bad, bad girl . . . or so I've been told,' she said in a low, breathy voice. 'Would you care to form your own opinion, Detective?'

She was standing too close to him now, recording his frown close up on her phone. He could feel her breath on his neck.

'I'd rather keep an open mind,' he said, stepping back. 'What have you done that's so bad?'

She laughed. 'What haven't I done?'

275

'I know you had a problem with substances for a while. But you're past that now. You got your degree. You're a grad student. Your parents must have been proud of you.'

'Must they have been?'

'They should have been. Looks to me like you've been getting your life together,' he said.

He went over by the window and looked out through the sheer curtain at the backyard. They were on the opposite end of the house from the professor's study and from the dining room. Charlie Chamberlain was standing on the brick patio in the rain, looking into the dining room through the French doors.

'Do you still belong to a program?' he asked. 'Do you stay in touch with anyone from your rehab days?'

'Like who?' she asked. She had started to follow him, then turned and sat down on the unmade bed, her back against the upholstered headboard, her legs crossed yoga style. She pulled a pillow into her lap, bent over, and breathed in the scent of one of her parents.

'A sponsor, a friend . . . ?'

'Ken says you're after some addict who might have done work on the house,' she said. 'Do you think he's a friend of mine? Some guy I fucked in rehab?'

Her tone had the edge of a challenge, like she wanted him to think she was offended, though he doubted she was. He didn't bite. 'Were you ever in the program at Rising Wings?'

'Where wasn't I?'

Another answer that wasn't an answer.

'My parents always wanted to give me back, you know,' she said.

'To the rehab? Which one?'

She looked at him like he was a sweet, dim child. She didn't mean back to a rehab, she meant back from where they had adopted her. She had probably heard them say it, or suspected them of saying it. Given the egotistical asshole her father had apparently been, it wasn't hard to imagine he might have said such a thing to her face. Maybe he said it Sunday night.

'Your brother said you had a big fight with your dad at his birthday dinner. What was that about?'

'He didn't like me. I didn't like him.'

'Did he think you were trying to sabotage him so Ken Sato could get the promotion?'

'Of course he did. Daddy always thinks the worst of me. Everybody always thinks the worst of me.'

'Yeah? Do they have good reason?'

She gave him the finger and then took a picture of herself doing it, making a comic tough-chick face.

'You were supposed to meet with him yesterday at the Office for Conflict Resolution,' Taylor said. 'Did you know he wasn't going to come to that meeting? He was meeting with his attorney instead.'

She didn't answer him right away. It made him wonder what she might be reliving in her head.

'What didn't happen doesn't matter,' she said.

What didn't happen didn't happen because Lucien Chamberlain died Tuesday night.

'You should be more fun, Detective Taylor,' she said, unfolding her legs and getting up from the bed.

'Where were you Tuesday night?' he asked.

She reached out and dragged a fingertip across his jaw as she passed him.

'I was in bed,' she said. She paused in the doorway and rubbed up against the doorframe like a cat. 'Dreaming.'

'Alone or with company?'

'I have to go pee now,' she announced. 'Can I use the bathroom at the other end of the hall, or is that a crime scene, too?'

Taylor motioned her on her way. He followed her into the hall but paused just outside the door of the master bedroom, his attention catching on a small key panel mounted on the wall — another keypad for the security system.

Mascherino had told them that, according to the security company, the system had been armed a little after seven Tuesday evening and disarmed at around twelve thirty. The Chamberlains had been in bed. Both sides of the bed had been used, the covers and pillows rumpled and tossed. Lucien Chamberlain had died in his fussy silk dressing gown. Sondra Chamberlain's blood had saturated her baby blue robe.

Why had they gone downstairs at all, he wondered. If they suspected an intruder, why didn't they stay in their bedroom and call 911 or hit the panic button on the alarm panel?

Analyzing the crime scene, they believed that the professor had gone downstairs first, and that Mrs. Chamberlain later either heard something and went to investigate, or became concerned when her husband didn't come back to bed and went downstairs to find him.

But neither of them had been worried about going downstairs because they didn't think anyone was down there waiting to kill them.

He flipped the front of the keypad down, revealing the numbers and emergency buttons. The panel was lighted. The system was unarmed but functional. If someone came into the house while the system was armed, they had half a minute to enter the code or have the alarm sound. During that thirty seconds, most systems beeped the countdown until the code was entered.

Before he could form another thought, a scream split the air.

Taylor bolted down the hall, even though the sound seemed to have come from downstairs. He went in the direction Diana had gone, remembering only as he turned the corner to the bathroom that there was a second staircase that went down to a TV room at the back of the house.

He cursed under his breath as he thundered down the stairs. Kovac was going to kill him.

One scream gave way to another and another.

Diana Chamberlain was on her knees in the dining room, in the middle of the huge bloodstain on the Oriental rug, screaming and screaming. Her white shirt was stained with her mother's blood where she had thrown her body down on the still-wet carpet. She had pressed her hands into it and wiped them over her face, painting herself with the last evidence of her mother's life.

Charlie Chamberlain knelt beside her, trying to comfort her. He had come in through the French doors, having knocked out the piece of plywood that temporarily covered the empty space where the Chamberlains' killer had broken out the glass and let himself in. He wrapped his arms around his sister and smothered her sobs against his shoulder, his hand tangled in her hair.

'Look what you've done!' he shouted, his glare going in the direction of Kovac and Sato, who had rushed into the room from the study, both of them looking shocked.

'Oh my God! Oh my God!' Diana sobbed over and over.

Sato spat out a curse as he went toward her. 'Di — '

'Fuck you!' Charlie snapped, exploding to his feet. His first punch caught Sato on the cheekbone, snapping his head to the side. The second one glanced off the professor's ear and temple. Sato stumbled backward, falling into Kovac. Momentum carried both of them backward into an antique sideboard.

Diana shrieked as her brother lunged after Sato, shouting, 'This is all your fault!'

Taylor ducked and moved, hitting Chamberlain in the midsection with his shoulder and driving the much smaller man off his feet and to the other side of the room like a tackling dummy. In one motion, he set Charlie Chamberlain down and spun him around, pushing him flat up against the wall.

From the corner of his eye, he could see Diana going toward Sato — and he could see Kovac coming toward him. He cringed inwardly as Kovac stepped up beside him, his expression like stone.

'You had one job, Stench.'

21

'That's some temper you keep locked away,' Kovac said.

They stood in the fussy sitting room, Charlie Chamberlain pacing one end of the room. Kovac had closed both sets of doors. He wanted the young man isolated, but didn't want him to have the cooling-off period of a ride downtown. He wasn't being arrested. Sato had no intention of pressing charges, despite the shiner he was going to be sporting in short order. The professor and Diana were in another room with Taylor.

Kovac wanted Charlie like this: hot, rattled, still emotional, embarrassed and upset that he had lost control. Nothing was worse to a control freak than losing his grip in front of people. Charlie was still breathing hard. He cradled his right hand against his belly as he paced. He wouldn't look Kovac in the eye.

'You'll want somebody to take a look at that hand,' Kovac said. 'You cracked him good. Could be broken. I don't imagine you get the opportunity to deliver a lot of beat-downs as a paralegal.'

'It's fine,' the kid said, flexing his fingers. They wouldn't straighten all the way. The hand was red and swollen.

'Then again,' Kovac said, looking at the framed photo of Charlie and his sister as kids in their karate outfits, 'for all I know, you're some kind of umpteen-degree black belt of whatever and you spend your free time breaking concrete blocks with that hand.

'Did you keep up with it?' he asked, gesturing to the photograph.

Chamberlain didn't respond.

'What was that about?' Kovac asked. ' "This is all your fault." What did you mean by that?'

Still nothing. He continued pacing, looking down at the floor. He chewed at a cuticle on his uninjured hand like a starving animal gnawing its own paw.

'Do you think Sato killed your parents? Why would he do that? Because of the job promotion? You need to help me out here, Charlie. Or is this about Diana?' Kovac asked. He sat down on the arm of a tufted leather chair, tired just watching this kid's nervous energy burn.

'He puts things in her head,' the kid said. 'He just uses her to get at our father.'

'So you know they're sleeping together, right? That bothers you — the idea of him and her sweating up the sheets?'

'Shut up!' Charlie snapped. He didn't want to hear it, but he didn't deny it, either. 'Of course it bothers me. She's my sister. He's taking advantage of her.'

'You're very protective of her,' Kovac said, going right back to the conversation they had had at the morgue. 'That must be exhausting, considering. She's not exactly a stranger to trouble, is she? Drinking, drugs, shoplifting, sex — '

'She's fragile,' he said in his sister's defense.

'You don't understand.'

'I'm trying to, Charlie,' Kovac said, keeping his voice even and soft. Annoyingly calm. 'Help me. Why is Diana so fragile? Did someone abuse her when you were kids?'

He wasn't going to talk about it. Kovac could see the stubborn set of his jaw, the muscles flexing as he fought to contain whatever unpleasant memories were coming to him.

Kovac pushed a little harder. 'Did your father abuse her?'

'He abused everyone,' Charlie muttered with a hint of a tremor in his voice. He stared hard at the floor, or at some memory only he could see. He was breathing like he was under the strain of a great weight.

'Physically?' Kovac asked. 'Sexually?'

The kid shook his head, but the movement was small, almost as if he was saying no to himself rather than to Kovac's questions. No, he would *not* talk about this.

'Do you think Sato put Diana up to going to the Office for Conflict Resolution?' Kovac asked. 'To mess with your father's chances at the promotion?'

'He certainly didn't try to stop her,' Charlie said sarcastically. 'She wants to please him.'

'And piss off your old man at the same time? Bonus. Did your dad know she was sleeping with Sato? Is that what they argued about Sunday night?'

If that was the case, Lucien Chamberlain could have used that information against Sato. Which would have been worse in the eyes of the university: a professor who created a hostile work environment with his bipolar grad student daughter, or a professor who slept with his rival's daughter as a power play? Kovac had to think Sato came out with the short end of that stick, no matter Sato's comment from the night before when he implied he had no fear of losing his job over his relationship with the girl.

'They were going to resolve their issues,' Charlie said. 'They just had to cool off. They were going to meet — '

'Only, your father had no intention of going to that meeting,' Kovac said. 'On Monday he called his attorney's office and made a Wednesday appointment for the same time of day. Now, in my experience, when a parent and an adult child have a big argument and the next day the parent is calling his attorney, that means one thing: he's changing his will. And when that parent turns up dead before that change can happen, we call that motive.

'Is that where the argument went Sunday night, Charlie?'

The kid shook his head vehemently. He was close enough that Kovac could see the tears rising in his eyes. His face was as red as if he was holding his breath against the need to scream.

'The old man had just had it with Diana's behavior, and said enough was enough,' Kovac suggested. 'He was disowning her, writing her out of the will. I can see that. He probably never wanted her in the first place, right? I mean, he doesn't strike me as a kid person, from what I've heard about him — especially not someone else's kid. And then it turns out she's defective, with the bipolar disorder. He probably wanted his money back.'

'Stop it,' Charlie said, his voice barely above a whisper.

Kovac knew he had hit a nerve. He felt a little rotten about it, but it went with the job. He had to keep poking until he found a raw patch, then dig in.

The tears were welling up and spilling over, streaking down Charlie Chamberlain's cheeks despite his efforts to hold them back. He scrubbed them away with the back of his good hand.

'Do you know who killed your parents, Charlie?' Kovac asked quietly.

'No.'

'Do you think Diana knows?'

He kept shaking his head. 'She didn't do this. It was a robbery. His picture was all over the news at noon. Why didn't you tell us about that? There's a manhunt for a suspect, and you never even mentioned it to us.'

'I don't know what the media is saying,' Kovac said. 'We don't know enough about the guy to even call him a suspect.'

'That's bullshit. This handyman did it, and you're wasting time accusing my sister — '

'I'm not accusing your sister, but who could blame her if she had something to do with it?' Kovac pressed. 'Your old man was a piece of work. You two couldn't do anything right. You couldn't make him happy. Kids deserve parents who love them. Diana lost out on that twice

— dumped by her birth mother, then gets adopted by a drunk and a tyrant who was ready to disown her. That's gotta hurt.'

'Stop it!' Charlie shouted. He glared at Kovac, tear-wet eyes narrowed. 'You don't know anything about us!'

Kovac lifted his hands in surrender. 'I'm trying to learn. Enlighten me, Charlie.'

A framed photo in the bookcase caught Chamberlain's eye. He stared at it for a few seconds then snatched it off the shelf and hurled it at the fireplace. The frame hit the brick and the glass shattered. He stormed out of the room and out the front door.

Kovac winced and swore under his breath as the door slammed. He watched through the bay window as the kid hustled down the sidewalk to his car. He might have pushed too hard. Charlie was a smart kid with legal training and connections. He had only to pick up a phone and one of his bosses would be recommending criminal defense attorneys. The second that happened, there would be no more access to the two people closest to the victims. If Charlie lawyered up, he would make sure Diana did, too.

'You okay?' Taylor asked, hustling into the room. 'He didn't punch you out, too, did he?'

'Not because he didn't want to,' Kovac said. 'I might have just screwed that up. I had him right on the edge, and I took one step too many.'

He went to the fireplace and picked up the now-broken picture frame Charlie had thrown. The glass was shattered. A spiderweb of cracks seemed to dissect the family in the photograph, separating the subjects from one another. The Chamberlain family: Lucien and Sondra, Diana and little Charles — the kids maybe eight and six respectively.

Fitting, he thought. It seemed they hadn't been as much a family unit as four individuals who happened to live under the same roof. Lucien Chamberlain had been the center of his own universe. Sondra Chamberlain created her own world of committees in the afternoons and wine at night. Diana lived in her own world, a victim of her mental illness and whoever wanted to take advantage of that. And then there was Charlie: the good kid, the peacemaker, trying to keep the family ship upright and balanced.

'The kid has twenty-four years of rage bottled up inside of him.'

'Do you think he might have unleashed it on his parents?' Taylor asked.

'I don't know.'

He tried to imagine Charlie Chamberlain in that role. It seemed anyone who had to butt heads with Lucien Chamberlain could have been driven to want to kill him. But want-to and follow-through were two different things. Could the boy who had always played the peacemaker, backing down and working around his father's ego rather than challenging him, have taken that giant leap to murder? Could he have chosen a sword from the wall in his father's study and hacked his mother to death? Sondra Chamberlain had been nearly decapitated. Her wounds had been so catastrophic that she had to have bled out in a matter of minutes. Could her own son have done that to her? He thought about Ken Sato's efficient movement with the sword in the study.

'He's spent his life trying to fly under the radar and maintain the status quo with the old man,' Kovac said. 'It would make more sense for him to take out Sato. He hates the guy messing with his sister. And if Dad gets the promotion, nothing else matters. That's all the professor cared about. If he had had clear sailing for the job, his conflict with the girl would have been moot.

'Did you get anything out of the other two?' he asked.

Taylor shook his head. 'They left. Sato was too pissed off. The girl was too hysterical. They went out the back door.'

Kovac set the broken picture frame aside and dug his phone out of his pocket to check his messages. There was no news from Tippen or Elwood.

'What did the girl have to say about her rehab history?'

'She was vague. She danced around every-thing: the rehab questions, the abuse questions. I never got a straight answer. She did say her parents always wanted to give her back to wherever they adopted her from. That's some-thing every kid wants to hear from Mom and Dad,' Taylor said sarcastically.

'Wow,' Kovac said. 'I threw that idea out at Charlie just to goad him — that the old man was going to change his will and disown the daughter. He should have punched me.'

'It's sad,' Taylor said, looking around the room, with its expensive antiques and its photographs of an unhappy family. 'These people seemed to have everything to give kids a good upbringing: education, financial security . . .'

'Money doesn't cure people of being narcissistic assholes,' Kovac pointed out. 'Get everybody's phone records. Landlines and cell phones for our vics and for the three amigos. I want a time line of every phone call, starting Sunday evening.'

'Done,' Taylor said. 'We should have the records by the end of the day.'

'Good.'

'You know they're all probably calling lawyers as we speak.'

'Probably,' Kovac conceded. 'I thought we were being clever bringing them here. Instead we're up for the Clusterfuck of the Year award.'

Taylor shrugged then winced and rubbed at his stiff neck. 'Seemed like a good idea at the time.'

'Yeah, well . . .' Kovac nodded. 'I've said for years that's going on my headstone.'

*   *   *

Kovac closed his eyes and dozed in the car on the twenty-minute drive to the office of the Chamberlains' insurance agent. As much as he hated to give up control and let the kid drive, he needed a rest, however brief. He was dog tired. Not for the first time (or the hundred and first time), he thought, I'm getting too damned old for this. In the next thought, he wondered what Liska was doing. He wondered how bored she was. He thought of cold case squads as the place old Homicide dicks went when they couldn't keep up anymore. Then he remembered with no small amount of depression that he was an old Homicide dick.

He looked at Taylor out of the corner of his eye: a man just coming into his prime, smart, fit, hungry, good-looking. All the things Kovac had been nearly two decades ago. Well, he admitted, he'd never been that good-looking. He had probably never been that fit, either. He had to grit his teeth against the urge to groan as he got out of the car at the insurance agent's office, his body protesting old injuries and the lack of sleep.

The agent, Ron Goddard, a short, bald Buddha of a guy, met them at the receptionist's desk with a friendly smile and showed them down a narrow hall to his small office, which looked out onto the parking lot. He closed the blinds with a twist of a wand and went around behind his desk.

'I can't believe what happened,' he admitted as he took his seat. 'Twenty years in this business and I've never had a client murdered. A college professor and his wife. A nice home in a good neighborhood. You just don't expect a murder.'

'They weren't expecting it, either,' Kovac said.

Goddard shook his head. 'I told Professor Chamberlain he'd be wise to upgrade his security system. The technology today is amazing.'

'Why didn't he?' Taylor asked.

'He didn't see the need. The system he had worked well. They had never had any serious crime in the neighborhood.' He made a sheepish face. 'And to be perfectly honest, he was cheap. Or maybe it's more accurate to say he was paranoid. He always thought people were trying to rip him off. I had to work to get him to insure the household contents for replacement cost. He thought I was just trying to make a bigger commission.'

'What about the collection?' Kovac asked.

'That was his passion. He was more reasonable about that. The collection had a separate policy.' Goddard placed three binders side by side on the desk and tapped each one in turn. 'Household, jewelry, and the collection. The inventories and appraised values. You can take those. I printed them out for you.'

Kovac picked up the binder for the collection and started to page through it.

'There's a DVD in each one, too,' Goddard said.

'The son gave us one of those,' Kovac said.

'Charlie. Nice young man. He tried to convince his father to upgrade the security, too. Typical twenty-something tech-savvy kid. If I didn't have one in my family already, I'd go out and adopt one,' the agent said with a chuckle. 'My phone is smarter than I am. These gadgets are going to take over the world.'

'When was the last appraisal done on the collection?' Taylor asked.

'Five years ago. I had it in my pending file to

suggest to Lucien that he might want to have it reappraised next year, just to be sure nothing had changed significantly. To my surprise, he called me Monday and asked about just that.'

'He wanted to have the collection reappraised?' Taylor asked. 'Did he say why?'

'He said he was planning to donate it to the university.'

Kovac came to attention. 'He what?'

'I was shocked myself,' Goddard said. 'He's spent his life building that collection. But the university is going to be doing a big expansion of the Asian studies program. Lucien felt he could donate it, get plenty of notoriety and whatever kudos the university would give him. He wanted to get the appraisal first to be sure to get every nickel of his tax deduction.'

'Had he told anyone at the U about this?' Kovac asked.

'I wouldn't know. But it would be like him to get the appraisal first. He liked his ducks beak to tail.'

'What about his kids?' Taylor asked.

Goddard made a little frown. 'He said it was his collection to do with whatever he wanted, not theirs.'

*   *   *

'There's the professor's end-around play,' Taylor said as they got back in the car. 'He could blow off the Office for Conflict Resolution if he thought he had something that trumped his disagreement with Diana.'

'He was going to leverage the collection for the job,' Kovac said. 'If he had had that *and* knowledge of Diana and Sato's affair, Sato wouldn't have been just dead in the water as far as the promotion was concerned. He could possibly have gotten rid of Sato altogether.'

'Smells like motive to me,' Taylor said. 'If Sato knew about it.'

'I tried to get Charlie to tell me what the big fight at Dad's birthday dinner was all about,' Kovac said. 'But he wouldn't spill it.'

'If Daddy threw his new big plan in Diana's face, she would have gone straight to Sato and told him,' Taylor said. 'Suddenly they're both better off with Lucien Chamberlain out of their lives.'

'Sato knows how to handle a sword.'

'But on the mother?' Taylor said. 'That's still a sticking point for me, no pun intended.'

'She's collateral damage.'

'That attack was so vicious.'

'Or it was the fastest, most expedient way to kill her. Sato told me the first strike would be at the neck and shoulder. Mrs. C was nearly decapitated. She would have died quickly.'

'Try selling that to her daughter.'

'I think Diana believes whatever she needs to believe to get the reality she wants. Don't you?'

Taylor thought about it for a moment. 'Yeah, you're probably right about that. She seems erratic, but that's her logic system at work.'

'And maybe all the wailing and screaming is grief magnified by guilt,' Kovac said.

'Neither of them has an alibi.'

'The phone records might tell a story.'

'I'll get right on it.'

'Good,' Kovac said, leaning back in the seat and closing his eyes. 'Wake me up when you've got something.'

22

'I'm really sorry to bother you,' Nikki said as the latest owner of the old Duffy house invited her inside.

'It's not a problem at all,' Bruce Larson said, wiping his hands on a dishtowel. He was a big burly bearded lumberjack of a man, a look contradicted by a chef's apron with DOMESTIC GODDESS embroidered on the chest. 'It's kind of exciting, to be honest.' He made a comical face. 'David, my partner, told me I probably shouldn't admit that out loud.'

Nikki toed her shoes off. 'Not everyone can say they had a famous murder in their backyard.'

'Do you really think it can be solved after all these years?'

'Never say never.'

'We are the biggest fans of true-crime shows,' Larson admitted. 'I was saying to David, we could end up being in an episode of *48 Hours* or *Dateline* or something. How crazy would that be?'

'Pretty crazy,' Nikki agreed. 'I just want to have a look out the window of the one bedroom, and then I'll be out of your hair.'

'Sure. I'll take you up,' he said, gesturing her toward the stairs.

'Don't let me keep you from your cooking. It smells amazing.'

'Not a problem. The meatloaf just went in the

oven. The best thing about this time of year is the menu, right? Comfort food. My famous Italian meatloaf and heart-attack-in-a-hot-dish macaroni and cheese. I'm a personal chef. I'll give you a card before you go.'

Nikki checked her watch as they went into the bedroom. The boys would be getting home, and she had nothing planned for dinner.

'Was the tree stump still here when you bought the house?' she asked.

'Yes, and was that thing a bitch to get out of there!'

'Can you point out where it was?'

He joined her at the window. 'Where the fire pit is.'

Visible from where they stood, but not if she backed up more than a few feet. Jennifer Duffy had been on her bed or in a chair, reading a book. She couldn't have seen anything. Nor could she have seen where the shots came from — especially considering it was nearly dark at the time of the shooting. Nikki had figured as much. She had wanted to get into this room more to imagine Jennifer in here, nine years old and hiding out from the chaos of her family.

'Cozy room,' she said, glancing around.

Larson and his partner had it ready to welcome a guest, with an antique iron bed with a small mountain of pillows, a patchwork quilt tossed across the foot. There was a small dresser and an upholstered armchair, and bedside tables draped in lace.

'Thanks,' Larson said, then his smile dropped. 'You don't think the killer shot him from here, do you?' he asked, torn between horror and excitement at the thought.

'No,' Nikki said. 'We know the shots came from the park. The victim's daughter was in this room at the time. I just wanted to know if she might have been able to see something.'

She imagined the world beyond the lacy curtains dark and cold, Jennifer tucked up against the pillows with her foster sister Angie reading in the amber glow of the bedside lamps.

That wouldn't have happened if they hadn't been close, Nikki thought. What teenage girl would go out of her way for a lonely little bookworm if she didn't feel a connection to the girl? Certainly little Jennifer had looked up to her surrogate big sister. Certainly she would have known if Angie Jeager had a boyfriend, or if she had been friends with the boy next door.

Nikki looked across the backyard to the second story of Donald Nilsen's house.

'How well do you know your neighbor? Mr. Nilsen?'

Bruce Larson rolled his eyes dramatically. 'Better than we would care to. He's a horrible, hateful old homophobic geezer. That's the Discovery ID show we'll probably end up on — the one where the neighbor from hell ends up killing us.'

'That bad?'

'You have no idea. The first thing he did when we moved in was tell us he doesn't approve of our lifestyle — and I'm phrasing that politely. Then we started remodeling the house, and he was a nightmare. He was constantly complaining about the noise, about the workmen's trucks. He kept reporting us for whatever imagined infractions he could come up with — which only prolonged the project of course.

'When we took that stump out, he tried to get us in trouble for that. We planted a vegetable garden. He complained about the tiller.

'Every time we have guests over for a cookout or a party, and we're in the backyard, he calls the cops to complain. And it's not like we're out there dancing naked and having a Roman orgy. We're quiet guys. We like to cook and eat, and drink good wine. Our friends are professional people. We talk about books and movies and politics. I'm sure Donald Nilsen hasn't read a book since *Mein Kampf*.'

'If it's any comfort, he doesn't like heterosexual couples with families, either,' Nikki said.

Larson shook his head. 'He hates everyone. He's the most miserable man on the planet.

'We had a big Labrador when we first moved here. Duck was his name. Nilsen constantly complained about Duck. The dog barked too much, the dog jumped over the fence and shit on his lawn. Nilsen actually threatened to shoot him! And he meant it! He was raving like a lunatic one day, waving a rifle around! It was crazy! I took pictures of him on my phone because I was afraid no one would believe us. David called the police. They talked Nilsen down and told us to keep the dog away from him, and put up a better fence. We should have pressed charges is what we should have done.

'We put up the privacy fence, and Nilsen

complained about that. I wanted to go over there and shit on his lawn myself.'

'What happened with the dog?'

'He died. I would bet money the old man poisoned him, but we couldn't prove it. What kind of person does that? Sick bastard.'

'You could move.'

'The hell with that,' Larson said. 'We've put heart and soul into this house. We like it here. The neighborhood is in an upward transition. He's an overweight old man with rage issues. He'll stroke out one of these days, and a gay couple will buy his house, and we'll all live happily ever after.'

'In the meantime, stay on your side of the fence,' Nikki said, moving toward the door.

'You don't think *he's* the killer, do you?' Larson asked, following her down the stairs. 'Oh my God!'

'I really can't comment on the case,' Nikki said, stepping back into her shoes. 'Thanks for your time, Mr. Larson.'

'No problem. Come back if you need to.'

He handed her a business card on her way out. 'Just in case.'

'Wishful thinking.' Nikki took the card and slipped it in her coat pocket. 'The only way I'm getting a personal chef is if I marry one.'

'Sorry, I'm taken,' he said with a smile. 'I bat for the wrong team anyway.'

'My luck,' Nikki said. She started to turn for the door, then stopped and turned back to him. 'Do you by any chance still have the photo of Donald Nilsen with the rifle the day he threatened to shoot your dog?'

'Sure, of course. I never delete photos unless I look fat in them. Everything else gets put in a folder on the computer.'

'Could you show me?'

'Sure.'

He led the way to a slightly messy home office and sat down at his computer. With a couple of clicks of the mouse, he opened his photo app and went directly to a file labeled REMODEL. There had to have been a hundred or more thumbnail snapshots, but he found the one he wanted quickly, and enlarged it to fill the screen. He had a series of five photographs of Donald Nilsen, red-faced, his expression contorted in anger, a small rifle in his hands.

A chill of excitement ran down Nikki's back. Goosebumps raced down her arms. Her heart had picked up a beat, but she kept her expression calm.

'Look at that lunatic,' Bruce Larson said with disgust. 'There are little kids in this neighborhood, and he's in his yard waving that thing around!'

He looked up at Nikki. 'That's not the murder weapon, is it? I mean, if he did it, he would have been arrested back then, right?'

'Mr. Nilsen had an alibi,' Nikki said. 'I'm just covering all the bases. Would you mind e-mailing those five photos to me?'

'Sure, no problem. I'll do it right now.'

'Thank you.'

*   *   *

Nikki went back out into the miserable drizzle, jamming her hands into her coat pockets and hunching her shoulders against the raw cold. What gray daylight they had had was fading. The streetlights had already come on. Lights had come on inside Donald Nilsen's house, but not on his porch. He wasn't inviting anyone to come knocking on his door. Nikki knocked on it anyway.

The old man came and peered out at her through the sidelight, his face sour.

'I don't have anything more to say to you,' he announced, cracking the door open. He glanced toward the house next door. 'Was that faggot complaining about me?'

He had seen her coming from Larson's house. He probably kept tabs on everyone in the neighborhood.

'I have some additional questions for you, Mr. Nilsen.'

'I don't have to talk to you,' he snapped. 'I know my rights.'

'Fine,' Nikki said. 'Then you know you have the right to remain silent and you have the right to an attorney — '

'You're arresting me?' Nilsen's face went bright red beneath his white crew cut. 'You can't do that!'

'I've got a badge here that tells me I can if I feel the need,' Nikki said, pulling her ID out of her coat pocket and holding it up, selling the bluff. Mascherino wouldn't approve, but Mascherino wasn't here.

'I've had a long day, Mr. Nilsen,' she said.

'And I'm tired and I'm bitchy, and I'm not messing around here. I have reason to believe you're in possession of a hunting rifle that happens to match my murder weapon. So, if you're not going to cooperate, I'll make your life inconvenient just because I can. From what I've heard from your neighbors, past and present, you're more than familiar with that tactic. So let's get on with it.'

He stepped back, stunned to silence for the few seconds it took Nikki to slip past him into his entry hall.

'I'll report you,' he threatened, slamming the door shut behind her.

'You do that,' she said. 'I could use a vacation. Meanwhile, until I get suspended, I'll get a search warrant and go through every piece of crap in this house on the grounds that you have a history of making terroristic threats to your neighbors, and because I believe you to be in possession of a rifle of the same caliber used to kill Ted Duffy. How about that? You want to try to trump that?'

'I had an alibi — '

'*Had* being the important word there. Your wife, who hasn't been seen or heard from since shortly after the murder.'

He didn't deny it. He went on the attack instead. 'I'll sue!'

'Well, everybody in prison needs a hobby, I suppose.'

'You don't have any grounds to arrest me!' he protested, as if saying it again and saying it louder made it so. 'I'm a law-abiding taxpayer!'

'Really?' Nikki said. 'Let's start with hindering a police investigation. You lied to me, Mr. Nilsen. You told me your son is dead. Your son isn't dead, is he?'

'He's dead to me,' the old man snapped, looking to his living room, where electric logs were glowing orange in the fireplace, and Fox News was playing on the television.

'That's not the same thing as actually being dead, now, is it?' Nikki said.

She glanced up at the wall over the small cabinet in the entry, at the senior-year photo of Jeremy Nilsen. He was a handsome kid, looking very serious in a suit and tie. A quiet boy, according to Barbie Duffy. Polite. He must have taken after his mother, she thought.

There was no photograph of him in uniform, which struck her as odd. She would have thought Donald Nilsen the type to be loud and proud to have a son serving his country.

'So the neighbor you didn't get along with gets murdered, and within two months, your wife disappears and your kid drops out of school and joins the army,' she said. 'Is there a reason nobody wanted to stick around for you, Mr. Nilsen?'

'He wanted to be a soldier,' Nilsen said. 'He turned eighteen and signed up. I couldn't stop him, and why would I? Saved me having to pay for college.'

'And maybe you gave him a little push out of the nest,' Nikki said. 'Maybe that's why you're lying to us now. You don't want us talking to him about what happened to Ted Duffy.'

'You don't know what you're talking about.'

'So what's your problem, anyway?' she asked. 'Your son served his country. You should be proud of that. What kind of father isn't proud of that?'

Nilsen made a bitter face and tried to turn away, waving a hand at her, as if to make her disappear.

Nikki put herself in front of him again. 'Are you ashamed of him because of the psych discharge?'

'He's weak,' he grumbled. 'Like his mother. He always was.'

'He joined the army,' Nikki said. 'He served in combat. That sounds like the opposite of weak to me.'

'You don't know anything about it!'

'You're pissed off at him because war wounded his mind?'

'He's an embarrassment! He always was.'

'No. I see who the embarrassment in this family is,' Nikki muttered.

Nilsen wheeled on her like a wild animal, coming at her, screaming in her face, 'You don't know anything! Get out of my house! Get the fuck out of my house!'

Nikki stumbled backward and banged hard into the small cabinet, knocking a pile of junk mail to the floor and tipping over the small lamp. Nilsen drew his fist back as if he meant to strike her. Nikki drew her gun and pointed it in his face.

'You need to seriously rethink your attitude, Mr. Nilsen,' she said calmly. 'Back off. Now.'

He took a step back, huffing and puffing, his eyes still bulging in his red face. 'You provoked me — '

'Shut the fuck up!' Nikki snapped, lowering the weapon. 'I'd ask if you're senile, but according to the Duffys, you were an asshole twenty-five years ago, so I have to assume nothing has changed.'

He started to grumble something else. She cut him off with a look.

'I should haul you in right now,' she said. 'You're damn lucky I didn't pull the trigger. If I made decisions the way you do, you'd have a hole in your head the size of Iowa right now.'

Her brain was already rushing ahead to the hassle of taking him in and charging him with attempted assault. It wouldn't be worth the paperwork. He would be seriously inconvenienced, but so would she, and at the end of the day he would get kicked loose anyway because he was an elderly taxpaying citizen no one would consider anything more than a harmless old nuisance who hadn't actually laid a hand on her.

She would miss dinner with the boys.

'Where's your son?' she asked.

'I don't know.'

'I swear to God, Mr. Nilsen — '

'I don't know!' he shouted. 'I don't want to know.'

'Where was he the last you knew?'

He looked down at the floor and mumbled, 'The VA hospital.'

'When was that?'

'Years ago.'

'You haven't had any contact with him at all?'
'No.'

Nikki stared at him for a long moment, wondering what could ever make her cut ties with one of her boys the way Donald Nilsen had with his. She couldn't think of anything. They were a part of her and she was a part of them, no matter what.

She wondered if Donald Nilsen's wife felt the same way, wherever she was. Maybe they were together someplace, mother and son, living in paradise without the man who had undoubtedly made their lives miserable. But Nikki didn't really believe that. In her experience, most stories like this one didn't have a happy ending. Damage didn't get undone.

Donald Nilsen had gotten a good look by previous investigators. None had considered him a strong suspect. At the time of Ted Duffy's murder, Nilsen's wife was around to give him an alibi. Later, no one believed he had sufficient motive. But he'd felt he had sufficient motive just now to haul off and clock a police detective for punching his buttons. He'd felt sufficient motive to threaten the neighbor's dog with a rifle for taking a crap on his grass. How much motive did a man like this need?

'Barbie Duffy told me you took a little too much notice of the two foster girls living with them, and that Ted had a talk with you about it. What do you have to say about that?'

Nilsen glared at her. 'Nothing.'

'If I go digging back into your history, am I going to find anyone who accused you of messing with young girls?'

'I never did!' he protested.

He didn't say no one had ever accused him. He denied the charge.

'Do you own a .243 deer rifle?'

'No.'

'Have you ever?'

'No.'

'You're lying. I just saw five photographs of you holding that gun. You threatened to kill your neighbors' dog with it.'

He couldn't argue that. He chewed on his frustration like he was chewing on a dirty rag, his mouth twisting at the taste.

'Would you mind showing me the guns you have?' Nikki asked, knowing he would say no. She knew once she was out the door she wasn't getting back inside this house without a warrant.

'Get out of my house,' he said, coldly calm now. 'I'm calling my attorney.'

Damn. Mascherino was going to kill her.

'You can call him from downtown,' she said, mentally kissing dinner with the boys good-bye. 'You're under arrest for attempting to assault a police officer.

'You know the rest of the song,' she said, pulling out her handcuffs, 'but let's sing it anyway. You have the right to remain silent . . . '

23

Lieutenant Mascherino stared at her across the desk. 'Is it possible for you to go one day without offending someone to the point that they threaten legal action?'

'Apparently not,' Nikki said. She felt like she was thirteen again and sweating it out in front of the principal for filling the Home Ec teacher's car with packing peanuts. Only the Home Ec teacher couldn't get her fired from her job.

'Mr. Nilsen's attorney has already called to inform us he will be suing for false arrest.'

'Yeah, he's got that guy on speed dial,' Nikki said. 'The ink's barely dry on his paperwork.'

Not equipped for transporting a suspect, she had called from her car for backup, and had turned Nilsen over to a pair of uniforms who had taken him to be booked and put in a holding cell. He could rot in there for all she cared. He had invoked his right to an attorney. She couldn't speak with him at any rate, being the victim of the charge against him. She had beat it back to the office and written up her report and the affidavit for the search warrant as fast as was humanly possible without forgetting to dot all the *i*'s and cross all the *t*'s.

'Anyway, it wasn't a false arrest,' Nikki argued. 'If I hadn't drawn my weapon, he would have punched a hole through my face. I'd probably be stored in his basement now with his missing wife and son.'

'He's seventy years old.'

'So? He's had a long time to perfect being an asshole and a bully. Ask Seley. He was aggressive and antagonistic the first time we saw him. Ask his neighbors. He has a history of bad behavior.'

'The press is going to portray you as the bully, Nikki.'

'The press?' She dismissed the idea. 'Nilsen likes to make noise, but I don't think he's going to want to talk to the media now. He's a suspect in a murder investigation. Feed that to the newsies.'

'Is he?' Mascherino asked. 'Really?'

'He is until I'm convinced otherwise.' Nikki ticked the reasons off on her fingers. 'He had a beef with Ted Duffy, he's a red zone rageaholic, he owned a rifle of the same caliber as the one that killed Duffy, and his alibi for the time of the murder hasn't been seen or heard from in twenty-five years. I want a warrant to find that rifle.'

'Nobody is going to give you a warrant based on your speculation.'

'I have photographs of him holding a rifle. He attempted to assault me while I was questioning him with regard to the homicide. He was subsequently put under arrest. I don't get a warrant off that? Are you kidding me?'

The lieutenant arched an eyebrow. 'Was that your reasoning for arresting him? To get your warrant?'

'Partly,' Nikki confessed. 'He was going to

make a big stink either way. I figured I had better have a paper trail documenting his behavior, even if the county attorney's office doesn't prosecute the charge.'

'Which they won't.'

'That's on them.'

Mascherino sighed the sigh of a long-suffering mother. 'Why do I get the uncomfortable feeling you're already familiar with this particular defense?'

Nikki shrugged. 'The best defense is a good offense. I've got Seley digging hard on Nilsen's past. Ted Duffy gave him a warning for taking too much interest in their teenage foster girls. I think Duffy might not have been the first person to look sideways at this guy. If Nilsen felt threatened enough, could he be violent? Absolutely.'

'Was he a serious suspect when the murder occurred?'

'At the time, he had an alibi witness. He got looked at later on, but no one thought he had sufficient motive. I disagree. I think there's something there. Before, the focus was on bad guys Duffy had put away, or was trying to, or it was on the brother and the wife — and that's certainly a viable theory. I'm not discounting that one at all. Both the wife and the brother made money off Ted Duffy's death, and lived happily ever after together. But in all this time no one has cracked their story.

'Meanwhile, I think Nilsen is hiding some-thing. He lied to me about his son being dead. What's the point of that?'

'What would his son have to do with this?'

'He was a senior in high school when the murder happened. He used to mow the Duffys' grass and shovel their sidewalk. He might have been friends with the girls next door. He was at a school event when the murder took place, so I don't know what his role in this might be, but the old man lied to us about him, and I want to know why. The son would have been well aware of the bad blood between his father and Ted Duffy. Barbie Duffy said he came to the funeral with his mother. Then Mom disappears and Junior gets shipped off to boot camp.'

'Have you found the son?'

'No. Nilsen claims he hasn't seen his son in years. There's bad blood there. Why?'

'Have you spoken with the Duffys' foster daughters? Did they make any accusations against Donald Nilsen at the time?'

'Nothing on the record. The one is dead,' Nikki said. 'She was found raped and strangled about six months after the Duffy murder. The crime was never solved. The case file was actually already in the stack on my desk.

'Seley just got an address for the older girl. She's my age now. I'll talk to her tonight — unless I'm executing my search warrant,' she said, raising her brows hopefully.

'Go talk to the woman,' Mascherino said. 'I'll call Logan and see what we can do.'

'Awesome. Thanks, LT,' Nikki said, getting up to leave. 'And I want to execute the search tonight. If he gets released, the first thing he's going to do is go home and get rid of that rifle.'

312

Mascherino gave her a look. 'Anything else? A red carpet to the front door?'

Nikki grinned. 'Naw, that'll do.'

'Please try not to strong-arm anyone else tonight,' the lieutenant said. 'You're turning my roots gray, and I don't have time to get them done. Please take Seley with you. So you have a witness.'

★ ★ ★

'Nilsen has never been charged with anything,' Seley said as they left the office. 'You would think if Ted Duffy had anything on him with regard to some kind of sexual assault charge, he would have done something with it.'

'Maybe he didn't get the chance,' Nikki said. 'How long were these girls with the Duffy family?'

'Less than a year. They got placed there in June. The murder took place at Thanksgiving time.'

'Tomorrow I want you to call Nilsen's former employer and see what they have to say about him.'

'I can't imagine anyone who was there twenty-five years ago is still around.'

'It's doubtful, but there should at least still be people there from his last years with the company. He can't have been retired for that long. If he's the kind of creeper who's looking at teenage girls, some client along the way might have complained. That behavior isn't something men outgrow or retire from.'

They got in the car and headed south, merging into the still-heavy traffic on 35W. The pavement glistened wet under the headlights. A steady drizzle was still falling.

Nikki wanted to be snug and warm at home. That had been the whole point of going to Cold Case: regular hours. Instead, she drove past the exit that would have taken her to her neighborhood. If this former foster child of the Duffys' had something to contribute to the conversation about Donald Nilsen, that could be the piece of information that locked in her search warrant for the Nilsen house. And there would go the rest of the evening ... But she couldn't take a chance on Nilsen's posting bail and going home to get rid of any souvenir he might have hung onto from all those years ago.

'If we get this search warrant for Nilsen's house, he'd better have his dead wife in a barrel in the basement,' she grumbled.

'Better hope he has that deer rifle.'

'I'll bet a week's pay he still has the gun. Hunters like their trophies. He'd still have the gun in lieu of Ted Duffy's head on his wall. Besides that, I'll bet he's a cheap old bastard. He probably hasn't thrown anything away since Reagan was president.'

They took the Crosstown Highway and exited into a neighborhood not unlike Nikki's — tree-lined streets and well-kept homes of a mix of styles popular in the forties and fifties; the kind of neighborhood where people lived quietly and raised their kids to go to church on Sunday.

'So, the story on this girl is what?' she asked.

'Angie Jeager was in and out of foster care growing up,' Seley said. 'Her mother was in and out of psychiatric facilities. She died of a drug overdose four months before the Duffy murder, so the girl was with the Duffys when it happened. When Barbie Duffy sent the girls back into the system, Angie was put into a group home. When she aged out of foster care, she had no family to go to, and apparently she ended up on the street. She has a yellow sheet full of petty drug stuff and prostitution.'

'She must have turned herself around at some point,' Nikki said. 'She's not turning tricks in this neighborhood.'

'My friend at DCFS told me she's a Chrysalis Center success story. They pulled her out of a bad situation. She ended up getting a degree in social work.'

'Good for her.'

'Actually, I think she was quoted in that article about Chrysalis in the *Trib* a week or so ago,' Seley said. 'Talking about girls aging out of the system.'

It broke Nikki's heart to see kids fall through the cracks. The social services system left a lot to be desired, but at least kids trapped in it got fed and had a roof over their heads. The second they aged out of the system, however, there was no safety net. They were thrown into the world like baitfish in a shark tank. They had no place to stay, no money, no means to support themselves.

Most homeless shelters wouldn't take them, reserving their spots for women with small children. A lot of them ended up on the street.

Most of them were barely educated because of the chaotic nature of their lives and the lack of adult support. The lack of education made job opportunities scarce. And most businesses wouldn't hire a homeless person anyway. Employers wanted stable individuals with real addresses, but it was impossible to get a real address without real money, and difficult to get money without a job.

Caught in a downward spiral, these kids were easy prey for drug dealers and pimps. Angie Jeager was lucky to have caught the attention of someone from the Chrysalis Center. Good on her for making the most of her chance.

'This is it, on the right,' Seley said, and repeated the address.

The house was a cute little English-cottage-style, like something found in the enchanted forest of a fairy tale. A fall wreath hung on the arched front door. Amber lights glowed in the multipaned windows.

'She's married now,' Seley said. 'Her last name is Burke. First name, Evangeline.'

Nikki rang the doorbell and they waited in the rain. They had not called ahead. She preferred seeing a person's honest reaction to a cop showing up on their doorstep.

A tentative voice came from behind the door. 'Who is it?'

'Minneapolis Police Department,' Nikki said.

She pulled her ID out of her coat pocket and held it up so it could be seen through the peephole. A second later, locks were being undone.

The woman who opened the door was Nikki's age, pretty in a girl-next-door kind of way, with light brown hair and big blue eyes.

'Did Kate send you?' she asked.

'Kate?'

'Kate Quinn. From Chrysalis.'

'No,' Nikki said. 'You're Evangeline Burke?'

'Evi. Evi Burke. Yes,' she said, clearly confused.

'I'm Detective Liska; this is Detective Seley. We have some questions for you.'

'This isn't about the note?'

'May we come in?' Nikki asked, ignoring her question. 'It's a little wet out here.'

'Oh. I'm sorry. Of course,' Burke stammered. 'I'm so sorry. Making you stand in the rain . . . '

She stepped back into the house and allowed them to come in, but Nikki could feel her resistance. Not many people were happy to see them. Even the perfectly innocent wanted them to go away as soon as possible, as if their presence might attract some dark force into their homes.

Nikki pulled her hood down, ruffled a hand through her hair, and unzipped her jacket, giving the impression she was ready to settle in for a while.

At a glance, she could see that Evi Burke's home had a cheery feel, with a palette of soft yellow, blue, and white. It had undergone a remodeling at some point, the walls having been opened up so that the spaces flowed one into another. From the entry she could see the living room, a section of the dining room, and the staircase that led up to the second-floor bedrooms.

'What a lovely home,' Seley said, smiling, setting a friendly tone.

Evi Burke wasn't buying it. She didn't smile back. She tucked a stray strand of hair behind her ear and crossed her arms in front of her defensively. 'Thank you. I'm confused. If you're not here about the note, I don't understand what you're doing here.'

'I know Kate,' Nikki said to further confuse the woman. 'I haven't seen her in a while. How is she?'

'She's fine.'

'She's a great advocate for victims.'

'Yes, she is,' Burke said, shifting her weight from one foot to the other, impatient.

'Why would she be sending detectives to your house?' Nikki asked.

'I work for the Chrysalis Center. We have a client about to testify against some potentially dangerous people.'

'You said something about a note?' Seley asked.

'Someone sent me a note that was vaguely threatening. My husband is a firefighter. He's not always here at night. Kate said she would ask for extra patrols in the neighborhood. I just assumed you had something to do with that.'

Kate would have gone straight to Kovac with that request, Nikki thought, knowing he could pull some strings and knowing he was incapable of saying no to her. He'd been half in love with Kate forever, though he would never admit it.

'Would you mind if we sat down?' Nikki asked. 'I'd like to know more about this note.'

It was the perfect hook to get them away from the door. Once they all sat down, it became harder to get rid of them without being rude.

Evi Burke nibbled at the corner of her lip. She wanted her problem taken care of, and here were two people who might be able to help her.

'Ah, sure. Yes, of course,' she said, still reluctant. 'Let's go into the dining room.'

She turned to lead the way. Now she had invited them into her lovely, cozy home, and she would feel obligated to be a good hostess.

'Would you like some tea?' she asked. 'I was about to make some for myself. I already put the water on. I just got my daughter down to sleep.'

'Tea would be lovely,' Seley said. 'How old is your daughter?'

'Five.'

'That's a great age.'

They shrugged off their coats and took seats at the small round oak dining room table. A woven basket of gourds and miniature pumpkins served as a centerpiece. A kindergarten Thanksgiving turkey craft project made from construction paper sat on an antique sideboard across the room.

'Would you like help?' Seley asked.

'No, no. I've got a tray,' Burke said, disappearing into the kitchen.

She was back within minutes, setting the tray on the table and pouring the hot water into a trio of pretty mugs.

'So, who's after this client and why?' Nikki asked, selecting an Earl Grey tea bag.

'Chrysalis pulled her out of a sex trafficking

situation with a very bad pimp by the name of Drago,' Burke said, taking her seat. She perched on the chair like a nervous little bird, ready to take flight at the first sign of danger. 'He's still on the loose. But she came out of a religious cult background with her family before that. She's going to testify to some pretty horrific abuse by her own brother.'

'What does the note say?' Nikki asked. 'Do you have it?'

'No, I gave it to Kate. It said, 'I know who you are. I know where you live.''

'That's it?'

'Yes.'

'Do you have any idea what that's supposed to mean?' Seley asked. 'Aside from the obvious. Do you feel like you're being watched?'

Burke made a little fluttering motion with her hands. 'I assume that whoever sent it knows I'm affiliated with Hope's case, and that they've somehow managed to get my address.'

'But there was no specific reference to the case?' Nikki asked. 'No actual threat?'

'No.'

'Have there been any other notes, threats, calls? To you or to anyone at Chrysalis?'

'No.'

'Has the girl been threatened directly?'

'No, but she's in a safe house.'

'So, why you?' Nikki asked.

She gave a little shrug, a little shake of the head, looking a little more worried than a moment ago. 'I don't know. I'm Hope's social worker.'

'Exactly,' Nikki said. 'You're her social worker, you're not her attorney, you're not her legal guardian — if she has one. You're not the figurehead of Chrysalis. Why would anyone come after you?'

'I don't know. I just know I got the note.'

'Is there any other reason someone would be targeting you?' Seley asked. 'Someone who might have a grudge against you?'

'No,' she said, looking genuinely baffled.

'I saw the feature on Chrysalis in the paper,' Seley said. 'Could this be somehow related to that?'

'I don't know.'

'When did you get the note?' Nikki asked.

'It was in yesterday's mail.'

Nikki sipped her tea and considered the timing as she jotted notes in her little spiral notebook. The newspaper article on the Chrysalis Center had come out a little over a week before. The announcement of the Cold Case investigation into the Duffy homicide had happened Tuesday. The note to Evi Burke had come in Wednesday's mail.

'Evi, we're actually from the Cold Case unit,' she said. 'We're investigating the Ted Duffy murder.'

Evi Burke sat up a little straighter. Her expression went carefully blank. She felt ambushed. She was thinking Nikki and her partner had weaseled their way into her home under false pretenses, and now she was trapped.

'I can't be of much help with that, I'm afraid. I wasn't there when it happened.'

'You were at a school function that night?'

'A basketball game. I didn't get home until nine thirty or ten.'

'Were you with Jeremy Nilsen?' Nikki asked.

'No,' she said, looking confused. 'Why would you think that?'

'Jeremy was supposedly at the game, too.'

'I saw him there. I wasn't with him. He was a grade ahead of me.'

'Were you friends?'

'Not really. Just to say hi, you know: small talk at the bus stop.'

'But you remember seeing him at the basketball game?'

'Yes,' she said. 'I remember because I had a crush on a guy he hung out with.'

Nikki paused in her scribbling and glanced up at her. 'What was his name?'

'Oh my God, you're kidding, right? It was twenty-five years ago. I can't even remember what he looked like.'

'What was it like, living with the Duffy family?' Seley asked.

She gave the little half shrug. 'It was okay. Better than a lot of places in the system.'

She fussed with her teaspoon. Her hand was trembling when she picked it up, and it clanked against her mug. She put it down. 'I don't like to talk about that time in my life,' she admitted. 'It's my past, and that's where I want to leave it. I live in the present now.'

'Yet you work with girls who have been in that same dark place,' Seley said. 'That's commendable.'

Burke seemed uncomfortable with the praise. She didn't know quite where to look. She made another small nervous gesture with her hand. 'I'm only doing what I wish someone would have done for me — what Chrysalis did do for me in the end.'

'You went by Angie back then,' Nikki said.

' 'Evangeline' seemed incredibly uncool at the time, so I became Angie.'

And when she hadn't wanted to be Angie — the foster child, the orphan, the homeless kid with a pile of horrible memories — she had become Evi, Nikki surmised.

'I spoke with Jennifer Duffy this afternoon,' Nikki said. 'She has some fond memories of your time with the family. She said you used to read to her. She's a librarian now.'

'That's good. I'm glad for her. She was a sweet girl.'

'She had a rough time after you left. She had a rough time over her dad's murder. I think it haunts her that it happened right under her window. Not that she could have done anything about it, but she was right there. Kids think the world revolves around them. Something bad happens, they think it must somehow be their fault.'

'I'm sorry to hear that.'

'What was your impression of the family? Did they seem happy? Was there any tension between Ted and Barbie?'

She sighed, uncomfortable again.

'Mrs. Duffy was . . . very demanding,' she said, choosing her words carefully. 'Penny and I were supposed to do all the housework and babysit the kids when she was at work or wanted to go out. Mr. Duffy was hardly ever there.'

'Go out where?' Seley asked.

'I don't know. In the summer she was gone a lot. Shopping. Lunch with her friends, I guess. She worked nights, slept until noon, and then would be gone a lot in the afternoon.'

'So, you and Penny Williams were basically servants.'

'Pretty much. Yes.'

'What was Mr. Duffy like?' Nikki asked. 'Did you get along with him?'

She looked down into her tea as if she might see the memory playing there like a movie on a screen. A sad movie. 'He was always tired and angry, and he drank too much. When he was home he didn't want to be bothered with the kids. He spent most of his time in his office with the door shut or in the basement. He had a workbench down there.'

'How did Mr. and Mrs. get along?'

'They fought a lot. Not big fights, just constant sniping. She nagged him all the time. He called her Barbie the Ball Buster. It was sad, really.'

Sad for Angie Jeager, too, Nikki thought. The one thing a foster child needed most was a sense of safety within a family. Safe was the last thing kids felt when the adults in their lives didn't get along.

'Did they argue about anything in particular?' Seley asked.

'Money. How he wasn't home enough, didn't

take care of things around the house. That kind of thing.'

'Did Mr. Duffy's brother come around a lot?'

'Sometimes it seemed like he was there more than Mr. Duffy. He came over and fixed things around the house when Mr. Duffy didn't get to it quickly enough for Mrs. Duffy's liking.' She shook her head a little. 'I'm surprised I remember that much. That was two lifetimes ago.'

'Did you ever think there might be something going on between him and Mrs. Duffy?' Nikki asked.

'I never thought about it. I never saw them kissing or touching or anything. Although, I did think it was kind of mean the way she would use one brother against the other that way,' she said. 'Like Ted wasn't a good enough husband, so she called in his twin. She wasn't a very nice person, but, on the other hand, she gave a home to two foster kids.'

'Did anyone ask you these questions at the time?' Nikki asked.

'Not really. They asked where I was when it happened. That was about it.'

As Nikki had suspected. The detectives on the case initially had been focused on who Ted Duffy was to them: a Sex Crimes top cop with a lot of enemies in and out of jail. Their other focus had been on the love triangle theory. They had discounted the viability of the kids as witnesses to the Duffys' relationship. The Duffy kids had seemed too young. The foster girls weren't considered part of the family. Angie Jeager had been out that night; therefore they thought she couldn't be useful.

'What can you tell us about the next-door neighbor, Donald Nilsen?'

'Oh, he was a horrible person,' she said without hesitation.

'Barbie Duffy told us he took a little too much interest in you and Penny. Did he approach you? Talk to you?'

She gave an almost imperceptible shudder of distaste. 'He was always staring at us,' she said. 'In the summer, Penny and I liked to lay out in the backyard to get a tan — and we weren't naked or anything. We wore shorts and bikini tops, and we stayed close to the house.

'He'd be looking at us from inside the house or he'd find some excuse to be in the yard, and he'd yell at us to go put more clothes on. He'd call us sluts. He was so creepy. If he didn't want to see us, why was he always staring at us? He was one of those: Think evil thoughts and blame the victim.'

'Did he ever do more than stare?' Nikki asked. 'Did he ever lay a hand on either of you?'

'He grabbed Penny by the arm once. She went right up to him in his yard one day and called him a dirty old man. He grabbed her by the arm, hard, and started screaming in her face. It was scary.'

'What happened?'

'Penny kicked him in the shin, and he let go. We ran back home.'

'Did you tell anyone about this?'

'We told Mrs. Duffy. She told Mr. Duffy. He

went over to the Nilsens' house and had a conversation with Mr. Nilsen.'

'Did you witness this conversation?'

'No.'

Nikki sat back again and had another sip of tea as she played the scenario through her head. Was that enough reason for Donald Nilsen to plot Ted Duffy's murder? It didn't seem to be, but they didn't know what Duffy had actually said or how he had put it. He could have issued a mild, vague warning, or he might have thrown his badge around and made a threat of jail time.

'What happened after that?'

'Mr. Nilsen stopped talking to us. He still looked. He still said things about us, just not to us.'

'Were there any run-ins with him in the week or two prior to Mr. Duffy's murder?'

'There was always something,' she said. 'He thought the Duffys overdecorated for Halloween. Their leaves blew onto Mr. Nilsen's yard. He was just a horrible person.'

'Did you interact at all with Mrs. Nilsen?' Seley asked.

'No. I hardly ever saw her.'

'What about Jeremy?' Nikki asked.

'What about him?'

'What was he like?'

Again with the little one-shoulder shrug. 'He was quiet. He was nice enough.'

'Not like his father?'

'He was *nothing* like his father.'

'Did they seem close — him and his dad?'

'It's hard to imagine Mr. Nilsen being close to

anyone. He was so angry all the time.'

'And you weren't friends with Jeremy?' Nikki asked again.

'No, not really.'

'That's funny,' she said, pretending confusion, 'because Jennifer told me this afternoon that you and Jeremy were close.'

'I don't know why she would have said that. But she was just a little kid. She probably just assumed. I said hello to him. I talked to him once in a while when I saw him. I'd take him something to drink when he was mowing the lawn. That kind of thing.'

'I suppose that's possible. She seemed very matter-of-fact about it,' Nikki lied, thinking back to the questions she had asked Jennifer Duffy — or, more accurately, how Jennifer Duffy had responded. She claimed not to know if Angie and Jeremy were friends, which didn't make sense. How could she not know? But why would she lie about it? Maybe there simply hadn't been anything to know.

Evi smiled a sad, fond little smile. 'Jenny liked stories with handsome princes who saved the day. I guess she imagined one for me and Jeremy. I never told her the world doesn't often work that way.'

'So I guess we can assume you haven't kept in touch with Jeremy over the years,' Nikki said.

'No.' She shook her head. 'I didn't even finish the year at that school. I got moved to a different district. It's hard to make friends when you move around that much. It's even harder to keep them.'

'Jeremy joined the army not long after you left,' Nikki said. 'He was discharged some years ago. We're trying to locate him, but we can't seem to find him.'

'Sorry I can't be of more help,' Evi said, getting up. 'Would you like more tea? I'll turn the kettle on.'

'No, thank you,' Nikki said, pushing her chair back. 'We've taken up enough of your time. I'll leave you my card. Please call if anything comes back to you. Anything at all.'

She placed her business card on the table near the centerpiece.

'As for your other situation, keep your doors locked. I'll put in a call and make sure the extra patrols are happening.'

'Thank you.'

Evi Burke followed them to the front door and locked it behind them. As they hustled through the drizzle to the car, a police cruiser rolled slowly past.

'Filthy weather,' Nikki muttered, starting the car and turning on the defrosters.

'Not a pretty picture of the Duffy family,' Seley said. 'They were coming apart at the seams. I'd love to know where Barbie was going every time she left those kids alone with her personal house slaves.'

'Yeah, and I'd like to know what Ted Duffy threatened Donald Nilsen with.'

'Something worth killing over?'

Nikki put the car in gear and pulled away from the curb. 'Let's go see if we can find out.'

24

Evi closed the door and turned the locks. She was trembling, and angry with herself for it. It had been so many years since she'd talked about that time in her life. Angie Jeager was someone she used to know, not someone she wanted to acknowledge still lived inside her. She had to think of it that way — that that girl was someone different from the girl who had lived on the streets, and the girl who done terrible things to survive on the streets was not the young woman who had finished college or the woman she was today. She tried to keep each version of herself in its own box, and kept all the boxes closed and locked as well as she could manage.

Two detectives had just pried the lid off one box and allowed the contents to spill out.

Evi knew from experience that every version of herself would come crawling out tonight in her dreams. She would see them, one looking accusingly at the next, all of them stalking the woman she had fought to become, doing their best to tear her down. Who did she think she was, having a nice life? Why did she think she deserved to succeed? She could call herself whatever she wanted, but beneath the façade of her too-perfect life she was still just Evangeline Grace Jeager, the abused, abandoned daughter of a drug addict. No matter what she did with her life, she couldn't change what had been done to her life. She couldn't change who she had been or the things she had done to save herself.

All those other versions of her had dreamed of the life she had now, and had seen it as a life not meant to be, nothing but the foolish wish of a lonely child. Now she had that life, and she did her best every day to believe it was real, that she wouldn't wake up as Angie Jeager, living in a filthy hotel room, smoking dope to dull the pain of her reality.

She went to the kitchen and busied herself cleaning up. She had just started the supper dishes when the doorbell had rung. Now she had to drain the cold water and start over. As the sink filled and the soap bubbled up, she stared out the window at the black emptiness of the backyard.

The memories rolled through her mind. She could see the chaos of the Duffy house — toys everywhere, the piles of half-read newspapers, the stacks of mail, the dirty dishes in the kitchen, the piles of dirty clothes in the laundry area in the basement.

The smell of the basement came back to her with the memory: vaguely musty and moldy. It was always just a little damp down there. Most of the basement was unfinished and dark. With the exception of the finished laundry/workbench area, the only light in the rest of the space was supplied by a couple of bare-bulb fixtures screwed to the floor joists overhead.

She had always hated going down there. She didn't do well in dark, creepy places where early memories could crawl out of the corners like snakes on the floor.

She had spent three days in a dirty old basement when she was little more than Mia's age, with nothing to eat but junk food and soda her mother had left in a grocery bag, and only some blankets and pillows, and her dolls for comfort. Meanwhile, her mother had partied upstairs. Three days of drugs so she could do what she had to do to make enough money to pay the rent. Evi had stayed in the basement, trying not to cry loud enough for anyone to come looking for her. The men who came to see her mother frightened her more than the dark and the bogeyman.

When Anna Jeager finally came off her high and sobered up enough to realize what she had done, she spent two hours sobbing and apologizing, holding Evi so tight she could hardly breathe. When the emotion subsided, her mother had calmly called Child Services to report herself, and then locked herself in the bathroom and tried to slit her own wrists, not the first of many suicide attempts.

Evi suffered through that memory every time she went into the Duffy basement to do their laundry, going down the old stairs into the dim maze of open stud walls dividing the space into potential rooms. Only the area with the laundry and Mr. Duffy's workbench was finished and well lit, a strange oasis in the dank and dark, like a stage set for a play.

Some nights, Mr. Duffy would come downstairs to sit at his workbench and clean his guns, which unnerved her. Growing up, she had learned early on not to trust men, and most especially not to trust men who drank. She would watch him from the corner of her eye as she rushed to do her work. He would sit at his workbench ten feet away, slowly taking a gun apart, carefully cleaning each piece as he smoked a cigarette and sipped at a glass of whiskey while old rock music played on the radio.

He had probably been handsome when he was younger, Evi thought at the time — which now seemed ridiculous to her as she stood in her kitchen washing dishes. She was older now than Ted Duffy was at the time of his death. He had been in his late thirties, but he looked older, harder, worn out by his life. Gray threaded through his black hair. Lines dug deep around his mouth and across his forehead.

'I'm just trying to escape,' he said one night a month or so after she had moved in. 'I'm not here to scare you.'

'I'm not scared,' she said, too quickly.

He gave her a look. 'You realize I get paid to know when people are lying, right?'

He smiled a little to himself when she didn't answer. His eyes were blue and sad behind the amusement. He had seen a lot, she supposed, doing what he did. He knew all about women like her mother. He knew all about girls like her.

'We're all just inmates, sweetheart,' he said, taking a sip of his whiskey. 'Trying to make it through our stretch.'

She folded a T-shirt on the counter and set it aside. She would have taken the clothes upstairs to fold, but Mrs. Duffy got mad when the clothes were wrinkled from being thrown in the basket warm from the dryer.

'You could just leave,' she said. 'If you don't want to be here.'

She didn't mean the basement. She had seen and felt the tension between him and his wife. She had heard the way Mrs. Duffy spoke to him, always critical, usually angry. He shot back with sarcasm. They were like snipers in a street war. Full-on battles were loud and nasty. But more often than not, he disengaged and stormed off to his office or to the backyard, where he chopped wood with vicious intent.

'Could I?' He lit a fresh cigarette and blew the smoke up at the ceiling. 'Naw . . . You can run from your problems, but you can't run from yourself. I just try to escape for a while. In here,' he said, tapping a finger to his temple. 'Down here,' he said, gesturing to the half-finished space around them.

The basement was one of the ongoing fights between him and his wife. Barbie wanted the space finished with a big family room, an out-of-her-hair place to corral the kids and their friends. So far, all that had been finished was this area. 'So far' had been going on for several years. But if the space remained unfinished, it could remain Ted Duffy's refuge. If he finished the space, it became something else.

'You know that's what your mom's doing when she takes drugs, right?' he said. 'She's trying to escape. She can't deal with the reality of her life, and so she tries to escape. But we can't escape who we are. That's the thing. We

334

can't ever really escape. We can just go to the basement for a while.'

'Do you know my mom?' she asked cautiously, watching him from under her lashes as she folded another T-shirt.

'No.' He picked a fleck of tobacco off his tongue and flicked it away. 'I know a hundred women like your mom,' he said, his voice tired and rough with a rasp of liquor and smoke. 'And a thousand men like me.

'We're a cautionary tale,' he said with a sarcastic half smile. He lifted his glass in a small toast, then tossed back the last of his drink. 'Find something to do with your life that doesn't make you hate the world, Evangeline.'

She had, but not before she had seen the worst the world had to offer. Not before she hated the world and everyone in it — herself most of all.

She wasn't afraid of Ted Duffy after that night. She just felt sorry for him. He was a sad man with a sad life who, in the end, died a sad death.

The water in the sink had gone cold again.

Evi pulled the drain plug and turned away, grabbing a towel to dry her hands. The weight of her past had exhausted her. She went and sat down in the dining room, elbows on the table, her head in her hands. That past seemed so long ago — three lifetimes at least. But one knock on the door, and here it was again, twenty-five years later, like it was yesterday.

She picked up the business card the detective had left on the table and stared at the name of the woman who had pried loose the hinges of that box in her memory, setting all those faces free in her mind.

SERGEANT NIKKI LISKA, DETECTIVE CRIMINAL INVESTIGATIVE DIVISION, HOMICIDE

Twenty-five years later someone had finally come to ask her what she knew about the death of Ted Duffy.

Evi closed her eyes against the tumult of memories and emotions, and thought, *Everything*.

And when she opened her eyes and looked around at the life she had fought so hard to get, she knew she would do everything in her power to keep her perfect present from being tainted by a past she couldn't change.

25

'Diana Chamberlain did twenty-eight days at Rising Wings a year ago,' Tippen announced. 'The straight and narrow is hard to walk when you're high on cocaine.'

'There's no arrest on her record from last year,' Taylor said, looking disturbed that he might have missed something. He pulled a file from the stack on the table and started flipping through the pages.

'That's because there was no arrest.'

'She went voluntarily?' Taylor asked with disbelief. 'Was she hot for one of the counselors?'

'Only the ones with penises. Substances are not her only addiction,' Tippen said. 'She was working as a research assistant for one of her father's cronies that summer while Dad was off communing with the Shaolin monks in the Songshang Mountains of China. She came to work high one day. He called her on it. She begged him not to tell her father. He said only if she went to rehab.'

'Who volunteered all this information?' Kovac asked, digging a fork into a carton of Mongolian beef. He felt slightly more human after a couple of hours of sleep, a shower, and a fresh shirt.

'She listed the professor as a contact on the paperwork the rehab administrator wouldn't hand over. I have an uncanny ability to read upside down, you know. One of my many hidden talents.'

'Most of which should remain hidden,' Kovac remarked. 'Did you talk to the professor?'

'Professor Roland Landers,' Elwood said, sniffing the aromas as he perused the open cartons on the table. 'He's writing a biography of Millard Fillmore. The girl was supposed to be helping gather and organize his research.'

'Jesus,' Kovac grumbled. 'I'd be doing cocaine, too.'

'Fillmore's wife, Abigail, had the first bathtub with running water installed in the White House.'

'Fascinating.'

'Landers was happy to fill us in,' Tippen said. 'With Professor Chamberlain dead, he didn't feel any need to be loyal to the daughter.'

'So the bottom line here is that Diana Chamberlain could possibly know Gordon Krauss,' Taylor said. 'You searched his room?'

'No ninja weapons, no samurai swords, no bloody clothing. He did have about twenty-five hundred dollars in a sock stuffed into the toe of a boot, and half a dozen different IDs — none of which belong to a Gordon Krauss,' he said. 'He could be James Gilliam. He could be Clyde Dodson. He could be Jeremy Nilsen — '

'So we don't even know who this guy really is.'

'We lifted fingerprints from the room,' Elwood said. 'Hopefully he's in the system.'

'If he's a vet, he's in the system,' Taylor said.

'There's probably a better chance of him being a criminal than being a veteran,' Kovac said. 'And if Diana knows this guy, then there's a connection through her for Sato or the brother, or any combination of all of them to hire this mutt as a hitman. They all benefit one way or another from Lucien Chamberlain's death.'

'But we don't know that Diana knew Krauss was working for Handy Dandy, or that she knew anything about her mother calling Handy Dandy to do the repairs. That could be a coincidence,' Taylor said.

Tippen and Elwood winced and howled like they were about to witness a car crash in an action movie.

'There's no such thing as coincidence,' Kovac growled. 'Never, *never* overlook anything in an investigation based on the assumption that it might be a coincidence. Assume every person of interest is, deep down, stinking rotten to the core,' he said, stabbing his fork in the air for emphasis. 'And always believe they all have the potential to be in cahoots with one another.'

'Yes, sir,' Taylor said.

Kovac gave him the stink eye, in case he was being a smart-ass. 'What did you come up with in the phone records?'

Taylor went to a large portable dry-erase board he had filled with columns — dates, times, names — all in meticulous printing with a different color marker for each person.

'Starting Sunday night we have multiple calls from the Chamberlain landline to Diana's cell phone. None of them lasts longer than thirty seconds.'

'Straight to voice mail,' Tippen ventured.

'They had the big blowout at dinner,' Kovac

said. 'That's probably Mom trying to connect, maybe trying to mend fences.'

'There's one longer call to Charlie's cell.'

'Mom crying on the kid's shoulder,' Kovac speculated. 'He's had to function as the adult in the family all along, watching out for his sister, keeping the peace between the parents.'

'Charlie calls Diana. Again, it doesn't look like she probably answered,' Taylor said. 'They connect Monday at twelve seventeen P.M. and speak for forty-three minutes. Charlie then calls the professor's cell number, and they speak for eight minutes. It looks like Mrs. Chamberlain tries throughout the day to get through to Diana, but she also calls the number for Handy Dandy Home Services at one-o-seven in the afternoon, and that call lasts twelve minutes.'

'Where the hell are you? Why haven't you fixed the whatever? Get your worthless asses over here and blah, blah, blah,' Kovac said. He looked to Elwood and Tippen again. 'What about the other handyman? Verzano?'

'We've got nothing on him other than the fact that he's been in the Chamberlains' house, and that the professor wasn't happy with the job,' Tippen said.

'He denies any involvement. He says he doesn't know where Krauss is, that he doesn't hang out with the guy, that he's worked with him only a few times,' Elwood added.

'He did hint that he thought Krauss was a bit of a twitch,' Tippen added.

'Oh yeah, sure,' Kovac grumbled. 'The missing guy is conveniently the twitch.'

'We took his prints,' Elwood said. 'He objected to that, citing his Third Amendment rights.'

Kovac rolled his eyes. 'A freaking constitutional scholar.'

'He seemed confused when I explained to him that our taking his fingerprints for elimination purposes had nothing to do with the quartering of soldiers in private homes.'

Elwood chose a carton of stir-fried vegetables and chopsticks and sat down to eat, his brow furrowed beneath the short brim of his porkpie hat. 'He could have theoretically made a Fourth Amendment argument. He would have lost, of course, but still . . . ' He sighed. 'I find it deeply disturbing that the average citizen isn't better informed.'

'The average citizen knows more about Kim Kardashian's ass than the Constitution,' Tippen cracked. 'For that matter, half the politicians running for president know more about Kim Kardashian's ass than the Constitution.'

'Can we discuss the decline of civilization later?' Kovac asked. 'You got his prints, and . . . ?'

'They're being processed now. His prints might legitimately be in the kitchen of the Chamberlain house,' Tippen said. 'But they won't legitimately be in the professor's study or in the dining room.'

Kovac looked to Taylor again. 'Go on.'

'There are no calls from Diana to Rising Wings, or from Diana, Sato, or Charlie to Handy Dandy or to Dan Franken or Gary Verzano,' Taylor said. 'There are still a couple of numbers from Diana's phone, and from Sato's phone, I've got to run down.

'This doesn't show the professor's call to his attorney or the call to the insurance agent regarding a new appraisal of his collection,' he went on. 'He probably made the calls from his office phone. We can get those records if need be, but because it's the university, there's extra red tape.'

'Did you speak to Forrest Foster?' Kovac asked.

'Yes. He had no idea Chamberlain was planning to give the collection to the university. They hadn't spoken about it. But he did say Chamberlain made a cryptic remark the day before about having an announcement to make at the meeting on Wednesday morning. It didn't mean anything to Foster at the time.'

'Yeah,' Kovac nodded. 'Chamberlain made that decision during or after the fight at dinner Sunday. That's my guess. He was getting set to put himself in the catbird seat for that promotion. Was there any indication of communication between Chamberlain and the daughter or between Chamberlain and Sato?'

'No. None. There were calls between Diana and Sato, but neither of them contacted or were contacted by Lucien Chamberlain.'

'Since we can only speculate as to the contents of any of these conversations, what else is interesting here?' Tippen asked. 'Is there anything odd or out of place?'

'Yes,' Taylor said, tapping his finger beside a call noted in pink marker. 'Sondra Chamberlain didn't use her cell phone at all from Sunday evening until Tuesday evening, when she called Charlie. He told us she'd left a message for him, which he didn't listen to until the next day, after his parents had already been killed.'

Tippen shrugged. 'So?'

'So that's the anomaly,' Taylor said. 'If she made all her other calls in that time period from the landline — including a call to Diana just minutes *after* the call to Charlie — why did she call Charlie on her cell?'

'Maybe she'd misplaced the phone and had just found it again,' Elwood offered. 'My mother has never gotten the hang of having a cell phone. She loses it, she forgets to charge it.'

'Maybe. But why switch back to the landline right after?' Taylor shrugged. 'I don't know what it means. It's just the odd thing. Looking back on the rest of the month, she made or received a few calls a day on the cell. There were no long gaps with her not using the phone.'

'Do you think the kid lied about the call?' Kovac asked. 'Why would he? I mean, there it is right there.'

'I don't know. He didn't have to say anything about it at all, so there wouldn't seem to be a point to lying about it. And he seemed genuinely upset about not having taken the call,' Taylor said. 'That just makes it stick out all the more.'

Tippen's cell phone rang. He pulled it from his pocket and stepped away. Kovac watched him, taking another bite of his Mongolian beef and chewing slowly.

'Dan Franken will have to change the name of

his business to Handy Dandy Home Invasion,' Tippen said as he ended the call. 'Greg Verzano's prints were on Lucien Chamberlain's desk, *and* Mr. Verzano has a record.'

26

'You've got your search warrant,' Mascherino said. 'Or, more accurately, I've got your warrant. Because of the situation between you and Mr. Nilsen, Chris Logan and I agreed it would be best from a legal perspective if I went with you on this.'

Nikki nodded, itching to go. 'I'm cool with that. You, me, Seley, and two uniforms. Let's do it.'

'Not so fast,' the lieutenant said, stopping Nikki mid-turn as she went to exit the office. 'We can search for the rifle and for ammunition for the rifle, and that's all. That's the scope of the warrant.'

'I can live with that. All I want is the gun. Where's Nilsen right now?'

'He's still in custody, but he won't be staying long.'

'Then let's get on it so we can get this accomplished without him ranting and raving in the background,' Nikki said. 'The sooner we're at it, the sooner we're done. I'd like to get home before my boys go to bed.'

'Are they home alone?' Mascherino asked as they left the office.

'God, no. Maybe I'll leave them unsupervised when they're out of college,' Nikki said. 'I'm renting out the other half of my duplex to a cousin of mine who's going through a divorce.

He's a private tutor. He works right there. His clients come to him. He's happy to check on the boys and hang out with them if I'm hung up on a case. The kids love him.'

She had always been clever and lucky arranging backup and babysitters for the boys. Her last tenant had been a graphic designer who worked from home. Marysue Zaytoun had become a great friend as well. Nikki had hated to see her go, when she got married and moved on with her life. Then Cousin Matt announced the end of his marriage, and the other side of the Liska duplex seemed the perfect solution for all concerned.

'I had hoped I wouldn't have to call on him much with the move to Cold Case,' Nikki said. 'But here I am.'

Mascherino gave her a look, a knowing smile turning her lips. 'If you wanted a nine-to-five, you wouldn't have put on a badge.'

'I know.'

'We didn't pick an easy ladder to climb, but that's what makes us who we are.'

'You have kids, too.'

'A boy and a girl. They're grown, with kids of their own now.'

'So, they didn't grow up to be serial killers,' Nikki said. 'They're not racking up hours on the therapist's couch because their mom is a cop.'

'They turned out just fine,' the lieutenant said. 'Yours will, too. The fact that you worry about it tells me that much.'

'I don't know,' Nikki said, scraping together a bit of humor. 'I still think Kyle and R.J. will exact their revenge on me when I'm old and decrepit.'

'Oh, they won't wait that long,' Mascherino said as they went out the doors of City Hall and into the damp cold. 'They'll sic their toddlers on you.'

They met Seley at the car and hit the road once more for Donald Nilsen's neighborhood. The rain had dissipated into a thick mist that slicked the windshield on the outside as the defroster struggled to clear the fog on the inside of the glass.

A radio car was waiting at the curb when they arrived. Nikki looked next door, at the house the Duffys had lived in, catching a glimpse of Bruce Larson as he stood in the front room of the house with a coffee mug in one hand, gesturing with the other as he spoke and laughed with someone out of sight. He would be thrilled to know the police were next door, setting the stage for a fresh episode of *Dateline*.

They went into the Nilsen house, leaving one of the uniformed officers to stand guard at the front door. The other paired with Seley to begin the search of the main level. Nikki and Mascherino climbed the stairs to the second floor. They went from room to room, methodically searching closets and drawers, looking under beds and behind dressers — anywhere that could conceivably hide a small rifle or a box of bullets.

There were three bedrooms and a bath on the second floor. Donald Nilsen's bedroom looked just as it probably had when Mrs. Nilsen was in residence: lace curtains and a floral bedspread, wall-to-wall carpeting so old the traffic patterns were worn like trails in the dingy beige pile. Nilsen had made a halfhearted attempt to make the bed, pulling the bedspread up and over the lumpy shapes of pillows. A few articles of clothing were draped over a chair, but other than that, the room was relatively neat. The furniture was a matching suite that had probably been purchased in a store with the word *Mart* or *Barn* in the name — a dresser with a mirror attached, a chest of drawers, a pair of nightstands, a four-poster bed, all made of inexpensive wood stained to resemble mahogany.

Nikki went to Mrs. Nilsen's dresser. Her perfume bottles still sat on a mirrored tray. An assortment of inexpensive jewelry boxes clustered together on the far right, a few pieces of costume jewelry scattered near them. A small dish held odd buttons, a thimble, a needle and thread.

It looked as if Donald Nilsen hadn't touched any of it in twenty-five years. Nikki wondered if he had left it in anticipation of his wife's return or out of apathy for the loss of her. Either way, it struck her as odd. She wouldn't have pegged him for a sentimental man. She would have expected him to get rid of this stuff, to clear out all traces of the woman who had allegedly left him. But the dresser's drawers still held a woman's lingerie and neat stacks of sweaters — all of it smelling vaguely stale, as if the drawers had not been opened, their contents left untouched for all that time.

'Not under the bed,' Mascherino said.

Nikki glanced over at her. 'The rifle or the wife?'

'Neither.'

'When Speed moved out of our house, I threw half his stuff out on the lawn and the other half in the trash. I couldn't clean out our bedroom fast enough,' she said. 'This guy just pretends nothing is different.'

'Maybe it's just easier that way.'

'It's making my skin crawl. If she left him, she didn't take much with her. The drawers are full, the closet has women's clothing in it.'

'Add another unsolved mystery to your stack of cases,' the lieutenant said.

'He never even reported her missing,' Nikki said. 'No one did.'

They moved from the master bedroom to a guest room Nikki couldn't imagine had ever been used. Who would go out of their way to visit Donald Nilsen? He was no one's kindly uncle. The bed was piled with old clothes. Nilsen's hunting coats and caps crowded the closet, but this was not where he kept his guns.

The third bedroom had belonged to Jeremy Nilsen. Just like his wife's portion of the master, Donald Nilsen had left this room just as it was the day his son left for basic training. A thick layer of dust coated the dresser. The bed was neatly made. A modest collection of sports awards was proudly displayed on a little shelf. A poster of Bruce Lee decorated one wall, Bruce Springsteen another.

Nikki felt a pang of sympathy. It couldn't have been easy to be the son of Donald Nilsen, a man hated by the entire neighborhood. It would have been especially hard for a quiet boy with nice manners, as Jeremy had been described. She thought of her own quiet boy, Kyle, always internally at odds with his brash and boisterous father. She wondered if Jeremy's mother had given him the sort of refuge a sensitive boy needed, or if she had been too overwhelmed by her husband to try.

Mascherino checked out the closet. Nikki searched through the dresser drawers. A small desk occupied one corner of the room, with pens and pencils in a Minnesota Twins cup. A U of M pennant was tacked to the bulletin board on the wall above. There was nothing but dust bunnies under the twin bed.

Knowing her own son, and his penchant for secreting things away, she slipped a hand between the mattress and box spring, her fingertips brushing across papers. No, she thought, not paper. Something slicker. Half expecting to find pornography, she lifted the mattress to find a small glimpse of Jeremy Nilsen's private life: two photographs. A chill ran through her.

'We're looking for a gun and bullets,' Mascherino reminded her. 'That's not a gun.'

'Isn't it?' Nikki murmured, picking the pictures up with one hand and lowering the mattress back into place with the other.

The two photos were of a slender teenage girl with long brown hair, smiling shyly for the camera of a school photographer; a pretty girl with sad eyes that had seen too much in her short life. Nikki would have put her at about sixteen.

'Do you know who she is?' the lieutenant asked.

'Yes.'

The friend who wasn't really a friend.

The girl next door.

Angie Jeager . . . Evi Burke.

A shriek of brakes and tires skidding on wet pavement broke Nikki's concentration. Mascherino went to the window that looked out on the street as a car door slammed.

'Here we go,' the lieutenant muttered, her game face firmly in place as she turned and started for the door. She looked at Nikki. 'Let me handle him.'

'I need to ask him about these pictures.'

'That can wait.'

They hustled down the stairs, a commotion on the front steps of the house rising to nearly drown out their footfalls. Donald Nilsen had been released.

' . . . my house, and I'll damn well go inside!'

'I'm sorry, sir, I can't let you go in while the search is under way — '

'I'll have your badge! I'm suing this department and everyone to do with this! This is an outrage! I'm a law-abiding taxpayer. You can't just come into my house — '

'I have a valid warrant, signed by a judge,' Mascherino said firmly as she stepped into the fray. 'This has all been explained to you thoroughly, Mr. Nilsen. You will not be allowed inside the house while the search is being

351

conducted, so you might as well calm down and sit down out there, or go sit in your car — '

'Mr. Nilsen would like to contest the validity of the search warrant,' Nilsen's attorney said, out of breath as he arrived at the front steps. He looked to be about Nilsen's vintage, but twice his girth, a morbidly obese man with a neck so large he couldn't button the top two buttons of his shirt.

'I'm sure Mr. Nilsen would like a lot of things,' Mascherino said. 'But he won't get that one.'

Nilsen's face was purple. Spittle gathered at the corners of his mouth like a rabid dog as he shouted at her. 'I want the name of your captain! I'll put an end to your career!'

Mascherino stood firm, the warrant in her purple-gloved hand, her Mother Superior posture ramrod straight. 'I'll put an end to your freedom for the evening, Mr. Nilsen,' she said. 'If you insist on trying to interfere with the execution of this warrant, I'll have this officer read you your rights and take you straight back downtown. Do you understand me?'

Nilsen sputtered, shrugging off the hand his attorney tried to lay on his shoulder. He peered over the top of Mascherino's head, his gaze fixing on Nikki.

'That one has it in for me,' he said. 'She's probably in there planting evidence.'

'She's doing no such thing,' Mascherino said.

Nikki let his insult roll off. He was a man in a panic. His insular little world was being touched and handled by strangers, his past being dug up like a garden that had been left to the weeds for twenty-five years. Like a cornered animal, he was going to lash out any way he could.

'I'll come out of the house if that makes you feel any better, Mr. Nilsen,' she offered calmly, surreptitiously slipping the two photographs she had found into her coat pocket.

Nilsen looked at Mascherino. 'I don't want that little bitch in my house.'

'It's okay, LT,' Nikki said, slipping past her superior. 'I'll wait outside. It's fine.'

The lieutenant gave her a flat look, her suspicion carefully hidden. Nilsen took a grudging half step to the side to let her out and then followed her down the steps and onto the sidewalk. Mascherino went back to the search, and the uniformed officer resumed his post at the door.

'I'm sure you'll find this hard to believe,' Nikki said as Nilsen and his attorney descended from the porch. 'But I'm very good at my job, Mr. Nilsen. My only focus is solving the crime. I'll do whatever I need to do to make that happen. If that means I wait out here so the search can be done in an expedient manner, then I wait out here.'

He walked past her without so much as acknowledging that she had spoken.

Nikki stood with her hands in her pockets, shoulders hunched against the damp cold, watching while Nilsen dispatched his attorney. The two men stood arguing at the nose of a black Lincoln parked at the curb. The lawyer finally threw his hands up, got in the car, and drove away.

Nilsen came back up the sidewalk, stopping just short of the steps and glaring up at the officer blocking the way into his home. He was breathing hard from aggravation, his face mottled red. He didn't want them in his house. There had to be a good reason for that.

Nikki stood on the lawn just a few feet from him, the damp soaking into her shoes. Hands in her coat pockets, she fingered the photographs of Angie Jeager. Just how angry would Donald Nilsen have been to know that his son had a crush on the tart next door?

'Your son, Jeremy, went to school with the Duffys' foster daughters, didn't he?'

Nilsen ignored her. She could see his pulse in a big vein on the side of his neck.

'Jennifer, the oldest Duffy girl, told me your son and Angie Jeager were friends. That must have been awkward, considering the names you called those girls.'

'That's a lie,' he snapped, unable to leave the bait alone.

'Really?' Nikki said. 'Why would she lie about something like that?'

He didn't answer. He shook a finger at the house. 'If there's one thing missing out of that house, I'll sue.'

'We're only looking for the .243 and ammunition for it. We don't have any interest in the rest of your things, though I find it strange that your wife left so much behind when she took off. She must have been in some big hurry.'

Nilsen glared at her, directing his finger her way. 'If you touched her things — '

Nikki held a hand up. 'I know, I know, you'll sue,' she said on a long sigh. 'So, did Jeremy try to keep it a secret that he was seeing Angie? Or was he one of those kids that just wanted something to throw in your face?'

'I don't have anything to say to you about my son or anything else.'

'I have to think you would have blown a gasket finding out he was seeing that girl behind your back.'

'He wasn't.'

'Then why did I find pictures of her in his bedroom?' Nikki asked.

He flinched just enough that Nikki knew she'd struck a nerve.

'I have two boys of my own,' she said. 'I know all their little hidey holes. The trick to that one is reaching all the way in between the mattress and the box spring.'

The pulse in his neck was pounding harder. She could see the wheels turning in his mind.

'He had a thing for Angie,' Nikki pressed. 'Was he in love with her?' she asked. 'Was that how he disappointed you? Or was he a stalker, like his old man? Was he looking over the fence at that ripe young body, thinking nasty thoughts?'

'Shut up!' Nilsen shouted, suddenly moving toward her aggressively.

From the corner of her eye Nikki could see Stevens, the uniformed officer, start toward them. She raised her hand to hold him off.

'What happened, Donald?' she asked, standing her ground, her focus on Nilsen. 'Did that little slut next door ruin your perfect boy? Or did

Jeremy just help himself to what he wanted?'

'You shut your filthy hole!' he shouted, his face purple in the bright motion sensor light that had clicked on at the corner of the porch.

He stopped short of touching her, his hands raised and clenched in front of him as if he might punch her or strangle her. He leaned down over her, trying to intimidate her with his size and with the hate in his narrowed eyes.

'Or what, Donald?' she asked quietly. 'You'll hit me? You'll choke me 'til I just stop talking? 'Til I just stop breathing? Is that what you did to your wife?'

'You're nothing but a dirty cunt,' he said, his lowered voice much more effective than his usual shouted tirade. Ranting Donald Nilsen was a man capable of throwing things, hitting things, striking out in a heated moment of rage. This Donald Nilsen, with the cold fury contained within, was the kind of man who would hurt deliberately and with malice aforethought.

'You all are,' he murmured. Then he turned and stalked off to the car parked in his driveway.

'You forgot 'brilliant,'' Nikki said as she watched him drive away.

27

'I told you, we saw the stuff through the window,' Greg Verzano said for the tenth time.

He flopped sideways on his chair, exhausted and frustrated. He was a smallish, wiry guy in jeans and a New York Giants jersey, a Yankees baseball cap backward on his head. Twitchy. Nervous. He was the kind of guy who wanted everyone to be light and happy, but this was not a light and happy situation.

Kovac sat across the table from him, stone-faced, unamused, arms crossed over his chest. 'How'd your fingerprints get in that office? Telekinesis?'

Verzano groaned and slumped forward, grabbing his head with his hands. Mr. Drama. 'We saw the stuff through the windows, and we had to go inside anyway to fix the cupboard door in the kitchen. What was it gonna hurt to go look? How many times do you get to see a samurai sword in real life? So I touched it. So what? I didn't steal it.'

'So, Mrs. Chamberlain was killed with that sword, Einstein,' Kovac lied. The sword Sondra Chamberlain had been killed with had yielded no usable fingerprints. 'And your prints are on it. Do you see how, despite the fact that you are annoying as hell, you're making my job easy for me?'

Verzano's eyes went wide, and he threw his

hands up in the air. 'I didn't kill anybody! She seemed like a real nice lady. The husband was a prick, but I didn't kill him, either. I'm not a violent person!'

'You have a conviction for assault in New Jersey.'

'That's because I'm stupid, not violent!' he said earnestly. 'I got into it with a guy over a girl. We were in a bar watching a hockey game. I had too much to drink! I was shit-faced, and here's this hot chick, and she's all smiles and batting her eyelashes,' he said, smiling and batting his eyelashes in his best imitation of a pretty girl. 'And here comes this asshole in a Rangers jersey — and I'm a Devils fan — and he's all 'Fuck off, dude.' Well, she never said she had a boyfriend, so naturally I took a swing at the guy.'

'You did more than take a swing.'

'I landed a couple of lucky punches. You know I used to box a little,' he said, pantomiming a flurry of jabs and hooks. 'And then I was going to switch to MMA and do the whole UFC thing, but then this Brazilian dude kind of fucked up my shoulder 'cause I owed him some money, and then this thing happened with the Rangers fan, and the guy was a dick about it, and he pressed charges.' He shook his head and looked away, speaking to an unseen audience. 'The girl wasn't even good-looking after I sobered up!'

Like that should be considered a mitigating circumstance.

'Franken told me he does background checks on his guys,' Kovac said. 'How'd you slip under the radar?'

'He married my sister.'

So Franken, who could have been looking like the mastermind of a burglary ring, was really just a guy trying to do the right thing, hiring his wife's hapless idiot brother and trying to help out vets and addicts with cash-under-the-table jobs.

'Tell me about Gordon Krauss.'

'What about him? I wouldn't say I really know the guy. I've worked with him a few times, but he's not one to socialize, you know? I mean, I guess he's not exactly gonna hit the bar and hoist a few brewskies with the guys after work — him having a substance issue and all,' Verzano said. He sucked in a quick breath and shrugged. 'He's quiet. It's that Minnesota thing, you know? Like the Vikings — the warriors, not the football team. You know, they don't say much, but don't fuck with them.'

'Don't fuck with Krauss?'

'No, man, the dude knows karate and shit. He was some kind of top-secret Black Ops agent or something in the army.'

'He told you that?'

'Dan told me. Gordon doesn't talk about it. Like I said: a man of few words. I wouldn't mess with him. He gets mad, he goes cold, you know? Internal. Scary.'

'How did he react that day when Professor Chamberlain was unhappy with the work?'

'He didn't like it. The professor or whatever was running his mouth, calling names, calling us idiots and this and that.'

'What did Krauss do?'

'Nothing. He just went cold. I could see it in his eyes. Me? I told the dude he was a douche and he should go fuck himself with his stupid fucking storm windows. Who the hell has storm windows in this day and age anyway? Cheap bastard.'

Kovac pulled a picture of Diana Chamberlain out of a file folder and shoved it across the table. 'Have you ever seen her?'

Verzano's eyes went wide. 'Wow! She is hot! Do you know her? Is she crazy? She looks a little crazy. Totally my type.'

'Jesus H. Christ,' Kovac muttered. 'Are you high?'

'No, not really. Well, I smoked a little weed after the other detective this afternoon, because he made me nervous, you know. I shouldn't have told you that, should I? I'm just nervous.'

'Why are you nervous if you didn't do anything?'

'Because I'm a fuck-up,' Verzano admitted. 'And I've got bad luck. I mean, I didn't do anything bad, and here I am, see? You're telling me I put my fingerprints on a sword that killed somebody. Who has that happen? Me, that's who.'

Kovac rubbed his hands over his face. He should have given this idiot to the kid, and gone home to bed. He leaned over and snapped his fingers in Verzano's face. 'Focus. Have you ever seen that girl?'

Verzano looked at the picture again. 'Yeah, sure. She was there that day.'

Kovac sat up straighter, suddenly wide awake.

'The day you were at the Chamberlain house, she was there?'

'Yeah.'

'You're sure?'

'Dude, seriously?' Verzano said. 'I'm stupid; I'm not blind.'

* * *

Taylor parked in a loading zone in front of Charlie Chamberlain's apartment building, got out, and took a slow walk around. He was supposed to be on his way home to catch some sleep. He'd lost track of the hours he had been going on nothing more than catnaps. But the questions tickling the back of his mind needed to be addressed. If he could get Charlie Chamberlain to speak to him for just a couple of minutes, he could sleep on the answers and let his subconscious mind work while his body recharged.

The building was a plain blond brick rectangle, probably built in the 1960s, four stories tall, eight units per floor. (He had counted the doors the night they first came to talk to the kid.). A utilitarian kind of place, there were no fancy signs in front naming the building, or lovely landscaping dressing the place up. A narrow parking lot ran along one side of the building, one slot per unit. All others had to take their chances finding parking on the street. Chamberlain's car was in its assigned slot.

Taylor walked all the way around the building, looking for visible security cameras, seeing none. Visitors had to be buzzed in the front door via an intercom system. He punched buttons until someone assumed he was the pizza guy. He didn't buzz Charlie Chamberlain's apartment. It was too easy to say no to a disembodied voice. And when he got to the apartment, he knocked instead of ringing the doorbell. Conscientious people were less likely to ignore knocking because of the potential for upsetting their neighbors. He knocked again, loudly.

On the third knock, the door cracked open and Charlie Chamberlain glared out at him. He looked like he'd run into a wall — and had probably had some help doing it. His face was a bruised and battered mess, with a blackening eye and a swollen split lip. His glasses sat slightly crooked because of the damage.

'What happened to you?' Taylor asked.

'Nothing.'

'Did Sato do that to you?'

'I don't have anything to say to you,' he mumbled, talking around the swollen lip.

'Charlie, this is over the line. You popped Sato a good one, but this is assault.'

'I tripped and fell.'

'Into a box of hammers? I know a beating when I see one.'

'Keep your voice down!' he said in a harsh whisper. 'I have neighbors.'

'I'm sure they saw on the news that somebody brutally murdered your family,' Taylor said. 'They shouldn't be surprised that there's a detective at your door. Or is it that you don't want them to see that somebody beat the shit out of you?'

362

Chamberlain swore under his breath as the neighbor across the hall opened her door and peered out.

'Come in,' he said, stepping back. 'But you're not staying. I have to be somewhere.'

'Where?'

'It's none of your business.'

'How's your sister?' Taylor asked, stepping into the apartment. The place was still as neat as a pin. Charlie had gone elsewhere for his beating.

'She's upset. We're all upset.'

He had wrapped gauze around the knuckles of the hand he'd clocked Sato with.

'Did you get that X-rayed?' Taylor asked.

'It's fine. It doesn't matter. What do you want?'

'I have a couple of questions about the last phone call you got from your mother. I was hoping you could help me get a clearer picture as I lay out the time line.'

'Fine. What?'

'Looking at the phone records, I see she called you from her cell phone that night.'

'Yes. So?'

'Did she say anything about having misplaced the phone for a couple of days?'

'No. Why would she?'

'There was a long period of inactivity in the usage records. Then she called you; then she called your sister on the landline.'

Charlie stared at him, looking confused and impatient. 'So what? Our mother was a drunk. She misplaced things; then she found them again. She probably lost the phone and by the time she found it and called me, the battery was ready to die.'

'That could be,' Taylor said, not convinced. 'Would she have been able to disarm the house security system from her phone?'

'She wasn't very good with gadgets — especially after a few glasses of wine — so, no. Why?'

'Do you know if their system has that capability — to run it from an app?'

'I wouldn't know.'

'I'm just trying to reconcile something,' Taylor said. 'The security company said the system was disarmed after midnight. Why would your parents have disarmed the system that late at night?'

'I don't know.'

'We were thinking the perpetrator let himself in through the dining room, then disarmed the system from the panel in the kitchen, but if someone came in through that door, all the control panels would have been beeping until the code was entered. If the system was beeping, why wouldn't your parents hit the panic button upstairs? They couldn't have been expecting company that late at night.'

'I don't know!' Charlie said, exasperated. 'How am I supposed to know? I wasn't there.'

'Could I listen to the message your mother left you that night?' Taylor asked, ignoring Chamberlain's growing sense of urgency.

'No!' Charlie said indignantly. 'Why would you ask such a thing?'

'You were one of the last people to hear from her. I'd like to know her state of mind.'

'She was sad. She was lonely. She'd been drinking.'

'I'd like to hear — '

'Well, you can't! I erased it!' he snapped, pacing now, back and forth, three steps one way, three steps the other way.

'Why would you do that?' Taylor asked. 'That was the last time you will ever hear her voice.'

'And listen to her say how disappointed she is, and how sad she is, and why couldn't I do something about it?' he said, building up a head of steam as he paced. His eyes filled. His voice strained. 'Why would I save that? I have enough memories of her being disappointed in me. I don't have to keep them on my phone.'

'Why was she disappointed in you, Charlie? You're the success story of the family. You graduated, got a good job, never in trouble — '

'Because it's never enough,' Charlie muttered. 'Nothing is ever enough. Something is always wrong or bad or not enough.'

'Well . . . it's over now,' Taylor said.

Charlie stopped his pacing and looked at him, a quiet fury in his eyes.

'You have to go,' he said quietly. 'Please go.'

Taylor hesitated, testing him.

'How did you feel about your dad donating his collection to the university?' he asked.

'What? What are you talking about?'

'We spoke with his insurance agent this afternoon. Your father called him Monday and wanted a new appraisal done because he was planning to donate the collection. Isn't that what you argued about at dinner Sunday night?' he asked. 'He was angry with your sister. Maybe he found out about her and Sato. Did he decide to trump her charge against him by giving his collection to the school?'

'He wouldn't have done it,' Charlie said, agitated. 'He was always making threats like that. He wouldn't have actually done it.'

'Well,' Taylor said with gravity, 'he won't now, will he?'

Charlie Chamberlain's body went rigid; his good hand balled into a fist. His mouth twisted with rage. 'Get out. Get out!'

'Thanks for your time,' Taylor said, stepping slowly toward the door. 'Are you sure you don't want a ride to an ER?'

'Get out!'

The door slammed shut behind Taylor as he stepped into the hall, and the neighbor stuck her head out again and looked at him. Taylor smiled at her and reached into his pocket for his ID.

'Miss, I'm with the police. Can I have a moment of your time?'

28

The nightmare would go on forever, Charlie thought as he paced his apartment, working around his swollen lip to chew on the cuticles of his left hand. His fingernails were already bitten to the quick. The trajectory of their lives, his and Diana's, had been charted before they were even born, without their consent, by women they had never met, and had been moved forward on that line by every event thereafter, hurtling them toward disaster for twenty-four years. This was the life they had been placed into.

What lucky little children they were, they had been told, to be adopted by parents who could give them opportunities and education and life experiences. They had looked like the perfect family from a distance. From within the bubble, their life experiences were learning how to survive in a house where children were not welcome, with parents who had wanted them for all the wrong reasons. They were supposed to be cute and quiet and well behaved, to reflect well on their parents, to be seen only on cue, to speak only when spoken to.

Don't bother your father . . . Mommy has a headache . . . Be quiet! Never touch the things in your father's study! . . . You're dirty! Go wash your face . . . Go change your clothes . . . You're an embarrassment . . . You're a disgrace . . . Behave or we'll send you back where you

367

came from! *Slap! Pinch! Go to your rooms!*

They had spent their childhoods trying to protect and comfort one another. Diana got the worst of it because she asked for it. Charlie always came to her defense. He learned to read the moods of all concerned, and worked to circumvent trouble before it could happen. Meanwhile, Diana ran headlong into it.

Their father belittled Charlie for trying. He called Charlie Diana's minion from the time they were small. Even when Charlie didn't know what that meant, he knew it was an insult by his father's tone and by the sneering face that went with it.

Charlie always thought of himself as his sister's hero — unsung, for the most part. He believed that was his purpose. He had been placed into the life he had to protect her. Diana, more often than not, had no lasting appreciation for his self-sacrifice. She was quick to use him when she needed him, and just as quick to dismiss him after. She used her love as a bargaining chip to get what she wanted from men, including him, and he fell for it every time because she was the only family he'd ever had, the only one who had ever given him any love at all.

There was a part of him that admired her and envied her for her recklessness, her passion, her violence. There had never been a line drawn that Diana wouldn't step across just to defy authority. She did what she wanted no matter the consequences. Charlie didn't have that in him. He was the dutiful son, the rule follower. He worked within the system like a good little drone, ever hopeful he would be rewarded for being a good boy. Diana had no system. She lived on emotion and thrived in chaos.

At times, he even envied Diana her mental illness. Her bipolar disorder was the built-in absolution for everything, from her erratic behavior to her hypersexuality. As much trouble as she got into because of it, she got out of because of it. *Poor Diana, she can't help herself. Poor Diana, the medication has such unpleasant side effects. Poor Diana, she's trying so hard to be good.*

As she moved into her teens, she collected the sympathy and empathy of their substance-abusing mother. She became the key pawn between their parents, a tool used by the passive-aggressive parent against the narcissistic one. But even as angry and vindictive as their father could be, even he couldn't resist Diana entirely — nor could she resist him. Even as she defied him, she wanted his approval. Even as their father tried to control her, he was drawn in by her magnetism, which was so seductive and so twisted.

And Charlie was lost in the shuffle, pushed to the side, called upon when needed by one side or the other. Charlie the Minion.

He stopped pacing and looked at his reflection in the mirrored doors of his bedroom closet. He hated that the detective had seen him looking like this. He felt ashamed and embarrassed. Exposed. He looked ghoulish with his battered, misshapen face and bandaged hand, like the survivor of a zombie movie. He felt just as battered psychologically. This was the internal ugliness of being a Chamberlain seeping outward like a stain.

He had gone to Diana's apartment after the disaster at their parents' house that afternoon. He wanted her forgiveness. He wanted to set her straight, to get her to see Ken Sato for the user he was. She needed to trust him — Charlie. He was the one who had always loved her. He was the one who had her best interests at heart. He was the one who would keep them together, and keep her safe.

She came to the door, her hair down in a wild tangle that tumbled over one shoulder, her makeup streaked with tears, mascara and lipstick smudged.

'I don't want you here, Charlie,' she had said, but she stepped back and let him in anyway. Typically Diana, a walking contradiction.

Her apartment was its usual mess, looking like it might house half a dozen refugees from some war-torn Third World country — clothes discarded everywhere, dirty dishes and glasses in the sink and on the counter, open bags and boxes of junk food sitting around. It smelled like she had forgotten to take the garbage out for a couple of days and then smoked a lot of weed to cover the smell.

'I can't believe you attacked Ken that way,' she said.

'All he's ever done is use you, Di. How can you not see that?'

'He loves me.'

'*I* love you. I told you not to go to the house, and I was right. It only upset you.'

'I'm upset because of you.'

'I broke in through a door for you. You were on the floor sobbing — '

'I'm in mourning!'

'For what? You hated them both!'

'How can you say that? She was the only mother we ever had!'

'That wasn't my choice or yours.'

'She picked me, Charlie,' she said, tearing up again. 'She came to the orphanage and picked me. And now she's dead! And Daddy loved me, too. We didn't get along, but he loved me.'

'Don't rewrite history, Diana. He loved himself,' Charlie argued. 'The rest of us were just there to amuse him or annoy him — you most of all.'

She struck him so fast his cheek was stinging before he realized she'd slapped him.

'It's *my* story,' she said, eyes narrowed as she leaned over him. 'It can be whatever I want it to be. They're gone now. I can remember them any way I like.'

'It doesn't change who they were,' Charlie said.

'Yes, it does!'

In the dark labyrinth of Diana's mind it made sense. Her perception was her reality, as fluid as quicksilver, and just as toxic.

'You were always a problem, Charlie,' she said with disdain.

'*Me*?! I've spent my whole life trying to save you!'

'Well, sorry for wasting your time,' she said, sneering. 'Why don't you go save yourself and leave me the hell alone? I don't need you anymore. I have Ken. He's a *real* man, unlike you, Charlie. You could never make me happy.'

'Don't say that!' Charlie cried. 'I'd do anything for you. You know that!'

'No, you wouldn't,' she said, her expression knowing and mocking.

Tears filled Charlie's eyes. The pain was worse than a knife in his heart.

'Di, don't!' Charlie begged as she turned away from him and started toward her bedroom. For all he knew, Ken Sato was on the other side, waiting to take his sister away from him forever. He would be left with no one. All he had ever wanted was to be loved and accepted, to belong. Fear froze hard in his chest. He reached out to grab her. 'Di, please!'

She spun on him, elbow raised, and caught him hard high on the cheekbone, snapping his head to the left. The second blow exploded against his mouth, the taste of blood like copper on his tongue.

Charlie staggered backward. Diana rushed him, jumping, hitting him in the chest with a knee that knocked the wind from him. He fell hard, the back of his head bouncing off the floor. Colors burst inside his brain, and his vision dimmed.

His sister was on him in an instant, sitting on his stomach, making it impossible for him to get a breath. She hit him again and again, using her fist like a hammer. Charlie raised his arms to block her blows. He begged her to stop, spitting blood and choking on his tears.

Her fury burned out like a flash fire. She got up off him and stood looking down at him as he cried, her eyes as cold and hard as marble. Charlie rolled onto his side and curled into a ball. The pain was unbearable — not from the physical beating, but from within, from his heart. He wanted to die right there.

'You're so weak,' she sneered, and walked away, leaving him on the filthy carpet that reeked of old cat piss.

She didn't love him. After all he'd done for her all their lives, that was the truth: She didn't love him. She wasn't capable of loving him the way he loved her.

It wasn't the first time she'd beaten him. But somehow Charlie felt with terrible dread that it was the last time. He always felt that way, he reminded himself. Every time Diana said she was through with him, he believed her. Then her mood would change like the wind, and she'd accept him as if nothing had ever happened.

It wouldn't be that way this time, he thought as he came back to the present and stared at himself in the mirror. The common cause that had bound them to each other was gone. Their common enemy was dead. He could feel the last of the bolts loosening as the shuddering vehicle that had held the family hurtled toward the inevitable crash.

With their parents gone, there was no reason for their alliance. Diana didn't need him. She was no more capable of loving him than their father had been — which was ironic, considering she and Lucien shared not one drop of blood. Perhaps she had been Lucien Chamberlain's perfect daughter after all.

Charlie felt as if his heart had been crushed inside his chest. He tried to tell himself he was wrong, that he always plunged into the darkest depths of depression after one of these fights with Diana. But the panic was stronger than the logic. He was shaking with it. This was the end.

They would be connected by the funeral, by the dispersal of the estate. Then what? Then nothing. Diana had already begun to plaster over their past in her mind. She would erase him, spin out of his orbit, and abandon him. The story of his life.

He had been her anchor, the hand brake on her recklessness. She wanted to be free of him now. She would destroy herself or be destroyed without him to protect her, and he would be left without the one person he had ever loved. Their family would cease to exist.

The idea terrified him, and yet, in the deepest, darkest corner of his heart he had to acknowledge what he had always secretly believed: They never should have existed in the first place.

They were four random individuals who had been brought together by whatever unseen force ruled the universe, thrown together by fate or karma; a social experiment in cruelty and mental illness staged for the amusement of some sadistic deity.

And now it was over. Now it would end. They would end.

He didn't want to live to see it.

29

Alice: How long is forever?

White Rabbit: Sometimes, just one second.

How terrible and true that was, Jennifer thought, even if it wasn't really a quote from the book.

She had spent the latter part of her afternoon helping a twelve-year-old girl search for the origins of the lines she had read in a Facebook meme. The lines had been attributed to Lewis Carroll, but only on social media, which the girl's teacher would not consider a real source. She was working on an art project that had to reference a literary work, and she had chosen *Alice's Adventures in Wonderland* as her inspiration. Even though Jennifer knew of several verifiable references to time in the novel, the girl stubbornly wanted the one they couldn't corroborate.

When Jennifer suggested that the girl actually read the book first, she was very rudely dismissed.

I hope your teacher makes you read it and it gives you nightmares, you nasty little bitch, Jennifer had thought, in no mood to be dealing with the public. Her visit from the police detective had rattled her and set her nerves on edge.

She didn't want to think about her childhood or her father's murder, or anything else from that time. She had worked too hard to pull herself out of the dark place she'd struggled in for too many years. It should have been over by now. People should have left it alone. Twenty-five years later, what did it matter? No one could bring him back to life. No one should have to pay for his death. That was how she felt.

How long is forever?

Sometimes, just one second . . .

One second was all it took to change everything. One second to see the wrong thing. One second to be in the wrong place at the wrong time. One second to discover that your deepest-held truth was the darkest kind of lie. Her childhood had been shattered in a series of one-second increments. The second it took to open a door. The seconds it took to overhear a conversation. The second it took for a bullet to end a life.

How long is forever?

One second after the next, after the next, after the next . . .

Her mother had quickly lost patience with Jennifer's mental fragility after the murder. She believed the mourning period should end as soon as the dirt was thrown on the grave and the last solicitous friends and relatives left the church basement reception. Her mother was not a sentimental person. Daddy was hardly cold in the ground when she officially started dating Uncle Duff. Life moved on for Barbie Duffy. She didn't understand why it wasn't the same for her oldest daughter, who was just a child.

She didn't understand, and Jennifer would

never explain it to her. The things she knew, she held inside. The caustic nature of those memories continuously ate away at her. No one tried hard enough or cared deeply enough to pry them out. It took her years to let go, to forgive herself, to climb out of the depression and anxiety that gripped her, and move on with her life. Tonight she felt like she had fallen all the way back to the bottom of the mountain.

She had come home at the end of her workday agitated and upset. She couldn't eat. She couldn't concentrate enough to lose herself in a book — her lifelong method of escape. She turned the television on, but couldn't settle to watch anything. All the local news stations wanted to talk about was the double homicide of the U of M professor and his wife, and the man wanted for questioning. All the news was bad. Violence, hatred, racism, bigotry — everyone was angry, everyone was outraged. The world was a terrible place full of terrible people doing terrible things.

She changed the channel to a decorating show and was immediately confronted by the phony drama and staged arguments of a real estate agent trying to convince his clients to sell their home while a decorator tried to convince them to spend thousands remodeling the dump. Even that was too much conflict to deal with.

Her arms wrapped around her as if she was freezing, she paced her apartment. Her mind was racing. Even earlier in the evening she had been dreading the night. Eventually, she would need to sleep, and sleep would bring the nightmares.

Not even sleeping pills would keep them at bay . . . unless she took one too many.

The thought slipped itself into her consciousness surreptitiously, like a snake slipping through a crack in a wall. As she recognized it, it frightened her. She hadn't thought that way in a long time. She shouldn't be thinking that way now. People who had never experienced suicidal thoughts didn't understand the seductiveness, the insidiousness of those thoughts. Her immediate, instinctive response was to distract herself with physical pain. She wanted to go to the kitchen and get a knife and cut herself to relieve the pressure and clear her mind.

Tears welled in her eyes. She had so many scars from cutting in her teens and her twenties that she would never change clothes in a gym locker room or allow a sales associate to see her in a department store fitting room. She didn't want more scars. She wanted to be free — and that thought took her straight back to the idea of the sleeping pills. The ultimate freedom was death.

The endless loop of destructive thoughts had begun, fueling itself from her fear and despair.

Maybe if she took another Valium.

Maybe if she took three . . .

How long is forever?

Sometimes, just one second . . .

The phone on the breakfast bar rang, startling her. She let the call go to voice mail and then dialed out and picked up the message.

'Ms. Duffy, this is Detective Liska. I'm sorry to bother you, but I need to ask you a couple of additional questions. If you could, please call me back at your convenience . . . '

More questions. As if the questions she had already asked hadn't caused Jennifer enough upset, awakening memories and stirring up emotions like stirring up the sediment at the bottom of a still pond. When she closed her eyes, she could see the faces of her past: her father, Angie, Jeremy . . . She had very deliberately not thought of them in years. Now here they were, come to haunt her. They would be waiting for her in her dreams, and they would be angry and accusatory and threatening.

You can never tell, Jennifer . . .

How long is forever?

The tears she had been struggling to hold back burst forth at that thought, like water from a crumbling dam, taking all resistance, sweeping away everything in its path. Sobbing, she hurried into the kitchen, pulled a paring knife from the knife block, shoved her left sleeve up, and . . . hesitated.

Her hand was trembling, the sharp blade a hair's breadth above her soft white flesh. She shouldn't. She had gone a long time without resorting to this. If she started again, she might not be able to stop. Just once always led to just once more to this is the last time . . . The rush of endorphins, the relief of releasing that inner pain was so tempting.

The pressure and the anxiety were just so terrible.

Just this once.

She'd been taken by surprise by the renewed

interest in her father's murder. It was only natural that she was upset. She'd been doing so well. If she could just relieve the pressure now, she'd right herself, and that would be all. She was stronger now than she had been before. She wouldn't need to do it again.

The sense of pain was clean and sharp as the blade sliced the delicate skin of her inner arm. The sense of relief followed immediately, followed by a quick, brief high as the endorphins were released in her brain. Then the high bottomed out, and the sense of shame welled up inside her like the line of blood rising on her skin.

Jennifer dropped the knife in the sink and turned the water on. Doubled over, lying against the edge of the sink, she stuck her arm beneath the ice-cold flow and cried and cried and cried.

She cried for her adult self, for the carefully constructed person she had become falling so easily back to the past, for losing all the ground she had fought so hard to gain. She was Alice falling down the rabbit hole and into an old familiar nightmare.

She cried for the nine-year-old girl she had been, the lonely, innocent girl who lived inside books, who witnessed something unspeakable, who listened to a murder . . . who never told anyone anything. The keeper of terrible secrets.

How long is forever?

Every day of her life.

30

They didn't find the gun.

Nikki was disappointed but undaunted. What she had found was potentially more important: the photos of Angie Jeager/Evi Burke. She knew Donald Nilsen had owned a .243 hunting rifle. She had a photograph of him wielding the weapon as he shouted at his neighbors and threatened to shoot their dog.

He'd had the means to shoot Ted Duffy. He'd had the opportunity to shoot Ted Duffy — if they discounted the statement of his long-missing wife. He wasn't lacking motive. The two had had runins. The discovery of the pictures hidden under Jeremy Nilsen's mattress, however, may have added a new dimension to the picture.

In her confrontation with Nilsen on his front lawn, she had thrown out the idea that Angie Jeager had somehow ruined or tainted his son. She'd done it just to get a rise out of him, but the more she thought about it, the more the idea appealed to her as an extra layer of motive.

Murder was a solution arrived at by different means, depending on the motive. In the heat of passion or rage, there was no forethought. It was an act triggered from a part of the brain where emotion and instinct lived. In other cases, the motivation for murder was built one step, one transgression, one insult at a time, layer by layer, until the mind could make an argument for a violent solution to an untenable situation.

Donald Nilsen didn't get along with his neighbors. By his reasoning, they encroached on his privacy and trampled on his personal world order. He was the kind of man who would keep score, remembering every little affront. He had deemed the Duffys' foster daughters a threat to his sense of decency. Ted Duffy had gone head to head with him on the subject of the girls. If Nilsen had found out Angie Jeager was tempting his son, or even that his son had a crush on her, that could have been the last straw. It only had to make sense to Donald Nilsen.

In need of movement and coffee, Nikki left her office and crept up the stairs to check on the boys. They had all been asleep in the living room when she got home — Kyle, R.J., and her cousin Matt — sprawled on the sofa and the floor like gunshot victims. One by one, she woke them and sent them off to their respective beds.

Kyle, her artist, had painted the door of his room red, black, and white, with a life-size samurai warrior — a fierce mask, a raised sword — warning the faint-of-heart not to cross this threshold. She cracked the door open and peeked in at him, sleeping soundly. He was her quiet one. He had broken up with his first girlfriend before Nikki even knew he had one.

She imagined Jeremy Nilsen the same way: quietly living his own life beneath his father's radar. Donald Nilsen would not have been an understanding parent. Knowing that, and knowing how he felt about his son now, would Donald Nilsen have killed someone because of his son?

Seley had been calling homeless shelters, looking for Jeremy Nilsen, hoping against hope that they would find him and that he would be able to fill in the blanks of the story. So far, he seemed to have dropped off the face of the earth after leaving the VA hospital.

Nikki couldn't imagine not knowing where her boys were, let alone not caring. She would have dug up every corner of the earth to find them, would have sacrificed everything she had to save them.

She closed Kyle's door softly and went back downstairs to the kitchen for a fresh cup of coffee — decaf, to begin to wind down. She was tired. Her head was swimming with everything that had gone on that day. Too tired to think straight, she admitted as she went to her office.

She sat back against the desk to look at her whiteboard and the notes she had made. She had put a call in to Jennifer Duffy, requesting a call back. No call had been forthcoming. She wasn't surprised. There was a reason Jennifer didn't want to go back to those memories, a reason she had struggled over the years with depression and whatever her other demons were.

Nikki thought back to the moment the dark cloud passed over Jennifer Duffy's memories as she spoke about sneaking into Angie's room to snuggle and read at night.

What did she know about Angie and Jeremy Nilsen? Angie had been like a big sister to a lonely little girl. Jennifer would have hung on her every word, would have wanted to imitate her, would have wanted to know about everything that went on in Angie's life — including whether Jeremy Nilsen was her boyfriend.

Why wouldn't she just say so?

And what did the answer have to do with Ted Duffy's death?

Nikki's follow-up call to Evi Burke had also gone unanswered. Evi Burke, who had been through two or three kinds of hell growing up but had managed to come out the other side and build a nice life, a meaningful life. It was no wonder she would rather pass on the opportunity to go back and dig up unhappy times.

'Sorry, Evi,' Nikki murmured as she stared at the time line of Ted Duffy's death. 'I'm taking you back there whether you like it or not. I think you might be my lynchpin in this.'

31

The dream took her back to a place she didn't want to go, to a time she didn't want to remember. Even in the memory, she felt so empty and so alone, the emotions creating a physical pain inside her.

She was alone in the world. She had no one. Her mother was gone. Gone for good, not gone to a rehab or gone to a hospital or gone on a bender. She was dead. She was gone and never coming back. As damaged as she had always been, as inadequate as her capabilities as a parent had been, she had been Evi's only relative, the only person to which she truly belonged — and vice versa.

It had come as a surprise, how hard it was to lose her. Evi had seen her sporadically as a teenager in and out of foster care. In many ways they had been little more than acquaintances and occasional roommates. Evi had done as much caretaking of her mother over the years as her mother had of her — probably more. Yet the loss felt as if a giant hole had been torn open inside her, and there was nothing to fill it. That emptiness had terrified her.

She had a roof over her head at the Duffys'. She had people around her, and she had school. But Barbie Duffy was not a mother to her, and Evi had no real friends. She was shy by nature, and ashamed of being in foster care. People looked at her differently, treated her differently, like there must be something wrong with her, something contagious that made her unlovable, or something intrinsically broken and dirty that attracted the darkness in the souls of men.

None of them reached out to touch her heart. All of them reached out to touch her body — young or old; in anger, as if it was her fault they wanted her; or in the guise of something kinder, as if it was their duty. She took what was offered because anything was better than the emptiness inside her.

She hadn't meant for bad things to happen. She had only wanted to be loved. She had only wanted to break the sense of feeling separate from everyone around her. She longed to feel she was a part of something, connected to someone. How could that be so wrong?

In the dream, everything was dark, all moonlit shapes and forms. Comfort came in secret. She grabbed it with both hands and held on. Hands and mouths and tangled legs, beating hearts and hot breath. But even in the attempt to connect to someone, she felt detached from her body, as if the essence of her being was just a tiny ball of energy trapped inside an empty shell. Frightened and confused, she held on tighter. She wanted something more, needed something she couldn't name because she had never known it.

She had never meant to hurt anyone, but in the end she had destroyed everyone she cared about most. As if her heart were Pandora's box: She had opened it and chaos had tumbled out like an avalanche, crushing everything in its path.

She had spent years in purgatory trying to pay for the damages. She was still paying on nights like this one, when she dreamed of sex and violence, and what her past could do to her present.

She woke up gasping for air, drenched in sweat, shaking, crying, dizzy, nauseated. She stumbled out of bed, tripping on the covers, and hurried into the bathroom to be sick. When her stomach was empty, she brushed her teeth and turned the shower on. Stripping her nightgown off and dropping it on the floor, she stepped under the water, gasping because it was still cold. She didn't care. She needed to wash the sensation of the dream away, the sensation of being dirty and defiled and disgusted with herself. She lathered herself with soap and scrubbed her skin with a loofah until it hurt.

Afterward, she felt weak and shaky. She wrapped herself in a towel and sat on the edge of the tub, trying to pull herself together. She wished Eric were there, and at the same time was glad that he wasn't. She didn't like to burden him with the aftereffects of her past. He knew a lot about her life, and the things she had been through, but there were memories she had chosen not to share with him. Things that haunted her. Things she regretted even all these years later that, as much as he loved her, she feared he wouldn't be able to understand or forgive. The prospect of losing him for the mistakes she made all those years ago was more than she could stand.

And yet, she knew there was no escape. Her past was part of who she was and who she had become. The past was like a stone thrown in a lake, the ripples going on and on and on. It was the ominous Other Shoe, and she felt the weight of it hovering over her, ready to crush her and all she held dear. And all she wanted to do was ignore it and hope that it would go away.

Detective Liska had called again and left a message saying she had a couple of additional questions. Evi hadn't called her back.

She thought of Jennifer Duffy, who had been like a little sister to her for that brief time. She had wondered for a long time after leaving the Duffys what would become of Jennifer. How much did she know? How much had she understood? Detective Liska had said Jennifer struggled for years after, another casualty of the past. Evi's heart ached for her.

My fault, she thought. She had only wanted what every child did, to be loved, and in the end she caused nothing but death. The death of a man, the death of innocence, the death of what might have grown into real love.

Needing to move, she got up, discarded her towel, and put on a fresh pair of pajamas. She left her room and went in to check on Mia. She always felt calmer looking at her daughter, her assurance that life went on and renewed itself with innocence. Evi felt a desperate need to keep her child that way: innocent and pure. Her mother hadn't been strong enough to do that for her.

Mia slept the sleep of a much-loved child,

sound and happy, snuggled with a favorite stuffed toy.

I can do this for you, Evi thought. She couldn't go back and change the past, but she could ensure her daughter's present and work for her future, and hope that that would make up for the choices she'd made so many years ago.

She went to the dormered window at the end of the room to look out at the night. The rain had subsided to a pea soup mix of mist and fog hanging low to the ground. The waxing moon played hide-and-seek behind black clouds scudding across the night sky.

She saw their faces in the moon, the face and expression changing every time a cloud slipped by — Ted Duffy, broken and defeated; Barbie Duffy, and cold and bitter; Jeremy, tormented and brooding; Donald Nilsen, angry and full of hate . . .

The motion sensor security light above the back door clicked on, and Evi flinched, her heart jumping in her chest. She told herself it was probably a stray cat cutting through the yard. Once, over the summer, they had a family of raccoons visit. She scanned the yard from side to side. One of the swings on the swing set was moving. The wind?

Only one seat was moving. The other was still.

A big oak tree took up one corner of the yard. Most of its leaves were gone, but the thick trunk still offered a hiding place. Near the tree was Mia's playhouse, which Eric had built for her birthday this year. They kept it locked. No one could get inside . . . but they could hide behind it.

Funny how something so sweet and pretty in the daylight could become so dark and sinister at night. Was that the shadow of a figure in the window? She held her breath and waited for it to move.

Her mind went back to the conversation she had had with the detectives, to the questions they had asked about why someone would be stalking her. She had assumed it might have to do with Hope Anders, but as Detective Liska had pointed out, Evi was no one of any real consequence in that case. She was a liaison. She gave the girls her counsel once a week. She had nothing to do with any of the investigations. She wasn't the figurehead of Chrysalis. She was a social worker. Why would anyone stalk a social worker?

Why would anyone stalk her at all?

Had someone seen her picture in the newspaper article and become fixated on her for reasons only a sick mind could know?

The sensations from her nightmares came back to her — the panic, the darkness, the feeling that she couldn't breathe or move. The shadows from her past stalked her every night. Had one of them come calling in person?

Liska had asked her if she'd kept in touch with Jeremy. She had not. She had been removed from the Duffy house and taken to a group home that seemed to have existed in another world. She never tried to contact him, did her best to put him out of her mind. Eventually, she succeeded. Years later. Just as she put his father out of her mind, and Ted Duffy, and the rest of them.

The ringing of the telephone tore through the silence, and Evi jumped and ran to answer it. A phone call in the middle of the night was never a good thing to a firefighter's wife. Her heart was hammering as she picked up the handset from the nightstand in her room.

'Hello?'

Her mind was already racing. Eric was hurt. She would throw on clothes and scoop up Mia. Would she remember how to get to whatever hospital he had been taken to?

'Hello?' she said again, realizing no one had spoken on the other end of the line.

'Hello? Who is this?' she asked, trying not to sound as frightened as she was.

'It all worked out for you.'

The voice was soft, barely more than a whisper. She couldn't tell if it was a man or a woman.

'Who is this?' she asked again, her voice trembling.

There was no answer. The caller was gone.

Evi tried to put the phone down, her hand shaking so badly she couldn't get it back in the stand, and it tumbled to the floor.

'Uh-oh, Mommy!'

Mia had come into the room, teddy bear tucked under her arm, her sandy curls tousled.

'It's okay, Mommy,' she said as she rounded the end of the bed. 'It didn't break. You don't have to cry.'

Evi scooped her child up into her arms and held her tight, choking back the sobs of sheer panic that clogged her throat. Holding on to her future as she tried to forget her past.

It all worked out for you . . .

32

'You got home really late last night,' Kyle said as he got the orange juice out of the refrigerator.

'We had to execute a search warrant,' Nikki said, stirring the eggs. 'It couldn't wait.'

'You said that wouldn't happen anymore.'

'It won't happen very often.'

'You missed jiu-jitsu,' R.J. said, putting the plates on the island. 'Matt took us.'

'I know. I'm sorry. I'll be there next week. I promise.'

'No classes next week,' Kyle said. 'It's Thanksgiving. No classes Wednesday or Thursday.'

Thanksgiving? God, how had that happened? Nikki kept the question to herself. She meant for their lives to be on a more normal track now. She didn't want them thinking she would forget holidays and important things like jiu-jitsu.

'I don't have wrestling, either, next Tuesday,' R.J. reminded her.

'I get out of school Tuesday,' Kyle added.

'Make sure all of this is on the calendar, please,' Nikki said, dishing up their eggs. She cut a glance across the room to the whiteboard calendar that was awash in a rainbow of colored marker for this school function and that activity.

'You're not gonna forget to buy a turkey, are you?' R.J. asked.

'No, I'm not gonna forget to buy a turkey.'

Mental note: Order a fresh turkey at Lund's.

'You're a turkey,' Kyle said, flicking scrambled eggs at his brother.

'You're a dork,' R.J. shot back.

'You're both going to be late for school,' Nikki said. 'Eat up and hit the road.'

★ ★ ★

She made phone calls from the car before pulling out of the driveway and heading downtown. Evi Burke: No answer. Jennifer Duffy: No answer. Donald Nilsen: No answer. No surprise.

Wanting to know the minute he came back from wherever he had stormed off to, she had put a unit on Nilsen's house the night before. She wished she could have put a tail on him the minute he left the property, but Mascherino had nixed the idea. Nilsen's itchy trigger finger for lawsuits had bought him his freedom for the evening.

She wondered where he'd gone. To a bar? To a girlfriend? She couldn't begin to imagine that. To a hooker? There was an ugly thought. Donald Nilsen, with his hatred and disdain for women, with his hair trigger for violence, was every prostitute's worst nightmare.

Immediately Nikki thought of the other Duffy foster child, Penny Williams, found dead in an alley only months after Ted Duffy's murder. Nikki had the case file on her desk. Had Penny Williams known something about the Nilsens, father or son? There had been no statement from or about her in the Duffy case file. There had been practically nothing in the file about Jeremy Nilsen, or Angie Jeager.

Either I'm a genius or an idiot, she thought as she headed into the office. She believed she was on the right track — the track no one else had gone down. But sometimes the road less traveled was less traveled for a reason — because it led nowhere.

In need of caffeine, and secretly hoping for camaraderie, she went into Kovac's war room.

He looked up at her from where he sat alone at the table, going through statements. He looked freshly showered and shaved, and not nearly as bleary-eyed as he had the last time she'd seen him.

'Oh my God, did you actually go home last night?' she asked. 'You're getting soft in your old age.'

'What?' he barked. 'They don't have coffee back in the broom closet?'

'Yeah, but it's not nearly as bad as this,' she said, pouring herself a mug of sludge. 'Have you caught your ninja yet?'

'Nope. This case is like a big grab bag full of broken glass and venomous snakes. Yours? Did Herb Peterson have anything for you?'

'Who?'

'Herb Peterson. The retired cop you were so hot to talk to yesterday when you tracked me down at Cheap Charlie's.' He gave her a knowing look. 'Tinks, I think you miss me.'

Scowling, Nikki slid down on the chair across from him. 'Of course I miss you. Don't be an ass about it.'

'It's what I do best.'

'You're coming to Thanksgiving,' she said bluntly, absently looking over the writing on the big whiteboard. 'It's next week, in case you've forgotten. Who has the neat handwriting?'

'Your boy, Magic Mike.'

'He's not my boy,' she said as she tried to forget the animal magnetism rolling effortlessly off Taylor as she sat beside him at the diner. He even smelled gorgeous, as she recalled. 'I don't date guys I could have theoretically given birth to.'

'Only if you were a slut in middle school,' Kovac said. 'He's not that much younger than you.'

'He's not my type.'

Kovac laughed. 'Yeah, right, those devastatingly good-looking guys are so not you,' he said sarcastically.

The smart-ass remark was half formed on her tongue when she saw the name. Her whole body jerked like she'd been given an electric shock.

'What?' Kovac asked, looking over his shoulder.

'Why do you have that name up there?' she asked. 'Jeremy Nilsen — why is that up there?'

'His ID was found in the room of a robbery suspect, Gordon Krauss. Why?'

'I'm looking for a Jeremy Nilsen. He was a neighbor of Ted Duffy's back when. Do you have the ID here?'

'No. It's in Property.'

'Does it match your guy? Is it him?'

'There's our guy,' Kovac said, pointing to a

photograph stuck on the wall.

The suspect's hair was overgrown, and a beard obscured the lower half of his face.

'I don't know,' she said, shaking her head. 'I don't have a recent picture of Nilsen. Every guy in a bushy beard looks the same to me. Have you run his prints?'

'He's not in the system.'

'Jeremy Nilsen served in the army. His prints have to be in the system.'

'Krauss allegedly served,' Kovac said. 'That's what he told people. But his prints don't show up as military or anything else. A known associate claims he was some kind of Black Ops assassin or some such bullshit.'

'Do you have him in custody?'

'No. I've got every cop in five jurisdictions looking for him.

'Do you think he's your guy?' he asked. 'Krauss could be an alias, but that ID was one of several Tip and Elwood found in his room at a rehab on the North Side. He came there from a shelter downtown as a charity case.'

'Seley from my office has been calling every shelter and soup kitchen in the Cities looking for Nilsen. He was a psych patient at the VA. But he's been MIA for a long time. This could be him.'

'Or he could have an answer for you,' Kovac said. 'This guy's crazy like a fox, not crazy like a loon. We don't know how he came by these IDs. Maybe he bought them off these guys for drug money, maybe he stole them. Hell, he could have killed them for all we know. I might like him for my double homicide. Could be the daughter of my vics hired him to off her parents.'

'Holy shit,' Nikki murmured. That would be the luck. She finally got a lead on Jeremy Nilsen only to discover someone killed him for his ID and his veterans benefits.

'Call me if you bring him in,' she said, getting up.

'Will do.'

'What the hell do you think you're doing?' The booming voice belonged to Gene Grider.

Nikki turned and looked at him as he barged into the room like a charging bull, knocking the door back so hard it bounced off the doorstop and nearly hit him on the rebound.

'I told you to leave the family alone!' he shouted at her.

Nikki stared at him, confused. 'What? What are you talking about? What's wrong with you?'

'He's in the wrong office, for starters,' Kovac said, getting up. 'Get out of my war room, Grider. No one invited you to the party.'

'Butt out, Kojak,' Grider snapped, coming forward, red-faced. He looked like his tie was too tight, choking him. He jabbed a thick finger at Nikki. 'I told you to leave the Duffys alone!'

Nikki squared off with him, leaning up toward him on her tiptoes. 'And I told you to butt the hell out of my case! You're not the boss of me, Grider. My case is the murder of Ted Duffy. I'm damn well going to speak to his family and anyone else I want to. It's called an investigation.'

'Well, great fucking job!' Grider shouted at

her. 'I hope you got what you needed. Jennifer Duffy tried to kill herself last night.'

*   *   *

'I had a conversation with her,' Nikki said, still in a state of disbelief. Her gaze skimmed around the lieutenant's office, looking for something to focus on. She settled on a picture of Mascherino with a granddaughter about the age Jennifer Duffy was when her father was killed.

'I asked her normal questions. It was very casual. I was persistent, but I didn't bully her. Is she going to make it? What did she do? Pills?'

'Sleeping pills and antianxiety meds. A neighbor heard her fall in the middle of the night and thought someone was breaking in. They called the police.'

'Oh my God,' Nikki whispered, rubbing her hands over her face, relief and shock and guilt all tumbling through her at once. 'Thank God.'

'She'll recover, hopefully no liver damage,' Mascherino said. 'She apparently told her mother over the phone earlier in the evening that you came to the library and she didn't want to speak to you.'

Nikki rolled her eyes. 'I'm a cop. No one wants to speak to me.'

'She said you threatened her.'

'That's a lie! I did not threaten her. She didn't want people to know who I was or why I was there, but she left the building with me voluntarily. Ask anyone at the coffee shop — I didn't have a gun to her head! We had cappuccinos, we talked. When she decided to stop talking, I left her alone. I tried to call her later. I had a few more questions. The call went to voice mail.'

The lieutenant sighed. 'Nikki, she was nine years old when her father died — '

'And she knows something, or she saw something,' Nikki insisted. 'I'd bet the farm on it. That's why she went off the deep end — I opened the door to her past, and she didn't want to look at what's on the other side.' she said. 'I need to know what she knows.'

'You're not getting anywhere near her,' Mascherino said. 'None of us are getting anywhere near her. The Duffys have circled the wagons.'

'Right,' Nikki muttered. 'Barbie Duffy had all the motherly love of a reptile when Jennifer was a kid. Now, all of a sudden, she's fucking Mother Earth.'

The lieutenant's face pinched at her language. 'Stay away from Jennifer Duffy.'

Nikki heaved a sigh. Now she had to wonder at the sudden show of family solidarity. Maybe she was off the mark. Maybe what Jennifer knew had to do with the family, and Jeremy Nilsen and his father were superfluous to the story.

Grider and Big Duff both had warned her away from the family. Barbie Duffy hadn't wanted the investigation into her husband's murder reopened at all.

'This is the strangest murder investigation I've ever been a part of,' she said.

'I guess Cold Case isn't so boring after all.'

'Not so far.'

Her head was buzzing from the possibilities — or from Kovac's coffee, she wasn't sure which. What she did know was that unless she could find Jeremy Nilsen, she was now left with one key to the whole thing: Evi Burke.

33

'How's my princess?' Eric asked as he came in the house, sweeping Mia off the floor and twirling her around, to her delight. 'Were you a good girl while Daddy was at work?'

'I was *very* good, Daddy!'

Evi watched them with a sickening mix of love and fear. She loved them so much it terrified her. She was still trembling from last night. *It all worked out for you . . .*

'And how's my queen?' Eric asked as their daughter scampered away in her pink tutu, twirling her glitter wand. He turned to Evi with a smile that faltered.

'Are you all right?' he asked, slipping his arms around her. 'You're as pale as a ghost.'

'I'm feeling a little off this morning,' she said, forcing a weak smile. 'It's nothing.'

'I hope it's a little something,' he whispered in her ear, hugging her gently.

Evi closed her eyes against a sudden rush of tears. They had been trying to get pregnant again for a while now — not such an easy feat at her age. They had both been thrilled at the idea of a second child. Now she saw that wonderful dream in her mind falling under a dark cloud. She tried to tell herself she was being ridiculous, but the fear was stronger than logic.

'Todd's wife had a little boy yesterday,' he said. 'Maybe it's contagious.'

He kissed her forehead and stepped back. 'I'll make you some oatmeal and tea for breakfast. That always settles your stomach. Come sit and tell me how your day was yesterday.'

'Nothing special,' she said, following him.

She spied Detective Liska's business card on the dining room table, swept it up, and tucked it into the pocket of her sweater. Given her job, it wouldn't have been unusual to find a cop's business card lying around, but the word *Homicide* jumped out. She dealt primarily with Sex Crimes detectives in her work with the girls at Chrysalis.

That truth struck her oddly today. Ted Duffy had been a Sex Crimes detective. Her life was running in some kind of weird circle as it turned back to that time.

It all worked out for you . . .

'Pete Heller's wife said there were a lot of cop cars in the neighborhood last night,' Eric said as he gathered ingredients and pots at the stove. 'Did you hear if there was something going on?'

'No,' Evi said, taking a seat on a counter stool. 'Oh, well, they're looking everywhere for a man who might be connected to that horrible murder of that professor and his wife.'

'They didn't come around knocking on doors, did they?' he asked, looking troubled. 'Good thing I'm home for a couple of days. I don't want you and Mia home alone if the cops think that guy might be in our neighborhood. I'll call Brad Dunn later. He'll have the scoop.'

A bolt of panic shot through Evi. Eric knew almost as many patrol cops as he did firefighters.

She hadn't even thought about that when Kate told her she would see that extra patrols came through the neighborhood. Would the officers have been told to keep a special eye on the Burke house? Would they have been told why?

Evi hadn't wanted to worry Eric over the note when she thought it might be connected to the Anders case. She had no intention of telling him anything about her connection to the reopened investigation of Ted Duffy's murder. There was no need to burden him with her ancient past . . . unless that past could put her family in jeopardy.

The idea turned her stomach over and over. A vague note and a late night phone call didn't constitute a threat, she tried to tell herself. That's what the police would say. What would her husband say if he found out she was keeping these things from him? Would he be hurt? Would he be angry? He had worked so hard to gain her trust over the course of their relationship, and here she was hiding something that could be potentially dangerous to them.

'We're going to need a bigger house,' he said, setting her tea on the counter in front of her.

Evi looked up, startled.

'You're a lovely shade of pale green,' he said, with a sweet, soft smile as he came around the counter to wrap her up in his arms. 'Looks like morning sickness to me.'

'I hope so,' Evi murmured, fighting tears.

She wrapped her arms around her husband's neck and buried her face against his shoulder.

It all worked out for you . . .

34

'He came in out of the rain to use the bathroom,' Tippen said as they watched the security video. 'Betrayed by his own bowels. It's one for the anals.'

He chuckled diabolically as everyone else groaned at his play on words.

'What time was this?' Kovac asked, squinting at the television screen. Even with his glasses, the time and date stamp was squiggly.

'Five seventeen this morning at the Super-America convenience store on Thirty-fourth Avenue, south of the Minnehaha Parkway,' Elwood said, pushing a pin with a red head into the map on the war room wall.

'You're sure it's him?'

'Looks like him,' Tippen said, referencing the photo on the wall. 'Same hair, same beard. The clerk was dead certain. Said he acted shady.'

'Him and every other street twitch sneaking into a bathroom meant for paying customers,' Kovac said. 'What do you think, Tinks?'

'I think this bearded lumberjack fad has to end soon, or I'm going to become a lesbian.'

'Is that supposed to be a threat?' Tippen asked, 'Or a tantalizing glimpse into one of my favorite fantasies?'

Liska threw a piece of stale donut at him, hitting him in the forehead. 'Not in front of the children, you disgusting pervert,' she returned without rancor.

Taylor was glaring at Tippen like a hungry guard dog, clearly unhappy with Tippen's apparent lack of respect for the lady of the group.

'Don't worry about Tinks, kid,' Kovac said. 'She could turn Tippen inside out by the scrotum if she wanted to.'

'Don't give me ideas,' Liska said. 'I don't have time to play. Let's get back on point, please.'

'Second possible sighting at Oxendale's Market, just down the street from the convenience store,' Elwood said, sticking another pin in the map. 'A truck driver delivering produce thought he saw Krauss hopping out of a Dumpster behind the store. That's two sightings, blocks apart, within an hour and a half of each other.'

Kovac scratched his head as he stared at the map. 'He's a long way from Rising Wings. What's he doing on that end of town?'

'Maybe he's from that area, knows his way around, is comfortable there,' Taylor speculated.

'It's a risk. That's a quiet residential area,' Kovac said. 'He's going to stick out more there than if he had stayed downtown.'

'But downtown is crawling with cops.'

'Maybe there's somebody he wants to see before he splits town,' Tippen offered. 'He's working his way south. He's got his pick of major highways from there. He can kiss an old flame good-bye and hit the road for anywhere.'

'The airport's right there, too,' Taylor pointed

out. 'Who knows what he might be carrying for an ID. It won't say Gordon Krauss, we can be sure of that. A shave and a haircut, and he's past TSA as Joe Schmoe.'

Kovac nodded at Liska. 'Fill them in on your deal.'

She got up and went to the map. 'I'm looking for a man named Jeremy Nilsen who may have information related to my cold case. He lived next door to my victim at the time. His father and the victim had an ongoing beef. Your guy, Krauss, had Jeremy Nilsen's ID.'

'And five others,' Tippen said. 'Do you think he's your guy?'

She shrugged. 'I don't have a current photo of Nilsen, but if it's him, you should have gotten a hit on his prints. He's ex-military.'

'Unless he's been erased,' Tippen said, excited at the thought.

Kovac tossed a pen in the air and rolled his eyes. 'Oh God, here come the conspiracy theories.'

Tippen pointed a finger at him. 'If you think it doesn't happen, my friend, you are doomed to an Orwellian future.'

'Yeah, I've got news for you,' Kovac said, '1984 was a few decades ago.'

'Here's what's interesting,' Liska went on. 'Jeremy Nilsen lived next door to Ted Duffy here, west of Lake Nokomis.' She stuck a pin in the map. 'His father — the poster boy for angry white men everywhere — still lives there. The kid had a crush on Duffy's foster daughter — now known as Evi Burke — who now lives here, east of Lake Nokomis.' She stuck a second pin in the map and then drew a finger in a triangle between her pins and Elwood's. 'We're talking about a relatively small area, a few square miles. And yesterday Evi Burke received a creepy, vaguely threatening note in the mail that said, 'I know who you are and I know where you live.''

Kovac sat up straighter. 'She works at Chrysalis?'

'Yes. She assumed the note was related to one of her cases. Maybe not.'

'So, the guy you want to question about a twenty-five-year-old homicide could be our suspect in a possible double murder-for-hire?' Taylor said. '*And* he's stalking the girl he had a crush on in high school? That's a whole lot of a word I'm not allowed to use.'

'An unlikely serendipitous collection of ideas,' Elwood offered.

'I'm not saying anything,' Liska said. 'But I am taking a picture of your guy over to Evi Burke, and I think it'd be a good idea to put an unmarked unit on her block until somebody throws a net over this guy.'

'Done,' Kovac said.

'Thank you. I'm out of here,' she said, giving a jaunty salute. 'Call me when you catch him, boys.'

As the door closed behind her, Taylor said, 'I stopped to talk to Charlie Chamberlain on my way home last night.'

'And he didn't tell you to call his attorney?' Kovac asked.

'I made speaking to me a better choice.'

'Good boy.'

'Someone had beaten the living crap out of him.'

Kovac's brows sketched upward. 'Sato?'

'He wouldn't say.'

'Not Sato.'

'My hunch? I think Diana did it,' Taylor said.

'The sister beat him up?' Tippen asked. 'Now, that's my kind of crazy.'

'She'd snap you like a twig,' Kovac said, 'and pick her teeth with your bones. She's a freaking Amazon, and a whole truckload of nuts.'

'He didn't want to talk about it,' Taylor said.

'If Sato did that to him, he'd be bringing charges.'

'Exactly. I also spoke with his neighbor across the hall. She referred to Diana as his tall girlfriend, and said there seemed to be a lot of fighting and making up between them.'

'And we have just crossed a line, even for me,' Tippen commented.

'I'm not surprised,' Kovac said. 'Even if he's not sleeping with her, her power base is sexual. She's had him wrapped around her finger since they were kids. He pissed her off popping her boyfriend in the face yesterday.'

'There was probably a sexual component to the father–daughter relationship, as well,' Elwood added. 'Actual or implied.'

'Charlie didn't come out and say so,' Kovac said, 'but he hinted there might have been abuse in Diana's background. Before or after she was adopted by the Chamberlains, I don't know. The damage was done either way. Add the result of sexual abuse to her bipolar disorder, and you've got a potentially explosive mix.'

'Sex and violence,' Taylor said. 'She goes off on her brother for taking a swing at her lover. Charlie looked like he went a couple of rounds with Mike Tyson.'

'They both studied martial arts as kids,' Kovac said. 'Imagine her reaction if Daddy told them he was giving away their inheritance.'

'Charlie denied knowing about that,' Taylor said, 'but I wasn't convinced. He said their father was always making threats like that, but that he would never follow through.'

'He was following through this time,' Kovac said.

'So Big Sis picked up the phone and called her ninja lover at Rising Wings,' Tippen suggested. 'Oh, won't you please slaughter my father for me, Gordon? He's so mean.'

'She saw Gordon Krauss at the house the day he was there to do the repairs,' Kovac said. 'Tweedle Dumber told me she was slinking around Krauss like a cat in heat.'

'She probably watched him do the deed,' Elwood said.

'Watched?' Kovac asked. 'Hell, she could have beaten her father to death herself. Whoever did it had a whole lot of rage. Then either Krauss or Sato took care of the mother.'

'Or Charlie,' Taylor said. 'After yesterday, we know he can lose control. And he certainly knows more than he's saying.'

'Were there any calls from Diana's phone that might have been to Krauss?' Kovac asked. 'To

411

Rising Wings? To a pay phone? Anything?'

'No, but she's smart enough; she could have used a burner,' Taylor said. 'Disposable phones are everywhere.

'I'm still bothered by the anomaly in the calls from the mother's phone,' he went on. 'I hope to hear back from the phone company today what towers those calls were pinging off. I asked Charlie if I could listen to the message his mother left Tuesday night. He said he erased it.'

'But we know the call was made,' Elwood said.

'But we only have his word about the message. What if Diana pocketed that phone Sunday night? What if the call was only for show?'

'Why steal her mother's phone?' Tippen asked.

'To disarm the security system from the app.'

'I like that,' Kovac said. 'Gold star for Junior.'

'You didn't drive to Dinkytown and ask the girl if she put a beat-down on her brother and hacked her mother up with a sword, Mr. Overachiever?' Tippen asked.

'The lights were off, and she didn't answer the door,' Taylor returned. 'I didn't see her car on the street. And she never answers her phone.'

'She was probably off eating a bloody steak with her bare hands,' Kovac said, pushing to his feet. He looked at Elwood and Tippen. 'You two stay on Gordon Krauss.'

He grabbed his coat and hat and nodded to Taylor. 'We're going to find Ms. Chamberlain and have a chat about her taste in men.'

35

Evi Burke had called in sick to work. Nikki mused on that on the drive south. Was she sick, as in the stomach flu? Was she sick, as in the work flu? Was she sick, as in afraid of a stalker? Was she sick, as in detectives came to her house and asked her questions that upset her?

'I'm freaking Typhoid Mary,' she muttered to herself, thinking of Jennifer Duffy lying in a hospital bed, recovering from a stomach pumping and suicidal intentions.

It made Nikki sick to think about it. Over and over she went through her meeting with Ted Duffy's daughter. Had she pushed too hard? She didn't think so. She knew what it was to go after a suspect like a tigress when it was the method that would yield the best result, but she prided herself on being able to read people and find the path of least resistance to get the information she needed.

They had talked about being the daughters of cops, how it was hard, how their fathers had been distant from them, how kids took things to heart. Jennifer Duffy had not spoken of her father in a sentimental way, and yet she had clearly absorbed some of the guilt the afternoon he died below her bedroom window. She had smiled a little remembering her secret bedtime reading sessions with Angie Jeager. Then a cloud had passed over her memories, and the

413

smile had faded away.

She knew something. Something she had kept secret all these years. Something that had sent her to therapy. Something that had driven her to take an overdose of pills.

And the family had rallied around her.

What the hell was that about? Nikki wondered as she pulled up in front of the Burkes' charming little English-cottage-style house.

Evi Burke's husband answered the door. He was a virtual Viking god in the flesh. In jeans and a faded navy-blue thermal shirt that hugged sculpted muscles, he looked like he could have been a few years younger than his wife. Jackpot, Evi Burke, Nikki thought as he invited her in.

'What's this about?' he asked, not letting her get any farther than the entryway. He crossed his arms over his chest and took a stance with his feet shoulder-width apart. The protector. 'We're looking for a person of interest in a homicide,' Nikki said. 'And we're trying to learn as much as we can about him.

'We think he might be connected to one of your wife's clients at the Chrysalis Center,' she lied. 'Mrs. Burke may have had an encounter with him during a home visit.'

'Do you think he's in our neighborhood? There've been a lot of radio cars on the street.'

'A clerk at the SuperAmerica on Thirty-fourth thinks he might have seen him this morning. We've saturated the surrounding area with patrol cars.'

Eric Burke took in her answer, thought about it, and nodded. She gave a mental sigh of relief.

414

Evi emerged from the dining room white as a sheet, with dark circles under her eyes, shuffling in a pair of fuzzy cat-face slippers, yoga pants, and an oversize sweater. She was preceded by an adorable blonde-haired moppet wearing a pink tutu and waving a glitter wand.

Nikki grinned at the little girl. 'Are you a princess or a fairy?'

'I'm Mia!' the girl exclaimed as her father scooped her up onto his hip.

'Mia and I will go up to the Magic Kingdom while you two talk.'

Nikki murmured her thanks. Evi watched her husband and daughter disappear up the stairs. She hugged herself as if she was cold.

'Why did you do that?' she asked. 'This suspect doesn't have anything to do with anyone at Chrysalis.'

'No,' Nikki said. 'But I didn't see a need to tell your husband this is about something that happened twenty-five years ago, either.'

'Thank you.'

They went into the dining room, taking the same seats they had the night before.

'You look like you had a rough night,' Nikki said. 'Did something happen after we left?'

Tears filled Evi Burke's eyes. 'I got a phone call,' she murmured. 'In the middle of the night. The person said, 'It all worked out for you.''

'What does that mean?'

She made a little fluttering movement of frustration and confusion with her hands. 'I-I have a nice life now. I didn't always.'

'Did you recognize the voice?'

415

'No.'

'Male or female?'

'I couldn't really tell. They whispered.'

'Did you tell your husband about this?'

'No. I don't like to worry him. I mean, it wasn't really a threat, was it? Just — *It all worked out.* I don't even know why I'm so afraid.'

'Because some faceless creep is reaching into your life without so much as introducing themselves,' Nikki said. 'That's scary. Knowing that you have a past, knowing that you work with at-risk women — that ups the ante considerably.'

'That's not why you're here, though, is it?' Evi said, trying to steer the conversation elsewhere.

Maybe, Nikki thought, but she didn't say it. Jeremy Nilsen had left the army on a psych discharge. Maybe he wasn't so happy life had finally smiled on the girl he had known as Angie Jeager. And Donald Nilsen had as much as said he blamed her for some imagined downfall of his family. Who knew where he had been in the middle of the night? He had nothing but time on his hands. He might have seen Evi's face in the newspaper article about the Chrysalis Center and recognized her. Nikki kept those thoughts to herself for the moment.

She pulled the photograph of Gordon Krauss out of her portfolio and put it on the table. 'Do you recognize this man?'

'He's the one you're looking for — for those murders. I saw the picture on television,' Evi said, looking confused. 'I don't understand. Why would I know him?'

'He's calling himself Gordon Krauss. A search

of his room turned up Jeremy Nilsen's ID. Could he be Jeremy Nilsen?'

Evi looked more closely at the photo, not touching it, frowning. 'I haven't seen Jeremy in twenty-five years. He was a teenage boy.'

'Imagine him without the beard,' Nikki said. 'What was he like back then? Was he troubled? Was he angry? Could he be violent?'

She stared at the picture. Her color worsened as she considered the questions and her answers to them, answers she chose to keep to herself.

'He seemed like a nice boy,' she said so softly Nikki almost had to strain to hear her. She looked as fragile as spun glass.

'Was he ever in trouble?'

'Not that I know of.' Her hands were shaking. She sat back and put them in her lap.

'Were you involved with Jeremy Nilsen, Evi? Did his father know about it?'

'No. I told you, we were just acquaintances.'

Nikki reached into the leather portfolio again and pulled out the photographs she had taken from Jeremy Nilsen's bedroom and put them on the table. 'Then why would I find these in Jeremy's bedroom? They were hidden under the mattress. All these years.'

Evi Burke's eyes widened at the sight of herself, sixteen and shy, her vulnerability captured by a school portrait photographer.

'I don't know,' she whispered, blinking against tears.

Nikki sat back and sighed. 'You have to tell me, Evi. You need this to be over.'

'I think you should go now,' Evi said. 'I'm not

feeling well. I need to lie down.'

'Jennifer Duffy tried to kill herself last night.'

Evi's face dropped. 'Oh my God. That's terrible. Is she all right? Will she be all right?'

Nikki shrugged. 'The family seems to think the conversation I had with her about her father's murder prompted her to do it. She's in the hospital.'

'I'm so sorry,' Evi whispered, closing her eyes and pressing a hand to her forehead as if feeling for a fever. Nikki wondered if she was speaking in general or specifically apologizing to Jennifer Duffy . . . for what?

'Evi, what could Jennifer have known that would have upset her to the point of trying to end her own life?'

'I don't know. I wasn't there.'

'You weren't there the night Ted Duffy was murdered. But what about any other night?'

'I don't know what you mean.'

'What was going on in that house, Evi? The Duffys have closed ranks around Jennifer. Whatever she knows about her father's death is staying in that circle. Why?'

'I wouldn't know.'

'You lived there,' Nikki said, frustrated.

'Please go now.'

Nikki sighed but made no move to get up. She could feel Evi Burke teetering on the edge. The harder it felt to hold the secret, the more tempting revealing the truth became.

'There's no reason not to tell me, Evi,' she said, gently. 'You were a child. You didn't have any control over what happened.'

Evi looked out the window at the cold gray day as if she was staring into her past. She looked utterly alone. Nikki wanted to reach out to her, but that wasn't her job, and it wouldn't get her the answers she needed.

Not finding an answer to an impossible internal question, Evi finally shook her head.

'I can't help you,' she said at last. She pushed the photographs back across the table. 'I don't know who that man is. I'm sorry.'

Nikki reluctantly put the pictures back in her portfolio.

'I will get to the bottom of this, Evi,' she said in the least threatening voice she could use. 'I know I'm close. I can taste it. I won't stop until I have the answer.

'I'm not out to hurt anybody,' she said. 'It makes me sick that Jennifer Duffy is lying in the hospital today. There was no reason for her to make that choice. Nothing is worth that. Nothing that happened back then, when she was just a child, could be worth paying that price.

'You have a nice life now, Evi,' she went on. 'You've been through enough. You deserve to be happy. I don't want to disrupt that for you. I just want the truth. That's what my job is: finding the truth. I won't stop until I get it. I owe that to my victim.'

'Good luck,' Evi said, pushing her chair back and screwing up the strength to stand.

They walked to the door together.

'Please call me if you decide you have something to say,' Nikki said, handing over another business card. 'Twenty-five years is long enough to keep a secret that doesn't matter anymore. Let it go. Set yourself free of it.'

'If it didn't matter,' Evi said, 'you wouldn't be here.'

Nikki couldn't really argue the point, she thought as she walked away from the Burke house. It seemed she was one of a small minority who gave a rat's ass what had happened to Ted Duffy or why. Maybe she would feel the same way by the time this was over, but that wasn't her choice to make.

★   ★   ★

Evi watched the detective walk to her car at the curb even as a patrol car rolled past on the street. Behind her and up the stairs she could hear the laughter of her husband and her child.

No, Detective Liska, she thought. Some secrets have to last forever.

420

36

'I don't have anything more to say to you people,' Diana said as she came out of her apartment and locked the deadbolt with a key. She was dressed for yoga in black leggings and a sloppy gray top hanging off one shoulder, revealing a lacy turquoise bra strap. Despite the damp chill of the day, she wore no coat.

'You don't want to give us your side of the story?' Taylor asked.

'My side of what story? You were there yesterday. You saw what happened.'

'I mean later, with Charlie.'

She narrowed her eyes and swept a messy chunk of hair behind one ear. 'What about Charlie?'

'Come on, Diana,' Taylor said. 'I saw him last night.'

'I'm not speaking to Charlie. I don't know what he might have said to you.'

'He didn't have to say anything. The cuts and bruises spoke for themselves.'

'I don't know what you're talking about. Did he have some kind of accident?'

'Yeah, he walked into some fists.'

'What happened to your hands?' Kovac asked, looking at the small cuts and the puffy redness of swollen knuckles.

Immediately she crossed her arms to hide them. 'Nothing. This weather gives me chapped skin.'

'Funny, beating the shit out of someone gives the exact same results.'

She had the nerve to look incredulous. 'Are you accusing me of hitting Charlie? That's ridiculous! I'm a woman. I don't go around beating people up. That's Charlie's department. Ken had to go get an X-ray on the way home yesterday.'

'You know, I think maybe we should go downtown to discuss this,' Kovac suggested. 'We've got an assault victim to consider. It's serious business.'

'Did Charlie tell you I hit him?' she asked. 'He wouldn't.'

'Because he's afraid of you?' Taylor asked.

'Charlie loves me.' She said it like it was a challenge. *I dare you to tell me he doesn't love me.*

'Yeah, well,' Kovac said, 'live a few more years and you'll figure out that doesn't mean what you thought it did.'

'What does that mean?' Diana demanded. 'Are you arresting me?'

'No, no. We just have a few questions for you,' Taylor said.

'I'm going to be late for my yoga class,' she complained, and pushed past them, headed for the front door of the building.

Taylor hustled ahead to hold the door for her, and then stepped out on the sagging front porch and cut off her angle to the steps down to the sidewalk. She gave him a nasty look.

'We need to have you take a look at a photograph,' he said.

422

'You know this guy,' Kovac said, showing her the photo of Gordon Krauss.

'No.'

'Oh, you misunderstand,' he said. 'I wasn't asking a question. You *know* this guy.'

'I do not!'

'Diana, we have a witness who puts you flirting with this guy at your parents' house the day they had some repairs done.'

'He's lying!'

'He's got no reason to lie.'

'So? People lie just to lie.'

'Some people.'

'Maybe she just doesn't remember him, Sarge,' Taylor said. 'She's a beautiful woman. I'm sure Diana has guys flirting with her every day.'

Kovac watched her out of the corner of his eye. Her demeanor toward Taylor instantly softened at the compliment. She couldn't help herself. Though she was clearly annoyed with the situation in general, she gave him a little smile, looking up at him through batting lashes.

'You've got a point,' Kovac said. 'My apologies, Ms. Chamberlain, if I seemed abrupt. We're all running on a lack of sleep trying to solve the murder of your parents.'

'Well, I don't know anything about it. I've told you a hundred times.'

'Let's try this again,' Kovac suggested, holding up the photograph. 'This is Gordon Krauss. You met him while you were a participant at Rising Wings, an outpatient drug rehab on the North Side. You met him again when you were at your parents' house the day they had repairs done. He is now wanted for questioning in the murder of your mother and father. Is any of this ringing a bell?'

'Are you saying I had something to do with him?' Diana asked, her face twisted with disgust. 'That's just gross.'

'He didn't try to ask you any questions about the security system at the house that day?' Taylor asked.

'No,' she snapped, done with it. 'I have to go. Get out of my way.'

She made a move to go forward. Taylor blocked her.

Kovac looked around at the sorry old house with the peeling brown paint and ill-fitting aluminum replacement windows, the porch cluttered with students' bicycles and a trash can full of beer bottles.

'I suppose you'll be moving out of this dump and back to the house as soon as we release the scene,' he said. 'Assuming you inherit.'

She looked offended. 'Of course we inherit. We're their children. Why wouldn't we?'

'Well, your dad was pretty fed up with you. He spoke to his lawyer on Monday,' he lied. 'Of course, the lawyer can't tell us what it was about, but it doesn't take a genius to figure that one out.'

'And we know for a fact he was donating his collection to the university ASAP to secure the promotion you were trying to keep him from,' Taylor said. 'So that's off the table as far as inheritance.'

'You don't know any of that.'

Kovac shrugged. 'Maybe they died before the paperwork was done, but yeah, I'd say you were getting chucked off the gravy train, sweetheart.

'But maybe Charlie will throw you a bone,' he suggested. 'He was the good kid, right? Always trying to pull your pretty butt out of the fire. You might want to reconsider using him for a punching bag. Maybe take up a career in the UFC instead. Put your rage in the cage. Earn a paycheck doing it. You'll need it.'

'I'm leaving now. Namaste,' she said directly to him, enunciating each syllable with venom. Her eyes were nearly white with anger.

This time when she started for the stairs, Taylor stepped aside and let her go. They watched as she dashed across the street, hiking the strap of her yoga mat up on her shoulder. She got into her car and pulled away, tires hissing on the wet pavement.

'Namaste,' Taylor said.

Kovac gave him a look. 'What the hell does that mean, anyway?'

'In this case I think it's yoga for 'Fuck you.''

★   ★   ★

From Diana's ramshackle student housing in Dinkytown they drove south to Charlie's neat, nondescript apartment building. He didn't answer his door, even though they knocked hard enough to rouse a neighbor from down the hall. His car was gone from its designated parking spot. Taylor tried calling. The call went straight to voice mail.

'He could be out making funeral arrangements,' Taylor offered as they went back to the car. 'Or getting a CAT scan.'

'Where did he say he worked?' Kovac asked, settling into the passenger's seat. He was getting used to being chauffeured. Getting soft in his old age.

Taylor consulted the notes he'd made in his phone. 'Obern and Phipps, family law. But he didn't go back to work with that face. I'd say he's feeling like a used piñata today.'

'No, but let's give them a call. He said he was online working the night of the murders. Maybe they can corroborate, and we can tick off a box on our list.'

Taylor called information for the number and then put his phone on speaker. A receptionist answered with a very professional 'Obern and Phipps, Family Law. How may I direct your call?'

'This is Detective Michael Taylor with the Minneapolis Police Department. I'm calling regarding one of your employees, Charles Chamberlain. May I speak with his supervisor?'

'One moment please.'

Classical music came on the line to fill the time until the call was transferred. A woman's voice broke in.

'This is Gloria Obern. How may I help you?'

Taylor went through the introduction again. 'I need to ask you a couple of questions about an employee, Charles Chamberlain.'

'Oh, poor Charlie,' the woman said. 'We all feel terrible about what happened to his parents. He's beside himself, the poor kid.'

'Have you spoken to him recently?'

'No. We've been e-mailing. He's a very quiet, private guy, but a terrific hard worker. I've never had such a thorough person doing my research. If there's a scrap of information to be had anywhere on the Internet, Charlie will track it down. I'm going to miss him.'

'Excuse me?'

'Charlie e-mailed me his resignation last night. It was the first thing in my in-box this morning. Of course I'll try to argue him out of it. He can have an indefinite leave of absence, as much time as he needs. I tried to call him, but it went straight to voice mail. I suppose he's busy making arrangements.'

A sense of urgency spiked through Kovac. He grabbed the radio mike and called Dispatch even while Taylor was concluding his conversation with Charlie Chamberlain's boss.

' . . . I need a BOLO on a Charles Chamberlain.' He gave the physical description as he fumbled through the pages of his little notebook. ' . . . driving a gray late-model Toyota Camry, Minnesota plates Charles Ida Victor eight-seven-seven. He's a suicide risk.'

He looked at Taylor.

'His parents are murdered, his sister beats him up, his inheritance is in question, and he won't answer his phone. How are your door-kicking skills, Junior?'

'Let's do it.'

They hustled back to the building. Kovac swore impatiently as Taylor punched buttons, hoping someone in the building would let them in again. Once inside, Taylor took the stairs two at a time. Kovac took the elevator. As he stepped into the hall on the fourth floor, Taylor was shattering the door of Charlie Chamberlain's apartment with a well-placed kick. The neighbor two doors down stuck his head out, wide-eyed.

Taylor was already rushing inside the apartment, calling, 'Charlie! It's Detective Taylor! Are you here? Charlie?'

Silence.

'Holy shit,' Kovac murmured, looking around as he stepped through the door.

The neat and tidy midcentury modern sofa and chairs had been destroyed, cut open, the stuffing pulled out, and strewn everywhere. Lamps lay broken, the shades smashed. Down the short hall, the bedroom was in a similar state, the mattress and bedding shredded, the mirrored glass closet doors shattered and hanging askew off their track.

Kovac stuck his head in the bathroom, where the mirror over the sink was cracked into an elaborate spiderweb of lines. 'There's blood all over the sink in here.'

'There's some on the door frame,' Taylor said. He picked a suit jacket off the floor and held it up. It had been cut and ruined. 'What the hell happened here?'

Kovac took another look around at the chaotic destruction.

'At the risk of being politically incorrect,' he said, 'this has Crazy Bitch written all over it. Get on the horn to the hospitals. See if Charlie Chamberlain made it to one of them.'

428

37

'I've been checking the homeless shelters and soup kitchens all over the area, asking about Jeremy Nilsen,' Seley said. 'A couple of the places downtown thought they remembered the name. One that tries to keep track of return customers had him on their roster, but not recently.'

Nikki sat back in her chair and rubbed at the tension in the back of her neck. She had driven past Donald Nilsen's house on the way back from Evi Burke's. The guys sitting on surveillance reported that Nilsen had not returned. Where the hell was he?

'I've got two missing Nilsens, an uncooperative witness, and I talked a woman into trying to kill herself,' she muttered. 'I'm batting a thousand here.'

'Don't forget multiple threats of lawsuits,' Seley added.

'Thanks for reminding me.'

'You shouldn't sell yourself short.'

'Where's Mr. Congeniality?' Nikki asked, nodding in the direction of Grider's empty desk.

Seley rolled her eyes. 'He made a grand announcement that he was going to try to help smooth things over with the Duffy family.'

'Oh, right,' Nikki said sarcastically. 'You watch. He's going to try to yank this case out from under me, so it can go nowhere for another quarter of a century. Asshole.'

'Then we'd better get it solved before he can make that happen,' Seley said, getting up from her desk and scooping up a file folder. 'I printed off a stack of the Gordon Krauss photos in case he's our man. Let's go check out these places where Nilsen might have been seen.'

★   ★   ★

For a city with months of inhospitable weather, Minneapolis seemed to have more than its share of homelessness. The truth of that pressed down on Nikki's heart like an anvil. And the fact that too many of the men living on the street had been discarded after serving their country made her angry.

At lunchtime on a raw, wet, cold November day, the line for lunch snaked outside the Daily Bread mission and partway down the street. Sullen men in dirty clothes hunched their shoulders against the wind and avoided eye contact while they waited for a hot bowl of beef stew.

'Minnesota has an aggressive initiative to eliminate homelessness among veterans,' the director of the shelter told them. Leonard Westin was a smallish balding man in his forties, with glasses and a polite expression. 'We've reduced our numbers by forty-seven percent since 2010. But it's still a problem, especially for soldiers coming back with significant psychiatric issues. If they end up on the street with paranoia, PTSD, drug problems, any and all of the above — that's a difficult situation. The programs are voluntary. We can't force people to accept help. And when a person doesn't trust anyone, or their primary objective in life has become scoring crack, that person isn't coming in here asking to sign up.'

They stood in the hall between the administrative offices and the dining room of the shelter, where the moods of the clientele had improved with calories, and conversations rose and fell and were interspersed with occasional laughter.

Seley held out the photograph of Gordon Krauss to the director. 'This is the man we're searching for. Does he look familiar?'

Westin squinted at the picture, frowning, searching his memory. 'Possibly. We get so many men through here, it's tough to remember faces unless they're regulars. Who is he?'

'He's calling himself Gordon Krauss,' Nikki said. 'But he was found to have half a dozen IDs in his possession, one of them belonging to a Jeremy Nilsen. We're trying to determine if the two might be one and the same.'

'I know we've had a Jeremy Nilsen come through here,' he said. 'I found the name several times in our roster from the last year. We try to keep track as much as we can. If we don't, who will? But I couldn't say I remember what he looked like. He wasn't a regular, and according to the list, he hasn't been in for several months.'

'Have you heard anything about guys getting their IDs stolen?'

'It happens. Life on the street is no picnic. Men get rolled for their drugs, for their pocket money, because they looked at someone the wrong way. Most of them don't want to deal with the police, so crime goes unreported. It's a transient population, so if we stop seeing a face, we assume they moved on, not that something happened to them.'

Nikki sighed, frustrated.

'I'm sorry I can't be of more help. That's the situation we're dealing with.'

'Thanks anyway,' Seley said. 'Do you mind if we show this around the room? Maybe someone will recognize him.'

'By all means, and good luck.'

They drifted up and down the rows of tables, trying to get people to look closely at the photograph of Gordon Krauss. Most weren't interested, glancing at the picture and passing it on, wanting nothing to do with cops. Then one man looked at the picture and sat up a little straighter.

'Do you know that guy?' Nikki put the man in his late fifties. With curly gray hair that had receded halfway back on his skull, he had the regal profile of an African king. The name on his army jacket read, KUMAR.

'Yeah. He's a bad dude,' Kumar said.

'Why do you say that?'

'Dude hit my friend Martin in the head with a hammer!'

'When was this?'

'Couple months ago. Down by the river. There's a camp down there in the summer. Some guys were passing a pipe. This guy brought some substances, if you get my drift.'

'This guy brought drugs to the party?'

'Yes, ma'am. And when they was all high — I don't partake, myself — this guy pulled a hammer and hit Martin a couple of licks in the head. BAM! BAM! Just like that!' he said, pounding a fist on the table.

'Martin had cashed his benefits check that day and bought some liquor. It was a nice party up until the hammer came out,' he said wistfully.

'Do you think he was going to rob your friend? Or was he just freaking out?'

'Oh yeah,' he nodded. 'I had my eye on him. He was hardly smoking. He was a man with a plan, for sure. We got more selective about our party guests after that.'

'And what happened then?'

'Cops heard the commotion and pulled up on the bank. Everybody went their own way.'

'Did you ever see this guy again after that?'

'No, ma'am.'

'Do you remember his name?'

He gave her a look. 'We're not big on names at the parties.'

'What happened to your friend?'

'He had seventeen staples in his head and went deaf in one ear.'

'That's rough. I'm sorry.'

'Well, I look on the bright side,' Kumar said with a smile. 'It knocked some sense into him.'

'Thanks for speaking up,' Nikki said. 'You've been a big help.'

'Despite all outward appearances,' he said, 'I always try to be a good citizen.'

'So, Jeremy Nilsen is either a thug rolling homeless guys or a homeless guy who got rolled by a thug,' Nikki said as they walked back to their car, leaning into the wind and spitting rain.

'And there were five other IDs found in Krauss's room,' Seley reminded her.

'Call the morgue and see if they've had any unclaimed John Does that match Jeremy Nilsen's description — or any of the men on those other IDs — in the last six months,' she said. 'Whoever this guy is, he could be worse news than anyone imagined.'

Her phone announced a text message with a bright *ping!* She dug it out of her pocket and looked.

'We'll find out soon,' she said, turning the screen to show Tippen's message: GOT HIM.

38

Gordon Krauss had nothing to say. Nothing at all. He had neither waived his rights nor invoked his right to counsel. He sat across the table from Kovac in the box, his back to the wall.

A suspect was put in that position, cramped behind the too-small table that was bolted to the wall on one end of the room, to feel as if he was cornered. Kovac had the option of increasing or decreasing the sense of pressure by moving closer in his chair, which was on wheels, or sliding subtly back away from the suspect.

He stayed back from Gordon Krauss, waiting. This was going to take time. Krauss appeared dead calm, his posture straight but not tense. He stared past Kovac into the middle distance, expressionless, observing his right to remain silent.

He had obviously been living rough since they had flushed him out of Rising Wings. His clothes were dirty and wet. He smelled like a Dumpster. His hair was greasy and flat from hiding under a watch cap. His beard needed a serious grooming. He had been caught trying to shoplift a pair of scissors and a pack of disposable razors from a drugstore.

They had not offered him fresh, dry clothes. Kovac wanted him uncomfortable. They had not offered him food. Kovac wanted him irritable, in the hope of eliciting an angry outburst, but none had been forthcoming.

They had been in the box for seventy-three minutes, mostly just staring. Kovac asked the occasional question that went unanswered. The afternoon was almost gone. It had grown dark outside by now. Most people would be thinking about going home and having dinner. His own stomach was grumbling. Krauss's face was gaunt. He probably hadn't had a decent meal in days.

'Everyone said you were a quiet guy,' Kovac commented. 'They didn't say you were a mute.'

He sat back in his chair, yawned, and stretched his arms over his head. He had all the time in the world.

'You're a real man of mystery, Gordon,' he said. 'We found six IDs in your room at Rising Wings. I don't think any of them are you. You convinced a bunch of people you're a vet, but we can't find your fingerprints in any system. So if you're a veteran, you must have been in the French Foreign Legion. Then again, I've got a guy who thinks you're some kind of shadow-world ninja assassin for the government. A poor man's James Bond, if you will. That would make a good movie,' he said. 'I'm not much for movies, but I would go to that.'

Krauss had no interest in discussing his potential as an action star.

'I doubt you're that interesting in reality,' Kovac said. 'I think you're probably just a garden-variety mutt. You're just another lazy mutt who took a low-end honest job so you could case some nice homes during the day and then come back after hours and steal what you could carry in a knapsack. There's nothing special about that. Just your average workaday thief.'

If Krauss was insulted, he didn't show it.

'Yeah, you're a little bit clever,' Kovac conceded. 'That's a good gig you landed with the rehab. That was smart. Too bad you had to meet Diana Chamberlain there. That chick is bad news. Bat-shit crazy. Look what she pulled you into. You're never gonna see the light of day as a free man again because of her.'

Krauss said nothing. He didn't acknowledge or deny knowing Diana Chamberlain. He didn't deny being a thief. He didn't say they had nothing on him or that he didn't belong in jail. His expression didn't change at all. He stared past Kovac, barely blinking. His eyes were empty, dead-looking, like a shark's eyes.

'What did she promise you, Gordon? Money? Drugs? Sex? All of the above? She's a party waiting to happen, that one.'

He opened a file folder and took out several photographs from the Chamberlain crime scene, gruesome close-ups of the victims, and laid them out on the table.

'Was she there with you? Did she help out with the alarm system that night?' Kovac asked. 'She's the kind of chick who would get off on watching this go down. But you know she's going to totally throw you under the bus on this, right?'

Krauss didn't look at the pictures. He seemed lost in some fantasy world. Meditating on murder. The guy made his skin crawl. Kovac had been in the box across from every kind of dirtbag known to man, but only a handful had given him the sense of being in the presence of something truly, darkly evil. Something in the blank, soulless stare made the hair on the back of his neck stand up.

'Yeah, well . . . ' He stood up and rolled his shoulders, picked up the file folder, but left the photographs on the table. 'It's been nice talking to you, Gordon. I'm gonna take a break here, go get a cup of coffee, grab some dinner, take a piss. Do you need anything, Gordon? Can I get you anything? No? Suit yourself. I'll see you later.'

He walked out of the interview room and went directly to the war room, where the whole gang had gathered to watch the show on a monitor.

'He's not much of a conversationalist,' Kovac said.

'But is he our killer?' Mascherino asked. Standing among the guys (and Liska), in her prim black suit and sensible shoes, she looked like the headmistress of a school for incorrigible overgrown boys.

'This guy probably killed his own mother and ate her the day he hatched,' he said. 'Whether he killed the Chamberlains or not, I don't know. I want to get Diana Chamberlain in here and see if we can play one off the other.'

'Be careful how you approach her, Sam,' the lieutenant said. 'After yesterday's fiasco, if you push too hard, she's going to use the L word. And not the one you're thinking, Mr. Tippen,' she added, arching a brow at the resident reprobate.

Kovac said nothing about their Diana encounter of the morning. He wanted her rattled but not over the edge. It was a fine line, especially if Taylor was correct in his hunch that Diana had handed her brother a beat-down — or worse. She was already teetering on the edge. They had yet to locate Charlie. He could have been dead in the trunk of her car as she drove off to yoga class that morning for all they knew.

'Work your charm, Magic Mike,' he said, looking to Taylor. 'She likes you. Reel her in.'

Taylor pulled his phone out and composed a text message. He read aloud as his fingers tapped the keys. 'Ms. Chamberlain: Good news. Suspect in custody. Please contact me ASAP.'

'Let's leave her alone for an hour or two,' Mascherino suggested. 'See if she's curious enough to make a move on her own.

'In the meantime,' she said, turning back to Kovac. 'How long are you going to keep him in the box?'

She nodded at the monitor and Gordon Krauss.

'As long as I can without him being able to claim we infringed on his civil liberties. We've got plenty to charge him with. Assaulting Junior here, for starters.'

'Don't forget the shoplifting,' Tippen threw in. 'Razors ain't cheap, you know.'

'Is that your excuse?' Liska asked sarcastically.

Tippen struck a smug pose and stroked his goatee with pride. 'The ladies love my goat.'

'They ladies you know?' Liska rolled her eyes. 'If you pay them enough, they won't care if you *smell* like a goat.'

'Nikki, you think you've got something on Mr. Krauss, too?' Mascherino asked.

'I've got a witness who ID'd Krauss for assaulting a homeless guy with a hammer a few months ago. I think if we dig into the rightful owners of those IDs that were in his room, there could be a list of charges. Assault might be the tip of the iceberg. That's a vulnerable community. A homeless guy goes missing, who even notices?'

'Owen Rucker from Rising Wings said Krauss came to them from a shelter,' Kovac said. 'He knows the ins and outs of that life. He'd know when people got their checks for Social Security, disability, whatever.'

'He's a predator,' Liska said. 'The homeless are easy prey.'

'It's safe to say Mr. Krauss won't be going anywhere for some time,' the lieutenant said.

'No, but I don't want him all snug as a bug in a jail bunk,' Kovac said. 'I'd rather take a shot at breaking him down now. Once he's arraigned and the court appoints him a mouthpiece, we won't get another shot.'

'Hey! He's moving,' Elwood announced, pointing at the screen.

They turned their collective attention back to the monitor to watch, as if Gordon Krauss was an exotic animal in a cage.

He shifted his posture on his chair, leaning forward slightly, changing the angle of his head to look down at the photographs Kovac had left on the table. He didn't touch them. He took a good long look, absorbing all the details of the carnage of Lucien and Sondra Chamberlain hacked and bludgeoned to death.

When he had seen enough, he sat back, and a slow reptilian smile curled across his face.

Is he a killer? Mascherino had asked.

Oh, yeah. Now Kovac just had to find a way to get him to admit it.

39

Nikki stopped on her way home and picked up lasagna and a big salad from their favorite Italian restaurant. In the old days, she would have stayed and tag-teamed the suspect with Kovac. She would have sat and watched the monitor while he tried all his tricks to get Gordon Krauss to talk. If anyone could get anything out of a suspect, it was Sam. But when she left the office, they were still at an impasse.

She had no obligation to stay. At this point, all she could ask Krauss was whether he was actually Jeremy Nilsen — which he probably wasn't — and if not, did he know where Jeremy Nilsen was. But he wasn't going to speak to her any more than he had spoken to Sam, and Sam had dibs on him anyway.

Still, there was a residual low level of anxiety humming inside her as she drove home. There was that rising sense of anticipation that momentum was building, in her case and in Kovac's, and that something big would happen soon.

But not tonight. Tonight she would have a nice family Friday evening with the boys. They would have lasagna and watch movies with insane car crashes, or watch professional wrestling, or whatever they wanted to do. They would all hang out in their pajamas on the big couch in the family room and fall asleep bundled up in afghans and blankets with sport team logos.

That was an infinitely preferable plan to sitting in a hard chair watching Sam have a stare-down with a silent suspect. Her mood lifted the closer she came to home, right up until she pulled onto her block and saw Speed's black Jeep Wrangler in her driveway.

Automatically annoyed, she parked at the curb and hustled up the sidewalk in the spitting drizzle, lugging what felt like forty-two pounds of Italian food. The front door flew open as she came up the steps, and the boys tumbled out onto the porch talking and laughing.

'Hey, Mom!' R.J. said in that overly excited tone he always got when his father had wound him up. 'Guess what? Dad scored tickets to the WWE! Ringside seats!'

'Wow!' Nikki said, looking at her ex. 'Two appearances in one week. If I had known, I would have worn a red dress for the occasion.'

'I just got the tickets this afternoon,' Speed said. 'I tried to call you.'

'You did not.'

'Mom! Jeez,' Kyle complained. 'Do you have to start a fight?'

'No,' she said. 'No, I don't.'

'Hey,' Speed said. 'You're the one who's always complaining that I'm not around enough.'

'And it's not even a school night!' R.J. said.

'No, that's great,' Nikki said, trying to muster a show of enthusiasm. 'I brought home lasagna. Come in and have supper before you go.'

'No time, Babe,' Speed said. 'These are VIP tix. We get a meet-and-greet with John Cena.

Gotta go! Don't wait up. They're staying with me.'

'Yeah, gotta go!' R.J. called, jumping off the porch. 'See ya, Babe! Don't wait up!'

And just like that, the three of them were bolting across the lawn and scrambling into the Jeep, where a perky-looking blonde waited in the front passenger's seat.

Nikki stood on the porch, struggling with her temper, hoping she didn't look as worn out and old and pissed off as she suddenly felt as she watched them back out of the driveway. Speed was free to have his overgrown juvenile existence. He had always had a blonde waiting for him somewhere. None of that was news. She had just been looking forward to quality time with her sons, that was all. Now she might as well be sitting downtown watching Kovac watch Gordon Krauss.

She put the food away, took a shower, put on yoga pants and a loose sweater, and set about adjusting her attitude. With the boys gone, she could spread out her work on the kitchen island. She could turn on the television and watch a show without a single exploding car. She could take a long hot bath and go to bed early.

All great ideas she couldn't get very excited about because the house was too quiet. Then it occurred to her that this would be what all her Friday nights would be like once the boys were graduated and gone. Those few years would go by in the blink of an eye.

'Oh my God, stop it!' she snapped at herself.

Needing to busy herself, she spread her work out on the kitchen island, then poured herself a glass of wine. She ate some salad and a square of lasagna, and put her mind to work, going over her notes about Evi Burke.

Her instincts were dead on. Angie Jeager/Evi Burke was the key to this case. If she hadn't been certain before, she was after their conversation that morning. She could hear it — not so much in what Evi had had to say, but in the heavy silences between. Evi knew what happened to Ted Duffy, and she knew why. And all these years later, she still felt that the burden of that truth was something she had to carry. Why?

If Angie and Jeremy Nilsen had been young lovers, what happened? Donald Nilsen would have blown a gasket, but why would he have killed Ted Duffy over it? He believed the relationship had in some way ruined his son's life. Jeremy had quit school and joined the army. Barbie Duffy had dumped the girl back into the foster system like an unwanted kitten. Nothing happened. The kids didn't run off together. There was no shotgun wedding. Would either of those things have happened had Ted Duffy been alive?

What if Angie had gotten pregnant? What would Ted Duffy, Sex Crimes detective, have done about it? Jeremy Nilsen was a minor. A statutory rape charge didn't apply. If Jeremy had actually raped her, why wouldn't Angie have given him up? Why wouldn't Evi give him up now? She worked every day with victims of sexual assault. Her personal story of overcoming her past was no secret.

If Donald Nilsen molested the girl, Duffy would have gone after him. Nilsen would have stood to lose everything, including his freedom. *That* was a motive. But if that had been the case, why wouldn't Evi Burke speak of it now? Why protect Donald Nilsen, who had gone on with his life unfettered after Ted Duffy's death?

What am I missing?

She thought about Jennifer Duffy lying in a hospital bed tonight. The burden of a secret had damaged her so badly that she had struggled with it her whole life. The weight of it had made her fragile and had nearly crushed her, now, all these years later.

Nikki slid off her stool and took her wine to her office, walking back and forth the length of the room as she looked at her time line for the day of Ted Duffy's death.

Donald Nilsen had been working from home. Ted Duffy had been chopping wood in his backyard. Jennifer Duffy had been in her bedroom, reading. Angie Jeager and Jeremy Nilsen had been at school, attending a basketball game.

The teenagers weren't really accounted for at the time. Their individual stories had been accepted as irrelevant facts. What motive would either of them have had for killing Ted Duffy? Was he trying to keep them apart? If that was an issue, surely Barbie Duffy would have mentioned it. Besides, star-crossed lovers ran off together; they didn't murder people. And if Angie got pregnant, Barbie Duffy would have, no question, brought that up. She had no love lost for the foster daughters she treated with all the compassion of Cinderella's stepmother.

If Angie Yeager caused a problem that led to the murder of Barbie's husband, Barbie would have been the first to say so, particularly when she herself had come under such intense scrutiny as a possible coconspirator in her husband's death.

Barbie had remarked that Jeremy — who had been so irrelevant to her that she had never even used his name in their conversation — attended Ted's funeral with his mother, and offered his condolences. Donald Nilsen had been conspicuously absent.

The puzzle was as intricate as a Gordian knot, so many strands interwoven and twisting around and around. Nikki's head was beginning to throb from attempting to untangle it all. She went back into the kitchen and scrounged around for a bite of something chocolate. If she was going to be frustrated, she might as well get fat doing it. Her secret hiding place in the vegetable crisper yielded half a Twix.

She sat back down at the island and ate her candy bar and had some more red wine. She wondered what her life would have been like if Speed had been murdered instead of just an asshole. She wondered if they were all having fun at the wrestling match. She wondered if the perky blonde had any clue what a heel her new boyfriend was.

Despite her ex-husband's less-than-stellar character, Nikki knew without a doubt that if someone killed him, she would, even now, be at the head of the line to hunt down his murderer. It was one thing for her to complain about his shortcomings and want to strangle him; having someone else do it was a declaration of war on her family.

Why wouldn't Barbie Duffy feel the same way? Ted was the father of her children, the father of the damaged daughter she now guarded like a tigress.

She thought again of the way Jennifer Duffy's expression had changed as she looked back on that memory of sneaking into Angie Yeager's room to read to her after bedtime . . .

Something Jennifer had said came back to her now, ominous and enigmatic: *In real life, good people can turn out to be bad people, and bad people can get away with murder . . . and worse . . .*

Someone had gotten away with her father's murder, and what could be worse than that?

Nikki looked across the room to the big whiteboard calendar on the wall. In less than a week it would be twenty-five years to the day since Ted Duffy was killed. Her calendar was a crazy mess of scribbled-in appointments, color-coded for each of them. Kyle was blue, R.J. was purple, she was hot pink. Appointments for doctors, dentists, lessons, sporting events, social events. Kyle had drawn a cartoon turkey on the date for Thanksgiving.

Add three more kids and a second adult, and the Duffys' calendar would have looked like an explosion at a crayon factory.

The Liska-Hatcher calendar week for Thanksgiving was double the usual chaos. Kyle got out of school Tuesday, R.J. on Wednesday. Regularly scheduled weeknight events had been canceled or moved because of the holiday. R.J.'s normal night for wrestling was Tuesday, but there would be no meet the Tuesday before Thanksgiving.

She thought back on her own high school years — when this crime had taken place. Boys' sporting events had been held Tuesday and Friday nights. Girls' events had been held Monday and Thursday.

Ted Duffy had been killed the Tuesday before Thanksgiving.

Nikki paged through the witness statements, looking for the name of the high school Angie Jeager and Jeremy Nilsen had attended, and then went to her office, sat down at her desk, and brought her computer to life with a move of the mouse. She typed in the name of the school and, once on the school website, brought up the calendar for the month of November. The Tuesday night before Thanksgiving was marked NO EVENTS.

There was no way of looking up the school calendar from twenty-five years in the past from this site, but the information was out there in the ether someplace. She would put Seley on it. If there was no basketball game on the night in question, then Angie's and Jeremy's alibi went out the window.

But why would they lie? Where had they been? Why had nobody really cared? If two teenagers had anything to do with the death of Ted Duffy, why would the people under the most pressure as suspects, Barbie and Big Duff, not have turned and pointed the finger at them?

It didn't make sense, but Jennifer Duffy and Angie and Jeremy were loose threads in the fabric of the story, and Nikki couldn't stand a loose thread. She would worry at it and tug at it to see where it led, and if the whole sweater unraveled in the process, so be it.

Of her three loose threads, she had access to only one: Evi Burke. Evi Burke, who didn't want her husband to know about this chapter of her past — which made little sense, because she had been through far worse, far darker chapters that were common knowledge.

It all worked out for you . . . a faceless voice on the telephone had said to Evi. The idea that her beautiful life was now somehow under threat had Evi Burke terrified.

'I'm sorry, Evi,' Nikki murmured. 'I need to know why.'

40

'You realize you're going away for a long time here, Gordon, right?' Kovac asked casually. 'We've got a whole grab bag of charges against you. Assaulting an officer, resisting arrest, fleeing the scene, attempted murder of a homeless guy last summer.'

There was a flicker of something in Krauss's eyes at that last bit, so fast that Kovac couldn't have named it. It was the first tiny crack he'd seen in Krauss's armor since they brought him in. They had been in the box now nearly four hours.

'We've got a witness who ID'd you as trying to beat his friend's brains out with a hammer.'

Still Krauss said nothing, but his expression had changed subtly. He looked less self-satisfied. He had played the Zen prisoner, saying nothing, asking for nothing, drinking nothing. Kovac had asked him several times if he wanted something to eat, but had gotten no response. But as cool as Gordon Krauss had played it, he couldn't keep it up forever. He was probably beginning to dehydrate. His stomach was growling loudly.

Slowly, Kovac had picked away at Krauss's show of confidence with small, sharp truths. He never raised his voice. He remained genial throughout, indifferent to Krauss's silence.

'Aaaah,' he said. 'You didn't know I had that in my pocket, did you? You were probably

451

thinking you were in the clear for that. It happened months ago. Just a bunch of homeless junkies having a party down by the river. Who gives a shit what happens to them, right? Nobody came looking for you.

'Turns out they weren't all high. We've got a good witness, sober as a judge, an honest-to-God war hero.' He embellished Liska's facts. Details made a more convincing story. 'And then there's the fact of those IDs we found in your room at Rising Wings. It's only a matter of time before we connect them to their owners — living or dead.'

He let that sink in and took a sip of coffee.

'You're racking up the prison time like a freaking Vegas slot machine on jackpot,' he said. 'And all that is just frosting on the cake, really, because I can put you with Diana Chamberlain at the rehab, and at her parents' house within days of the murders. And she is gonna fucking bury you to save herself. We both know that.'

The corners of Krauss's mouth turned ever so slightly downward.

'I realize you probably haven't gotten to watch much TV in the last few days,' Kovac said, 'but I have to tell you, she's a very convincing grieving daughter on camera. Ooooh, those big eyes, that pouty mouth . . . Of course, crazy girls do make the best actresses.'

He rocked in his chair, looking off wistfully, as if picturing Diana Chamberlain shining in all her bipolar glory. He came back to the moment with a sigh.

'I'm gonna go down the hall here in a minute,

and she's gonna tell me how you took advantage of her when she was at her most vulnerable, and how your beady little eyes lit up when you saw her parents' house that day. She'll probably turn on the waterworks and tell me how she's overcome with guilt for recommending Handy Dandy to her poor dead mother . . .

'I think I'll stop in the break room and get a bag of popcorn to take with me for that show,' he said, smiling.

A fine sheen of sweat glistened on Krauss's forehead. He looked *at* Kovac now, not past him.

'You're sure you don't want anything to eat, Gordon?' Kovac asked as he got up. 'I could bring you some popcorn, too. No? Suit yourself.'

He was almost to the door when Gordon Krauss spoke for the first time since he had been taken into custody.

'She asked me to do it,' he said. He had a voice like smoke and gravel. 'I told her no.'

Holy. Fucking. Shit.

Kovac turned around slowly, as if afraid a sudden move might rewind what he'd just heard. It was all he could do to maintain an expression of mild curiosity. 'You'll give me Diana Chamberlain?'

'I want a deal,' Krauss said. 'And I want a lawyer.'

★ ★ ★

'That was seriously impressive,' Taylor said as he pointed the car in the direction of Dinkytown.

The rain had subsided. Clouds scudded across

the big moon, pushed by a brisk wind bringing a fresh band of crappy cold weather from the west.

'It's all about patience,' Kovac said. 'You won't get anywhere screaming at a guy like that. You're not going to scare him. He's playing the odds. He knows he's smart. He knows he's been careful. He doesn't believe you have anything. You show him one card at a time before you throw in the big bluff.

'Bully the ones that are already scared,' he said. 'Like that guy that shit in the wastebasket the other day. He's a mouse. Mice scare easily. Krauss is a rat. He's clever and ruthless.'

'He thinks he can leverage Diana Chamberlain into leniency on the other charges,' Taylor said.

'Or mitigate the damage to him in this case.'

'He says he didn't accept the job.'

'He can say he was born of a virgin for all I care,' Kovac said. 'It doesn't matter if he took the job, didn't take the job, or is lying through his teeth. We can use him against her.'

The interview with Kovac over the second he requested an attorney, Krauss had been taken back to a holding cell to wait. Kovac's heart was still beating like a bass drum. The adrenaline was gushing through his system like water out of a fire hose. That high was one of the reasons he had stayed on the job after all these years.

Now they just had to hope Diana Chamberlain wasn't running. She hadn't answered Taylor's text regarding the suspect in custody. He had hoped that information would reel her in, that she would be curious and want to insert herself into the situation and start spinning the

454

story for damage control.

'No word of Charlie?' Kovac asked.

'None.'

That worried him. The state of the kid's apartment worried him. The fact that he — or someone — had e-mailed his resignation to his boss worried him. Kovac had locked down the apartment as a crime scene. He and Taylor had checked out the Chamberlain house in case Charlie might have gotten the idea to go home and kill himself where his parents died. The uniforms guarding the house hadn't seen him.

They pulled onto Diana's street to what was a worse-than-normal glut of cars. Someone in her building was having a belated Halloween party. Despite the chill in the air, costumed revelers spilled out of the big house, onto the wide porch, down the steps, and onto the sidewalk and lawn, drinking and dancing.

Taylor double-parked. The patrol car that had followed them there parked behind them. As they got out of the cars, Kovac directed the uniformed officers to go around the house and cover alternate means of escape.

Friday night — one of the last there would be before winter smacked its frozen fist down on the city and forced everyone indoors until spring. Students were out celebrating their couple of days of freedom from the drudgery of academia. Kovac and Taylor had to thread their way through a mob of ghosts, ghouls, vampires, and zombies to get to the door of Diana Chamberlain's apartment.

Taylor knocked hard. 'Diana? It's Detective Taylor!'

He had to shout in the attempt to be heard above the music and the voices of the partygoers. Recordings of screams and shrieks and moans emanated from a dozen or more smartphones, adding to the atmosphere.

Taylor pounded on the door again. 'Diana?'

'Kick it in,' Kovac ordered, pulling his weapon and positioning himself to the side of the door.

The old door frame gave way with little effort on Taylor's part.

'Police! We've got a warrant!' Kovac called and then ducked inside and to the left, back to the wall, gun out in front of him. Taylor followed.

The apartment was dark and still. And cold, Kovac realized. He could feel a breeze from the windows on the other side of the room. The cheap curtains and moonlight fluttered inward.

As his eyes adjusted to the lack of light, it became clear that Diana's apartment, a mess to begin with, was in an even greater state of disarray than he remembered. Chairs had been overturned. Trash littered the floor. The sofa and heavy armchair had been cut and disemboweled in much the same manner as Charlie's furniture had been.

Holding his gun in one hand, Kovac pulled his phone out of his coat pocket and turned on the flashlight. As he began to shine it around the room, a couple of drunken partygoers stumbled into the apartment, laughing. Taylor wheeled on them, gun first, and barked, 'Get the fuck out! Police business!'

Their eyes bugged out comically, and they backpedaled, tripping each other and falling into the hall. Taylor shut the door and turned the deadbolt.

Kovac moved toward the lone bedroom. The door was closed but not latched. He stood to the side and pushed it open with his foot. Nothing happened. No one shouted. No shots were fired. The room held the same cold, eerie feeling of stillness, save for the curtains and moonlight drifting inward. The breeze pushed the scent of blood and feces toward them. A figure lay motionless on the bed.

He shone his light on the body that lay spread-eagle among the tangled sheets, naked and painted in blood, drenched in blood, so much blood no skin was visible at a glance.

The victim was a male of medium stature. He had been eviscerated and castrated. The intestines spilled out of the body cavity and onto the sheets.

'Holy God,' Taylor murmured, lowering his weapon.

'I think we might have just found Charlie,' Kovac said, though it was merely speculation on his part.

The victim's head was nowhere to be seen.

41

'Holy ninja, Batman,' Steve Culbertson said as he stood over the body. 'Someone cut off this man's giblets with a Ginsu knife!'

'That would appear to be the least of his problems,' Kovac said.

They stood around Diana Chamberlain's bedroom in Tyvek jumpsuits so as not to contaminate — or be contaminated by — the gruesome scene. The lights were on now — the shitty overhead light and a couple of utility lights on tripods brought in by the ME's investigator. The scene was only more horrific in the harsh light, the victim's intestines gleaming wet as they spilled to either side of the body, the blood a vibrant dark red as it soaked the white sheets.

'Is the head lying around here somewhere?' Culbertson asked as he examined the abdominal wounds.

'Nope,' Kovac said. 'Head and genitalia are MIA.'

He had seen more decapitated bodies than most people, yet it always amazed him how his brain wanted immediately to reject the image as not being real. The sight so went against nature that the brain would try to come up with an alternate explanation, no matter how far-fetched, rather than accept the terrible truth. He had often heard people say, about finding dead bodies in general, that they had thought it was a mannequin in the ditch, in the river, wherever it had been found, as if random mannequins littering the landscape were a common occurrence.

It certainly wasn't natural to see a death like this one. As hardened as all the people in this room were, this wasn't normal even to them. Each would react and cope with it in his or her own way, which might sound callous or disrespectful or inappropriate to regular citizens, but it was how they learned to cope with the horrors they had to deal with on a daily basis. They all understood that, even their proper lieutenant.

'Decapitated first or eviscerated first?' Mascherino asked.

Kovac had alerted her to what they had found. He hadn't expected her to show up. She had crossed herself upon seeing the body, but hadn't turned a hair at the brutality of the scene. He gave her a gold star for being tougher than he had given her credit for.

'Eviscerated first is my guess,' Culbertson said. 'But he must have been unconscious. There are no ligature marks on the wrists or ankles, no defensive knife wounds on the hands or arms that I can see. Nobody's going to just lie down and take this. I mean, Mel Gibson in *Braveheart*, but in real life? No.

'It looks like the blade went in here about three inches to the right of the navel,' he said, tracing the path in the air above the body, 'and was pulled across to the left. Then inserted in the middle and pulled up toward the sternum.'

'*Seppuku*,' Taylor said.

Everyone looked at him.

'*Seppuku*,' he said again. 'The ritual suicide of the samurai. They disemboweled themselves.'

'And they cut off their own heads?' Kovac asked. 'That's a special trick.'

'No. Somebody else did that for them.'

'Why do you know these things?'

'I told you. I grew up on martial arts movies. In ritual suicide, the samurai kneels and makes the first cut across the abdomen then pulls the blade up toward the sternum, literally spilling his guts. Then a chosen swordsman whacks the guy's head off with a single slice.'

'What about the boy bits?' Mascherino asked. 'Is castration part of the ritual?'

Taylor shook his head. 'Not that I know of.'

'That's an angry crazy woman,' Kovac said. 'That's what that is.'

'You really think Diana Chamberlain is capable of doing this?' the lieutenant asked, sounding dubious.

'Taylor thinks she beat the hell out of Charlie yesterday,' Kovac said. 'And she would certainly know how all this was done. She's a graduate student in East Asian history. She grew up in a houseful of the weapons the samurai used. And if Gordon Krauss is to be believed, she solicited him to murder her parents. And if he didn't take her up on it, then who did? I don't think this kind of violence is beyond her.'

'Have you contacted the other professor?' Mascherino asked. 'Her lover?'

'Calls go straight to voice mail,' Taylor said.

'Could be they're in this together. They both benefit. Sato gets the big job at the U. If Charlie's out of the picture, they share the spoils: the collection, the inheritance, the house — everything.'

'And they're free to be lovers without Charlie's disapproval,' Kovac said.

'If this is Charlie,' the lieutenant said.

'If this is Charlie. This could be the mailman, for all we know.'

'Then where does Krauss fit in?'

'Maybe he doesn't. Maybe he didn't take the job. Maybe he's a liar and an opportunist. I suggested to him that Diana might have asked him for a favor. Maybe he just took the ball and ran with it. Or maybe Diana was setting him up as a scapegoat. We know Sato knows how to use a sword.'

Mascherino nodded. 'Put out an APB on all three of them: Ken Sato, and Charles and Diana Chamberlain. Armed and dangerous.'

42

'I had to kill him. It had to happen that way to close the circle.'

There was comfort in inevitability, once one accepted that truth and let go the need to control. As it turned out, surrender of control led to freedom. Control wasn't freedom at all. Control was a burden. Acceptance was freedom. In acceptance, chaos fell into silence, and the Way became crystal clear.

So beautifully simple. So very *Bushido* . . .

Lucien Chamberlain claimed to have appreciated that philosophy. *Bushido*: the way of the samurai. The essence of life is found in death. If he truly believed that, he would have died happy.

Of course, he didn't truly believe that. The things Lucien coveted from the way of the warrior were the obvious and wrong things: power, control, force, superiority, and violence for the sake of all those other things. And because of that, death was the necessary end to the cycle of abuse.

I love you — I hate you. I give — I take. On a whim. For a laugh. To punish you. To belittle you. To give false hope for no other reason than to take it away again just to prove a point. I'm stronger than you. I'm more powerful than you. I'm more ruthless than you. I will control you. I will hurt you because I can — to keep you down, to make you crawl, to make you beg . . . for love.

You don't belong here anyway; we just keep you because we can . . .

Around and around, and around and around. It was time to close the circle.

'I know, deep down, you understand. We're supposed to be together, you and I. Our fates are intertwined. We were put together for a reason. We have to accept that. In acceptance we find freedom.'

They drove south on surface streets. They didn't have far to go. It was a small world, after all.

One more stop. That was all. One more stop, and the circle would be complete. In order for the circle to be complete, one had to find the beginning. The very beginning.

The search had taken time and patience, starting and ending long before the killings, but with no end purpose in mind. Just the need to know, to have a name, to imagine a face, to ponder the why. But the pieces had fallen magically into place. The universe had a plan. It wasn't always clear, and it wasn't always kind, but in the end a pattern emerged. The circle of life: birth, conflict, growth, enlightenment, death. And in death one found the meaning of life.

There was comfort in acceptance of truth. Accepting the inevitable created simplicity. Simplicity was a beautiful thing, even drenched in blood.

The side street was dark and empty. The neighborhood was quiet.

'I'm sorry you can't come with me, but this part is mine. We'll be together again soon. Then we'll be together forever.'

The kiss was long and lingering, with no one to judge. There was freedom now. It didn't matter that the lips were cold or that the body was lifeless. The spirit lived on. Their spirits would live on together once the circle was complete.

43

'Thank God they caught the guy,' Eric said.

They had watched the story of the murder suspect's capture on the local news at five and six. The station was featuring the story in their promo for the news at ten. The crime had been so horrific, the capture of the suspect had the entire Twin Cities population breathing a collective sigh of relief, and clamoring for details at the same time. Had he known the couple? Had he killed before? How had he gained entry to their home? Could this happen to us?

The suspect had worked for a handyman service. Already the news on channel eleven had put together a companion piece on how commonly used household services like handyman services and carpet cleaners, and even home security companies, could be staffed by dangerous criminals.

Evi didn't want to think about any of it. She had spent so much of her life feeling afraid, being in danger. The last two nights had reminded her: She didn't want that emotion in the life she had now. She wanted to feel safe. Tonight she couldn't remember what that felt like.

How fragile perfection was. Like a snowflake, beautiful and unique, and gone in the blink of an eye with the touch of a finger. Just days ago she had looked at her life and dared to believe that

465

happiness could last. Tonight she felt the weight of dread on her shoulders.

'I don't like that you could have met that guy,' Eric grumbled.

'I didn't meet him,' Evi said. 'I told you.'

'But you could have. The home visits scare me. You know that. Some of those girls know some rough customers.'

'And I would know more about that than you, wouldn't I?'

'I know you do. I know you're aware. I know you're careful. But we both know none of that stops somebody else from doing something terrible. I just — '

Evi reached up and put a finger against his lips. 'Can we not talk about this anymore tonight? I'm tired. You're tired. I just want to sit here with you and relax and stare at the television.'

He smiled and wrapped his arm around her shoulders and kissed the top of her head. 'Yes, ma'am.'

They sat on their cushy couch with their stocking feet up on the big ottoman. Eric snuggled Evi into his side and used the remote control to cue up a show they both liked, which they had recorded while having their evening playtime/bath time/bedtime with their daughter. The first thing to come up when he pushed the Play button was the promo for the ten o'clock news, the photograph of Gordon Krauss briefly filling the screen.

Detective Liska had asked Evi if this man could be Jeremy Nilsen grown up and gone bad.

She honestly couldn't say. In twenty-five years her memory of him had faded to a blur. She remembered thinking he was handsome. He had a strong jaw and straight brows. His hair was brown. He was lean and athletic. Beyond that, she couldn't recall. She'd known him for such a short time and then had never seen him again. She had become a different person, and the memories that belonged to the girl she was had been buried or thrown away. Better for both of them.

The man in the photograph Detective Liska had shown her, the one that kept popping up on the TV screen, was bearded and dirty-looking. When she studied his face, she saw an animal, something clever and hungry, and dangerous. Was that who Jeremy had become? If it was, how much of that was her fault?

'Earth to Evi. Earth to Evi. Come in, Evi!'

She snapped back into the moment, embarrassed. 'I'm sorry, what?'

'You went away from me for a while there,' Eric said, looking into her eyes. 'You had that 'Long, long ago, in a galaxy far, far away' look. Are you okay?'

'I'm sorry,' she said again — an old habit that never died: apologizing for everything. 'I just drifted away for a minute.'

'Stay with me,' he murmured, kissing her cheek. 'This is a happier place.'

'Yes,' she said, finding a smile for him.

She nearly jumped out of her skin as the phone on the end table rang. Eric picked it up and answered.

467

'Burke residence.'

Evi's heart was in her throat, beating so fast she thought it might burst.

Eric looked perplexed. 'Hello? Who is this?'

What was he hearing? Could he see the guilt on her face for not having told him about the call last night? Would he know by looking at her that she was keeping something from him? What would she say when he ended the call?

'Hello?' he said again, then shrugged and put the phone back in its cradle. 'Wrong number, I guess.'

'What did they say?'

'Nothing.'

'I'm going to make some tea,' Evi said, popping up from the sofa. 'Would you like some?'

'No, thanks, sweetie. Do you want me to get it?' he asked. 'You still look pale to me.'

'No, no. I want to stretch my legs,' she said too brightly, already heading for the kitchen.

She wasn't sure her legs would carry her that far. They felt like limp noodles beneath her. She turned and went into the kitchen, immediately rushing to the sink and bending over, her head swimming, her stomach flipping. She thought she would vomit. She was shaking and sweating and cold all at once.

What if the caller had spoken? What if the voice had whispered, 'It all worked out for you?' Would Eric have taken one look at her and known she'd heard it before?

Why couldn't this all just go away? No one could change the past. The years had grown over those secrets like vines hiding a ruin from another lifetime.

'Ev?'

She bolted upright at the sound of her husband's voice coming from the dining room. She fumbled to turn the faucet on, grabbed the kettle off the stove.

'Ev? Is everything okay in here?' Eric asked as he walked into the kitchen.

'Yeah, fine. It's all fine.'

He took the teakettle from her and put it on the stove to heat, then turned back to her, his expression serious.

'What's going on with you? You almost jumped out of your skin when the phone rang,' he said. 'You're a nervous wreck. What's up?'

He put one gentle hand on her shoulder and tipped her chin up with the other. 'You know there's nothing you can't tell me. You know that, right?'

She looked up at him, so handsome, so earnest, her knight in shining armor. What should she tell him? The lie that it was nothing? The lie that there was something going on at work? Should she tell him about the note that had come in the mail, or the shadow she might have seen in the backyard, or the call she had kept from him?

It all worked out for you . . .

Should she tell him she had knowledge of a murder and had kept that secret for most of her life?

'Evi . . . ' He said her name on a sigh, like he was disappointed in her or frustrated with her.

He had every reason to be. He had always been so patient with her, and still she didn't trust him?

No. It wasn't that she didn't trust him. It was that he had trusted her, and she didn't deserve it. She didn't deserve him.

It all worked out for you . . . But it shouldn't have. The mistakes that had been made all those years ago couldn't be abandoned and forgotten. The effects of those mistakes continued to ripple forward through time and touch the lives of all concerned, and the lives of every person *those* people had touched, like Eric, like Mia . . .

Could she even stop it now with the truth?

She drew a shuddering breath to speak, still not knowing what she would say.

The teakettle screamed, startling her.

Eric turned and took it off the burner, turning off the flame.

'Let's go sit down,' he said.

Evi felt like she had already missed her window of opportunity to do the right thing, that anything she said now would be viewed as the result of coercion, not something volunteered because she knew he had a right to hear it.

Something banged against the back door as she poured the steaming water into her mug, and she flinched and splashed water on the counter.

'What the hell?' Eric asked. He leaned over the sink and looked out the window, trying to see past his own reflection.

'It's getting windy,' he murmured. 'I meant to put that patio umbrella in the garage a week ago.'

'Just leave it,' Evi said. 'It doesn't matter.'

'No. We'll hear that thing thumping all night,'

he said, going into the laundry room/mud room. 'It won't take five minutes. I'll just stick it in the garage and deal with it tomorrow.'

He grabbed a heavy jacket off a hook on the wall and threw it on, and stepped into a pair of work boots with the laces undone.

'I wish you'd just leave it,' Evi said.

'I'll be right back. You won't even have time to miss me,' he said, shooting her a wink as he opened the door.

But in the next instant, time went into slow motion, and what must have been only seconds seemed to last an eternity.

Eric didn't see the monster coming. He was glancing back at her as he opened the door. Evi saw what rushed at them out of the darkness. The face was surreal: a horrific white mask with blood-red details and a demonic grimace twisting the black mouth into the shape of a horseshoe. Two black holes stared where the eyes should have been. A bristling black mustache sprouted sideways beneath the elaborately flared nostrils of the red nose.

Evi screamed.

Eric turned toward it and threw his arms up to protect himself as something glinting silver swung down at him. Blood sprayed against the white wall and cupboards, and across the white washing machine. The momentum of the attacker pushed them backward, farther into the room as the monster slashed and hacked at Eric.

Her husband's blood sprayed across Evi's face and arms. She screamed again, but the sound

471

seemed far in the distance, dulled by her pulse roaring in her ears.

She stumbled to the side, arms thrust up in front of her, watching in horror as Eric, his face a mask of blood, pushed forward at the assailant. The demon stepped back, letting Eric's momentum carry him out the door. It struck Eric again, across the back, sending him sprawling face-first down the steps of the deck.

'*Eric!*'

And then the monster was rushing at her. For the first time, she realized what the weapon was, but immediately her brain tried to tell her it wasn't real. It couldn't be.

She had to run. She had to get to a phone. She had to get this thing out of her house, away from her daughter. If she ran out the front door, would it follow her? If she ran across the street, would a neighbor let her in?

But the demon was on her before she could even turn to run. It hit her hard in the sternum with the hilt of the weapon, and pain exploded through her body, shutting down every other signal. She fell backward, her head bouncing hard off the floor. Her vision dimmed as if someone had thrown black lace across her eyes.

Then the assailant was on top of her, staring down at her with its sightless eyes and toothless grimace. The demon's whispered voice was one she had heard before.

'I'm here for you, Evangeline. Aren't you lucky now?'

It all worked out for you . . .

44

Nikki drove the Crosstown Highway for the second time that day, hoping she wasn't making a big mistake. She felt so close to having an answer, just a piece or two away from finishing the puzzle and having the complete picture of the events that had led to Ted Duffy's murder a quarter of a century past. Evi Burke held those pieces, the weight of them pulling on her, pressing down on her. The strain had been there in her eyes as she had looked out the window that morning.

The questionable alibis of the teenagers were the fine cracks in the time line of that day. Nikki wanted to put pressure there to see if the cracks would deepen and split apart. She had tried earlier to call Evi Burke on her cell phone. The call had gone straight to voice mail. That was fine. She didn't want to speak to the woman on the telephone. She wanted to see her face-to-face. She wanted to do what she and Sam called 'a Columbo': *Just one more question, ma'am.* Just a little more pressure. Just another quarter turn of the screw that tightened the nerves . . .

And the second she thought it, she saw Jennifer Duffy in her head. She pictured Jennifer Duffy in a hospital bed with a heart monitor beeping.

Evi Burke wasn't Jennifer Duffy. Evi Burke had fought her way through tougher times than most people could ever imagine in their worst nightmares. But that didn't mean she wasn't fragile in her own way. It was clear she didn't want her past tainting the life she had now — a career she loved, a husband she loved, a beautiful little family.

It all worked out for you . . .

A faceless voice on the telephone had whispered those words, an allusion to the past. Why? It seemed everyone from the time of Ted Duffy's death wanted those memories left in the shadows where they had been all these years. If the call was related to that part of Evi's life, then who? Why? Why now?

Nikki turned off the highway and into the Burkes' quiet neighborhood. With her husband home, Evi would have to feel safer than she had in the last couple of days. All the more reason for Nikki to drop by unannounced. She didn't want the woman sleeping too soundly. She wanted her thinking about Jeremy Nilsen and the Duffy family, and whatever she knew about Ted Duffy that she had kept to herself all these years. Even if she wouldn't answer the question tonight, the seed would be planted — but gently, just slipped under the surface; something to worry at, like a sliver just under the skin.

The lights were on in the Burkes' living room. Softer lights illuminated the second story, glowing through the curtains. Nikki parked at the curb and went to the front door, knocking instead of ringing the doorbell. She expected Eric Burke to answer, as he had that morning. She would have to talk her way past him.

She was there to inform them personally that the suspect who had been at large was now in custody, and they had determined he was not in any way connected to Evi's case at the Chrysalis Center. That was her in. That was her cover story. Lame, but it would get her in the door.

If anyone ever came to answer the door.

She knocked again, a little harder, and rose up on tiptoe to try to see in through the glass panes arranged in a fan shape at the top of the door. A futile effort. She could hear voices. The television, she decided as the volume rose with what sounded like a commercial: animated, rapid-fire staccato voices and a quick blast of music.

She knocked again.

They might have gone to the kitchen. They might have gone upstairs to check on their little girl.

She rang the bell and waited. She looked to see if they had a security camera pointed at the front steps. Were they ignoring her because they recognized her and simply didn't want to deal with her?

She didn't see a camera.

Unease began to scratch along her nerves. She'd made enough noise that she should have gotten a response of some kind by now. She pulled her phone out of her jacket pocket and called the house number. As the phone rang in her ear, she could hear it ringing in the living room a second later. Six rings, and the call went to voice mail.

Slowly Nikki moved off the steps and onto the

grass. She tried to see through the partially open blinds and into the living room. She could see a lamp on an end table, a corner of the sofa, the television sitting on a console.

Around the corner, she could see into the dining room, where a pair of small lamps glowed on an antique sideboard. The soft white under-cabinet lights were on in the kitchen.

Where were Evi and Eric Burke? Why weren't they answering the phone? Why hadn't one of them come to the door?

Maybe they were otherwise engaged, Nikki thought again as she made her way to the back of the house. Maybe she was thinking like a cop while the Burkes were thinking like a happily married couple on a Friday night. Eric Burke was a firefighter. He worked a twenty-four-hour shift and then had two days off. The night was young, and they could sleep in tomorrow.

What would I be doing if I had a hot fireman husband and no work tomorrow? she asked herself.

Yeah.

She almost turned to go back to her car, thinking she should just go home and have that hot bath she had promised herself. Tomorrow was another day.

She decided she would complete the circle around the house, and if she didn't catch a glimpse of someone inside, she would leave.

The backyard was awash in moonlight that came and went as clouds sailed across the sky. The wind had picked up, brisk and cold. The temperature would drop below freezing tonight.

476

The tree branches rattled like bags of bones. The swings on the little swing set were swaying, chains squeaking. At the back of the property sat a child's playhouse.

A wooden deck that overlooked the backyard ran the width of the house. The hulking shape of a gas grill filled the near corner. The wind rattled a patio umbrella in its stand and bumped it against the house's siding.

Nikki rounded the end of the deck and stopped cold at the sight of a body sprawled head-first down the steps.

She pulled her phone out of her pocket, turned on the flashlight, and pointed it as she crept closer, lighting up the bloody face of Eric Burke.

★ ★ ★

'Who are you? Why are you doing this to us?'

The demon didn't answer. He shoved her forward, up the stairs.

Evi's heart was quivering like a frightened bird trapped at the base of her throat. Her legs were so weak with fear she could hardly lift her feet. She tripped going up the stairs, and had to catch hold of the railing or fall on her face. Her assailant shoved at her back with the hilt of the sword.

A sword. This had to be a nightmare. Had she passed out? Had she lost her mind? This couldn't possibly be happening.

I'm here for you, Evangeline. Aren't you lucky now?

It all worked out for you . . .

As she stumbled into the hall at the top of the stairs, she turned and hurried past Mia's room, hoping and praying her daughter stayed asleep. Even as she hoped that, she heard Mia call out in a sleepy voice, 'Mommy?' and her nightmare memories of childhood flashed through her mind: hiding in a closet, trying not to cry while she listened to the sounds of what men did to her mother for money, for drugs, for punishment, for fun.

The monster shoved her through the open door of her bedroom. She tripped and fell, and then scrambled to her feet, backing up until she ran into the wall.

Downstairs, someone was knocking at the front door.

Down the hall, Mia called again, 'Mommy?'

Her assailant stepped close, the bloody sword held across its chest. The voice hissed behind the hideous mask. 'I'll cut your throat like I cut your husband's. Then who protects the pretty little girl?'

Evi bit down on the urge to sob, the terror lodging in her throat like a fist. It was all she could do to keep from choking on it.

Was Eric dead? She had seen his blood spray across the laundry room. She had felt it hit her face and arm.

She touched a trembling hand to her face as the demon stepped back. Her fingers came away smeared with her husband's blood. She pressed her hands to her mouth to keep from screaming.

'It doesn't matter who it is,' her tormentor

mumbled, taking a step back from her. 'This is your destiny. You can't escape who you are. You can't escape what you've done.'

Evi wasn't sure if the words were meant for her or for the monster, who began to pace in front of her. Dressed all in black from head to toe, with a wide cloth belt banding the waist, a long knife in a scabbard hung from the belt, this looked like a character from a movie, but it was all too real. She had seen her husband fall. Her throat was raw from screaming. Her child was crying down the hall.

The knocking came again.

Had someone heard her screams? Could Eric have gotten to a neighbor's house?

The phone on the nightstand rang like a sudden alarm. Evi jumped and looked toward it. If she could pick it up, she could yell for help. But she couldn't get to it. It was too far away. She would die trying, leaving her daughter at the mercy of a madman.

Somewhere there was a person on the other end of that call sitting in a comfortable chair waiting for her to pick up. Maybe a friend. Maybe a telemarketer. Whoever it was, it would never occur to them that she wasn't answering because a masked assailant would hack her to death with a sword if she tried.

The ringing stopped as the call went to voice mail.

She couldn't expect help. She couldn't wait for help. She had no way of fighting, but she had to try something. Maybe if she could make her attacker see her as a person instead of a target, she could buy some time.

'Who are you?' she asked, her voice trembling. She needed to sound calm. She swallowed hard and tried again. 'Please, tell me why you're here. What did I do to you?'

If she was going to die, she wanted to know the reason.

The monster stepped closer until the grotesque mask was inches from her face. It tilted to one side and then the other. Deep inside the black-rimmed eyeholes, blue eyes burned bright with madness.

'Do I know you?' she asked.

'You should. Jeager, Evangeline Grace.'

'You owe me this, Evangeline.'

'Please tell me why,' she pleaded. 'I don't know who you are. How did I ever hurt you? Please tell me.'

He pulled the mask off and tossed it on the bed, then looked at her and waited, as if he thought she would surely recognize him. His face was a battered mess, swollen and bruised. His lower lip was fat and split. He was young, twenty-something, with blue eyes and brown hair. She had never seen him before in her life.

She stared at him until her eyes burned, praying for some spark of memory. Was he connected to a client? Someone's boyfriend? Someone's brother? Her client Hope Anders had a brother she had accused of molesting her, but he was big and red-haired.

How could someone she had never met be so angry with her?

'You don't know me?' he asked.

Evi said nothing, afraid of his reaction. The sound of her breathing filled the silence that stretched between them.

'You should,' he murmured. 'You gave me life.'

45

'Don't you fucking die on me, Fireman!' Nikki ordered, leaning over Eric Burke.

She had pulled him onto the grass at the bottom of the deck stairs. He had a pulse. It was weak, but it was there. He had been cut badly across the face with some kind of blade. One eye was gone. She could see his cheekbone; she could see his teeth through the gaping wound.

'That's gonna leave a scar,' she said to him, saying anything just to keep him connected. 'Don't worry. Women go for that shit. You get an eye patch, and you're all set.'

With one hand, she pressed hard on a badly bleeding wound at the base of his neck; with the other hand, she fumbled with her phone to call Dispatch.

Having no idea where the assailant might be, she kept her voice low as she rattled off the required information about her rank and her badge number and location. Her voice was trembling from the adrenaline rush.

'Listen to me carefully,' she said. 'I've got a badly wounded man here. I need a bus at this location ASAP, but absolutely no lights, no sirens. Got that? I've got a situation ongoing. And I need two backup units. I say again: no lights, no sirens. Tell them to come up the alley behind the house. I'm with the victim in the backyard.'

She made the dispatcher repeat her instructions back as she looked down into Eric Burke's remaining eye. She could see his fear. She knew that look. He could feel his life draining out of him.

'Eric, you hang on,' she said. 'You're not gonna let a cop be the last thing you see, are you?' You're a fireman, for God's sake!'

That was always the running joke between the professions: Firemen thought they were better than cops, and cops thought they were better than firemen. The ribbing between them never ended.

Eric Burke's lips moved, but he made no sound. She could feel his body starting to shake. He was going into shock.

'You stay with me here, Fireman. I've got your buddies on the way to haul you out of here. Don't you punk out on me!'

His mouth moved again. 'Ev — Ev — '

'Evi,' Nikki said. 'I know. I'll make you a deal, Fireman. You take care of you. I'll take care of Evi. I'll take care of her now, and you can take care of her later. Right?'

She could see him losing the focus in his good eye. She bumped him in the side with a knee to jostle him back, to make the synapses fire in another part of his brain.

'Eric, do you know who did this to you?'

No response.

Shit, shit, shit.

'Eric, is he still here? Is he in the house?'

He stared up at her. She was losing him.

She leaned harder against the wound. Her

hand was slick with his blood; it seeped between her fingers.

'Damn it, Eric! Stay with me! You've got a pretty wife and a beautiful little girl to live for. Fight!'

★ ★ ★

His words tried to penetrate Evi's brain at the same time as her brain tried to reject them.

You gave me life.

Jeager, Evangeline Grace. Her name, as if read from a legal document.

It couldn't be.

'You don't recognize me?' he asked with sarcasm and a bitter little smile. 'I'm Baby Boy Jeager. Father: Unknown.'

Oh my God . . .

Down the hall, Mia called for her again.

'I'm the one you didn't want,' her tormentor said.

Evi thought she might faint. She pressed herself hard against the wall to keep from falling as the floor seemed to sway beneath her feet.

Baby Boy Jeager. Father unknown.

Son of Ted Duffy, come to avenge a father he didn't even know. The father who had died because of him.

She had gone to great lengths to bury those truths so deep inside she would never find them again. She had lost herself on the streets, and had been plunged into a terrible purgatory of degradation, drugs, sex, and despair. It had somehow seemed fitting to try to forget one nightmare by living in another, losing herself in the process. But here she was, all these years later, with that past staring her in the eye, ready to cut her throat.

You can't escape who you are, he'd said. *You can't escape what you did.*

She said the first thing that made any sense to say: 'I'm sorry.'

'No, you're not,' he said. 'You're sorry I'm here now. It all worked out for you. Here you are with your nice little life and your nice little family. It all worked out for you.'

She wanted to ask him his name, but she didn't dare. She hadn't given him a name when he was born. If she'd given the baby a name, it would have been harder to try to forget. She saw him once after giving birth, then he had been whisked away to a better life than she could have given him, to parents who had no memory of his conception or of what had transpired because of it.

Even as she remembered, the smell of whiskey and smoke and man filled her head. Her mother had died. She felt so alone, so empty. She wanted comfort. She needed connection. He came to her room to check on her. He held her while she cried. It was late. The house was quiet. He'd had too much to drink. The job was draining the humanity from him. He refilled himself with whiskey to dull the pain.

She didn't understand what she shouldn't want. She knew what she felt, and she knew what she didn't want to feel: alone, abandoned. He kissed her. He touched her. She couldn't think. She didn't want to. Was this what it had been like for her mother giving herself over to a man? A welcome escape from the pain and emptiness of her life?

He didn't force her. She didn't fight him.

He cried afterward. He sat on the edge of her bed with his head in his hands and sobbed, ashamed, apologetic. She looked past him to see Jennifer's small face, wide-eyed as she peered out of her hiding place in the closet. And then the shame was Evi's . . .

She couldn't tell this man any of that. This man, her own child, who had come here to kill her.

'I couldn't keep you,' she said. 'I was seventeen. I didn't have a home. I didn't have a family. I couldn't give you anything but a better chance.'

'You don't know anything about what you gave me,' he said.

'I gave you more than I had.'

She hadn't hated the baby she carried. She'd hated the circumstances that had created him, and the tragedy that followed. She blamed herself for needing things that had never been meant for her — comfort, safety, love — but she gave the child a chance to have those things. It never occurred to her that he might grow up to hate her for it. Not in her worst nightmares did she ever foresee this.

'You gave me to a nightmare!' he shouted, lunging at her, pressing the sword to her throat.

Evi swallowed hard. She felt the blade scrape

against her skin. Tears blurred her vision and spilled down her cheeks.

'I'm here to give it back,' he said. 'I'm done with it. It's time to close the circle.'

46

Nikki entered the house through the open back door, weapon drawn. She had charged the first uniformed officers to come up the alley with keeping Eric Burke alive until the ambulance arrived. One was keeping pressure on his neck wound while the other started chest compressions as he began to slip away.

The lights were on in the laundry room/mud room, a cheery white space splashed with Eric Burke's blood. The spatter arced across the room on the ceiling, on the wall, on the washing machine, on the floor. What the hell was this assailant fighting with? Burke's face had been laid open like the belly of a gutted fish — sliced too cleanly for the weapon to have been an axe or a hatchet. If it was a knife, the blade was long.

She thought of Kovac's samurai sword murders. What the hell was wrong with people?

Drops of blood pooled on the kitchen floor where the attacker had paused for a moment.

Where was Evi? Where was little Mia?

A faint cry of 'Mommy!' from overhead cut along Nikki's nerve endings like a razor. Her blood pressure spiked so hard she could hear her blood rushing across her eardrums. At least the child was alive. Was she crying over her mother's dead body? Was the assailant still in the house?

Leading with her weapon, she moved into the dining room. There was no sign of a struggle, save for the drops of blood on the hardwood floor that led the way into the living room and up the stairs to the bedrooms.

The patrol sergeant in the backyard had argued for her to wait for a SWAT unit. Nikki refused. What were they supposed to do? Sit around on the deck waiting while Evi Burke and her daughter were raped and slaughtered inside the house? No.

The sound of voices upstairs rose and fell. She couldn't make out how many or what they were saying.

From where she stood at the bottom of the stairs, she could see nothing. She would be a sitting duck if there were a bad guy in the hallway.

The child's voice wailed, the sound piercing Nikki's ear like a needle. 'Mommy! Mommy!'

She swore under her breath. Kovac would kill her for going in alone — if someone else didn't kill her first.

She started slowly up the stairs.

⋆   ⋆   ⋆

The hit on the BOLO for Charlie Chamberlain's car pulled Kovac and Taylor out of the crime scene in Diana Chamberlain's apartment. Mascherino had taken charge of the scene, sending them on their way.

The Toyota was found parked on a side street in a quiet neighborhood east of Lake Nokomis, not far from where Gordon Krauss was apprehended earlier in the day. Kovac asked for the reporting officers to sit on the car from a discreet distance and wait for them to get there.

Was there supposed to have been a meeting there? Kovac wondered. Was this the place chosen for a payoff to Krauss, to buy his silence about the solicitation with enough cash to get him out of town?

The radio crackled with coded bursts as they sped south on Hiawatha, dash strobe running. Reports of a home invasion in the area. Units were on the scene and multiple units were en route. Not my monkeys, not my circus, Kovac thought as they turned off the main drag and were instantly swallowed up by a neighborhood of small, neat older homes. He killed the dash light.

There was no sign of the patrol car that had called in on the BOLO and should have been sitting watching, waiting for the Toyota's driver to return. They had responded to the home invasion call-out.

Kovac and Taylor walked up on the Toyota, one on either side, each with a Maglite held high. The keys were on the driver's seat. Bloody fingerprints and handprints marred the pale gray interior on the dash, and the interior of both doors. Blood smeared the passenger's seat.

'Well, that's not a good sign,' Kovac muttered.

'You want to wait for a crime scene unit?' Taylor asked.

'We'll be here all night.'

Kovac opened the driver's-side door with a gloved hand, reached in, and pressed the button to pop the trunk.

He didn't know what he had been expecting. He had suspected the corpse at Diana's belonged to Charlie, that Diana and Sato had killed him to get him out of their way. But when he and Taylor both shone their flashlights into the trunk of Charlie Chamberlain's car, it was Diana Chamberlain inside.

She looked like she was resting, lying on her side with her eyes half closed. Her throat had been cut from ear to ear. Placed next to her, staring up at them, was the head of Ken Sato, his penis sticking out of his mouth.

47

'Mommy! Mommy!' Mia ran into the room, sobbing.

Evi looked at her daughter and, heedless of the blade at her throat, shouted, 'Run, Mia! Run!'

But her daughter, just five years old, and never having known danger in her whole brief life, didn't understand. Mommy was her safety. She stood ten feet away, confused and terrified, wailing, her precious little face red and wet.

Rage rose up like a wall inside Evi. Whatever mistakes she had made in her life, this would not be one of them. She wouldn't let her murder be the last thing her child saw before a madman butchered her.

She reached up and clawed at her assailant's eyes. Startled, he pulled back in reaction, lifting the blade from her throat.

Evi kneed him in the groin and ducked to the side as he doubled over, her focus on Mia. If she could grab her child and run —

He caught her by the hair, nearly yanking her off her feet, and slammed her back against the wall, shouting, 'NO! No! You will *not* ruin this for me!'

The back of Evi's head banged hard on the frame of the window. Her knees went weak, and her vision swam. She saw him turn toward Mia. She reached out to try to grab him and dropped to her knees, too dizzy to keep her feet beneath her.

She watched in horror as he scooped up her daughter. He had dropped the sword in favor of the long knife that hung from his belt. He put the point of the blade to Mia's throat.

'You're going to do what I tell you!' he shouted. 'Or I'll slit her throat, and you can watch her die!'

★ ★ ★

'Police! Drop the knife! Drop it now!' Nikki yelled. She entered the room gun first, taking a stance maybe five feet from the assailant. 'Drop it now or I'll blow your fucking head off!'

'No!' He hiked the child up higher against him so that her head overlapped the lower half of his battered face. The point of the knife pricked the tender flesh of the little girl's throat, and blood began to trickle down.

Evi was on her knees, sobbing, pleading. 'Let her go! Please! She's just a little girl!'

Mia was screaming and kicking, trying to wriggle from the grasp of her captor.

'Stop it!' he snapped into her ear. 'Stop it right now!'

'Mia, be still!' Evi cried.

'You hurt that child, I'll make you wish you'd never been born,' Nikki promised.

He laughed, a sound that was strangely tragic. 'I already wish that,' he said quietly. 'That's why I'm here.'

'What does that mean?'

493

'You're not a part of this,' he said. 'You don't belong here. Get out. This is between me and her,' he said, nodding toward Evi.

'Then let the little girl go,' Nikki said. 'There's no reason to hurt her.'

He shook his head, hefting Mia up and adjusting his hold on her.

'She's getting heavy, isn't she?' Nikki said. 'Put her down. Let her go. Let's end this now. Nobody has to get hurt.'

'No,' he said. 'You're wrong.'

'I'll stand here like this 'til hell freezes over,' Nikki told him. 'Can you hold her that long? Come on. Put her down. We can all walk out of here.'

Come on, asshole, give me something to work with here, she thought. She had to keep him talking. The longer she kept him talking, the heavier that child was going to feel in his arms.

'What's your name?' she asked, readjusting her grip on the Glock in her hands.

He laughed again, a sound full of nothing but sadness, and nodded toward Evi. 'Ask her.'

Evi was sobbing quietly into her hands, rocking as she kneeled on the floor, just out of reach of her daughter.

Nikki could hear cars pulling up outside. There were no sirens, but someone was running lights. She could see the flash of blue, red, and white through the window.

'Put the child down,' she said softly. 'Let's end this.'

'Let's,' he said, but he made no move to let Mia Burke go. Instead, he lowered himself and

494

the child to the floor, putting her on her feet and kneeling behind her, the knife still pressed to her throat.

Strange knife, Nikki thought in the back of her mind. Exotic. It was long, maybe eighteen inches, and gently curved from end to end. The soft amber nightlight played over the surface of the blade. The handle was elaborately wrapped in some kind of fine blue cord.

'Give her the gun,' he said, nodding toward Evi.

'No. I can't do that. You let the little girl go.'

'Give her the gun or I'll kill this child right now.'

To prove his point, he cut an inch-long line on Mia Burke's throat. Blood bloomed along the line and ran down the blade of the knife.

Evi screamed, 'No!' as her child screamed and cried and called for her mother.

'Give her the gun!' the assailant shouted.

The telephone on the nightstand rang. Nikki thought she could hear the distant *whop-whop-whop* of helicopter blades beating the air.

'Give her the gun!'

Fuck. She had to buy them time.

Nikki took the Glock in her right hand and moved her arm to the side slowly as she stepped toward the bed.

'I'll put it right here,' she said, placing the gun on the foot of the bed.

A thousand scenarios raced through her mind. The last thing she was supposed to do was surrender her weapon, but she couldn't shoot him without endangering the child, and she

495

couldn't stand there and watch him slit Mia Burke's throat.

'Get the gun, Evangeline,' he said. 'Get it and bring it over here.'

Evi pushed herself to her feet. She was trembling visibly. She looked at Nikki with desperation in her eyes.

'Get the gun!' he shouted. 'I'll cut her again! I swear to God! I don't care any more about this child than you ever cared about me.'

'Do what he says,' Nikki told her. 'It'll be all right.'

How could she even say something so stupid? What part of this was all right? But she kept her voice calm and strong.

'Do what he says.'

She watched Evi pick the gun up like it was a dead rat, distaste and fear twisting her face. Her hands were shaking so badly she could barely hold on to it.

'Stay calm, Evi,' Nikki murmured to her. 'It's going to be all right. Just stay calm.'

*   *   *

Evi looked at the gun in her hands. Stay calm? Every cell in her body was trembling. She had never been so terrified in her life. It felt as if her nerves were wrapped around her throat, growing tighter and tighter. She could hardly breathe.

'Bring the gun over here,' he ordered.

She looked at the weapon in her hands then at the stranger holding a knife to the throat of her daughter. Both of them her children. His father had died because of him. Now her daughter might die by his hand. None of it should have happened. Her mother shouldn't have died of an overdose. She should never have put Evi in a position to be taken advantage of by a man she should have been able to trust. Ted Duffy shouldn't have come to her room that night. Evi shouldn't have leaned on him. So many decisions by so many people had brought them to this moment, and the result was this battered animal holding a knife to Mia's throat, a madman with an agenda only he could understand.

Evi walked toward him, holding the gun in front of her like some kind of offering.

'Put it to my head,' he ordered.

'What?'

'Put it to my head,' he said again.

'I don't understand.'

'It's time to close the circle, Jeager, Evangeline Grace,' he said. 'I came here to close the circle. It started with you. It ends with you. I didn't come here to kill you. I came here for you to kill me.'

★ ★ ★

She had brought him into the world. She would take him out of it. That was the circle, Charlie thought. She had given him to the cycle of madness that had been his family. He had ended their lives: The father who had tormented them, who would have disowned them. The mother who had never protected them, never nurtured them. Diana. He couldn't leave her to

497

self-destruct or to be destroyed by a man who only wanted to use her. Charlie had always loved her best. He had always protected her. He had been protecting her even as he cut her throat with the *wakizashi* he had taken from their father's collection, the knife he now held to the throat of the child. A quick, painless death. A kiss to take her to the afterlife.

All that was left was for him to die.

That was the circle.

He had begun his search for his birth mother with no clear picture of what he wanted from her. He had known only that he had to find her, the woman who had brought him into the world and given him away like a puppy to the first stranger who would take him. Or maybe she had done it for money. Maybe that was what their father had meant when he used to say, 'You're more trouble than you're worth.'

As the other pieces fell into place, his purpose for finding her had become clear. She could do this one thing for him, this one kindness. It would be their one perfect moment as mother and son. She had given him life and now she could give him the essence of life in death.

This was how it was supposed to end. He would be gone, and she would live with the memory of him forever.

He could hear a helicopter getting close. More police. It didn't matter. It would all be over soon.

'Do it,' he said.

She looked back at the policewoman.

'Do what he says, Evi,' the cop said. 'Stand to the side of him. Put the gun to his temple.'

'No. No,' his mother said, crying. 'Oh my God . . . '

'It's all right, Evi. Just do what I tell you,' the cop said. 'Stand to the side of him. Put the gun to his temple.'

'No. Please! I can't!'

'Do it,' he said. 'Do it!'

He tightened his hold on the child as he shouted, scaring the girl. She wailed for her mother. For *their* mother.

Evi raised the gun, her hands shaking so badly he thought she would strike him with it before she could put it to his head.

'Do it,' he said.

'I can't!' she sobbed.

'Do it or I'll kill her!'

'Mommy!' the child wailed.

'DO IT!'

★ ★ ★

Nikki heard the chopper coming closer. *Whop, whop, whop.* From the corner of her eye, she could see the spotlight sweeping back and forth. She kept her focus on the bizarre tableau in front of her.

Evi Burke was sobbing, her hands trembling violently as she held the barrel of the Glock to the temple of the man who held a knife to her daughter's throat, the man who might have murdered her husband for the sole purpose of getting her to blow his brains out.

Nikki calculated her odds of being able to get her second weapon out of her ankle holster in the split second she would have when he realized the gun to his head wouldn't fire. She had set the safety.

'*Do it!*' he screamed. 'I'll kill her!'

'*Mommy!*'

Evi closed her eyes and braced herself.

WHOP, WHOP, WHOP, WHOP.

The police chopper swung in close and flooded the room with stark white light that struck the assailant in the face, blinding him.

'*Evi! Run!*'

Head down, Nikki exploded forward. With her left hand she shoved Mia Burke to the side as she brought her right knee up into her tormentor's face. Momentum carried her forward. She ducked a shoulder and rolled, coming back up to her feet in a crouch, ready to block his attack.

He grabbed the knife off the floor as he turned over and came up onto his knees again, blood gushing from his broken nose.

Expecting him to come at her, Nikki went for the gun strapped to her ankle.

She pulled it free and brought it up, shouting, 'Drop the knife! Drop it!'

He didn't drop the knife.

He didn't come at her.

He plunged the blade into his own stomach, screaming.

⋆　⋆　⋆

'Jesus H. Christ, Tinks. I let you out of my sight for five minutes and suddenly you're freaking

Rambo. Or is it Rambette?'

Kovac. Nikki looked up as he came into the bedroom, parting the sea of SWAT uniforms milling around the doorway like some kind of film noir Moses in a trench coat and fedora. Taylor followed him, his handsome face set in stern lines as he scanned the room, zeroing in on the dead guy lying on the floor in a pool of blood.

'That'll be Wonder Woman to you, Kojak,' Nikki said, ridiculously relieved to see him. It made no sense for him to be here, but she didn't care.

Her head was spinning. Everything had gone in fast-forward from the moment she moved on the assailant. He had plunged the knife into his stomach and collapsed to the floor, and then SWAT was charging in, and paramedics, and the room was filled with light and noise, and commotion.

'You leave my squad, hijack my suspect, and solve a one-man crime wave while saving a mom and her kid,' Kovac said. 'Wonder Woman it is.'

He looked down at the dead man and sighed.

'Your suspect?' Nikki asked, confused. 'Who is he?'

'Charlie Chamberlain,' Taylor said, squatting down beside the body.

'He came here to die,' Nikki said. 'He wanted Evi Burke to kill him. I don't understand any of it.'

She heard a little tremor in her voice. The aftermath of the adrenaline dump. Clear as a bell in the midst of the crisis, now she felt the delayed surge of confusion and fear. So many things could have gone wrong. Mia Burke could have been killed. Evi Burke could have been killed. *She* could have been killed.

'But you're okay?' Kovac asked.

'Sure,' she said, automatically, as if it was that simple. She looked down at herself. Her hands and clothes were covered in the dead man's blood. Her hands were trembling. She had gone to him as he lay on the floor, dying. He had bled out before the SWAT team even made it up the stairs. There was nothing left for the paramedics to do but cart his corpse to the morgue.

'He must have hit an artery,' she murmured. 'It happened so fast.'

Kovac wrapped an arm around her shoulders and gave her a brotherly squeeze. 'Let's get you out of here, Wonder Woman. You've got a date with a shitload of paperwork downtown.'

Nikki leaned into him, grateful for his presence and his friendship. 'You always know just what to say to a girl. And here I was thinking you didn't care anymore.'

His mouth turned up on one corner in his trademark sardonic smile. 'I wouldn't let you off that easy, Tinker Bell. Let's go,' he said, turning her toward the door. 'I'll even buy the coffee.'

48

'I never hated him,' Evi said quietly. 'I've always been ashamed of that.'

They sat in a private meeting room at the Hennepin County Medical Center, a drab gray room with drab gray modern furniture, and a wall of glass that overlooked a courtyard several stories below, where snow was accumulating on the trees and bushes. Just down the hall in the ICU, Eric lay sleeping. His condition was stable.

'I shouldn't need to tell you it wasn't your fault,' Detective Liska said gently. 'You were a child. He was an authority figure. Consent was moot.'

'It was nobody's fault,' Evi said, knowing her colleagues would have pounced on her for her answer.

Ted Duffy took advantage of a vulnerable girl; the culpability was his. That was true. Of all the people who should have known that, he was at the top of the list. The decorated Sex Crimes detective had committed a sex crime against a child in his care. She should have hated him. Anyone would have vilified him, crucified him, sent him straight to hell.

Evi knew, though, that hell was a place of one's own making, and both she and Ted Duffy had served time there for their own reasons. He was dead because of her, because of what he'd done, and while that may indeed have been justice, all Evi saw when she thought of him was a broken man, ruined by his life, begging her forgiveness, sobbing with his head in his hands. What use was there in hating him? She had hated herself enough to know it didn't serve any purpose.

Her emotions at the time had been so tangled and confused. She had made an uneasy friendship with Ted Duffy as she did the Duffy laundry in the basement and he sat at his workbench sipping his whiskey. He asked her about her days at school. He gave her advice about boys. He was kind. She felt sorry for him. She had never had a friendship with a man. She had never had a father figure. She didn't know how those relationships were supposed to work. She didn't understand how or where to draw boundaries.

If she had asked for love, then she didn't have the right to say no, did she? If she believed she could trust, then she had to accept betrayal of that trust, right? That was what she believed because she didn't know any better. How could she have been expected to know what love was and what love wasn't when her only example of love was a woman so tormented by life that she had ended her own?

'He wasn't a terrible man,' she said. 'He did a terrible thing.'

'Did you tell Barbie?' Liska asked.

'Only when she found out I was pregnant,' she said with a sad smile. 'She called me a liar, said no one would ever believe me. It would be my word against his — against hers.

'And you didn't try to tell another adult? A guidance counselor, a teacher?'

'Why would they believe me? I was just a foster kid. I hadn't been in that school half a year.'

'You didn't trust anybody.'

'Why would I?'

She looked to the other end of the room, where Eric's mother sat reading quietly to Mia in an oversize chair by the window. Her daughter's only physical scar from their ordeal would be the mark on her throat where Charles Chamberlain cut her as a threat. Emotionally, the damage would go deeper than a surface wound, and the guilt Evi felt for that was choking. But Mia would always be surrounded by people who loved her, people who would do their best to protect her and care for her. She would never know that terrible yawning emptiness that Evi had lived with for most of her life.

She reached up and brushed a tear from her cheek. She had that family now. Eric's parents loved her unconditionally, without judgment. Even with their son lying in the ICU hooked to tubes and monitors because of her, they loved her. It was difficult for her to believe she deserved that, but they helped her work at it every day.

She felt that she had so much to make up for. She had never trusted Eric with the details of her time with the Duffys, and the product of her time there had appeared in their lives like a monster from a nightmare and nearly killed him.

The doctors estimated he had lost a third of

his blood supply the night of the attack. The paramedics had brought him back from cardiac arrest in the ambulance. The ER staff revived him a second time. He had lost an eye. The wound to his face would require multiple plastic surgeries. The cut across his back, which had sliced through his heavy jacket, required more than a hundred stitches to close.

And yet, the first thing he said when he opened his eyes and saw her was 'I love you.' And when she told him the terrible truth she had kept to herself all these years, the first thing he said when she finished was, 'I love you.' And that would make all the difference in both their lives and in the life of their child.

She had often wondered what her life would have been like if she had had that kind of love as a child. Now she couldn't help but wonder what a difference it would have made in the life of the child she had given up. What kind of horrible pain had he carried within to do the things he had done? She had given him the only thing she could: a chance at something better, never imagining that chance could become a nightmare.

'Tell me about Jeremy Nilsen.'

Jeremy, her first real crush. She had been his first girlfriend, a secret from his father. And he had been her secret from the Duffys. Romeo and Juliet.

'He was a sweet boy. He had a difficult relationship with his father, trying to live up to his father's idea of what a man should be. I suppose that was where the trouble started.

'When I found out I was pregnant, I was so afraid. I didn't know what to do. I didn't know what would happen to me. I was afraid they would send me away. I told Jeremy what had happened.

'He was so angry. He wanted to do something. He wanted to confront Mr. Duffy. He wanted to have him arrested. I told him we couldn't do any of those things. I told him they'd send me away. He wouldn't let it go. He wanted to be my hero. He thought he should defend my honor.'

She put her hands over her face and leaned against the table.

'He said he would kill Mr. Duffy for what he'd done. I didn't believe he'd really do it.'

'But he did.'

'I tried to find him after school,' she said. 'I couldn't find him.'

She started to tremble, remembering her growing panic as the afternoon darkened. She remembered how she had stood outside the Nilsen house, afraid to knock on the door, afraid Mr. Nilsen would answer. She could hear Mr. Duffy chopping wood next door.

'We used to meet in the park and walk on the trails in the woods. It was the place we could be together without anyone knowing. I thought maybe he had gone there to think. It was almost dark.'

She remembered the bitter day, damp and cold. A spitting, freezing rain pelted her face like tiny shards of glass. It was changing to snow as she hurried down the trail. She was crying, afraid, filled with dread. What had she done? Why had she told him?

'And then I heard the shots,' she said, and an overwhelming sadness filled her. It filled her now, and she wanted to cry for everything that was lost in that moment. Their lives had just been set on a path over which they would have no control, and any hope for their budding love would be dashed, all because a troubled boy had done the wrong thing for all the right reasons.

★　★　★

' . . . They came up with the story of having been at school at the basketball game,' Nikki said.

They sat in Logan's office in the government center: Nikki, Candra Seley, Logan, and Mascherino. Logan's desk phone was lighting up like a pinball machine. He ignored it. The news media had gone rabid for details of Charlie Chamberlain and his wake of death.

'Any other week, there would have been a game on Tuesday night. No one bothered to check,' she went on. 'No one really questioned them. They were just kids. Everybody thought Ted Duffy was killed by someone he had put away, or that Barbie and Big Duff had pulled it off. There were so many more realistic possibilities. If Barbie had any suspicions, she kept them to herself rather than risk the world finding out her husband, Mr. Sex Crimes Detective of the Year, had raped their sixteen-year-old foster child. She and Big Duff closed ranks around the family, and she sent the foster girls back into the system. Jeremy Nilsen turned eighteen and joined the army.'

'Do you think Donald Nilsen knew?' Mascherino asked.

Nikki looked away. 'Can I plead the Fifth on that?'

'Off the record, then,' Logan said.

'Jeremy Nilsen was an honor student,' she said. 'He had already been accepted to several universities. How many parents would let that kind of son drop out of high school to join the army?'

'You think it was the father's idea?' Logan asked.

'Do you have kids, Logan?' she asked him.

He shook his head.

'I think Donald Nilsen is a sad old man who did what he could to protect his only child for killing a man who raped a teenage girl. I can't say I wouldn't do the same,' she confessed. 'I think he packed his son off to the army and hoped for the best. That wasn't what he got, but I think that was his intent. And I think his wife probably left him over it.

'Do you want to pursue any of that?' she asked.

'Do you think Ted Duffy doesn't deserve justice?'

'I think life dealt out crueler justice than any of these people had coming,' Nikki said, the sadness of that truth heavy on her shoulders. She tried to shrug it off. 'But I'm just a cop. I do what I'm told.'

509

Mascherino arched an eyebrow, but made no comment.

'Where's the son?' Logan asked.

'His dental records are a match for a John Doe death last summer,' Seley said. 'A body found snagged under some branches in the Mississippi. A probable homicide victim. His ID was found in possession of Gordon Krauss, a man who has been identified as having committed assault on a homeless man near the river in June.'

Logan sighed and swiveled his chair. He had jerked his tie loose at the end of the day. His shirtsleeves were rolled up as if he had been doing physical labor. 'So what you're saying is you've got nothing for me to prosecute.'

'Who's left?' Nikki asked. 'Evi Burke? The then teenage rape victim of a celebrated detective? Do you want to open that can of worms? What do you try to pin on her? Conspiracy? Accessory after the fact? What's the point? I think if you talk to the Duffy family, they won't want you to pursue this. They didn't want the case reopened in the first place.'

It was Logan's choice. As the county attorney's number one, he had prosecutorial discretion, the power to pick and choose cases. But he was a realist and a politician, and there was nothing to be salvaged from this sad mess of a case. He nodded and smiled, conceding defeat graciously. 'Happy Thanksgiving, Detective Liska. Close the case. Pick a winner off the pile when you come back from the holiday.'

49

'Man, that's cold,' Tippen said as they stared at the computer screen.

The photographs had been pulled off Charlie Chamberlain's cell phone: One close-up of Lucien Chamberlain's crushed, bloody skull, eyeball dangling from the socket. And one taken from slightly farther away to include the murder weapon, the nunchucks that lay within reach of the professor's hand, as if he had done this to himself.

In a way, he had, Kovac thought. He had spent twenty-four years breaking down the psyche of the son who had turned on him.

They were in the war room, putting the case to rest. The whiteboards had been erased, the paperwork filed and boxed up. The case that had consumed their every waking moment for days was officially over, but they rehashed the details as they wound down, trying to make sense of it all as the adrenaline receded. As if there was any sense to be made of the dark twists and turns taken by the human mind and heart.

Diana Chamberlain, so fond of shooting spontaneous videos on her phone, had been recording her father's birthday dinner when the argument began. They started with potshots at one another, she and Lucien, taking aim like snipers. Then a quick show of mother's nervous disapproval, and Charlie scowling at the camera

511

even as he tried to play diplomat.

Bit by bit, the foundation of civility eroded away beneath them. Lucien berated Diana for making the complaint to the Office for Conflict Resolution. He called her names, questioned her intelligence, and speculated about her true parentage, since she clearly was no daughter of his.

She struck back with 'I'm fucking Ken Sato.'

As family fights went, it was as nasty a verbal bloodbath as Kovac had seen in a while. There were few cutting instruments on the earth as razor-sharp as an articulate tongue fueled by bitterness and alcohol. The words cut to the bone and lacerated the heart.

Diana had tried to drag Charlie onto her side of the argument. He tried to remain the voice of reason. She lashed out at him like a viper. The pain in his expression was more eloquent than words.

'He killed them for her, though,' Taylor said. 'He stole his mother's cell phone that night so he could access the security system through the app. The call from Sondra's phone to Charlie's phone the night of the murders pinged off the tower nearest Charlie's apartment.'

'He got plenty of satisfaction out of it, though,' Kovac said, gesturing to the images on the computer screen. 'He probably fantasized about it for years. He took the pictures so he could relive the thrill.'

Liska had told them that during the stand-off in the Burke house, Charlie spoke repeatedly of 'closing the circle.' He killed the father who had constantly belittled him, and the mother who had allowed that to happen. He slit the throat of the sister he loved too much, and then tracked down his birth mother to end it all.

John Quinn, Kate's husband, a renowned criminal profiler, told Kovac that Charlie Chamberlain ticked off many of the boxes of a type of killer known as a family annihilator. Abused as a child, feeling inadequate and powerless, having the need to exert strict control over as many aspects of his life as possible. While he had undoubtedly killed his parents in retribution for their abuse, he could very well have killed his sister out of a twisted sense of love and protection. He had tried to protect her all his life; how could he leave her to the world to be destroyed without him there to defend her?

If Gordon Krauss was to be believed, Diana Chamberlain had tried to solicit him to murder her parents more than a week before they were killed. Had Charlie been a part of that plan? Had Diana's death always been a part of Charlie's plan? They would probably never know. They did know, from searching Charlie's computer at work, that he began methodically searching for the truth of his parentage in the spring, and knew about Evi Burke since late summer.

'Shakespeare would have had a freaking field day with these people,' Kovac declared.

' "The gods are just, and of our pleasant vices make instruments to plague us,'' Elwood quoted. ' 'The dark and vicious place where thee he got cost him his eyes.

' 'Thou hast spoken right, 'tis true. The wheel

is come full circle . . . ' '

'Oh talk Shakespeare to me, baby,' Liska said, walking into the room, her hands tucked in the pockets of her coat, ready to leave for the day. 'I miss you, Elwood.'

'What?' Kovac asked, getting up from his chair. 'Gene Grider doesn't do poetry readings in the broom closet?'

'Gene Grider is noticeably absent from the broom closet following the closing of the sad case of Ted Duffy. Poor guy,' she said. 'I feel sorry for him, to be honest. None of that panned out the way he thought it would.'

'Another hero bites the dust,' Tippen said as he shut down the computer.

'No heroes in this story,' Liska said. 'Just humans, good, bad, and otherwise.'

'The world's overrun with them,' Kovac said, shrugging into his overcoat and grabbing his hat. 'It's our job to sort them out.'

'Yeah, well,' Liska said, backing toward the door. 'Before we have to do it all again, let's go drink a toast to the survivors.'

Acknowledgments

Special thanks go out to several people for their incredible generosity to causes near and dear to me.

To Candra Seley for her generous winning bid to play a role in *The Bitter Season*. Her donation goes to Play for P.I.N.K. (www.playforpink.org), a fantastic organization that raises funds for life-saving breast cancer research via sports events such as the Challenge of the Americas dressage event held annually in Wellington, Florida. And to Rona Mascherino Garm and Kent Mitchell for their generous donation to the extraordinary Vinceremos Therapeutic Riding Center (www.vinceremos.org) in Loxahatchee, Florida, for Rona's mother, Joan Mascherino, a longtime avid reader, to also play a role in this book.

Thank you all for your generosity of heart and spirit in donating to these worthy organizations.

We do hope that you have enjoyed reading this large print book.

Did you know that all of our titles are available for purchase?

We publish a wide range of high quality large print books including:

Romances, Mysteries, Classics
General Fiction
Non Fiction and Westerns

Special interest titles available in large print are:

The Little Oxford Dictionary
Music Book
Song Book
Hymn Book
Service Book

Also available from us courtesy of Oxford University Press:

Young Readers' Dictionary
(large print edition)
Young Readers' Thesaurus
(large print edition)

For further information or a free brochure, please contact us at:
Ulverscroft Large Print Books Ltd.,
The Green, Bradgate Road, Anstey,
Leicester, LE7 7FU, England.
Tel: (00 44) 0116 236 4325
Fax: (00 44) 0116 234 0205